WHEN GIRLFRIENDS LET GO

SAVANNAH PAGE

OTHER TITLES BY SAVANNAH PAGE

Everything the Heart Wants

A Sister's Place

Bumped to Berlin

WHEN GIRLFRIENDS SERIES

When Girlfriends Break Hearts

When Girlfriends Step Up

When Girlfriends Make Choices

When Girlfriends Chase Dreams

When Girlfriends Take Chances

When Girlfriends Let Go

When Girlfriends Find Love

WHEN GIRLFRIENDS LET GO

Published by Pearls and Pages

ISBN-13: 978-1494740474
ISBN-10: 1494740478

Information about the author and her upcoming books can be found online at
www.savannahpage.com

For Emma

1
_____

"She *can't* give up. She can't just stop—stop—trying!"

I blink long and hard, fighting the path where my thoughts are headed. I resist the temptation to consider my own relationship—my marriage—and how it's nothing like I imagined. Giving up actually doesn't seem like such a bad idea.

"That's giving up too soon. Too soon."

I look down at my wedding ring—the Tiffany five-carat, custom-ordered, round solitaire, which is exactly what I'd always dreamed of. I thumb the platinum band and give a sniff, trying to dismiss the negative path my mind is beginning to wander down.

Cramming my hands in the pockets of my tangerine-colored sweater dress, I pull my chin up and return my attention to the topic actually at hand.

"It's too soon, don't you think? Right?" Claire Whitley, one of my closest friends from college, is looking at me expectantly. "She can't give up. Right, Jackie?" She scrunches a handful of her tight golden curls at the back of her head.

"Yeah, yeah," I say quickly.

I brush my fingers across the row of colorful book spines in front of me and find myself amusingly distracted. Titles like *Your Baby,*

Your Birthing Plan and *Do You Doula or Not?* and *From Utero to Universe: The Better Birth* do more frightening than marketing. I don't know how any pregnant woman would be persuaded into picking up one of these books based off of the corny titles. I don't know what constitutes a "better birth" or how someone can really *plan* one. And what's a doula, anyway?

"You agree with me?" Claire says as she also pulls a book from the wooden shelf. "That it's too soon to tell? To make any rash decisions? That she'd be giving up if she tossed in the towel already?"

I pull at random one of the many pregnancy self-help books. "Maybe," I say to Claire, glancing to my left at Sophie Wharton, who's got her nose in the utero book.

"Maybe?" Claire repeats, hanging on my response with those patient but always excited crystal blues of hers.

"Maybe Lara's giving up too soon...true," I say slowly. "Or maybe she just doesn't see the relationship going anywhere," I give a one-shouldered shrug, "so she figures why not pull the plug now? Stop stringing along and end the suffering?"

"They've only been living together for what? Three or four months? Something super short." Claire raises a questioning brow. "That's too soon to really know, I think."

She quickly scans the cover of the book in her hand and her eyes grow wide. "These titles are so creative!" she gushes in her ever-peppy way. She gives me a toothy smile and immediately flips open the book.

I suppress the urge to offer up my differing opinion; babies are more Claire's department than mine. These books are definitely more marketed towards women like her, certainly not me.

Claire continues to pore over the book like it's the Kama Sutra—something actually interesting. She juts out a curvy, blue-jeaned hip, the book pressed to her waist and tightly clutched in one hand. She flips page after page, twisting her lips from side to side and occasionally purring out sounds like *Ahh* and *Oooh*.

"Well," I exhale, turning round and round my wedding ring, "I've lived with guys for less time than Nathan and Lara have lived together, Claire."

Claire manages to pull her attention from the evidently fascinating book and looks at me, still wearing curious and wide eyes. "And?"

"And I was able to realize the relationship was headed for Disasterville." I glance down at the book in my hand and immediately return it to the shelf. The image on the cover is one of those illustrations of the inner workings of what makes a female a female—the same illustrations that cover every OB-GYN's walls. I shiver.

"Nathan doesn't seem like some of the bozos you've dated, Jackie," Claire says. "No offense."

"Never any taken."

"Nathan and Lara have been together for a while." She claps the book shut and returns it. "They've invested so much time in one another. Surely they're only having those normal hiccups you can have when you change your living arrangement."

Lara Kearns, my best friend in the whole wide world, (right up there with Emily Saunders, both fab girlfriends from college) has been seeing this guy Nathan for a year now. He moved into her apartment last fall and everything had seemed to be going really well prior, hence the sharing of the abode. But lately Lara hasn't been feeling so sure about their arrangement...or their entire relationship. She says she can't really pinpoint the reason behind the feeling and their growing distance, but that maybe that's just it: There's distance between them, and it's, well, *growing.*

I can understand her hesitancy about staying in a committed relationship when she's on the fence about the guy, though. To stay or not to stay, hoping it'll get better? Or will it get worse? I mean, I've had my *un*fair share of dazzlers-turned-douches, all of whom started out amazing and eventually crashed and burned, or at least fizzled out. Relationships can be the most mind-blowing and amazing adventures, yet they can also be the most heart-wrenching and horrible experiences of your life.

I say, if Lara's feeling so-so with Nathan and they've already been in a relationship for so long, then certainly that relationship can't last. Can it? She's given it a long and fair chance—plenty of time—and if she called it quits now, she wouldn't be "tossing in the towel...giving up" would she? If there's no longer anymore fun in the relationship (as Lara has firmly stated), then what the hell's the point?

Then again, hiccups are totally normal in a relationship, as I am always reminding myself. Maybe this one is just a really lengthy hiccup. Eventually it'll stop and things will be back to normal. Right?

Oh, I don't know! Who am I to give advice? I'm Jackie Kittredge, the girl who *goes* to Lara—and all my other friends, for that matter—for advice.

"I'm torn," I say to Claire. "Maybe she should think a *short* while more about it, or..." I pause, pursing my lips. My thoughts begin to drift back towards that path. That path where I begin to consider my relationship with my husband. When is a relationship old and stale enough to begin thinking of alternatives to happiness? When is it all right to consider giving up and moving on? Is it ever all right when you've made a commitment to someone? A big commitment, like marriage...

"And?" Claire waits with bated breath.

"Hmm?" I sound, lips pressed together tightly.

"You think Lara should wait it out a while *or...*"

"Or..." I glance down at my wedding ring, give my tongue a quick bite, then blurt out, "Maybe she should say 'to hell with it' and kick Nathan to the curb! I don't know." I wave a dismissive hand.

Claire nods slowly, pensively. "Playing it on the safe side and waiting it out a bit is probably a good idea," she says. "See where things go. I mean, she and Nathan have been *great* together...and Lara's been wanting a solid relationship for so long." A sullen expression creeps across Claire's face. "I'd hate to see her hurt and single again." I nod as she shouts out abruptly, "And! Once you let someone go, there's no getting them back." She gives me a blank look. "Better to play it safe and give it more time."

"All right," Sophie's voice trills as I feel my brow furrow over

4

Claire's comment. *No getting them back...* And yet again my thoughts are drifting to that path.

"Found one finally?" Claire asks loudly. She sets a hand on my shoulder and leans over me, looking at Sophie, eager.

Sophie, just as proactive and bossy as she was the first day we met back in college a bajillion years ago (actually it's more like ten), waves a book in the air and proclaims, "This one! This book is filled with information that pertains *specifically* to Robin's situation."

Claire nods in a matter-of-fact way and reaches out to examine the book herself.

"There are two whole chapters that talk exclusively about Cesareans and breeched babies," Sophie waxes on lyrically. "There's also a chapter all about having to change birthing plans at the last minute." She gives one sharp nod. "Definitely the book for Robin."

Sophie looks satisfied with our trip to Randy's and ready to go. She's standing here tall and proud—slim, impeccable posture, and towering a good nine inches over my five-feet-nothing. Her glossed lips form a subtle and content smile, but one that's hinting at the tiniest bit of impatience. She puts one hand on her hip and scratches at her lightly freckled nose in an expectant way. "It's a great find," she says assuredly. She places her other hand on her hip, posture still perfect, and adds, "Our search is done. It's definitely the right book for Robin."

"Oh, yes," Claire says. She's thumbing through the book at a rapid pace. "Very good, very good." Her voice is becoming a muted and absorbed mumble.

Sophie, Claire, and I are at Randy's, an old college hangout where we used to all go with our homework in tow when we were studying at U Dub (the University of Washington for those who aren't familiar with the most awesome college ever). If I could count the hours we'd spent in this bookstore, poring over our homework... Well, it'd be nothing in comparison to the hours we spent here ignoring said homework and exchanging gossip, laughing, and ordering one frappé after another.

We just spent the last couple hours tonight doing the very same things (chatting and drinking tasty beverages, that is) over at our friend Robin's place, and now we're here at Randy's looking for preggo books, because poor Robin's birthing plan has been shot to hell. A natural birth with breeched (and rather largely-sized) Phillip may not be in the cards, and Robin's faced with possibly having to have a C-section.

Robin's all panicked, naturally; Sophie's confident she can solve this; Claire's way too interested in all of it; and I'm along for the ride in sisterly support. By Sophie's insistence to find the best self-help book pronto for our friend in need (who can't quite fit behind the wheel anymore), I find myself looking at suggestive books that give tingles up and down my spine—something I would never do if it weren't for my best friends. I know I can appear selfish and kind of spoiled at times (as they'll hint at now and then, and as my husband is always quick to point out), but honestly, I'd do anything for my girlfriends. They're my family, and if that means Robin needs help making her uterus plan or whatever, then I'm game.

"Are we *sure* a book is going to help Robin prepare, though?" I ask Sophie with skepticism.

"It's the least we can do," Sophie replies assuredly. "Better to be informed. Besides, she's got no reason to panic. She's going to be a rock star with this birth, natural or otherwise."

I shrug and say, "If the books'll help, then...by all means."

Robin Sinclair, also one of my college friends whom I've known for eons, is supposed to have her second baby, a boy, in something like four weeks. She had a natural birth with her two-year-old daughter Rose and planned to do the same for Phillip. I suppose Robin figures she did it natural once before, so why not again? Plus, she's that kind of a woman, Robin. She used to be sort of meek and not very confident, kind of taking a backseat in her own life. But ever since she had Rose, dealt with the aftermath of the one-night-stand that led to Rose, and met her dreamy fiancé, Bobby Holman, at the publishing house they both work for, she's taken the lead role in her life. She's still quiet and meek, but I take my hat off to her for taking charge of her life and growing a backbone.

"This is great," Claire exclaims. She hands the book back to Sophie, who is now engaged in something on her iPhone.

"Let's roll," Sophie states, not removing her eyes from her phone as she slips the book under her arm.

"Wait!" Claire shrieks. "I want to look a little more."

"Oh dear," Sophie groans. "This again?"

Ever since Claire and her husband Conner exchanged vows last summer, Claire's had babies on the brain. The fact that Robin is expecting doesn't help matters, nor does the pessimism of Lara, the slightly more senior among our group of girlfriends. Lara thinks all hope of having a baby some day is lost now that she's convinced a lasting relationship with Nathan probably won't come to fruition. Oh, and that she'll be thirty-two this year and her eggs will probably expire by the time she finds a replacement for him. It's not even like she wants to have a baby anytime soon since she's married to her advertising career, but she wants to keep her options, like her stock, open. Lara's thoughts on the matter only incite more panic in twenty-six-year-old Claire, who's determined to pop out kids before she's even sniffing in Neighborhood 30.

"I only want to *look*," Claire says in a high-pitched voice.

Sophie heaves a long, drawn-out sigh as she types on the phone's screen. "Make it quick, Claire. It's getting late and I really need some sleep. I've got a long and early day tomorrow and I *still* need to finish the rest of the day's menu." She waves her phone about for emphasis.

Sophie owns her own café/bakery, The Cup and the Cake. She's really made a name for her small startup here in Seattle, where there is some *serious* competition among cooks and bakers. We're a culinary capital over here with some well-known and well-established bakeries and cafés, but Sophie's joint is contending well.

"I just want to see if they have the book I heard about on the radio the other day." Claire is scanning her eyes up and down, left and right about the shelves. "About how to convince your husband that now's the time."

"Remind me that next time we're in the car together I turn *off* my radio," Sophie says, mock-petulant.

"Dear god," I groan, sliding down the opposing bookshelf and onto the floor. "You're not still thinking of dragging Conner to that fertility clinic, are you, Claire?" I pull my knees to my chest.

"Oh, I was only thinking out loud," Claire replies. "My man's fertility is *not* a problem. Remember all those pregnancy scares back in college?" She pauses her intrepid search to give me a direct look, then Sophie.

"Yeah," Sophie says, still focused on her phone. "Only because you're not so great at remembering to take your pill, honey."

"Or remembering where you misplaced them," I quip.

"Whatevs," Claire says, returning to her search. "Just you wait, girls. Before you know it Robin won't be the *only* preggers one around here."

2

I take a long, slow drag on my cigarette as I lean against the ice-cold, steel railing of the balcony that wraps around my luxurious townhouse. The muffled post-five-o'clock traffic sounds that travel up these twelve floors have retired for the evening. At quarter past eight on a Friday *most* businessmen, however stressed and strapped, are home from the office.

Those unsettling thoughts of my marriage that crept up at Randy's are still plaguing me, nearly a week later. They were there before—long before, actually; perhaps a little more light was shed on those thoughts during the discussion of Nathan and Lara. Right now, it's just me and these disconcerting thoughts as I stand alone in the crisp winter night. Just me, wondering how the hell I went from the altar as an excited, blushing bride, to a woman too often unhappy in her marriage—looking for a fix, maybe even a way out.

The story of how Andrew and I met and fell in love wasn't exactly something out of a Cary Grant film. No meet-cute, no coy romance, no charming repartee. Yes, there was me, a damsel so often in distress; yes, there was the knight, Andrew, in very shiny armor. There was attraction, there was fondness, there was love—but an affair to remember? Ha!

No, the way I met, fell in love with and eventually married my knight was not in the style of one of my many beloved romantic, black-and-white films. It was me, Jackie Anderson, a twenty-six-year-old hostess, desperately trying to hold onto one of the only jobs I'd survived long enough to earn a full payroll, always on the prowl for a potential relationship—someone to save me from myself, or at least boredom...or poverty.

And then there was Andrew Kittredge, a successful, attractive, and sophisticated businessman, nearly twice my age, looking for a bite to eat but ending up getting much more than he paid for. There was a bit of flirting, a wad of cash handed to my boss to get me off my hostess duties that night for a date, and sparks that danced spiritedly over drinks, dinner, and dancing. Lather, rinse, repeat—you get the picture. Hot attraction and flirty fun, but certainly not a classic Hollywood romance.

Taking another drag, I survey the deep blue Elliott Bay, on past to Puget Sound. Two ferries are leaving the city, probably filled with happy couples who have made plans for a weekend of R&R in Bremerton or a romantic evening on Bainbridge Island. I blow out a steady stream of smoke and lightly chuckle at the imagery of a damsel in distress, high up in her tower, waiting for her knight to ride on in and scoop her into his arms. Oh, irony and it's not-so-subtle ways.

Some might think our love story is actually charming in its own way. Some of my best girlfriends think it a bit crazy that I was kind of "bought" for our first date. I think it set the precedent for what would eventually become our marriage. Andrew sees what he wants, he goes after it, and if that means paying whatever price, so be it. When I see a man who's willing to offer me love (and lasso the moon), I'm no fool. When we fall in love and exchange vows, well, maybe we're both the fools, then.

I rub out the nub of a cigarette and immediately smack another one out of the pack.

Whatever started back at that jazz bar two and a half years ago eventually culminated into what is, thirteen months later, my marriage to Mr. Andrew Kittredge. Often they call marriage "taking the plunge," but I think the plunging begins a couple months into the marriage. I don't know; every couple's different. God knows Claire, who's been married to her college sweetheart Conner for nearly half a year now, would say that "the plunge" only applies to people who aren't marrying their soul mate.

Even if some plunging does occur in my marriage, and regardless of when, I honestly do believe that Andrew's my soul mate. I've dated a lot of assholes and wasted plenty of time on men who were boys. Andrew's the real deal; the best I've ever had. I do believe he loves me, he does try to treat me like a princess, and I know he'd never allow for another man to come between us…or for someone to hurt me. And I love my husband. I married him for his charm, his care, his passion, and his expressed and deep love for me. And, yes, I won't lie—his copious amounts of wealth made signing that marriage certificate a little easier.

I come from a broken and poor home. Getting showered with expensive gifts and whisked off on exotic trips is the royal perk of being the apple of a rich man's eye. But it certainly isn't what made me decide to marry Andrew, no matter what those judgmental onlookers might think when they see a mature man with a twenty-something on his arm. If I was looking for marriage for money, I could've run off to Vegas with Phil the thick-walleted car salesman from West Seattle or decided to "take the plunge" with the U Dub golfer and Tau Sigma honors student senior year, trust fund, adenoids, and all.

No, I love Andrew. He's the one I was meant to marry. Can I *stay* married to him, though? That's the question that's gnawing so deeply at me.

Is being soul mates enough in a marriage? Does it mean you stay together when the relationship that made you believe you were soul mates to begin with has changed beyond recognition? When people change, when situations change, when life changes… Can you love someone with all your heart but let go and love from afar? What do you do when your marriage becomes a stranger, when you begin to think you just might be better off alone?

Leaning farther against the cold balcony railing, both forearms pressing hard down onto the top bar, I take another pan of my picturesque surroundings. Seattle is stunning any time of the day or night. Of course, it could be *more* beautiful if a certain someone were home on a Friday night. If a certain someone could share this view with me, wrap his arms around me, be here to tell me he loves me...

I flick some ashes over the ledge and watch as the amber flecks flitter about, falling down, down, down.

On the one hand, being married to a rich and handsome and powerful man and having that stability I never had growing up is really nice. I don't have to work—and thank god, because I'm the world's worst employee. I live in a palatial home. I want for nothing materially. I'm a very lucky girl, I know that, and my husband makes all that possible.

On the other hand, sometimes I simply hate my situation. I hate that what makes for this stability is a career that requires the vast majority of Andrew's time and attention. His obsession with his professional life, his lack of time for me, the missed calls and my unanswered messages left with his half-wit secretary, and of course the entering of a PIN in exchange for a shiny something as his answer to quarrels and unhappiness all make me feel like I'm drowning. Like I'm plunging. Like life is a pool party, my marriage the pool. I'm drowning with a whole poolside party going on above. I'm screaming and gurgling from time to time, I'm flailing helplessly, and they're all carrying on with their silly shindig as if nothing's happening. Like I'm the crazy one for drowning during a fun pool party.

It's not all the time that I feel this way, all helpless in my marriage. Some days we're really great together, like when Andrew and I were first going out. Then others I'm up here, probably catching cold twelve stories up, contemplating the meaning of love and marriage. And it's those ups and downs, those incessant hots and colds, that bring me right back to that question of when enough becomes enough. When has a relationship run its course? When is enough neglect and enough loneliness and enough unhappiness license to move on? Because you know that just around the corner another high point will come, and you'll be head-over-heels for your husband once again, scolding yourself for ever having had such nasty thoughts of desertion.

Oh, but when will all of the neglect become too much? When will all of that waiting for the next high point to happen become too painful? When will the suffering become unbearable? And is love really enough?

What happens when that consistent passion, those sweet gestures or deep talks, the willingness to do something for your significant other that *you* may not want to do but do anyway because it means the world to them fade away? What happens when you're more often unhappy than content? When you spend more time complaining than being grateful? When the days you wish you were anywhere but here happen more and more frequently? When all the chips are down, do you walk away? Or do you find a way to keep on playing, keep on hoping for that next happy moment?

Andrew and I had quite a rough patch not too long ago, and I actually thought our marriage was doomed. I thought I'd seen my final drowning.

Andrew's in investments. He's a broker, and while I don't really know what that means, I do know that it's a really demanding career and requires just about *all* of his time. His neglect and inattentiveness thanks to his heinous hours was finally enough to make me research divorce law. My friends said I was much too rash, and maybe I was, but at some point a woman can only handle so many out-of-town business trips, so many nights of bringing work home, so many canceled dates, so many missed or unanswered calls because of some meeting, deadline, or something more important.

Andrew and I are one of those couples that manages to bicker far too often—a real hot and cold, high and low couple. But when it comes down to a discussion about us spending time together and my husband understanding that I'm not *just* some trophy wife we can get into some pretty heated fights.

Somehow, though, we talked—though only briefly, and I did *not* mention my research project. We talked about how I needed him to give me more attention. I needed to feel not like the kept wife who sits around the house all day with nothing to do.

All right, I've got five of the best friends a woman could ask for, and we do get to hang out frequently. But they all have lives of their own—pool parties where they're *not* drowning. They all have jobs, and husbands or relationships...busy lives.

When I'm not spending hours getting facials and pedicures or stuffing my walk-in closet with gems from Balenciaga, Prada, and Chloé, or sitting around here by my lonesome, I do get to hang out with my girls, and then I get to wonder when the hell my husband will be home—and, when he is home, if he'll have time for me. He's always got his fingers on the computer or in a pile of paperwork.

But, once we talked, Andrew had made steps to improve. There were more home-before-dinner evenings, weekend getaways, and he'd even include me on out-of-town business trips now and then. It was, well...like the beginning of our love story.

Then, somehow, we wound up back here, yet again. Back to the unanswered phone calls, back to the endless meetings, back to setting the polished trophy back up on the mantel and, what? Planning on making another polishing appointment six months later? A year?

Though I thought I'd sunk my lowest researching divorce law last year, and though I thought things were really starting to turn around again, I now find myself wondering if Lara's the only one who has a relationship conundrum to face, if she's the only one with a tough decision to make when it comes to love.

I bring the cigarette up to my glittering, pink lips and am about to inhale when I hear the front door close and my pet name called out. "Baby doll? Baby doll, do you have a window open?"

I quickly extinguish my cigarette, feeling a mixture of relief that Andrew's home at last and disappointment because it's not like anything's changed. His coming home was bound to happen at *some* point, so why bother getting excited? As I walk through the wide-open balcony door I glance at my silver, diamond-encrusted Chanel watch, one of the many "I'm sorry I have to travel for work" presents from Andrew. *8:40*, the glittering gift reads.

"It's freezing in here," Andrew says. He drapes his full-length wool coat over the back of the sofa, his black briefcase following suit. He briskly crosses the room to close the large glass door, and I can't help but smile as I watch him.

Andrew's so attractive, with his determined and mature strut, and his slim but well-proportioned build. He towers over my five-foot self a good ten inches, has even bluer eyes than mine, skin a color between almond and caramel with hints of freckles, and the most dreamy salt-and-pepper hair, emphasis on the salt. Come this time each day his face has got an equally salt-and-pepper-ish shadow. He always smells of the muskiest of colognes and, when clean-shaven each morning, of a rich aftershave, thanks to Ralph Lauren. His wardrobe is impeccable—suave and with an air of importance, just like the man in the suit. With the exception of the rarely worn pair of linen pants or loosely-fitted shirts, it's nothing but crisp, collared button-downs from only the best designers, with smart sport coats and evenly-pressed dress slacks, Cartier cufflinks, exorbitant ties, and Italian-made loafers to match.

"Hey," I say in a soft voice, holding my arms out for him to give me a hug.

"Hey, baby," he coos, wrapping me in a strong and warm embrace. He leans down for a kiss, my lips instantly tingling. We definitely aren't lacking in the attraction department.

"I was waiting forever for you to come home," I say in between kisses. My lips may be tingling, but my stomach feels a little unsettled, no thanks to the distressing thoughts running through my mind lately. I force a bleach-white smile and run my fingers through his hair.

"But I'm home now," he says. Then his brow slightly rises. "Jackie, were you out there in this weather?" He points to the balcony. "*This* cold wearing *that?*" He motions at my rather scantily clad self.

Andrew's got his prim and pressed designer wares, and I've got my Samantha Jones meets Beyoncé designer wardrobe. Glamorous, maybe inappropriate to some, but always fun.

I look down at the shimmery gold and cream spaghetti-strap Marc Jacobs dress that perfectly conforms to my slim lines and flat chest.

"Looks better on me than the hanger," I say coyly.

"*That,*" he says with a kiss, "I can't argue. You look ravishing."

"And..." I sing, taking his hand in mine as he walks back to the sofa. He retrieves his briefcase. "...maybe, since I look so ravishing, we could go out?"

He charges towards the office, flipping lights on in a flash. "Sorry, darling." He lets go of my hand and sets his briefcase down on his massive, glass-topped desk. With a *click-click* of the case and a flurry of papers and files, he says, "I've got to work this whole weekend. If I don't give this client my full and complete and *immediate* attention, I'm going to be in hot water."

"Great," I mumble. I begin to rub absentmindedly at the office's doorframe. "I thought we could go somewhere, do something. *Anything!*"

"Baby doll." His tone is impassive. "I have work to do. I'm sorry."

"You *always* have work, Andrew. We never do *anything* fun." I move from rubbing the doorframe and on to the figure-eight-shaped oriental vase on the pedestal nearby. I finger the reflective material. "I'm bored."

"And I'm busy." His eyes are focused on the piles of paperwork. "And what about the other weekend, huh? What about that trip to Jamaica? We have fun."

"Andrew." I glare at him. "That was *Thanksgiving.* Two months ago!"

"Baby," he says in a low, drawn-out way, "I love you, but I'm doing this for us. Okay? I have no choice. I've got to get this work done."

"Fine," I say. I flick the top of the vase with an acrylic nail, and a high-pitched ping sounds. "Whatever."

With a sharp turn on my bare heel I make my way back to the living room, diving headfirst onto the cozy sofa. I take a sip of the neglected martini I whipped up in disappointment once it was already past seven and Andrew still wasn't home. With a small smack of my lips I flip on the television, then say under my breath, "Maybe *I* have no choice."

3

"Have you talked to Lara lately?" Emily asks over the phone. "Left a couple texts to see if she wanted to hang out. I've been so bored lately," I say. "Says she's busy at work."

I was going to call Lara last night, in fact, to ask if she'd thought any more about what she was going to do about Nathan. I'm afraid to hear her answer, though, so I've done the most unlike-Jackie thing of all and haven't rung her up or texted a zillion times. Discussing Lara's situation with her only reminds me how perhaps her problems aren't so different from my own, and *that* reality hurts. Besides, does Lara really want my prying or shoddy attempts at advice? I can't with a clear conscience tell her what I think is best for her when I don't even know what's best for myself.

I mean, you never really know if you're making the right choice about a relationship. If you stick it out, maybe it'll work, maybe it won't. If you bail, then you'll never know if it possibly had the legs to stand. But did you just save yourself more potential heartache, more disappointment, by calling it quits? Or did you just screw yourself out of something that could be amazing?

"This still about Andrew?" Emily says.

I'm an open book to this girl. Well, it probably helps that I run to and confide in her like bees flock to honey.

"Jackie," Emily says before I can say anything. "You need to have an open and honest discussion with Andrew about your feelings. It won't get any better until you do. Plus, it isn't fair to him—to either of you—to keep this bottled up."

"He just thinks I'm spoiled." I try to pick clean the back of an acrylic nail. "Being dramatic."

"Well, that you are," she says with a laugh.

"Spoiled or dramatic?"

"Both."

"Ha, ha." I pick at another nail. "I'm being serious."

"Being a pampered princess is besides the point, Jack. Your marriage is obviously bothering you a great deal, and things aren't going to look up if you keep complaining, keep hiding your feelings. You're a frank woman. Be open!"

"I think Lara should dump Nathan," I cut in acutely.

"And Andrew?" Her tone, and question, is direct.

"Ugh!" I begin picking at the back of another nail. "You know what happens if I say we need to talk! We'll just wind up in the same position we always wind up in. Apologies, a flood of gifts, saying we'll work through it, empty promises, and after a while the charm wears off. Back to square one."

"You make amends and effort sound so horrible," Emily says, her sarcasm not lost on me. "Apologies and gifts..."

"Well," I say with a whine, "I *do* like the gifts, I guess. But enough's enough at some point, you know? Nothing's improving in the end. I just wind up unhappy all over again...the distance grows."

"Look, hon," Emily says. She suddenly sounds rushed, distracted. "I'm going to give you the same advice as always: Talk with Andrew. And before you can say you already have and it doesn't work, talk some more. If you feel his promises are empty and you're unhappy, you *have* to talk."

I heave a heavy sigh into the phone.

"And as for Lara," she says.

"Yeah, what do you think Lara should do? Have a pointless talk with Nathan?" I suppress a playful roll of the eyes.

Emily says in a slightly higher tone, "I think Lara needs to make her *own* decision, just like you do. I know she and Nathan have talked about things—their distance—and I know things aren't getting better." She pauses. "Maybe breaking up with Nathan is the best thing for her..."

"Same story over here, Em," I point out. "I've talked before; things aren't getting better."

"Yes, but you made a *promise* to Andrew," she says in a soft voice. "You're *married*. You can't just give up on that like—like—nothing."

"What's with the sudden March for Marriage attitude?" I say with a laugh. "You couldn't care less about the tradition."

"But you *do* care, Jackie," she quickly counters. "I'm not married, Lara's not married, but you *did* make that choice. And you did it because you love Andrew. I don't want to tell you what to do or judge, and I'm not saying that just because you're married you *have* to stay married forever. It's not so cut and dry. But I don't think there's any harm in fighting to keep something you have, something that I know deep down you want."

I pull out of my relaxed position on the sofa and snatch up the clicker. "You're probably right," I say. "I *do* want my marriage to work."

"You just don't want to have to *do* the work, right?"

I can picture the understanding and playful smile that I know is on Emily's lips right now. "Probably," I mutter through my own crooked grin. "It shouldn't be so impossible, you know? Love...relationships..."

"Love's not an easy thing," she says, "and relationships are far from easy. But when you have the right one, it's worth the work."

"God, gettin' all mushy on me."

"I'm serious."

"Yeah, well..."

"Actually, I've been reading this book about finding your inner Zen. It's really enlightening."

This time I do roll my eyes. I love Emily, but could she get anymore Kumbaya?

"Well, I'm gonna give Lara a call in a bit," I say without much resolve. *Not that I have any wise words to help,* I think glumly.

"I think that's *exactly* what you should do," Emily says. "Maybe you two can share your troubles with relationships. You can help each other out. You're both going through the same thing, sort of—feeling unsure and all…"

"I guess." I rub roughly at the side of my face.

"One step at a time." Her voice is soothing and encouraging. Classic Emily. "Take my advice. Oh, and check your horoscope, babe! You could totally be missing out on *very* informative and helpful advice, you know?"

"Yeah, yeah," I say with a chuckle, actually making a mental note to consider this tip. Like Emily, I'm a believer in peeking at the writing in the stars from time to time.

"Okay," I say at last. "I'm gonna go; call Lara eventually."

"And until then?" Emily asks. "Right now?" Her voice sounds distant, then I hear her shout out to someone in the background, "I'll be up there in a sec."

"Today?" I flip the TV on. "Right now?"

"Yeah. What are you up to today?" she presses.

"Probably smoke a joint and stare out the window, watch the seagulls fly across the Bay." I select HBO and turn down the volume as soon as the program comes on, blasting at full volume.

"Jackie," she says in a low voice I find comical.

"Kidding! You know I quit ages ago."

"Hey, I'm not one to turn up a nose at sparking up, but you can really do something more productive with your day."

"Then ditch work and come rescue me from boredom." I pick behind another nail. "Puh-lease!"

"I wish I could, but I can't." She sighs. "In fact, I've really got to run. Sophie needs help up front, and Gatz has class this morning, so he's not in yet." She sighs again, but this time it somehow rings with optimism. That's Emily for you: ever the optimist, no matter the stress or situation. "Think we're headed for Monday madness over here, so I've got to hunker down."

Emily has been helping Sophie at her café for a while since Sophie needs it and can't quite yet afford hiring anyone in addition to Gatz. Emily dabbles in part-time freelance photography for a local Seattle magazine, and since she's loaded thanks to a trust fund, she spends a lot of her time at The Cup and the Cake, lending her baking hand for free.

All that will change, however, when Emily zips off to Zambia in March—I am *so* not looking forward to that! But, in the meantime, I'm sure the perks of Emily working at the café now go beyond the routine taste-tests and getting to hang out with one of your best friends. Gatz is there.

Gatsby Carter is the jack-of-all-trades, barista/baker/student/I-don't-know-what, who apparently aspires to be a writer or a poet or something literary-like. He and Emily have been dating for a couple weeks. She invited him to her book club, and I guess the two had more in common than literary preferences. Go figure.

Of course, how long she'll keep this guy is a mystery to all. I'm betting Gatz'll be around for the long haul, because they really do seem perfect for each other, but with Em we never really know.

Emily has a long dating record, and I can totally see why. She's free-spirited, accepting, understanding, super fun, and pretty—like in that all-natural way. She has that perfectly sun-kissed skin and those let-your-hair-fly-about-in-the-breeze locks that are long and fresh-earth-brown (unless she's in a mood and goes for Corvette Red or Alien Green or winds up in dreads). She wears gobs of jewelry, usually of the wooden and shell families, and thinks tattoos and multiple belly button-rings and earrings are more necessary than much (or any) makeup when considering a day's ensemble. She sees nothing wrong with simply smacking on some lip balm, shampooing her hair, throwing on a hand-knit scarf with a down to earth outfit, and considering herself ready for a date. With her simple beauty and free spirit, it's no wonder she doesn't really have to try. She just glows.

I think Em's open mind and heart are big reasons why she's found it difficult to really get serious with one guy. I guess if I were traveling all over the globe and liable to meet a hottie around any corner, always open and eager to meeting anyone new, I'd probably have a tough time making a commitment, too.

But Gatsby. Gatz seems to have caught Emily's eye, and I think there's some serious potential with this one. Lord hope there's potential, seeing how the girls and I all created this giant Operation Blind Date game last year where we tried to get Emily into a serious relaysh. That was an adventure!

"Have a fab day, Em," I say, slowly beginning to feel chipper as I think about how I'm going to take Emily's sober advice and talk to Lara. I turn up the volume of the TV. "Sounds like you've got your hands full, so I'll let you go."

"Do something productive," Emily says, that warning and "big girl" tone of hers ringing through thickly.

"Yes, Mommy."

"I'll talk to you later, Jackie," she says as I pick up on Sophie's garbled voice in the background. "Be smart, be safe," Emily adds.

"Yeah, yeah. Love-ya-mean-it. Bye, girl." I make a kissing noise before clicking off.

"Goodness." I toss my phone aside.

Emily worries about me. Okay, okay, all the girls tend to worry about me. Sophie and Claire worry that I'm a bit reckless. I just like to have a good time and go to clubs and party, that's all.

Robin worries about the same, and Lara's always afraid I'll fall off the wagon and need help. To be fair, she has all the right in the world to fear that, because, well, she's picked my ass up somewhere in the ballpark of a million times. I can't even begin to tell you how often Lara's paid an outstanding bill of mine or made that emergency counseling appointment for me or stocked my kitchen cupboards. What can I say? I like to live life with abandon.

Emily worries that my mind will dull. Idle hands are the devil's workshop and she's probably right on that one, come to think of it. When I'm bored or lonely, I do stupid shit. The last thing I did that really pissed Em off was falling into a drunken sleep with a lit cigar and kind of burning a hole in her futon.

She's such a doll, though, that Em. She wasn't the least bit P-Oed about the ruined futon (which I replaced, by the way, with a *really* swanky European piece). She was worried to death over the fact that I fell asleep with a smoldering cigg, endangering my life. God, I love that girl. She's always thinking of me, looking out for me.

So it's a real bummer that she's not around more often. Emily Saunders has a permanent case of wanderlust. She's really well off thanks to her dad inventing something (or was it investing in something?), and her parents have always encouraged her to see the world and make something of her photography hobby. That means she's always wandering from place to place, and this spring she's going to Zambia! Africa!

She's going to help build wells or water pipes or something, and will do a smashing job at it, because Emily always does. She's a do-gooder with a solid heart of gold, and sometimes I envy her. But not like I used to envy Robin's close relationship with Lara, the friend who's always been able to take care of *me* and put *me* up.

When single and pregnant Robin found herself in a bit of trouble, Lara rushed to the rescue, and I sort of felt like I was playing second fiddle. But I'm over that now. Lara can be just as good a friend to me as she can to Robin, no matter the circumstance; and I was super immature back then, anyhow.

No, I envy Emily's upbringing. I couldn't imagine what it'd be like to have loving parents who actually *care* about you and your future, encouraging you and making it possible for you to be the very best you can be. My parents always told me that they just hoped I wouldn't become a crack whore, and if I did that I'd find someone who could put me up in a rehab facility, because they sure as hell weren't going to foot the bill. Charming, eh?

I also envy Emily's penchant for doing good and being so selfless. I've tried to be selfless like her. (No, not in the feeding-starving-African-babies way.) I tried to volunteer down at the women's Y a couple years ago. The second day I was volunteering to help the nutritionist educate elementary school girls on healthy eating, there was an outbreak of lice. After some days I was told it was contained and I could return, but I kind of lost interest after that. Besides, I had no business helping teach young girls healthy eating habits. My idea of staying trim for bikini season is to live off Bloody Marys and Ritz crackers.

"Hmph," I sound. I rub my hands up and down my arms, trying to abate the sudden case of goosebumps. I wrap a chenille throw around my shoulders and will myself to stand.

I have no idea what I'll do today, but I'm sure there's a sale on something somewhere. Or maybe Robin will be free to hang out. Or maybe Andrew will get home from work early and have a fancy dinner date planned. Hah! Aren't I the comedian?

I crank up the volume on the television for audible comfort and saunter towards the bedroom.

"Not likely," I grumble to myself, nudging aside a throw pillow with one foot.

My Teacup Yorkie named Bella, another one of those "sorry you're lonely when I travel often" presents from Andrew, stirs from sleep at the foot of the unmade California king-sized bed.

"Not likely, huh, Bella?" I say sweetly. I throw open the door to my walk-in closet, and the automatic lights come to life.

"Guess we better hit the town before the housekeeper gets here."

4

I kill the engine of my Mercedes and wait patiently in the darkness of the car.

Lara told me to come meet her at her office in Downtown once I got around to calling her earlier during lunch. "I'm too swamped to chat," was her reply when I rang. "We need to do drinks after work."

Lara and I haven't been out for drinks in a while. She's got this really difficult client who's been zapping all her energy, and she's got the stress of dumping Nathan (or not dumping Nathan) hanging over her head. This is one of many reasons why I don't have a job. What would be left of me if I had to work like Lara? That'd be the end of my social life! My shopping! My ability to strike up even an infinitesimal relationship with my husband! All that, plus I'm the world's worst employee.

"Let's get our drink on!" I exclaim the instant Lara opens the passenger door.

"Hey," she groans, heaving her attaché and handbag onto the car floor. She tucks a piece of short, brunette, gently highlighted hair behind her pearl-clad ear. "Thanks so much for doing this with me."

"Thank *you* for suggesting," I say, starting the engine.

Lara fastens her belt in an exhausted fashion, pulling the belt far from her chest. "Finally. I'm out of there!" She opens her black suit jacket and undoes the top pearlescent button of her dress shirt.

"You work much too hard, sister," I say.

"It's this effing client." She snaps the belt across her chest. She scoots her seat back farther to accommodate her lengthy legs—legs that she could really use to her advantage if she wanted. She could really get some hot action at one of the bars the girls and I hit up if she tried. Lara has beautiful cobalt eyes, a soft and creamy complexion, has great manicure and hair salon habits, a healthy body—she jogs and actually has a treadmill in her apartment! More than I can say about my gym habits (of which there are *none* to speak). Lara says her ass is growing wider with every year she falls further and further away from what was once the daunting 3-0 but is now the "oh, back when I *was* thirty" (which was only last year). So melodramatic for no reason. If I were a dude, I'd do her.

But Lara doesn't like to get too wild and crazy, even though she's got somethin' to shake. Sure, we can go out and have fun, but she's pretty reserved. Show her a spreadsheet and I'm sure she'd get all hot and sweaty; tell her to dress up in a mini and stilettos and try to get lucky she'd turn beet-red and say I'm off my rocker.

Sometimes I've been able to coerce her into a tight little skirt, a pair of high heels, some vibrant eyeshadow or lipstick, and some jewelry that *isn't* of the Julia Child collection. Those are the nights Lara gets hit on and I just say, "Duh!" She rolls her eyes and says it's too much. And she wonders why she thinks she has no luck when it comes to relationships?!

"So, where to?" I ask excitedly.

"Anywhere," Lara answers with a sigh, sinking down into her seat. "Anywhere that'll help me fight the pain I'm feeling."

"This career of yours sounds like it's killing you."

"It's not the client," she says. "It's Nathan."

I come to a stop at the light, grip the wheel firmly, and look at her. "You're breaking up with him, aren't you? You've decided?"

She shuts her eyes. "He's cheating on me, Jackie."

"Uh, we're going to need another one of these, please," I say to the bartender. "And make it double." I motion to Lara, who's sitting next to me on the barstool at a place that makes a mean cosmopolitan. "Need to get her *tanked.*"

The bartender winks and says, "I'll take care of her."

I'm about to say that I'm sure he could, seeing how things with that loser of a boyfriend of Lara's have ended up, and how this bartender has ripped biceps that look like they could sustain hours and hours of lifting and swinging and positioning and—

"Can you *believe* him?" Lara says, snapping me back to.

"Nathan?" I take a sip of my cosmo.

She brings her head up from the depressing position on the bar, nods, then drops her head back down, her hair spilling around like a wide-open fan.

"I try not to make much sense of anything guys do," I say in all honesty. "Good or bad."

Throughout the rest of the ride to the bar, I sat in almost complete silence, mouth hanging open like a doped up patient, totally bowled over by Lara's news. Sure, anyone's capable of cheating. But Lara's boyfriend? Can't she catch a break? She's been so down and out on love for so long, and Nathan came along and seemed like a catch. Then he goes and does something stupid like this and—

"*Cheating!*" Lara shouts as she brings her head up quickly. "*Cheating!* Can you believe this?!" And down again goes her head.

"Thanks," I say with a coy smile to the bartender as he sets the stiff drink next to a pile of Lara's hair.

See, sometimes riding out that bump in the relationship leads you right here—a pathetic victim of infidelity, knocking them back with your BFF in total despair.

"Here, babe," I say, tapping her shoulder. "Drink up. It'll cure everything."

"Yeah, right," she says into the bar.

"Okay, it helps. It doesn't cure." I shrug, then take a sip of her drink.

"Turning to the bottle doesn't solve troubles, Jackie." She looks up to give me a dry expression—an expression I know all too well over the years from when she's rebuked me for turning to Captain Jack or the likes of JD when I'm feeling low and desperate.

"Then why the hell are we here?" I take my cosmo in one hand and cross my legs. I hike up the shimmery aubergine tube top I threw on for happy hour.

"It helps, I guess. Eases the pain." Lara pulls cautiously and list-lessly on her cocktail. "But drinking is *not* the answer, Jackie."

"Okay, okay," I say, flicking away the issue with my wrist. "I don't need a lecture about my *occasional* drinking habits." I roll my eyes. "But don't deny this is the kind of place to be—the thing to do—when you find out your *asshole* of a boyfriend is two-timing you. The nerve!"

"Right you are there." She raises her glass and takes another sip.

"How do you know, anyhow?" I ask. I scratch at my platinum blonde pixie cut with a freshly filled, Barbie-pink acrylic nail.

"That Nathan's cheating?" She looks nonplussed.

"Yeah. Is it a hunch or did you catch the bastard? And how long has it been going on?"

Lara fishes in her handbag, shaking her head, and withdraws a crumpled piece of paper. "Read it and weep." She returns to nursing her drink.

I open the wrinkled paper and my jaw drops. "No!"

"As evident as the Earth is round."

"He left you this?" I'm so thunderstruck I can't believe I'm actu-ally able to form words.

"That's what I woke up to this morning, Jack," she says without any luster in her voice. "The asshole writes me a *note* to tell me that he's been seeing someone else and will be all moved out while I'm away at the office. Can you believe that?"

"Shit," I whisper, setting the note on the bar. But before I do I notice there's print on the opposite side.

"What?" I say under my breath. I smooth out the note, squint, then look at Lara, tapping it roughly with a stiff finger. "A receipt?" I gasp. "He left you a fucking breakup note on the back of a receipt?"

"That's not even the worst part," she says, squiffy. "It's a receipt for the new flashy, copper, something-super-special pan he'd been wanting but didn't have the cash for."

"Huh?"

"I know, I'm a sap." She takes another pull of her cocktail.

"No, he's an ass!" I wag my head in sheer disbelief. Any of my own problems or complaints about Andrew are minor infractions compared to this doozy. "Honey, how could you focus on anything else all day?" I ask in surprise. "I would have...like..." I furrow my brow. "I would have had an appointment with the noose or something!"

"Thanks," she says dryly.

"Seriously. You poor thing. You should have called me, not gone to work. I mean, you have sick days, don't you? This definitely qualifies as a sick day."

"Going to work was all I *could* do not to face the pain." She takes a strong gulp and wipes at her lips with a cocktail napkin. "The reality."

"I'm so sorry, Lara." I give her arm a squeeze. "Should we go over there and key his car or something?"

"Ha!" Her drink sloshes about its glass from her excitement. "I don't think that's the wisest of moves, or very mature."

"Screw maturity!" I cry. "Let's give this asshole what he deserves. He gives you a receipt," I wave the receipt about, "for something *you* bought him, you give him vengeance."

"Jackie." She rests her hand on mine and gives a small smile. "I love your passion to stand up for a friend, but let's slow down here. No one's going to *key* anyone's car, all right?"

"Well," I huff, tapping my nails on the bar, "I think you're missing out on the perfect revenge opportunity."

"I just want to get on with my life, Jackie, and put him behind me."

"With*out* revenge?" I really can't believe this. The things I've done to guys in the past who've cheated on me, or broken my heart, or stood me up on a date, or said something really uncool when I was in the throes of PMS!

"It's kind of ironic, isn't it?" Lara asks with a snicker. "How I was once a mistress, and now I'm the victim, the one being cheated on?"

"There's nothing ironic about it," I state adamantly about the once-upon-a-time affair Lara had with a married man. "Nathan turned out to be an asshole, but this has nothing to do with irony."

"Bad luck?"

"Exactly! Bad luck, that's all."

"Bad luck, irony, or whatever," she says with a flutter of the lashes, "it doesn't make it hurt any less."

She stares down silently into the swirl of the bright pomegranate-shaded beverage that doesn't seem to be doing much help here.

"I really thought I was headed for a happy ending," she says finally. She tosses up her hands, fatigued. "I thought Nathan could be...you know? The *one*."

"We've all been there before, honey." I give an understanding grin, feeling myself soften at the conversation, no longer consumed by fanciful images of getting revenge on Lara's behalf.

"I really, honestly, truly thought it could work out—that we were headed in that direction," Lara bemoans.

"Except for the whole part about you having second thoughts since he's moved in," I point out.

She nudges forward her glass and makes a ho-hum motion with her head. "Yeah, well... It was nice to pretend...dream..."

"On the bright side," I say, my voice rising an octave in pep, "at least you have an easier decision to make now. You don't have to give your relationship a second thought. He's done!"

"Thanks," she says, her voice thick with sarcasm.

"Some day, girl. Some day." I give her a warm and encouraging pat on the shoulder and consider Emily's advice to help a friend in a similar situation—talk to Lara about my own second thoughts with

Andrew. Although, in this situation, now that Nathan's a cheating bastard and there *is* no choice for Lara to make, I'm not really much help here. So rather than trying to dispense some shifty-at-best advice, I say, "Your true love is out there somewhere, Lara. I just know it!"

"Well, right now I'd rather not think about *any* men." She slumps her chin into her palms.

I raise my hand to the bartender and am about to order Lara another drink when she quickly puts her hand on top of mine. "I'm good."

"You sure?" I make an inquisitive expression. "Drinks are on me. I'm ready to help you, dear. You need it."

"You being here helps," she says, dabbing at her mouth with her napkin.

"I can help out in another way, too..."

"No." Lara draws a line in the air with a hand, the napkin fluttering along. "We're not going to find the girl and go key *her* car. I don't care—"

"No, silly." I whip out my credit card and click it on the edge of the bar. The bartender snatches it, and I toss back the remains of Lara's drink. "I'm talking about a replacement. We all helped Emily find a man. Well...actually she kind of found Gatz on her own, but *anyway*, that's not the point."

"Uh-uh, Jackie," she says, drawing another line with her hand. "No dating games for me, thank you."

"Not that way," I say in my best convincing tone. "I mean that I bet we can find you a really nice and eligible man if you just put on something slinky and hit the bars, the clubs. Have some fun out... Hell, I'd *love* to be your wing gal! I'm *so* in need of some fun!"

Lara stands and slings her handbag over her shoulder as the bartender hands me the padded folder with my receipt and credit card. "I won't find my winner that way, hon," she says. "I can promise you that."

"That's how I met Andrew!" I state while scribbling my signature on the receipt. I hurriedly thank the bartender and grab my belongings. Lara's already headed for the door.

"You got lucky. One in a million, babe," she calls out as I trail sloppily behind, my oversized Prada handbag loosely hanging open and off one shoulder, my card and receipt and the bartender's pen in one hand. "One in a million."

"Oh, shoot," I say under my breath, turning back to the bar. "Your pen." I wave the pen at the bartender.

"Keep it cutie," he says with a wink, flipping a hand towel over his shoulder.

"Aww, thanks." I put a hand on my hip, slightly sticking my hip further to the side.

"She's married!" Lara calls out loudly.

I roll my eyes, turn on my high-heeled toes, and make a trot to the door. "Thank you!" I call out, waving goodbye behind me.

I link an arm with Lara's and lean into her as we exit the bar. "Can't a girl still get compliments when she's married?"

"Not when the bartender looks like *that* and when you're dressed like *that* and *tipsy* and...all cute and bubbly and stuff." She wags her head. "Uh-uh."

"I can be sweet on a guy for *you*, Lara," I say in a low voice, trying to sound serious and not burst out laughing over her protectiveness. "Let me run back in there and grab his number. You'll have a date in no time!"

"No more men for me for a while, Jackie," she says, walking us to the edge of the street, her grip firm.

"Well where's the fun in that?" I jam the receipt, pen, and credit card into my handbag.

"Not everything in life has to be fun, Jackie. Life is not a party."

Lara hails a distant cab, and I shrug my bare shoulders.

I don't know about that. What's the point of life if there isn't a party going on or one to be had soon enough?

5

"That was a great idea, Jackie!" Robin says. She strokes Bella's head, which is sticking out of the top of the chic Louis Vuitton dog carrier that's set on its own seat in The Cup and the Cake.

With Andrew off on an overnight business trip to LA leaving me all alone, and with Robin busily planning her upcoming wedding to Bobby, I jumped at the chance to lend a friend a hand and help tick off the florals on her wedding to-do list.

"I was only going off of the list of wedding flowers you had pre-prepared, Robin," I say.

"But you knew my vision!" Robin looks like she's glowing, and not just the pregnancy glow. She's looking at me like I've discovered the cure for cancer or something, because she's so happy with my suggestion at the florist's this afternoon. "You have an eye for this."

"Simple is...simple," I say with a light laugh. "Besides, you're the artist."

It's true. Robin's a book cover designer by trade, and in her rare free time, she paints and sketches. I appreciate art and design, in particular interior design, but could never imagine being able to make a craft a trade, like Robin.

"Well, I love it!" Robin gushes.

Rose, Robin's two-year-old daughter, who's sitting in the antique high chair that Sophie keeps on-hand for her tinier customers, is loudly banging her collection of small, colorful toys on her tabletop.

"Hydrangea with roses and some eucalyptus greenery," Robin says, going all starry-eyed over her chosen wedding florals. She puts a hand to her cheek in a rapt gesture.

Robin's wedding to Bobby is going to be so beautiful. She wants something not at all complicated, but still very pretty, obviously. No big shindig, like Claire's wedding, but not too understated, like mine.

Andrew and I had a courthouse ceremony. It was super simple, with no frills whatsoever. I didn't even wear a traditional wedding dress. Neither of us wanted to make a big deal over our wedding, and I think a tiny part of Andrew didn't want to deal with any potential ridicule that could come as a result of him robbing the cradle, as some may say. I didn't care either way—big shindig or simple ceremony and fête afterwards. So long as I got to become Mrs. Andrew Kittredge. Our New Year's Eve party was the perfect reception, and looking back I wouldn't have done it any other way. Simplicity at its best.

Robin's wedding is going to be easy and sweet and sentimental. She and Bobby are getting married in April in their backyard, so long as the familiar April showers of Seattle stay at bay. A ceremony and reception at home, with an intimate group of close friends and family. I think it's a really smart idea, seeing how Phillip will be just a tiny thing and Bobby and Robin have such a gorgeous home in Phinney Ridge, a family-friendly neighborhood in north Seattle.

"Wait," Sophie says, having joined the conversation soon after Robin and I downed our first beverages. We're now already working on seconds as we discuss deeper the Nathan-Lara issue. "I don't understand." She abruptly shakes her head, her curled brunette bangs and long, silky ponytail wagging along. "She honestly had *no* idea that Nathan was seeing someone else? No inclination?" Robin and I nod our heads. "Yet she was *still* feeling wishy-washy about their relationship?"

When Robin and I weren't gushing over her wedding details during today's car rides, we talked the Lara and Nathan issue to death. We've got to help her out some way, but keying cars is apparently not allowed, and Robin told me on the way to the florist *and* on the way to the café that I am not permitted to call Nathan and give him a piece of my mind under any circumstances. (Dammit.)

"Yup!" I say to Sophie enthusiastically. "I didn't believe it either, but over a couple of cosmos during happy hour girl time, Lara gave me the whole story."

Lara, like most women, couldn't have fathomed that the wedge that was driving its way between herself and Nathan was another woman. She thought perhaps the reason they'd been steadily growing apart was because of work-related stress; kerfuffles that can mount when you share a home together; or petty disagreements that combust into relationship-doomers. Sometimes comfortable relationships can turn down that road—that edge of the cliff. Sometimes an affair to remember turns into that affair you'd rather forget. Sometimes you have to let go and move on.

Sure, at first Nathan and Lara's relationship was great. They spent nearly all of their free time together, and whenever they were at home, it was *all* about being together. Dinner together, movies and TV together, walks around the neighborhood together, even apartment projects and to-do lists together. It's what my women's magazines call young love, or "the honeymoon stage." Everything's new and fun, and you kind of feel like you're on top of the world and impervious to anything bad, sad, or potentially mood-dampening. Oh, it sounds *so* familiar!

Then come the routines, the humdrum and makes-you-want-to-kill-yourself-sometimes days. It's when that usual walk through the neighborhood or the late-night rerun of *How I Met Your Mother* with greasy, take-out burgers is no longer fun and exciting and viewed as valued and enjoyed time together, but becomes your life. Your predictable and mundane life.

All relationships go through this dip down into boring routine, as my women's magazines also point out, but if there isn't true love and hope to fall back on, then you're kind of where Nathan and Lara are. The charm's worn off, the love isn't really there or it's fizzling out, and then what? You're staring at each other over a cold plate of spaghetti that you've prepared together in silence, perhaps in an effort to rekindle that spark you used to have when you made meals as a couple in the beginning. Neither has anything to say—or anything they *want* to share, especially if they're off giving it to another woman—and that mind-numbing slump slowly but surely becomes your life, your relationship, your...drowning moment.

"They even talked about doing something to change things," Robin says to Sophie, thumping the table with one hand. "Said Nathan told her he was fine with the way things were, even if they *were* a little boring." She looks to me. "I got that right, didn't I, Jack?"

I nod in approval.

"Damn," Sophie mutters. Her hands fall into her aproned lap. She sinks her slender shoulders forward, then says, "And Lara? She told him she wasn't fine? Before she discovered the affair?"

"Yup," I jump in, fiddling with the wrapper of the carrot and ginger spiced cupcake that Sophie insisted we try—a tasty new recipe of hers. "Lara said she confronted him several times about being unhappy, and each time he said he was fine with the status quo."

"Status quo." Sophie makes a squished face. "Yikes."

"Yeah," I say with a scoff. "*Status quo.* Any guy who uses those words to refer to your relationship...beware."

"I've heard that line before. *No bueno* for sure." Sophie shivers, then absentmindedly smooths out her teal apron, running her hands up and down her long legs. "Poor Lara. Just when she thought she'd scored with this one—"

"He turns out to be a chump," Robin finishes with a full mouth.

"Well," Sophie says in a high-pitched tone. She sits up even taller in her seat. "All we can do is be super supportive and hope and pray she gets out of this one without too many scars."

"I still think we should go find the bitch and key her car," I say, picking at the crumbs on the table.

"Do we know who this bitch is?" Sophie looks from me to Robin.

"Language, please," Robin says. She abruptly covers Rose's ears, a piece of cupcake awkwardly in one hand. A small dollop of frosting is now on the side of Rose's forehead, some of it caught up in her wispy, gold tufts of hair. Robin thumbs at the icing and licks it, making a small smile as she swallows the sweet treat.

Sophie mouths a "sorry" as I say, "Apparently it's some girl he works with. She's some floozie assistant cook or something. Lara knows of her—says she couldn't care less at this point."

"Lara said when he started his new job things *really* started to fall apart," Robin adds.

"Obviously. He goes and meets the home-wrecker. How could she not know?" Sophie pulls a perplexed face. "I mean, I guess the signs aren't *always* obvious." Sophie and Robin share a quiet and small moment.

I won't get into the yucky details, but Sophie used to have this boyfriend, right out of college (no doubt the "status quo" asshole). Then there was this really drunken and stupid and totally forgiven accident—Robin kind of hooked up with him one night. It sounds really crazy, and a lot of people might think Sophie's insane to ever have forgiven Robin for something like that, but life and relation- ships and friendships are funny things. Some are just so damn strong and important that even the things that move mountains can't move anything as monumental as a bond you have with a friend.

Anyway, Sophie didn't see the cheating signs when that happened; why would Lara see them with Nathan and this ditzy coworker? Sometimes all of the signs are pointing and screaming so loudly at you, but you just can't see them, or hear them. And maybe sometimes you don't want to...

"Isn't it often the slinky coworker?" Sophie says, a puzzled look in her eyes.

"Usually," I say. Both girls look at me with expecting gazes. "My magazines say that, anyhow."

"Well, now more than ever we need to be supportive of Lara," Sophie says with determination.

"That's right," Robin agrees. "The best thing for that girl is to just hold her head up and move on—and know we're here for her."

"And probably busy herself with work until it's put far behind her," Sophie says pragmatically. "That or get therapy. It worked for her with the last guy."

"Speaking of which," Robin says, resting her hands on top of her watermelon of a belly. "You're seeing that new therapist, aren't you, Jack? How's that going?"

I set down my frilly, floral-patterned teacup and look at Sophie, who's now standing, wanting to stay and chat but needing to get back to work.

"You're right!" I say. "I haven't even told you girls about my new therapist yet. Dr. Pierce."

"Fab?" Sophie asks with a grin, bringing out her pen and pencil as a young college-aged couple walks through the café's door.

"I'd say." I make a thumbs up.

"Okay. I'll be back in a jiff, and I want to play catch-up some more." Sophie picks up the scattered pieces of trash on our table and stuffs them into her apron pocket. She makes her way over to the couple who've just seated themselves near the large front window that's painted with a cherry-topped cupcake and the words *The Cup and the Cake* printed in a pretty, swirly font in pink.

"What happened with Dr. Milbanke again?" Robin blurts out, drawing my attention away from the newly arrived couple, who are sitting with their fingers entwined, foreheads pressed together. "That's his name, right?"

"Yeah," I say. I look to Robin. "Dr. Milbanke said he couldn't really help me anymore. Said it was time I moved on to a recommendation of his."

"Oh, *yeaaah*." Robin tilts her head back in recollection.

"Anyway." I jiggle my foot, sliding my chestnut-colored, stiletto-boot up and down a bit. "I'm really liking the new shrink. I've only been seeing him for going on two weeks, but he's really helpful. Insightful." I smile to myself as I think about what Dr. Pierce said at our last session. "He thinks he can really help me learn to grow and deal with my pain."

"That's really great, Jackie," Robin says. She gives me a small but genuine and understanding smile.

"And he also said he's going to help me learn how to appreciate my life." I pause briefly. "And Andrew. 'Cause, you know, things are so rough." I give an awkward shrug.

"Wonderful." She tries her best to reach over the table, but her watermelon tummy is keeping her from making much progress. I hold my hand out to hers, and she squeezes it. "That's wonderful, Jack."

"And," I say rather loudly, looking proudly from my left to my right, "he's going to help me realize that divorcing Andrew is *not* the answer to my problems."

"Okay," Sophie says, rushing back over to our table. "What'd I miss? I think I've got five minutes." She plunks down into the seat next to me, startling Bella from her sleeping position in her carrier nearby. "Your therapist. The new one. Dish, dish."

6

I t's no secret. Okay, so it's only a secret to Andrew, the second-most important yet fully unaware other party in the whole divorce discussion. The girls all know that a couple of months ago I kind of ran off the ledge, full lemming style, and researched divorce law in Washington state. I don't know why they made such a big deal about it when I told them what I was up to. It was only *research*. And it's not exactly the easiest of things to Google or search for in the library, let me tell you. Just getting a library card so I could access the library was the biggest hassle of all. I can't imagine what an actual divorce would be like!

I ended up copying a few papers on the topic, hurt my brain trying to understand a fraction of what they said, and after a really hot night under the sheets with Andrew and a new Tiffany brooch, and eventually a chat about how we needed to keep our marriage in front focus, I decided I didn't want to divorce him after all. The whole idea was no longer up for discussion, and I told the girls I was happy in my marriage once again and would not be visiting a divorce court any time soon. And even when I got down in the dumps about my marriage, like oh-so-recently with Andrew jetting off to LA so abruptly, I'm not running back to the library and going into research mode again.

Fast forward a wee bit, on the chaise longue of my new therapist, Dr. Pierce, and somehow I got to spewing forth my trip yet again, however brief, down Divorce Drive. Of course, Dr. Pierce wanted to further explore that greying area on day one of our sessions, and what could I say? Every now and then we'll reference it, but I'm working on healing.

The big 'D' is not the only thing Dr. Pierce and I talk about in my therapy sessions, though. God knows I have more that's plaguing me than minor issues of researching divorce law.

Dr. Pierce and I talk about all sorts of things. Well, really I talk and he listens, but that's the beauty of the doctor-patient relationship. I get to talk and talk and he gets to answer on occasion, and always with really helpful advice. When I want to talk to Andrew I'll often get a, "Let's do this later, baby doll," or "I'm really tired, let's get some sleep and visit this tomorrow." And occasionally it's, "Can't you talk to your therapist about this? I bet he could help. I pay him enough." Ugh!

I've been going to therapy for years. Ever since I met Andrew, actually. He suggested I try it out since I have a lot of pent up hostility for my parents and upbringing and shit like that, and then there's the part about me getting really bored and liking to hit the bottle or the clubs, or often both simultaneously, when the going gets tough. I wasn't so sure about therapy at first, but all my girl-friends said it was the best idea *ever*. Plus, Andrew said it was either try therapy or his stupid Scientology shtick, and there was no way in hell I'd be doing that. I mean, did Katie Holmes not teach *People* magazine readers *anything*?

I was going to Dr. Milbanke for the longest time. But then a couple months ago he told me he'd done all he could do for me and thought it best I seek out another therapist—someone with more credentials and experience with situations like mine, so he said. I say I got promoted! Guess I was doing so well that he decided to grad-uate me to my next level of shrink sessions!

"We're looking very nice today, Jackie," Dr. Pierce says as I take my seat on his plush chaise. I like Dr. Pierce's choice of furniture much more than Dr. Milbanke's, whose was so typical psyche-doctory—cold, sterile, and a deep cherry wood, as if to embody intelligence or seriousness.

Dr. Pierce's furniture isn't necessarily aesthetic and does nothing for the bland eggshell walls that could *really* use some paintings or frames or sconces or anything to look at when I'm lying about, but the chaise sure is comfortable. Almost too comfortable. Sometimes I feel like I could doze off, and last session I think I actually might have.

"Thanks," I say to the good doctor as I settle in to my usual position. I cross my ankles and prop them under a few pillows at one end of the chaise, resting my head at the other end.

"You and your husband have a nice date planned, I take it?" Dr. Pierce says, taking his own seat across from me. "That's excellent."

"Oh, Dr. Pierce," I say through a throaty laugh. "Ever since Andrew got back from that stupid meeting in LA he's been consumed by paperwork. At the office late all the time. No time for the little wife. But," another laugh, "isn't that always how it goes?"

I abruptly pull myself into a seated position, crossing my recently tanned legs. I can still smell the sweet coconut- and mango-scented bronzing cream. "I just felt like getting dressed up a little more than usual," I say candidly as I look down at myself.

I'm wearing a shift dress in a canary-yellow, with a pair of sexy black, leather, heeled boots. I first had my stiletto boots on, but even I, who has a penchant for wearing fun and loud clothing, thought it looked a little too Julia-Roberts-*Pretty-Woman*-esque. That'd no doubt give Dr. Pierce something with which to begin our session, and I don't have the patience.

Instead, I opted for the lower heel, and since it's winter, I slipped on some black Nylons and grabbed my long black and white fur coat Andrew got me from a business trip in Europe. I look like I'm ready for a date, sure, but I long ago gave up on dressing up *only* for moments when you plan on going out and doing something. I've spent many a day doing absolutely nothing around the house, and sweatpants are not befitting to anyone, whatsoever.

"Feeling down and wanting to uplift your spirits by getting up and dressing up?" Dr. Pierce smiles complacently. "Very nice."

"Well," I bite at the corner of my lip, "not exactly. Although I suppose there's always *something* to feel down about, right?" I laugh in a hiccup fashion, then slouch back into the chaise.

"What'll it be today?" Dr. Pierce rests his hands relaxedly on his legs. "You start? I offer the topic? Pick up where we left off last week?"

"No," I growl, closing my eyes. "I'm *so* done with talking about how I considered divorce. *Please*, Dr. Pierce." I open my eyes and meet his, a firm gaze. "*Anything* but that, okay? I'm already pissed that Andrew's back to treating me like a piece of furniture as it is."

"A...broken-lamp piece of furniture?" Dr. Pierce's face now reads of concern.

"Oh, god, no."

Okay, so a *few* times Andrew and I have had really rough arguments. Arguments that lead to, as Dr. Pierce knows and is inferring, broken furniture. But Andrew would never hurt me. He never has! And I'm not pulling a denial technique to cope. It's true. We just get a little...heated, if you will, and the furniture can unfortunately take the brunt of those passionate fights.

"Doctor-patient confidentiality, Jackie," Dr. Pierce says. His voice and face are pulled into such a serious expression.

"I promise," I say honestly. "Do you see any bruises?" I sit up and shrug off my coat, then hold out my arms and twist them over and back around, then around again. "See? No bruises." I twist my legs. "And none here, either. Just tanning bronzer."

"Thank you." He holds up one hand and looks off to the side. "I'll take your word for it."

I'm about to slip my coat back on but decide to roll it up as best I can into a pillow for my head. I swing my legs back up around and lie down.

"Actually, Dr. Pierce, a friend of mine, Lara," I look over to him and he nods, "she recently found out her boyfriend was cheating on her. The bastard."

"And you're concerned because..."

I scrunch up my brow and jerk my head in his direction. "Because she's my bloody friend, that's why!"

He looks taken aback, so I quickly add, "Sorry. *Bridget Jones's Diary* was on TV again."

No response.

"Lara's my friend, that's why I'm concerned," I continue, calming my rattled voice. "And cheating's just so wrong. So horrible! I could gouge his eyes out for making my friend hurt like this."

"What makes you bring this up today?" Dr. Pierce asks calmly, coolly. "Is that what you'd like to discuss? Infidelity?"

"I bring it up because it's been bugging the hell out of me." I rub a soft pinch of coat fur between my fingers. "Infidelity's been on my mind because of, you know, it being a recent thing with Lara and all." I let go of the fur and fold my hands awkwardly on my stomach. "Got me thinking about my dad," I say in a small voice. "About my mom. About affairs."

"About your father's unfaithfulness to your mother. Go on."

"About both of them!" I say loudly. I dart my eyes to the doctor across the room. "They're both lowlife scum who cheated on each other left and right."

I swallow the sudden lump that's beginning to form in my throat. I don't get *too* emotional when I talk about my family or home life as a kid, because when you've told the same sob story over and over you get pretty immune to the pain and the emotion that usually comes along with talking about angry fathers, philandering mothers, and jailbird brothers.

Even though my parents divorced when I was young, they'd done enough damage to last two lifetimes. Even after they ditched the piece of paper saying they were husband and wife, they didn't stop paving a path of destruction for their children, forcing their poisonous lifestyles onto any semblance of normalcy I may have had going for me.

My brother, Mark, whom I haven't heard from in something like fifteen years and couldn't care about less, was in and out of jail since the age of twelve. He'd done it all—anything from vandalizing Mom and Pop shops and petty theft at liquor stores to domestic abuse and drug-dealing. Mark was the last person I could turn to at home.

Dr. Milbanke had asked me on more than one occasion if my brother had ever sexually molested me or come on to me in any way, and for that matter if my parents had, either. He told me that could have been the reason I was so sexually promiscuous in college and, well, up until I met Andrew.

I told him no (I was being honest), then said wasn't that one of the perks of going to college and joining a sorority? You get to meet a lot of guys, have a lot of parties (and tons of fun), and find out what you like and don't like? We spent another three or four weeks discussing nothing *but* how I should try to view myself as a person of value offering more than what's between my legs, and on my chest—though up top I'm barely an A cup, so...

I guess if you look at it the way Dr. Milbanke put it, I'm really fortunate. I actually knew of some girls in junior high who had dads and uncles who did things that dads and uncles should never do. I'm not sure where all those girls are today, but I know their roads weren't smooth growing up, and the paths ahead only looked to be bumpier.

I heard that Lizzie, a girl I knew in seventh grade who grew up over on Hayden Avenue, is living in a trailer park in West Seattle with three bastard kids and her pimp. Of course, it could just be a rumor, but it's a believable one. My road could've been hers, but I was fortunate.

I was one of the lucky ones, and not just because I didn't have a perv of a father feel me up. I knew getting into college was one of my only chances to escape the life that fate forced upon me. I applied to the University of Washington, and I actually got in! I was admitted on a probationary status because of my less-than-stellar high school grades, but if I could maintain at least a 2.25 GPA my freshman year then I'd be able to attend college on one of those "We're sorry you're poor and come from a crappy background, so here's some money for your education. Don't become your parents, please" scholarships.

I completed my first year with a 2.75 GPA, became friends with my bestie, Lara, and even joined the Delta Gamma sorority! I pursued my degree in what would be, come my junior year when I *finally* got around to declaring a major, Communications. (Not much of an academic, but certainly a social butterfly, and with more Facebook friends than anyone I knew on campus, Communications was the most obvious choice.) That first year at U Dub paved the way for the next, when I was crowned Phi Delta Theta Fraternity House Sweetheart (probably because I slept with the house president, but I took the tiara and title, anyway); I legitimately earned my first (and only) 'A' in college; and I met the rest of my best friends! Life was definitely *much* better once college arrived. Not easy, but better.

Somehow I was able to pull myself up and do my damnedest not to repeat the mistakes my parents made. But nobody's perfect. Both Dr. Milbanke and Dr. Pierce had warned me time and again how my turning to the bottle when bummed out or reaching for a joint or getting a tad too wild on the dance floor with some skeezy guy was dangerously close to behavior my mother and father might approve of.

"This is why we're doing these sessions together, Jackie," Dr. Pierce says after I spend what feels like an hour ranting about how unjustly my parents treated their children. "You're leaps and bounds ahead of the game just by acknowledging that their lifestyle—what they put you and your brother through—was wrong, damaging, and is *not* the path for you. You can fight it. You don't have to follow in their footsteps."

"Who says I'm following in their footsteps, Doctor?" I shoot out, more rudely than intended.

"I'm not saying you are, Jackie," he says with a soothing calmness. "I'm saying it's good that you recognize their problem and that such a lifestyle is not for you." He raises both hands. "You've risen above this. Let's stay up there."

"Right," I mumble, returning to fingering my coat's fur. "Yeah... Stay above it."

"Your parents' infidelity," he opens yet again. "Do we want to explore that?"

"Do I *want* to explore it?" I give an ironic laugh.

"Shall we discuss it?"

Dr. Pierce and I spend the remainder of our session talking about how each month it seemed like my mother had a new asshole dropping by the house to "talk business," as they referred to the relationship they carried on in my parent's bedroom.

We talked about my dad and how he checked out early in the game, saying he discovered having a family just wasn't his cup of tea. He preferred the young and single pole dancers and cocktail waitresses.

The last day I saw my father was a cold, winter morning before school, back in the second grade. He brushed past me at the kitchen table. I was holding up a box of Apple Jacks, and his abrupt movements caused the box to loosen from my small grip and subsequently spill all over the sickly green and cracked laminate floor. He muttered a few choice words (I specifically remember him calling me a "stupid shit"—a kid can't erase those words no matter how much Clorox she may sniff in junior high). Then he grabbed his navy-blue work jacket, angrily stuffed the newspaper inside a pocket, and declared he wouldn't be coming home for dinner.

I cried all throughout snack break, recess, lunch break, and after-school daycare that day, unable to shake the import and cruel reality of my father's words that morning. And come seven o'clock that evening, my tiny tummy growling and my mother locked away in her bedroom after having slammed down a can of Spaghetti-Os in front of my brother and me, saying, "Eat up then go to bed," I looked to my brother from across the table and said, "I don't think Dad's coming home."

I don't think I hated or disliked my brother any time before that moment. Sure, his pulling the heads off the two Barbies I'd ever owned and stabbing out the glass eyes of the hand-me-down doll my mom had picked up for me one *happy* day down at a flea market conjured up feelings of resentment for my brother. Any five-year-old would be pretty pissed. But I'm fairly certain that the day my father didn't come home was the same day I began to hate my brother.

What was his response when I said, teary-eyed and scared, that I feared Dad wouldn't be coming home?

"No duh, you stupid shit."

All in one night I'd lost my father, lost my brother, and I'm pretty sure realized I'd lost my mother, although that had more than likely happened long before. It was me against the world, and it was a cruel one, but eventually I knew I could pull myself through it. Eventually that light at the end of the tunnel would shine. I couldn't settle for the sham of a life I'd been forced to start in this world.

I'm still waiting for that light to really shine and make all these horrible memories feel so distant I'll question if they even belong to me. They still feel pretty real, but they don't hurt as badly. The light *is* getting brighter. And my best friends—Lara, Emily, Sophie, Claire, and Robin—all have something to do with it. And, Andrew, too, of course.

"You don't have to internalize your friend's unfortunate brush with infidelity and mix it up with the pain your parents caused you, Jackie," Dr. Pierce says.

"I know. I'm not *internalizing* it." I sigh. "Just reminds me of crappy people, crappy behavior. Makes me wonder if we all end up that way, if that's written in my destiny after all..."

"You can't control what other people do. You can only control what *you* do, and how *you* react."

"Yeah, yeah, I know." I pull myself up into a seated position once more and slip on my coat.

"Don't make your friend's problem your own, imagining that you're headed for the same scenario." He clears his throat.

I bite down on my bottom lip and fix my gaze on the floor.

"Jackie? Do you *think* you're headed for the same scenario?"

"I don't know." My voice is small, because I'm not so sure where I'm headed.

"Is there something you want to talk to me about?"

I blink twice and press my coat tightly to my chest. "No," I say. "No, I'm fine."

I consider the likelihood of Lara's story, my parents' story, far too many unfortunate women's stories, becoming my own. Andrew's an attractive, successful, and charming man, and so long as you're not the wife sitting around waiting for him to come home, he's the total package. What woman wouldn't want him? Especially the kind who are around him more than I am. Like the kind who work with him.

"If the question of your husband's loyalty is something that's bothering you," Dr. Pierce says, "then you should be open and honest with him."

"I'm fine, Doctor," I say sternly.

I can feel my face become hot with discomfort. It's one thing to think your husband's having an affair, but it's another to move past conjectures and actually discuss ways to deal with a cheating spouse.

"I'm probably internalizing, that's all." I give a weak grin. "I'm fine. I can handle it. Thank you."

7

The pink bubble grows and grows until I hold my breath and carefully let it go...*snap!* I lick the deflated bubblegum from my lips and chew, prepping for another bubble. Maybe this one'll be bigger.

My attention's drawn from my masterful bubble-blowing skills to the small chandelier hanging in the antique shop window's display. It's got the largest of teardrop crystals draping about the bottom, with smaller ones climbing upward. It's exquisite!

I can't help but press my forehead to the glass windowpane of Pioneer Square Antiques to try to get a better look. I imagine the chandelier must cast the most romantic golden glow when it's turned on and all those crystals come to life. It'd look so beautiful hanging above a dark-wood dining table, or in a narrow hall or entry, or—

Suddenly, my cell phone vibrates in my hand, and its clamoring ring sounds, startling me from my fantasies.

"Andrew?" I answer the call quickly and blindly.

"No," comes the nasally voice. "This is Nikki."

"Oh," I say, disappointed. "Hi."

Nikki Dowling is Andrew's obnoxious, rude, stupid, bit— Okay,

I'm really trying to be nicer to her. I'll just refrain from using any flavorful adjectives.

Nikki Dowling is Andrew's secretary.

"Where's Andrew?" I get straight to the reason why I called my husband's office thirty minutes ago and left a message with Nikki, the girl who couldn't deliver a message if her life depen—

"I'm sorry, Jackie," her grating voice cuts through my thoughts, "but he's still got his hands tied." Her voice is so nasally I can feel my own nose start to uncomfortably plug up.

"So he's, what?" I say, backing away from the antique shop window. "Busy?" I take a seat on a wooden bench nearby.

"Yes, busy," Nikki says. "He's still in with a client, and I don't anticipate he'll be out for at least...another hour."

"An hour?" I bellow.

"Yes."

Incensed, I drop my turquoise Ferragamo handbag next to me, then cross an arm over my chest. "Well..." I smack my gum. "I guess just tell him to call me whenever he's finished. Like my last message." I roll my eyes.

"Will do. Have a great day. Bye-b—"

"Wait!" I say briskly, leaning forward in my seat in urgency. "I'm not done!"

"Yes?" Nikki's voice is unappreciatively curt.

"Please tell him I'm probably going to Emily's," I say to what seems like dead air. "Hello?"

"I'm here," Nikki says, monotone.

"Tell him that, Nikki. Okay?" I inhale deeply, beckoning relaxation. "Please. I don't know how long I'll be at Em's, but if Andrew's looking for me, that's where I am." I withdraw the pack of Parliaments from my handbag. "That's all I wanted to say."

"All right. Have a nice day, Jackie. Goodbye."

The line clicks dead before I can slip out another word.

I look at my phone with a curiously raised eyebrow. "She's such a bitch," I mutter. I toss the phone into my handbag.

Nikki Dowling and I don't exactly get on too well, if you haven't noticed. We try to be civil, but it's difficult when there's such a strong undercurrent of nastiness every time we talk. It's that passive-aggressive bitchiness that runs really rampant up sorority row amongst the houses. As a DeeGee sister, I can smell it a mile away, and Nikki reeks.

I could live my life quite happily without Nikki in it, thank you very much, but Andrew won't fire her, because apparently she's a really fast typist and very reliable. Reliable at what? I'm not so sure, seeing how Andrew misses about half the messages I leave. But whatever. Andrew says I'd dislike anyone who was his secretary because they'd be a natural roadblock to me being able to ring up and access him any time I pleased. Point well taken, I suppose.

I'm sure Nikki could live her life happily without me in it, too. I think she hates me. Of course, I did drunk dial her once upon a time and told her that she was a total bitch who should kiss my ass. She kind of had it coming, even though Andrew still seethes a tad whenever that memory's brought up.

See, Nikki's a fellow shopper and lover of all-things-designer, especially when on sale, so she used to give me little tips on special sales she found and stuff. The gestures were kind, and I guess she figured it wouldn't hurt to be sugary to her boss's wife. So when I'd call the office to reach Andrew (because he gets upset if I call his cell phone when he's working—so stupid) she'd tell me, "Hey, by the way, there's a sale on sandals at Nordstrom!" or "Did you know there's a BOGO at Anthropologie?" Very helpful and critical information like that.

Only trouble was that sometimes that information was totally false. If I told her afterwards that there was no such sale at Kate Spade's, she'd act all surprised and say things like, "Oh, I'm *so* sorry, Jackie. I must have gotten the date wrong."

I've always thought it fishy to send me on these wild goose chases. I mean, what the hell's the point? Just don't tell me *anything*. Andrew (and all the girls, actually) think I'm being petty and that the whole passive-aggressive thing Nikki and I have going on is ridiculous. Andrew says if missing out on a discounted pair of peep-toes tops my tragedies list then I need a hobby. To which I reply, "Shopping...hobby...what part of this are you not understanding?" To which he'll often reply that I don't need to chase sales anyway with my bottomless allowance.

Anyway, I don't know what Nikki's got for brains, but I'm pretty sure if you took a trip inside her skull you'd lose a few of your own wits stumbling about in that dark. There's no reason for her to lie to me or have a beef with me or...erm...okay, minus the drunk dialing... But she was bitchy *before* that little episode. She had it coming. I just don't get her behavior. What did *I* ever to do to *her*?

Now, ever since that little episode with the phone one shnockered night, Andrew's insisted that Nikki and I both put our best foot forward and be as civil as possible. I'm trying. I really am.

I continue to huff and puff as I sit in the square, even mumbling aloud to myself, grousing how I wish Andrew would come to his senses and fire her. I bet he'd get more of my messages then. He may even call me back now and then. Now there's a novel idea...

Or maybe Nikki'll grow so tired of having to deal with me she'll quit! I think excitedly. I blow one last bubble, then toss my gum into a nearby trashcan. "She's impossible!" I cry.

I withdraw a stick from my nearly emptied pack of cigarettes and place it between my ruby-lipsticked lips.

"Honestly," I say in an angry whisper. I light up, take in a puff, and blow a ring of smoke out up into the cloudy sky.

There's a slight breeze whirling through the square, the bushes and thin tree limbs swishing and swaying. The sun's at the perfect position, in a long stretch of no clouds and able to scatter its rays all about the red-brick buildings and square.

I love Pioneer Square. It's the best place to come to think and unwind. In the old pioneering days it used to be the heart of Seattle, and today it's filled with all of these historic, turn-of-the-century brick and stone buildings. It's a short drive from home and kind of looks like an old Hollywood movie or TV set. It's a charming part of town that's kind of plunked down in the middle of the modern, rush-rush part of the city.

I used to come here growing up whenever I wanted to escape whatever fight was breaking out at home. If it wasn't my parents arguing, then it'd be my dad and my brother, or my mom and my brother—always someone wanting to throw the first punch or strike below the belt. Running to Pioneer Square provided that escape, that imaginative release. Feed the pigeons, sit and think, imagine that I was in an old movie with Cary Grant, Bette Davis, and Doris Day. I'd gawk at what was for sale behind the antique and gift shop windows. How often I'd wander through the old bookstores and secondhand shops.

I never felt like Pioneer Square belonged in Seattle—it's so displaced with its historic charm. And I never felt like I belonged in my family. Suppose that's why I ran here in the first place.

I still like to come here from time to time—old comforts that are conveniently located near home. It's the kind of place where you can burn time, ponder, smoke, or even shop. A place of escape.

My phone rings to life once again, and I immediately retrieve it, hoping on a wing and a prayer that it's Andrew. It's not that my message is of any importance, but it'd sure be nice to know that Nikki listened to me and Andrew cares enough to do even the smallest of things I ask.

"Andrew?" I answer in a blind hurry.

"Nope," comes Emily's reply.

"Oh, hey," I say, trying not to sound too disappointed. "What's going on?"

"Your crap, that's what," she replies dryly.

"My *crap?*" I yank on my handbag and stick my cigarette in my mouth, trotting off through the square. "What are you talking about?"

"Jack, I love you," she says with a laugh, "but I've got a ton of your clothes over here. *Still!* My bedroom floor is beginning to disappear. *Again!* Are you on your way yet?"

"That the only reason you want me over, eh?" I tease.

"The main one." Emily—always honest. A doll, but honest.

Emily's got a simple one-bedroom apartment over in Fremont,

the peculiar part of town. The neighborhood's motto of "*De Libertas Quirkas*" fits Emily's hippie and quirky personality and lifestyle to a T. It's Seattle's funky corner, with junk shops and head shops, eccentric public sculptures and art, and there's never a shortage of dusky coffeehouses or grungy pubs. It's filled with a mix of ancient hippies, up-and-coming young business types, and even the few, like Emily, who enjoy being granola on top of a giant trust fund.

Em's had her place in Fremont for years, even when she's off traveling the world, and often I'll call her *casa* my *casa*. It's not unusual for my stuff to collect at her place. (It just sometimes gets a little out of hand.) Whenever Andrew's out of town I'll usually crash at Em's. I've lived there when she's been gone traveling and also countless times when I've been between boyfriends.

"All right, I'm coming," I say to her. I take one last puff, then stamp out my cigarette.

I'm about to make my turn out of the square when a vintage hatbox in the antique shop window catches my eye.

"Oh, Emily." I peer inside the window, shielding my eyes from the reflecting sun with one hand between. I press my face up closer so I can get a look at the gorgeous, worn, striped pattern on the box. "I just found the most lovely little hatbox. Can't believe I didn't see it before!"

"Hanging out in Pioneer Square again, are you?"

"Yes," I say, my voice all gushy-sounding as I stare at what would be the most perfect decorative piece for a sitting room or entry hall. It's like one of those pieces they'd use in a *Vogue* photo shoot, where the models are all dressed up like Victorian dolls, with pastel parasols, and they're in a San Franciscan carriage house or something. Something elegant and turn-of-the-century.

"Gatz is coming over when he gets off work later tonight," Emily explains through what sounds like the munching of chips. "So if you're looking for some girl time and you're bored..." She clears her throat. "Or if you don't mind coming over and taking home some of your crap, then now is the time."

"I'm coming," I say, pulling myself from the window. "Was only gawking."

Andrew would never hear of putting something that wasn't modern or white or steel or ridiculously expensive in our home as décor. I wouldn't really know what to do with an old hatbox, anyhow.

8

"How does this even cover what it's supposed to cover?" Emily asks, holding up one of my shift dresses. She's got a bemused look on her face and begins to press the dress up against her body. "Guess you have to choose..." She pulls it up higher over her boobs, then lower to above her knees.

"It stretches when you put it on," I say with a laugh.

"I should hope so!" She tugs at the silvery cloth.

"Don't stretch it out!" I caution, reaching up for the dress from my seated position on Emily's bedroom floor, which, by the way, is *not* as bad as she made it out to be. You can still see at least half the floor.

"I thought you said it *stretched*, silly," she says, dropping the dress into my open arms.

"There's a right and wrong way to stretch material."

Emily tosses a pair of my fishnet stockings into the laundry basket in the center of the room.

"I want to keep these here," I say, showing her a handful of some simple shirts and a pair of dark jeans.

"You can keep some stuff here, Jack." She folds a pair of my pants. "You know half that dresser," pointing across the way at it, "and half that closet," pointing over at it, "are yours, anyway. My door's always open for you, honey. I just need *some* space for myself." She places the pants in the basket and holds up a U Dub sweatshirt. "Yours or mine?"

I twist my mouth to the side in consideration. "Not sure."

"Well, you're a stick," she says, "and I've got the curves and bosom." She presses the baggy sweater against her chest. "Probably mine."

"Whoever's it is, just keep it here." I shake out a balled-up white minidress and guffaw when I realize what it is. "My god, do you know what this is?" I hold the dress against me.

"1990s *Clueless* throwback dress?"

"Ha-ha." I hold the dress out at arm's length and examine it. "I bought this like three years ago, thank you."

"Guess the 90s *are* back in style." She casually tosses another pair of stockings into the basket.

"This is the dress I wore on my first official date with Andrew." I smile and fall back on my heels, legs tucked underneath.

"It's been here that long?" Emily looks thunderstruck. "No way."

"Of course not." I shake my head. "I've worn it since then, obviously." I hold the dress to me and sigh. "Oh, memories..." I hug it tightly. "That was when things were exciting and fun and—"

"New," she cuts in. "When things were new."

"Exactly. Relationships can be *fabulous* when they're new."

Emily cocks her head to the side—that warning look of hers that says I better not argue with her. "Things still can be fabulous, Jackie, even if they aren't new. It's a different kind of fabulous, you know?"

"Yeah, yeah." I take one more look at the dress and give a small smile. "Well," I say in a high tone, "enough about my husband who refuses to return my calls."

"He's a busy guy."

Emily always gets an earful about my slumps with Andrew. She's always understanding and patient, and she lets me talk and talk, and will offer sage advice, kind of like Dr. Pierce, but better. God, it's going to suck when she goes to Africa next month...

I fold the dress with a pout, force the image of a departed Emily from my mind, and set the dress in a Dolce carrier bag.

"He's got a lot to do at his firm," Emily continues, "with a lot of stress and a lot of responsibility."

"With a secretary who I know will *not* deliver my messages, no matter how much I plead...or how often." I let my shoulders sink forward. I pick up a sandal, glance about for its partner, and when I can't spot it immediately I give it a toss into the darkness of the closet.

"Don't work yourself into a tizzy over Nikki," Emily says. "She's not worth it."

"I've left messages with her twice now, Em. *Twice.*"

"You've left more before, and Andrew's called you back. Eventually." She stops folding another pair of my pants and tells me to keep my chin up. "Give him time. He's busy, and when he's done, he'll call you back."

"Do you think he's cheating on me?" I ask suddenly. The question came up in my mind, however briefly, at Dr. Pierce's earlier; I've had it a couple times before, but only faintly; now it comes spewing forward given the recent events that have unfolded in Lara's life.

I twist the rock of a wedding ring around my finger twice. I'll never forget that trip to New York with Andrew, when we went to Tiffany's so I could pick out a dazzling tennis bracelet, just because. We took a little detour to the engagement rings, and Andrew not-so-surreptitiously pried at what struck my fancy. It was a round solitaire—*the* Tiffany Setting—that made my eyes wide, my heart beat, my stomach go all flippy at the thought that *I* could become Mrs. Andrew Kittredge. At the thought that I could walk around those country clubs I pictured being a member of when I hit middle age, strutting about with my giant, glitzy diamond, swinging a tennis racket and thinking, "Look how far I've come!"

I look at the weighty ring, and my heart goes from dreamy beats to heavy thumps. A lot can change in a year-and-a-half. Cloud Nine with Tiffany's one day, then on Emily's floor the next, touching on the topic of infidelity, wondering if I'd made the right choice marrying Andrew...

"Andrew?" Emily says, aghast. "*Andrew? An affair?*"

"Yeah. You think it's possible?"

"Well," she says slowly, her warm brown eyes locked on mine. "Anything's possible—"

"Oh, great!" I exclaim, tossing up my hands and the melon-colored chiffon scarf that's in them.

"Let me finish." Emily's voice is cool and collected. "Anything is possible, but I don't think that a man who loves a woman *so* much— the way Andrew loves you—would cheat."

"If he loved me so much he wouldn't neglect me like he does, Emily," I say sourly.

"I know you're frustrated with your situation, Jackie." She gives me a small and sympathizing grin. "I know if you had it your way you'd have Andrew home by five every night."

"And he wouldn't be married to his damn career," I add.

"And he wouldn't be married to his damn career."

"And he wouldn't have Nikki as his bimbo secretary." I stick out my tongue and make a childish face.

"In a perfect world, yes, there would be no Nikki and there would be no late hours at the office. There'd be no arguments, no disagreements, and always a party."

I chuckle. "True. That'd be a perfect life, wouldn't it?"

"Yeah," Emily says, her face lighting up as the conversation trends away from "I'm in a pit of marital despair" to "maybe I'll manage this like I've managed the other rough patches." She continues, saying, "But this isn't a perfect world, and no one has a perfect life. There's *no such thing*, Jackie."

"Okay, I'm *so* not being lifted up by this pep talk, Em." I fake a laugh.

"Maybe that's the point." Her face folds up slightly in vindication. "Not everything's going to be pretty and perfect. Andrew being busy and having someone you don't like take his calls are some of those things. For god's sake, Jack, you want the glitz and glamour life, and that comes at a price. Andrew is wealthy and not from nothing. He works crazy hours because he wants to provide for you." She wags her head and begins to fold another pair of pants. "Besides, you were well aware of his dedication to his career before you married him. This should come as no surprise."

"I know," I moan, having heard and thought this all before.

"A man in his fifties," she carries on, "never been married to anything but his career...what can you expect? Life is great, but it ain't perfect."

"You don't have to tell me how life isn't rainbows and unicorns," I say, my tone and words unwavering.

"I know that." She inches her way across the floor on her hands and knees until she's right beside me. "I know you're going through a difficult time in your marriage right now, Jackie, but this is life. It'll get better again."

"*Another* difficult time." I look at her, deadpan.

"When God handed out lives, She didn't assign only *one* difficult hurdle per person, babe."

"Well." I turn a loose sock inside out, then back again.

"It'll get better," she reassures once more.

"You promise?" I sniff back the teary feeling I suddenly have.

"Yeah, I'll promise that." She gives me a squeeze. "It *will* get better again. You just need to stick it out and stay strong."

"*Get* strong is more like it," I say with a long blink. I sink further onto my heels, and Emily gives my shoulders a friendly shake.

"And," she says with very slight hesitation, "I think you really should be open with Andrew and have a heart-to-heart with him. I know you've ignored my advice." She raises her eyebrows. "Am I right?"

"Em, it won't do any damn good."

"I'm just saying." She holds her hands up. "Just saying it's the least you could do. *Try* to talk. Let him know how you're feeling."

I scratch at the back of my head and nod, knowing that she's right, that I probably will eventually gather the nerve to talk to Andrew. Just not right now. Not yet. Besides, maybe this valley will see a little peak again? Just maybe? And maybe this will be the last of the slumps. I'd hate to get into a roaring argument over nothing.

"What brought this cheating topic up, anyway?" Emily asks. "You think Andrew's, what? Having an affair with Nikki?"

"Oh, god, I don't know," I groan. "The thought's crossed my mind a few dozen times." I lie down on the floor, removing a flip-flop from underneath my back. "I sure as hell hope not." I toss the shoe across the room. "I think I've just got it on my mind because of what Lara's going through."

"Bullshit, isn't it?" Emily wags her head disgustedly.

"Talked about it to my shrink, too. Talked about my parents and..." I give her wide eyes. "*You* know that spiel."

"You know what?" She pulls her knees to her chest, large swathes of her tan skin peeking through her ripped jeans, and glances around the room. She begins to rock slowly. "I think we should do something for Lara."

"Like drive over to Nathan's and egg his place?" I say in excitement, pulling myself up on my elbows.

"No, you crazy girl. Something *for* Lara not *to* Nathan."

"Doing something bad *to* Nathan would be just like doing something good *for* Lara. Besides," I say, lying back down, "I called her this morning," I place my hands underneath my head, "bugging her because I was so bored, seeing if she wanted to go out and do something after work."

"And?"

"Said she's too busy." I sigh. "No time, and said she doesn't want to talk about Nathan anyhow."

"Come on," Emily says, leaping up. She holds her hand out to me, wiggling her bejeweled fingers, fingernails painted a dark (chipped) shade of green. "We're going to do something for Lara whether she has the time or not. It'll be good for her, and it'll be good for you. Get you out of this is-my-husband-cheating-on-me slump."

"She's going to love it!" I sing, holding one end of the large gift basket Emily and I've put together for Lara. We went to Pike Place Market, the world's best outdoor market, and filled it with all sorts of frilly things sure to make a girl feel better after heartbreak.

We've got the bottle of wine (the essential in gift-basket-making), the dried Chukar cherries and sweetened almonds, boxes of cookies, chips, and, of course, *several* bars of dark chocolate, some lavender bubble bath, and this organic olive oil soap that Emily always has in her shower and insists should replace all other body soaps. We found this new organic hair conditioning treatment when we stopped to grab some of Lara's favorite body cream, so we threw that in too. Then of course we had to swing by Randy's to pick up the latest Dean Koontz and James Patterson hardbacks that we know Lara's been wanting to get her hands on. It's the perfect get-over-your-douche-of-an-ex-boyfriend-make-you-feel-like-a-million-bucks basket!

"And look," Emily says, pointing at Lara's sleek Audi across her apartment parking lot. "She's home, so it looks like we won't have to camp out on her doorstep."

"Wait!" I stop abruptly in my tracks and point at the bright red Jeep two cars down from Lara's.

"What?"

"It's him." I point my finger harder, as if to emphasize my surprise. "*Him!*"

"Him who?"

"Nathan, who else?" I lock my jaw, clamping down tightly, trying to contain the rage that's beginning to boil.

"That Jeep?" Emily asks. "You sure?"

"Of course I'm sure! No one forgets a bright red Jeep." I turn to Emily and say, "Hold this. I'll be back."

"What are you doing, Jack?" She looks a smidgen frightened. She takes the heavy basket on her own, balancing it awkwardly, while I pry my keys from my handbag. With the keys in hand I boldly march up to the blindingly red car.

"Jackie, *no!*" Emily shrieks. "Don't do it!"

I can hear her chase after me, the rustle of the basket's shrinkwrap growing louder and nearer. But she's not going to stop me. Nothing's going to stop me! I'm that lemming over the ledge again. There's nothing but me, my keys, and the asshole's car.

"I've had it with cheaters," I say under my breath, wielding the longest key on my ring. With it firmly in my grip, I press it deeply into the glimmering red at the car's rear. "No one hurts my friend like this!"

I begin, slowly and steadily at first, dragging the key across the car, flicks of paint dusting into air. I pick up my pace, my line growing longer and more jagged with each bold step I make along the car. Emily's pace quickens too, but by the time she reaches me, one hand gripping my working arm, I'm already halfway done.

"It's a half-done job, Emily," I say gruffly, key still boring into the car. "I'm mad as hell and I need to do something about it."

Emily, worry covering her face, sets the heavy and awkward gift basket on the pavement. "What happened to taking some Pamprin, or watching a Hugh Grant film and crying into your pillow or something?" She roughly sets her hands on hips.

"No, Em," I say, returning to my piece of artwork.

"You're taking out your anger over Andrew and Nikki—"

"Don't forget Nathan!" I cry loud and dramatically, dragging an even deeper and more jagged line across the driver's side of the car. "He's screwed one of our best friends over. This means revenge, no matter what Lara says!"

"All of this anger about all of these things and people is being taken out on *one* guy," Emily nearly hollers. "Jackie! You're acting insane."

I make a strong slash across the rear of the Jeep, doing a little leprechaun's jig as I finish—a leap in the air, my Manolo Blahniks clicking.

"There," I say, twirling round and blowing the tip of my red-tipped key like it's a smoking gun. "Insane or not, that'll teach him to never cheat."

"No," Emily says in a deep and *uh, duh!* kind of tone. "That'll teach him he needs a car alarm system."

"Oh, Emily." I help her pick up the basket and heave it up high to get a good grip on it. "Don't be ridiculous."

"Or to get a car cover," Emily waxes on as we ascend the stairs to Lara's apartment. "Or to park in the boonies."

"Or not to fuck with one of our best friends," I say, indignant.

Emily wags her head. "Or that, yeah." She gives a loud moan. "Seriously, Jackie. That is totally unacceptable and immature behavior. There *are* better ways to achieve contentment. Ever heard of meditation?"

"Oh, Em."

"Deep breathing?"

I roll my eyes, adjusting my grip on the heavy basket.

"Yoga, repeating a mantra..." she runs on. "Ugh, Jackie. What are you thinking?"

"I did what Lara should've done a long time ago," I say curtly.

"Jackie..."

"Come on, Em." I give her a quick, sideways glance. "It's not the first time you've seen me go ape-shit on a guy's car before."

"Yeah, well," she says off to the side, "some things never change; some things should."

We reach Lara's front door, and Emily's about to knock but I quickly pull her hand down. "Wait," I say. "He's in there."

"Yeah," Emily says, eyes round and wide. "Nathan's in there, so I wouldn't exactly bring up the whole I-keyed-your-car thing right now."

"Should we wait?"

"This basket's getting heavy. If we sit out here on the front step, it's just...no. No, it's weird. We're here, we're her friends, we're going to see her."

"Yeah!" I stamp my foot in approval. "That's right! And I'd like to give Nathan a piece of my mind, anyway."

"Dear god, *no*, Jackie." Emily's eyes grow even wider—I didn't think that was possible.

"Well, we'll see about it," I say. "You're right. Let's go see Lara."

I raise my hand to knock, but before I can the door flies open and a tall pile of man pushes into me, nearly knocking me over. I lose my grip on the basket, and Emily clutches the whole thing in her arms. Emily and I stumble backwards a bit, the shrinkwrap rustling loudly.

"Oh," the man says, alarmed. He brushes at his hair and scans my face, then Emily's, then mine again. "Sorry. I—I—didn't see you." He steadies his stance and turns to the doorway, where Lara's standing, arms over chest, mouth drawn into a tight line.

"Nathan!" I cry. "Why I oughta—"

"Goodbye," Emily says, quickly stepping in between Nathan and me, the gift basket obscuring her vision, its ruffles of shrinkwrap towering. "Bye now."

"I'm out of here," Nathan says in an agitated way as he jogs towards his car.

"Jackie!" Emily says, turning to face me, smiling a frozen, forced grin through the shrinkwrap. "Let's go inside, shall we? *Inside*..." She makes a sharp motion towards Lara standing in the doorway.

"Not a bad idea," I say, pulling tighter my leather coat. I take a fast glance at Nathan. He's not yet near his car. *Oh, but when he is, and when he sees the damage I've done—*

"Lara," Emily says, chipper, still wearing that tight smile as she turns to greet Lara. "Hi!"

"Girls!" Lara looks at us in bewilderment and excitement. "This is a pleasant surprise."

"We're going to come in right now," Emily says, pushing her way into the apartment. "Right now. Come along, Jackie." She looks back at me and motions with her head to follow her inside ASAP.

Part of me is tempted to run out to the parking lot and lay one into Nathan, but I'm feeling pretty pleased and content with my art job, so I decide to follow Emily's wise orders and get my butt inside. Enough damage done for one day.

9

In just a few days' time Lara's saying she's on the slow but steady path to recovery, especially after having seen Nathan one last time to exchange a few forgotten items. (And I'm sure the gift basket played a part, too.)

Andrew's come home from the office at a decent hour a measly one time this week, bringing with him pizza for dinner. It was one of our many stay-at-home dates I wish I could exchange for a *real* night out on the town.

In the meantime, I'm learning just how gratifying revenge can be. It's been a while since I've tasted the sweet nectar and release of the 'R' word. Venting at my shrink session this week, getting the gift basket for Lara, and, of course, giving Nathan an original Jackie Kittredge piece of art have all come together to help me feel so much better about the whole sordid mess that is life.

My shrink, Dr. Pierce, of course, told me seeking revenge or searching for peace shouldn't necessarily be found at the expense of someone's car, but what the hell? The bastard's gone from our lives now, and we're all the better for it.

And the fool! I don't think he even noticed what I'd done, seeing how there was never any resentful banging on Lara's door that evening. We poured some Chardonnay and tuned in to Netflix to help her get over the loser. Emily's agreed that it's probably best we keep my ditty with the keys a secret between us; no need to get Lara's panties in a twist over some guy who shouldn't have anything to do with her...or her panties.

As for having a heart-to-heart with Andrew, I've decided to leave that on the back burner for now—for a few days or so. I'm probably daft to think there's anything going on with Nikki, or any woman for that matter. Lara told me I was definitely insane, and that's coming from a woman who's just been burned! Not to mention, things have been fairly pleasant between Andrew and I. Well, not exactly enjoyable or fun or anything like that, but at least we're not bickering, and at least he's not spending *all* of his evenings at the office.

Besides, Valentine's Day is just around the corner, and I'd hate to get into a giant row before the possible festivities. I have a feeling Andrew's got something special planned for us. I'm not sure what, but I did see some flight search tabs opened on his laptop the other night, and guess what the destination entered was? Hawaii! Oh, how dreamy would that be?

I'm already fantasizing about lounging on white sand beaches wearing skimpy designer bikinis, sipping fruity, neon-colored beverages with little umbrellas and wedges of pineapple in them, Andrew rubbing oil all over my body, us making passionate love in a bungalow or a regal resort, hell, the ocean, even—but then my cell phone startles me, bringing me back to reality.

I don't recognize the caller ID, so I answer slowly, "Hello?"

"Jackie!"

"Bobby?" I say, puzzled. "What's up?"

"It's Robin."

"What?" I blurt. Bella leaps from my lap as I jolt forward from the living room sofa.

"She's in labor." His voice is a peculiar mixture calm and frazzled.

"What? *Labor?*" I put a hand to my forehead. "How? She's supposed to have a C-section next week. How can she be in labor?"

"Phillip's decided today's the day," Bobby says with nervous laughter. "Robin wanted me to call all the girls and let you know if you want to come. We're at Swedish Medical. Ask for Sinclair."

"Is he here yet?" Claire asks, rushing around the corner of the bland, cream- and turquoise-colored waiting room at the hospital. It's a sterile area with cold, hard chairs that look like something from a futuristic airport lounge.

"We got here as soon as we could!" Claire shrieks. She quickly catches her breath. "Go figure! The one day this week I'm *not* scheduled to work at the hospital, I'm not in the area, and Robin goes into labor." She plops down into the sterile seat next to me, clearly distraught.

Claire's also, like Emily, one of those soft souls, do-gooder types. She works in the medical field as a healthcare worker. She tends to elderly patients at the hospital and goes around from home to home providing in-home care, too.

Claire's husband, Conner, follows two steps behind her, his slightly disheveled, sandy-blonde hair looking much more askew than usual.

"Did we miss it?" Conner pants, clutching his chest. "Please tell me we didn't miss it." He collapses into a seat next to his wife, whose eyes are the size of ping pong balls. "Claire will be devastated if we missed it."

"Nope," Emily says, looking up from her camera, which she's been staring at for the past forty-five minutes, scanning through photos. "Still waiting."

"Good!" Claire says loudly, fanning her ruddy, peaches-and-cream skin. "I can't wait to meet this little guy. Can you believe this is happening?"

"Eventually the kid's got to come out," Conner says lazily, picking up a *Mommy and Baby* magazine.

Claire playfully slaps him on his cut, tan bicep. "Oh, stop it." She shakes her head, her pillow of curls bouncing about.

I take a peek at my cell phone, hoping I've somehow magically missed an expected return call from Andrew.

No such luck, I think when I see the empty home screen. *Always the same story.* I scratch at my head and toss the phone back into my bag.

Immediately after Bobby called with the exciting news, I rang up Andrew's cell phone, deciding this was much too urgent a matter to leave in Nikki's trust. As I anticipated, though, he didn't pick up. The damn thing went straight to voicemail, which tells me that he has the thing set to *Do Not Disturb* mode.

"Is Lara coming?" Claire asks. "I already called Sophie to see if she was on her way." She withdraws a thick book from her bag. "She's going to leave the café just as soon as Gatz gets back from class."

"I *assume* Lara's coming," Emily answers.

I bite my bottom lip in anxiety and pull my phone back out. I turn on the home screen. Still no missed calls, no text messages, nothing.

When I couldn't get a hold of Andrew, I finally resorted to calling his office. I'd left a message with Nikki. It was filled with urgency, and I told her that if she could interrupt whatever important meeting Andrew had going on with my message—if any message then *please!* this one!—it would mean the world.

"I'll do what I can," she said in her nasally tone. "He's really swamped, Jackie. There is a very important client meeting with him today."

Yeah, yeah, what else is new? But Andrew promised he'd be by my side when Robin delivered Phillip. I asked him to commit to that, and since it was important to me, he said he'd be there.

But now, as I pan about the hospital's waiting room and nervously check my phone an umpteen amount of times, this is looking to be yet another promise Andrew will have failed to keep.

Before long, Sophie arrives on the scene in a flushed mess, one cheek actually dusted with a swipe of flour, her stained apron still on.

"Not having an update is tough," Claire says, closing her book, her thumb holding her place in between the thick bind of pages. "I hope Robin's doing all right." A small look of panic begins to cover her face.

"I'm sure she's doing very well," Emily says assuredly.

"I wonder if she's actually able to deliver," Sophie says, her apron now gone, revealing a cute ensemble of black, slim-fit jeans and a white, three-quarter-length cotton blouse rolled to the elbows. "What with Robin needing a C-section and all."

Claire holds up her book and says, "If what I've read is correct, it's actually possible. Difficult, but not *impossible.*"

"You brought a how-to book with you?" I ask with a disbelieving laugh. I don't know why it's hard to believe, though, seeing how Claire is deep in pram-pushing/pacifier-popping mode.

Conner motions towards the long hallway that we've been forbidden to enter per the notification of the husky nurse at the desk. "Claire's having my semen sampled as soon as Robin's finished up in there," he kids.

Claire gives Conner a petulant look. "I am not, you big goof." She opens her book and thumbs past a few pages. "I'm reading this for *informational purposes.*"

Conner chuckles to himself and returns to skimming through his women's magazine.

"Looks like you're reading for *informational purposes,* too, Conner," Emily says teasingly, leaning over and poking at his magazine.

"Nah," he says breezily. "Just reading this for the bare boob pictures."

"Ugh," Sophie groans, resting the side of her head in her palm. "There's nothing sexy about breastfeeding."

"I beg to differ," Conner says, eyebrows raised.

"Hey," Lara's voice appears suddenly.

"You made it!" Emily cries. She pats the hard, open seat next to her.

"The girl with a million things to do at work is actually here," Sophie says in jest.

"Yeah, yeah," Lara says. "Take it easy on me. I'm in recovery mode still." She takes a seat next to Emily, unbuttoning her cappuccino-colored power suit. "I'm excused from all teasing for...at least one month." She smiles and sits up eagerly. "So I didn't miss it, did I?"

"No," Claire says, looking up momentarily from her book. "We don't know if she's delivering or is having the C-section or... anything." She scrunches up her face, then returns to her reading.

I retrieve my cell phone, hoping Andrew's seen the two texts I've sent him, or at least received the two messages I left with Nikki since I learned of the labor news.

"Ugh," I groan when I'm not surprised by the ever-blank screen.

"Andrew will call you when he can, Jackie," Emily says in a drawn out way, as if she's had enough from my matinee dose and doesn't want to see the evening showing.

"I know," I whine. "But this is a big deal. He said he'd be here." I drop my bag to the floor and turn sideways in my chair. I prop my heeled feet on the armrest.

"Babies can come suddenly like this," Emily says kindly. "Could be tough on his busy schedule, the spontaneity of it and all."

"True," Sophie says, removing her messy bun from atop her head. She waves out her long, silky hair, then methodically begins to wind it into a fresh bun.

I know it's important to Robin that her best girlfriends be here when Phillip's born, and I know she probably doesn't feel one way or the other about the husbands coming along for the ride, but Conner's here. Conner and Claire love each other, and his being here for her is a testament to that, however small.

"Don't let Andrew spoil your evening," Emily says.

"Yeah, you're right," I agree with a small smile.

"Here." Conner tosses a magazine my way. "Get your mind off it by reading one of these. For the articles, of course," he says with a giggle.

"I've got something to get your mind off of Andrew," Lara says rather abruptly. She turns sharply in her seat and her eyes bore into mine slightly threateningly.

"What?" I squeak out.

"A little matter involving, oh..." She places a dark red fingertip on her lips, tilts her head, and melodramatically says, "...a key, a car, and a *very* pissed off ex-boyfriend."

I press my lips together tightly and avert my eyes to Conner.

"Jackie!" Lara says. "It was you, wasn't it? You keyed Nathan's car, didn't you?"

"Now, girls," Emily says calmly. She sets her camera aside and rests a hand on Lara's shoulder.

"Jackie," Lara says again.

"Conner!" I say in a quaky voice. "I'll see that magazine about the boobs right about now."

"Jackie!" Lara crosses her arms over her puffed out chest.

"Lara, it was for your own good," I rush out, reaching for Conner's magazine, but he's holding it back and laughing.

"He got what he deserved," I tell Lara. "You need to stand up for yourself, and what are friends for? I can't stand by and watch him do that to you!"

"So it *was* you." She claps a hand to her head.

"Duh, it was me." I slink back, giving up on trying to retrieve a magazine distraction.

"He's seriously pissed!"

"Good. He deserves to have his feathers ruffled, the jackass."

"Oh, Jackie." She wags her head heartily. "I love you, but sometimes you can be so...so..."

"Let's not say anything anyone'd regret, girls," Claire says willfully. "Happy time. This is a happy time."

"Hey," a deep voice sounds from across the room. The discussion is too hot for anyone to pay it any attention, though.

"She was only doing what she thought was best, Lara," Emily

comes to my defense. "Yes, it was a stupid thing—a very, very *stupid* thing—but it's done and over with."

"He could sue," Lara says, mouth drawn tight.

"Did you tell him it was me?" I ask, edgy. Andrew would kill me if he found out I'd gone and gotten myself into a potential lawsuit. And if Nathan knew it was me—loaded Jackie—he'd really have my head.

"No," Lara says. "I told him I didn't know what he was talking about, but..." She sighs. "Jackie, you can't just go all loose-cannon-like and—"

"Girls!" the deep voice sounds again, but this time louder. It does the trick, and everyone looks over in its direction.

It's Bobby. He's dressed in blue scrubs, one of those doctor face-masks attached around his ears and curled under his chin. He looks at us in a collective way, expression serious yet gentle.

"Omigod!" Sophie exclaims, leaping from her seat. "Is he here?"

"Phillip!" Claire begins to clap, her book falling to the floor in a clammer.

We all wait on with bated breath as Bobby says, "She's going into surgery right now."

10

I don't even bother turning on the lights. As I step foot in the foyer, the small stream of golden light from the twelfth-floor hallway creeps farther in—inch by inch. The marble flooring is cold on my bare feet. The air isn't much warmer, and neither is my mood. I let the door click closed behind, and the dark swallows me.

Eventually the crescent moonlight sprinkles into the home, sparkling off of Elliott Bay and bouncing off of the various glass and metallic vases, frames, and minimalistic décor.

I feel my way through the foyer and into the living room, my fingers grazing the light switch. I power the bar upwards so that only a low glow similar to the one in the outside hallway fills the room.

09:23 reads the digital clock on the oven.

I don't need the time or the darkness of the townhouse to tell me that my husband is spending after-hours at the office. Again. They're only loud and painful reminders.

With abandon, I drop my bag onto the floor, along with the high heels I took off the instant I stepped into the lobby, too tired to make it another step in those high numbers after four long hours at Swedish Medical, waiting on pins and needles for Phillip's arrival. I make a beeline for the kitchen cupboards and retrieve a glass.

Everything went well with the birth. Robin and Bobby are now the proud parents of the cutest bundle of boy joy, and Rose is a big sister.

After Robin was taken to her recovery room, and once Phillip was looked after, we all got to meet the wrinkled guy, and my-oh-my is he a sweetheart! I didn't think it was possible to feel my heart ache —almost thinking I wanted a baby of my own—when I held the helpless bundle. The way he cooed and slightly stirred in my arms was the most endearing thing in the world. I remember holding Rose for the first time and having similar feelings—as if the rest of life's troubles kind of melt and drip away, like ice cream down a cone on a hot August day. And you don't even feel the residue down your hand or get perturbed. Every trouble that plagues you plunges into some unknown depths, and you're all alone with the most beautiful thing life can produce—life itself.

Then Phillip began to wail, as I recall Rose having done when I first held her, and I quickly handed him off to an awaiting and proud Bobby.

As Phillip was calmed down and passed from Sophie on to Lara and on round the circle of his aunts and Uncle Conner, that ice cream cone of worries went in rewind. The melty parts zipped back upwards onto the cone and became frozen. They started to build higher and higher, in fact. It was like my world's troubles were back, and no new nephew could cure them. The troubles seemed to be even more evident, more compounded, more troublesome.

Eight o'clock was approaching, and I *still* hadn't heard from Andrew. Come nine o'clock, as I was on my way out of the First Hill medical district and heading into Downtown on my way home, I decided I was not married to a chronically late, career-obsessed man; I was married to a philanderer. What other explanation could there be for him not returning my most urgent of calls? To ignore the *four* text messages I sent him?

I throw back the shallow pour of whiskey and stare through the vast floor-to-ceiling living room windows and out across the midnight-blue bay. *He's cheating,* I think to myself. *There's no other explanation.*

I pour another helping of whiskey, this one not as shallow, and bring the glass to my lips but stop when I hear the jingling of keys in the front door lock.

I set the glass down on the counter, ignoring the loud clank it makes when it lands, and race into the foyer.

"There's my baby," Andrew's voice trills. Still maneuvering his keys out of the lock, his wool coat slung over a bent arm carrying his briefcase, I do all I can to contain the words on the tip of my tongue.

But I can't.

"You asshole!" I holler.

He whips suddenly around, brow knit in confusion.

"You asshole!" I raise a hand to hit him, but he drops his keys and catches it.

"Start again," he says, tone low. "What's the problem?"

I wriggle free from his firm grasp. "You know *exactly* what my problem is, Andrew." I can feel my body start to shake, but now's not the time to chicken out. Now, in fact, is the time to have that talk—that long-awaited, much-needed talk. I may be a bit sloshed from the whiskey, my judgment not the keenest, but I'm so incensed I can't think of anything I want to do more than tell my husband just what I think of him, of us, of our sham of a marriage!

Andrew walks right on past me, heavily sighing and stepping over his fallen keys. "Judging by the whiskey on the counter, I *do* know what your problem is," he says snidely.

Just the same, he proceeds to fetch himself a glass.

"This isn't a *joke*, Andrew!" I storm into the kitchen, coming up to him and pulling his outstretched arm down, away from the cupboard.

"Just what do you think you're doing, Jackie?" he says tersely. "You've obviously had enough booze for the evening."

He yanks free from my grip and pours himself a glass of whiskey.

"Don't change the subject," I say, my voice registering at a lower level of volume now that I'm way past angry and headed towards delirious rage.

"I'm sorry I'm home so late," he says in an overtly exhausted fashion, but not in a way that conveys he's actually tired from a long day at the office. He's obviously tired of having to have the same damn discussions. And frankly, so am I.

"It's not that," I say, wagging my head vehemently.

"Okay then. I'm sorry that I didn't have time to return all of your calls?" He gives me an interrogating look.

"Bingo!" I stick a pointed finger at his chest.

"Jackie," he says with an easy sigh. He takes a drink, pauses for a moment, then takes another drink before removing an envelope from his suit jacket pocket. He retreats to the living room, to his favorite chair in the corner.

"Robin had her baby today," I say in a trembling voice. The cold of the kitchen floor, like the marble foyer, is ice to my bare feet. I'm forced into the living room, nearer to Andrew, where I can find some comfort on the plush, white rug.

"Good for Robin." He takes another sip of whiskey.

"And you missed it. This was important to me, Andrew. You promised you'd be there!"

"On the nineteenth, yes, when the surgery was scheduled."

I take a timid seat on the armrest of the sofa. "Why didn't you call me back?"

"Business, baby doll." He smacks his lips after another drink, then casts me a smug grin.

"It's always business with you."

"Mmmhmm." He shakes open the contents of the envelope, his eyes dancing across the page.

"But not tonight, was it?" I say declaratively. "Not tonight!"

He doesn't respond, but just looks to be more involved in the envelope's contents.

"Tonight," I say, staring down at my bony, trembling fingers. "Tonight was not business, was it?"

He shakes his head, confusion written all over his face. "What the hell are you talking about, Jackie?" He pulls himself forward onto the edge of his chair, the paper held loosely in his hand. "Just how much did you have to drink?"

"Don't pretend I have a drinking problem, Andrew!" My voice rises in anxiety. "It's not fair and it's not true and I hate when you do that!" I can feel the swelling of tears begin, but I tell myself not to break. Not yet.

"I *know* I drink to try to fix things. Sometimes." I pause, regaining my composure so I don't fall into a sea of tears. "But it's not so bad anymore. I'm really trying." Another pause. "And that's not even the issue, Andrew. Don't change the subject. Don't make this about me."

"Isn't it always about you, baby doll?"

I can feel my cheeks redden in rage.

"I'm sorry I've obviously upset you," he blurts out effortlessly.

"I have *one* little drink in the evening because I'm emotional." I bite my bottom lip, the tears aggressively fighting their way forward. "Everyone acts like I'm a screwed up mess or something!"

Andrew stands and puts a hand on my knee. "Jackie, baby," he whispers. He pushes up my chin. "It's been an emotional day for you." He gently kisses my forehead. "Robin had her baby, you weren't able to get through to me—"

"Exactly!" I sniffle, the tears really ready to burst from the starting gate with each word I speak.

"Let's get you ready for bed and call it a night, okay?" He searches my watery blue eyes and is about to press his lips to mine when I jerk back.

"No," I whimper, moving behind the sofa.

"No?" He holds out his hands in supplication. "Jackie, I think it's time you calm down and get some sleep. You've been drinking, and you're upset and—"

"No!" I bat away the warm tears that are trickling down my cheeks. "No more games, Andrew. No more!"

"Okay," he says with a surrendering hand motion. "I'm not up for *this* game you're playing, so I'm going to take care of some more business, take a shower, and *I'll* call it a night." He returns to his seat.

"You're sleeping with her, aren't you?" I did it. I finally got out what I wanted to say all along. Dr. Pierce, Emily, everyone had told me to be honest, so here's honest!

Andrew's eyes narrow, needle-thin, and he looks breathless. Guilty, perhaps?

"You are," I say, feeling my whole body begin to quiver.

"What the hell are you talking about?"

"You know!" I scream. "You know *exactly* who and what I'm talking about!"

"You're ridiculous. I don't know what the hell you're talking about."

Andrew's so calm I can't help but think that I've hit the nail on the head. He's in shock that I've found him out, so now he's just going to play it cool.

"I'm right," I sneer. "I'm right and it *kills* you." I hold my arms open. "Go on!" I coax. "Be honest with me. *Tell* me you were with her tonight. That you've been with her *every* night. Oh!" I throw my hands up flippantly. "But not the nights you've come home early for your poor, pathetic, unsuspecting *wife!* Throw her off the scent now and then—"

"Okay," he says, standing and tossing the paper into his chair. He strides over, whiskey glass in hand. "I don't know *what* you're talking about, Jackie! You're obviously intoxicated, and I think it's time for bed."

He reaches out with his free hand for my arm, but I stumble back. "No!" I scream. "I'm not drunk and I'm *not* going to bed!"

"Jackie." His voice is hoarse. He approaches me again.

"No!" I quickly pick up the cerulean glass vase from the end table and hold it out to my side. "Just tell me the truth, Andrew. You'll hurt me more by denying the truth."

"Oh this is absurd, Jackie!" He folds his face into a knot of complex emotions. "Put the vase down and let's go to bed. I'll go with you. Business can wait until tomorrow."

"Because it also waited for tonight," I accuse, my lips curling in a contemptuous way, "when you were too busy fooling around with *her* and ignoring *me!*"

"Enough!" he yells. "You're not making any sense. *Who* was I with, Jackie? Huh? Tell me! *Who?*"

I lick my lips and slowly shake my cocked head. *I can't believe it,* I think. *He's a liar.*

"Tell me, dammit!" he shouts, causing me to jump.

I raise the vase higher. "Tell me the truth—*admit it*—or I'll smash this."

Abruptly his whiskey glass goes flying, crashing to the marble floor, and as my eyes follow the sea of shards flying about, Andrew has his hands firmly gripping the vase.

"Knock it off, Jackie!" He tries to yank free the vase from my hands.

In a flurry of emotions, and a small portion frightened of what Andrew will do now that he's thrown the first of what I fear will be a few more glass items of the evening, I let go of the vase and slip under the space between him, his raised arm, and the sofa.

"No!" I scream. I begin a mad dash to the kitchen.

"Dammit, Jackie!" he howls, vase still raised. "What is this all about? This paranoia?"

I take cover behind the large island, as far from Andrew as possible.

"Nikki," I spit out, the name leaving an acrid taste in my mouth.

"What about Nikki?" He looks positively flummoxed.

He plays the part so well, I can't help but think.

"You're sleeping with her. I know it! That's why you miss my calls. That's why she doesn't pass the messages on. That's why she's such a bitch to me!" I pick up the half-empty bottle of whiskey on the counter and hold it upside down by the neck. "You're fucking her." I wave the bottle. "Confess or I'll break this!"

"Dammit!" he shouts, unexpectedly throwing the vase across the room, where it shatters loudly in the far corner of the living room.

I suck in a quick breath of air—definitely did not see that

coming. Then I dart my attention back to Andrew. He's nearing me, fury filling his eyes, covering his face, shading crimson his cheeks.

"No!" I shriek at the top of my lungs, slamming the bottle against the granite counter. Whiskey and glass fly all around, and the amber liquid and confetti-like pieces of the bottle caught in the booze begin to course down my legs, my arms.

I'm in shock. All I can do is stand here in the toxic puddle and stare at the broken chunk of glass in my hand.

Shaking, I slowly pry open my hand to see a small, fresh slice in my flesh, blood dripping down my wrist.

"Christ, Jackie!" Andrew says in angst, immediately at my side. He takes the glass piece from my hand and tells me not to move. He reaches for a kitchen towel.

"What the hell are you doing, baby doll?" He carefully bandages my hand with the white towel and picks me up, the crunch of the glass popping underneath the soles of his loafers.

He sets me on the cool counter and instantly tends to my bare feet.

"Thank god you didn't move," he says, examining my soles and in between my toes, carefully spreading them apart and dusting away any possible glass pieces. "I don't think you've cut your feet."

"Just tell me," I say, staring at the now rose-colored patch of cloth that's covering my hand. "You're sleeping with Nikki, aren't you?"

Bent down, blowing soft breaths on the bottoms of my feet, he puffs out a heavy breath and slowly looks up at me. His face is of the serious kind—the type of face you expect to be greeted with when your husband says, "Yes, I've been seeing her for some time now."

"Just tell me," I repeat, voice steady and icy. *We've gone through all this mess, let's finish this business once and for all.*

Andrew crumples up a paper towel after drying off my pinky toes and gives them one last glance for any signs of lodged glass. With both hands placed on my kneecaps, he looks deep into my eyes and says with such simplicity, "No."

The tears that I can no longer hold back spill forth in a surge.

"I don't know where you got this idea, Jackie," he says. He moves some broken glass around with his foot.

"She doesn't give you my messages; you don't return my calls." I sniffle and rub at the tears on my face. "Something that was so important in life—important to *me*—you missed tonight. And you say it was because of work."

"It was!"

"Then I don't know what's more pathetic." Another sniffle. "You not being there for me because of work or because of your mistress."

"I don't have a mistress, Jackie!" he growls, slamming a fist on the counter. "And you can't expect me to leave multi-million- and -billion-dollar deals to be there when your friend has a baby!"

"It's not even the fact that you weren't there tonight, Andrew," I say, beginning to gain enough composure to hold back fresh tears. "It's that you didn't even have the decency to spend thirty seconds to call or text me. You just *ignored* me!"

He doesn't say anything for a while. His eyes are trained on the small disaster on the floor. "You're really going to have to grow up, Jackie," he says solemnly. "You're going to have to accept that I work. I live to work."

"And Nikki," I scowl. "Just accept that you're fucking her?"

He fixes me with a chilling stare.

I wait, on tenterhooks, both eager and frightened of what will come next.

Then he says in an icy voice, "And you're going to have to accept that Nikki is my secretary."

Another loud crunch of the glass, and Andrew makes his leave of the kitchen.

"And your mistress!" I shout. "I have to accept that she's your mistress, hah?"

"Goodnight, Jackie."

"That's it?" I plead, twisting around on the counter towards him. "Goodnight? No more discussion? Place is a wreck, goodnight?"

"I don't know what more to tell you." He turns around, his shoulders sagged and face long. "Be careful when you get off the counter." He removes his cufflinks and saunters off to the bedroom.

When I'm sure he's concluded the evening and so-called conversation, ready to pop a sleeping pill and crawl into bed, he says from down the hall, "Call Marta in the morning and make sure this mess is taken care of."

11

Relieved of the closing duties after a long six-hour shift at the café, Emily removes her teal-colored apron, imprinted with *The Cup and the Cake* in pink stitching, and places it on the center of the café table. "So you're, what?" she asks me as she takes a seat. "Just not talking? At all?" Her lips are slightly parted.

Sophie, apron still on as she and her extra set of hands, Chad Harris, are closing up shop for the night, takes a brief seat in between us.

"Not talking, period?" Sophie tosses in quickly, a baffled look flashing across her face. She darts her attention for a moment towards the kitchen when a loud clang sounds—Chad making himself undoubtedly known as he washes and puts away the pots and pans. She rolls her eyes and returns her attention to me. "How long can this go on, Jackie?"

"Yeah, well," I say nonchalantly, but deep down I'm torn up. Andrew and I have quarrels, as all couples do. But throwing-things, breaking-things, accusing-of-cheating, not-fessing-up-to-cheating, and no-longer-on-speaking-terms-for-*days* kinds of quarrels? That's not healthy; we've gone too far.

"You need to move immediately into reconciliation," Sophie says with determination. "Learn from me and my pathetic relationship experiences: Silence is *not* golden in situations like these."

"Get talking again," Emily says. She twists at her heavy collection of leather cuffs and bracelets on both wrists. "And, Jackie, when I said *serious* heart-to-heart with Andrew, I didn't mean to do it when you were high on emotion, distressed, and sipping the sauce."

I lightly chuckle and say, "We've had fights like this before, Em. Broken glass isn't anything new."

Speaking of broken glass, another loud *bang-bang-clang* sounds from the kitchen, and Sophie lets out a loud groan. "Dear heavens..." she mutters. She cranes her neck around and shouts in the direction of the kitchen, "Chad, you break it, you replace it."

"It's all good!" Chad's deep and raspy voice shouts back, eliciting a heavy roll of the eyes from Sophie.

"That boy," Sophie says under her breath. "Someday I'm going to be able to afford real help—no offense at all to you, Em," she claps a hand on top of Emily's, and Emily nods. "I appreciate him offering to help me out around here, but sometimes he really gets under my skin."

"Chad and Sophie," I say, feeling prickles of relief as the topic of conversation is changed, however temporarily and briefly. "The day you two *don't* get under each other's skin." Emily shares a giggle with me.

Chad Harris is Conner's best friend, and so naturally a mutual friend among us girls. He's got a career in marketing and in his off time paints, even selling some of his work here and there. But on the occasional evening or weekend he'll lend a few hours to the always-in-need-of-help Sophie at the café. He doesn't need the work, nor the extra cash, but like Emily he wants to help out a friend.

"Anyway," Sophie says, the balls of her cheeks turning a twinge pink. She smooths her apron and sits up taller. "That's neither here nor there. We're off topic." She knocks on the small tabletop. "You and Andrew have *got* to get your shit figured out. Pardon my language, but seriously. This is ridiculous. You're *married*."

"Married people go through bumpy patches, too," Emily pragmatically points out. "This too shall pass."

"I don't know," I mumble, scratching at the base of my neck where the tips of my bleached-blonde hair come to an end. "I want to believe that, but I'm just *so* tired of this hot-and-cold, hot-and-cold crap."

"You're Jackie," Sophie says with a wide smile, "if you weren't hot and cold—up and down—you wouldn't be you."

"The mentally imbalanced friend," I say in jest. "Oh what a grand honor."

"What I think she's saying," Emily cuts in, "is that you and Andrew have always been high on drama—living life in the fast lane, so to speak. It's glitz and glam, it's really bad lows, it's passion... It's not anything new for you two. It's just particularly difficult right now. I'm not making excuses, just trying to put things into perspective."

I nod.

"But it's *nothing* you can't work on," Emily adds, flashing a warm smile. "If you try."

"I'm so sick of trying, girls," I bleat. "So sick of it."

"You can always try harder," Emily says.

Again, a loud clang sounds from the kitchen, this time louder than the previous noises. Sophie bites her tongue, her cheeks turning red now, but as the noise subsides so does her apparent frustration.

"All through Valentine's and *no* conversation," I carry on. "That's pretty bad, girls. We didn't do a damn thing for the holiday! And I *so* thought he had a trip up his sleeve..." I sigh, plunking my chin into my hands. "Thought we'd be going to Hawaii or something. We didn't even *talk!* So effed up, huh?"

"Yeah," Sophie rasps. "That's rough."

"And how much longer will this silence go on?" I say. "I think the longest we've gone without talking was like a week or something." I try to rattle free from my mind the longest spat to date. "But he was out of town."

"On business," Emily says in an understanding tone.

"Or out screwing his secretary," I offer lifelessly.

Sophie rolls her eyes. "Pure conjecture, Jackie. And not substantiated by anything more than pure paranoia because of Lara and Nathan and..." She squeezes her lips together and looks like she's silently apologizing before saying her next piece. "Maybe boredom."

"Or unhappiness," Emily says in an amazingly cheerful way.

"Or both," Sophie treads lightly.

They're probably right. If Andrew's not two-timing me then I'm probably acting like this because of paranoia, unhappiness, and discontentment in my marriage. And, yeah, all right, I'm probably a teensy bit bored, but I can be pretty good at abating that. There are the trips to Pioneer Square; hours and hours of addicting television; spa treatments and mani-pedi appointments; tons of shopping to be had in the Westlake Center, Pacific Place, and along Broadway; and we can't forget cupcake nibbling and coffee sipping at The Cup and the Cake.

"You two really need to have a serious talk," Sophie says. "One without erupting into a fight and smashing things. That's really not healthy."

"I know. I've tried. Got me nowhere. My marriage is toxic. Nothing about it is healthy."

"You talk to your therapist about all of this?" Emily queries concernedly.

Of course I talk to my therapist about this kind of stuff. He knows all about the spats and rough patches, even the really ugly ones. And each time we discuss it, or each time I bring up the latest altercation, he'll ask if Andrew's laid a hand on me, saying, "I just want to make sure, Jackie." I say, as I always do, "No. Andrew takes his anger out on the furniture."

I laugh out loud to myself. On the comical side of things, I suppose if Andrew and I continue these nasty fights eventually there won't be anymore furniture left in the house and then I'll be able to buy all sorts of Old World knickknacks and pieces to decorate our place. I could actually make the place a home for us, not the sterile as-found place it has been since I first moved in.

I heave a heavy sigh as my mind dances with mixed images of Andrew reading his newspaper, broken glass on the kitchen floor, sterile furniture, sterile life, sterile love...

"You'll figure this out," Emily assures me. "Honestly, this too shall pass, and if you try and make a real effort to get your marriage on track, you two will be in a much better place."

"Someone has to step up," Sophie says, smoothing her apron some more. "Or this void's just going to grow and grow, Jack. Silence is *not* the answer. Talk. For *real* this time."

"Andrew could step up," I say in a weak voice. "Why can't *he* make the first move, huh?"

"He said, she said, he's it, you're it." Sophie stands up and lets out a noise that's a combination of shrieking and groaning. "I don't care who does it, just fix this. You and Andrew have only been married a year—"

"Thirteen-and-half months," I correct.

She looks on at me with pleading eyes as she grips the top of the chair back. "Come on, Jackie." Her voice turns soft. "Don't give up. We're here to support you and help you, but if you don't start helping yourself...and Andrew...there's nothing anyone can do."

"Yeah." Emily pats me on the back. "No one said marriage would be easy. But it is possible."

"Sorry to interrupt the love fest," Chad's voice comes suddenly from behind. "I finished the dishes."

"Thank you," Sophie breathes out. She turns on her heels to face him. "Break a few along the way?"

"*Break a few along the way,*" Chad says in a mimicking tone. "No, Anna-Sophia, I didn't *break* a few along the way." He unties and removes his apron in a swift movement, then flashes her a lopsided grin. "Biscotti for tomorrow are all done, the ovens are cooling, dishwasher's running, and we just need some more to-go boxes prepped."

He rolls his apron into a ball and tosses it on the front counter between the cash register and the cupcake display case. He stretches his thick, tattoo-covered arms over his head, then behind his back, making one loud pop.

As he rolls his neck about, making grating crackle and pop noises, Sophie says, "Thanks, and don't worry about the to-go boxes." Any appearance of incandescence is gone. She now pushes a long strand of auburn hair behind her ear and gives Chad an appreciative smile. "Gatz or I can do them tomorrow."

"Nah," he says with a lopsided grin. "Don't worry. I can do some."

"You can go home now," Sophie insists.

He runs a strong hand over his lightly greasy, haphazard, dirty-blonde hair as he walks to the espresso machine behind the front counter.

"Don't you have to work tomorrow?"

Chad shrugs, flicking at his lip ring. "Five minutes won't kill me."

Sophie, too, gives a simple shrug, then turns her attention back to the table.

"Hey, what'd you want me to do with those leftover cupcakes you've got set out on the plate back there?" Chad asks while he fiddles with the espresso machine's dials.

"Leftovers!" Emily beams.

"For Robin," Sophie says, deflating Emily's happy balloon. "I'm taking them to her tonight as a welcome home present." She looks to me and Emily. "She and Phillip were released home today. I know she'll need a ton of help with cooking and dinners and stuff. Figured I'd start with the best part first—dessert."

"Always dessert," Emily says.

"Phillip's healthy? And Robin's still good?" I ask. Last I heard, which was just the day before last, Phillip was healthy, at a strong weight, and all the vitals and stuff were top-notch. Robin was in good shape, too.

"Phillip's healthy," Sophie says proudly, "and Robin looks beautiful. Saw her yesterday after work." She presses a hand to her tan cheek. "Looks amazing. Hard to believe she just had a baby. So!" She says this last word in a disjointed way. "You're going to do something, right, Jack?"

"Yeah," Emily pipes in. "Talk to Andrew? Not to push, but it sounds like things are kinda bad."

"You going to get over this messy mess and be all in love again?" Sophie flutters her lashes and giggles.

"Seriously." Emily fixes me with a sincere gaze, that look she gives me when she and I both know her sage advice is only for the best, and that I better heed it—or else.

"Anyone want anything while I'm here?" Chad asks over the cacophonous steaming of water.

"Yeah," Sophie shouts. "A solution to life's problems."

"Hmm." Chad scratches at the few days' worth of stubble on his face. "I thought sex was the answer to that conundrum," he meets Sophie's teasing.

"Ha, ha," she breathes through a sigh of annoyance.

"Sex is where all the trouble begins," I say drolly, "and that's coming from *me.*" I'm the girl of our close-knit group who's always put an emphasis on testing out the goods before any commitment's really made. I'm not saying I'm a wham-bam-thank-you-ma'am kind of girl, though. I do have my standards, and *frequently* hopping into bed on the first or second date is not always advisable. When you do, it can sometimes lead to some *very* wretched "hindsight is twenty-twenty" moments.

"Wish I could help you and join your pity party," Chad says, the machine's hissing dying down. "But sex and I are like best buds. I'd never turn my back on it."

"Anyway," Emily says, "we've already found life's solution." She rubs my arm. "Or whatever. We found your solution, your next step, Jackie. Talk to Andrew. Have a real and *deep* discussion. *Seriously* this time."

"Without accusations," Sophie adds in.

"No assumptions," Emily says.

"No blaming and screaming."

"No throwing things, either."

"Deal?" Sophie says, holding her hand out for me to shake. Emily makes the same gesture.

12

I'm ready. I'm ready to have this talk—a *real* talk—and put all of
this behind me. So the last talk didn't turn out so well; it doesn't
mean this one won't. Besides, the last talk wasn't even a talk. It was
more like an episode of retching—insulting words and accusations
just spilling from my mouth without any thought, running on pure
emotion (and, in all fairness, a wee bit of Bushmills Irish Whiskey).
This time I'm going to tell Andrew how I really feel—that I'm
unhappy, that I'm lonely, that we need to do something serious
about our marriage.

"Ugh!" I moan as I light a cigarette.

Okay, I'm not as ready as I thought, so instead of driving home
straight from The Cup and the Cake I took a detour by way of
Pioneer Square. I need some alone time to get my ducks in a row
before I go back home and face the man who has my heart, and who
also drives me completely mad.

Sitting on one of the many benches in the square, chewing some
gum, smoking a cigarette, chewing some more gum, then smoking
another cigarette, I begin to reflect on other times where I've found
myself in the same precarious and totally unnerving situation.
When you tell yourself you know what you need to do, and that you

can do it, but you're too worried about all of the what-ifs that you just wind up sitting immobilized, wandering down memory lane.

I blow out a large smoke ring and watch it dance into the chilly night air as I go back to my junior year at U Dub—the winter week my sorority house had its biggest gala and fundraising event of the year. The Delta Gammas were known to rake in the dough during their philanthropic week, and it was mostly because of one single, two-hour-long event. All of the fraternity guys gathered, setting aside any house conflicts someone might have for one brief but exciting event. In fact, nearly every guy on campus crawled from underneath their books and homework, their booze, joints, and girlfriends, to come to the Delta Gamma Anchor's Away Date Auction.

The name says it all, but I'll divulge the gritty details anyway. Basically, just about every DeeGee sister pledged to put herself and one *clean* date up for auction to the highest bidder. Unfortunately, this could lead to some raunchy cat fights regarding popularity and dibs-on-guys rights, and some girls had boyfriends who were none too pleased with the tradition, even in the name of philanthropy, so sometimes brawls could erupt afterwards. What happened after the event or as a result of it was never much of a DeeGee concern, though—Greek houses can get pretty good at skirting issues so long as the accused happens outside of the house and not within the party or member meeting.

Anyway, the dates were auctioned off with the written and verbal understanding that the dates were nothing more than dinner, or a movie, or maybe dancing, perhaps a moonlit walk on campus, or lunch in the cafeteria. Basically a date, sans anything sexual.

My freshman year the Theta house had a close run in with the campus police, and their charter was under a slight investigation after rumors had spread that there was a girl doing certain things for certain fraternity guys so she could have her house dues paid. Since then, the Delta Gamma Anchor's Away Date Auction had watched its Ps and Qs carefully.

Somehow, though, some numbskull bidder didn't pay any attention to those Ps and Qs, and he obviously hadn't taken heed of the loud warning that while the Thetas may have swung that way, DeeGee girls did not—at least not officially and definitely not at public events.

I went up to the platform and a chorus of bids sounded along with a strong starter bet from Chad and Conner, Pi Kappa Alpha brothers who promised they'd get the ball rolling and save the day in the event I didn't have any takers.

But takers I had, and I was sold for a whopping eight-hundred and twenty dollars, a lot, but nothing compared to Stacey St. Clair, who went for a thousand-and-a-half! I was bought by a tall, dark, and handsome jock named Kurt. I think he was on the basketball team, or maybe it was football, but it didn't matter. He was a jock, and, as it turned out, a Grade-A asshole. Oh how often those two sadly go hand-in-hand.

Kurt and I agreed on dinner in the nearby U District at one of the cheap eateries right off the Ave. I was dead-ass broke, as always, and he wasn't too hung up on extravagant dinner plans. He was more interested in the movie afterwards. Or, rather, what *he* had planned after the movie.

The dinner was enjoyable, and we actually got on well. Easy discussion, a dramatic Leo DiCaprio film, then a walk back to campus. I could see my sorority house in the near distance and was ready to kiss him goodnight and consider my DeeGee philanthropic duties paid. Kurt was a nice enough guy, and though I wasn't horribly attracted to him or looking for a little piece of something on the side, I thought I'd be sweet on him and give him a simple kiss goodnight, followed by a thank you.

But the kiss turned deeper, harder, and before I knew it Kurt had one hand making its way up my skirt, thumb under my panties. I jumped back, so alarmed I couldn't speak. He drew nearer, grinning this horribly fiendish grin, and he started to grope me again. I squirmed, I swore I'd scream if he didn't stop, and it only turned him on more. He pulled me tight and told me that he'd get his money's worth, that I shouldn't fight what I flaunt all around campus, wearing my halter tops, miniskirts, and high heels.

I tried to jerk free, forcing him to grip my arms with both of his hands—at least free of further molestation at that point—and then he said I should have no problem doing the job he'd paid for, seeing how I'd been with half of fraternity row anyway. It was a sordid and flagrant lie. Okay, maybe a few guys, a few dates, maybe at a drunken house party or two, but *not* half the row. And what business of his was it anyway what I did with my free time? With my body? It's *my* body to do with as I wish, and I told Kurt *no*.

I don't know what would have become of the sham of a date had it not been for one of Conner and Chad's fellow Pike brothers walking by on his way home from the library, stepping in to put things to an end.

That night I cried myself to sleep, not breathing a word of what happened to anyone. How humiliating to be known as a campus hussy, wrongly accused just because I may dress a certain way and be a little free-thinking with a few dates, and then exploited, abused. Part of me felt dirty and ashamed, and I wanted to burn all of my clothes and vow to join a convent or something over-the-top; the other part felt angry and vengeful. I wanted to buy more of the clothes I liked, date more of the guys I liked and *wanted* to date. Who was Kurt to shame me and make me feel badly about myself? I'd had enough of that growing up, thank you very much. I had enough demons to deal with, enough guilt and enough problems. I didn't need some deadbeat assaulter quashing my spirit, my voice, my self —hampering me from trying to move on and grow up and figure life out.

My secret didn't stay a secret for long, though. The next day Conner and Chad were let in on Kurt's number on me when my guardian angel that night recognized me as one of the guys' friends. Conner and Chad have never been very explicit on what went down once they found out, but I saw Kurt on campus a couple days later and his face was black and blue, one arm in a sling.

I blow out another smoke ring, watching as it disperses and spreads thin. Even if I'm reflecting on painful pasts, it's still refreshing and sobering to come to Pioneer Square. It's comforting to be one with my thoughts, especially when I have to do something big and scary and really difficult, like have a serious talk with my husband.

I didn't have the courage to ever face Kurt after that, and I couldn't bring myself to tell my girlfriends of the details. They could get what they wanted from Conner and Chad, but that evening's story ended when my eyes fell shut and I was able to drift to sleep and dream of anything but what had happened that night. And now, here I am, unable to bring myself to talk to Andrew, to have an open and honest discussion with the man to whom I pledged my eternal and undying love.

"How strange this silly world is," I mumble to myself as I stamp out my cigarette. I dab with my pinky the lone tear in the corner of my right eye and stand.

It's the damnedest thing, life. There's no rulebook or lesson plan to guide you, and even the best damn therapist in the world can't prepare you for all the curveballs. Especially the curveballs you somehow manage to throw at yourself.

Wrapping tighter my black, crushed velvet jacket, I make my way to my car and begin my slow and silent journey back home. To do what needs to be done—what should have been done long ago.

13

"If you keep pacing like that you're going to burn a hole in your slippers," Andrew says from his chair in the corner of the living room. He turns the page of the newspaper he's reading.

"Hmm?" I sound, continuing my pacing. I scratch my head, pause at the end of the room, then spin back around.

I can do this, I tell myself. *I can talk to my husband, have a serious conversation that will not start off with accusations, that will not become a yelling match, and will not end up like a scene straight from* Who's Afraid of Virginia Woolf.

"You feeling all right?" Andrew asks, peeking only briefly around his crisp paper to give me a discerning look.

I sound another *hmm* and continue to pace, continue to scratch, continue to procrastinate.

"Okay, Jackie," he says at last, dropping his paper in a crinkle onto his lap. "You're making me nervous. What's going on?"

I abruptly stop pacing and look at him. "Well," I start. I bring my thumb to my mouth and avert my eyes to the expansive view of the dark Bay.

"Jackie." His voice is low, crisp.

"I've been wanting to talk to you," I say, keeping my eyes focused dead ahead out the window.

"About where you were tonight." I sense a slight hint of discomposure in his voice.

When I arrived home from my contemplative break in Pioneer Square, it hadn't even been ten seconds before Andrew asked where I'd been. I told him I was with the girls and left it at that. He didn't pry further, but the abrasive tone I used in response set him on edge. He returned to his newspaper and kept silent. Only now that I'm pacing in nervousness does he speak again.

"I was at the café with the girls," I say, removing my thumb from my mouth and waving the topic away, "and I got to thinking." I move timidly towards the sofa, across from him. "I took some time out for myself, then. Went to the square."

"At this hour?" Andrew looks aghast. "With the bums and the delinquents and other men who could do you harm? Do you know how dangerous that could be?" He blows out a low and deep puff of air. "Sometimes, Jackie. Where's your head?"

I want to tell him it wouldn't be the first time I'd gotten myself into trouble in the dark of the night, but there's no need to open up that can of worms. I've divulged plenty of my past to Andrew—he is my husband, after all, and I wasn't about to walk down the aisle with any old guy just because I saw security and care sparkle in his crystally blues. I wanted a partner I could share things with, confide in, turn to, and be comfortable with in my own skin.

Instead, however, I reply with, "My head's frustrated, Andrew."

No, that didn't come out right. I scrunch my brow, then brush off my choice of words.

"So I take it we're *finally* talking now?" He gives me an expecting expression. "No more silent treatment?"

I take his cue and say, "We have to work on our marriage." I swallow the frog that's rapidly formed in my throat. "It's a disaster, to say the least."

My eyes search his, waiting for a response, but after what feels like a lengthy minute of silence, I decide to continue. "I need more from you. I know you're busy at work and too overloaded with stuff to apparently even give me a return call," I roll my eyes, "even when it's something that's really important to me." I twiddle my thumbs unassumingly, staring down at the small curlycues that design the cigar box on top of the coffee table. *Please say something. Please.*

"A marriage is work on both ends, Jackie," he says at last. In my peripheral vision I can see him fold up his newspaper, slowly and rather sloppily. "You need more from me, I need more from you." His voice is so calm it's actually soothing, in an odd way. I'm grateful for the comfort it provides, because my stomach is flipping this way and that, and I can feel my armpits become increasingly damp with each breath. "It's like we're not playing on the same team," he says.

"What more do you need from me?" I cry out in a whisper, keeping my focus on anything but Andrew's eyes, which I can feel staring at me.

"I *want* to play on the same team as you, baby doll." His voice turns even gentler. "I hate not talking, I hate arguing," he chuckles unsettlingly, "I hate having to replace vases around here. You need to grow up a little and realize that there's more in my life than just you. I'm a very busy man, and I'm trying all the time to be the best husband I can be for you."

Slowly I meet Andrew's eyes.

"I love you, Jackie, but you've got to meet me halfway."

"*You* have to meet *me* halfway, Andrew," I whimper, swallowing another frog. "You don't know how it feels to be ignored! It's *me* waiting for *you*; it's what's convenient for *you*; it's *me* having to be understanding for *you*, *your* schedule, *your* work life."

"I'm trying." He folds his newspaper in half and taps it against his knees.

"You need to try harder."

He rubs long and hard at the grey stubble on his chin. "I'll try harder if you try your part, too. Be patient, be trusting. And relax!"

"Fine," I say, empty, confused. "Whatever."

"Not whatever." He tosses the newspaper on the coffee table. "I will try my damnedest to give you more attention, but my career isn't easy, Jackie. If we want the kind of lifestyle we have, then I *have* to work heinous hours! It's—"

"You can start by firing Nikki," I say in a tone more juvenile than I intended. "You want me to trust you? Fire her. Please."

It's the meat of the problem: Nikki Dowling. I can't ignore what happened to Lara, what happened to my mom, my dad... I will not be one of those victims. I already have to battle the fact that my husband works around the clock; but having to stir in the wee hours of the night wondering if Nikki has something to do with his magnetic pull to that office is just too much to bear. The girls told me to be honest and step up and be the bigger person, breaking the wall of silence, well here it is: honesty in its repulsive and painful form.

"What?" Andrew squints tightly. "No. No." His voice is firm. "No, I will *not* start by firing Nikki. Where is this *coming* from, anyway?" He loosens his mauve, pinstriped tie. "I will try to be more attentive, but you—*you*, Jackie—need to trust me."

He roughly runs a hand through his short, grey-white hair. "And what the *hell* is your neurotic obsession with thinking Nikki and I are," he wags his head brusquely, "having an *affair*? It's insanity!"

I run my tongue across my teeth. I'm frustrated and confused about why he's so reluctant. If I'm uncomfortable with Nikki and she's a big reason why I'm freaking out over our failing marriage and Andrew's commitment to that office of his, then why not get rid of her? Why the obstinance about this? And he actually wonders why I think they're having an affair!

"You need to be more understanding and more trusting," he says. "I need to be more attentive. If we both start there I can assure you our marriage will be far better off."

"You've tried to be more attentive time and again, Andrew." I fold my hands in my lap and cross my legs, leaning back into the plush sofa. I feel like I'm in a constant, unnerving state of repetitive circular movement. "How many times you've promised to come home sooner, or given me diamonds and vacations to say you're sorry, and we always end up here! Same shit, same story!"

"Marriage isn't a one-time-try kind of arrangement, darling," he says with a small, patronizing laugh. "It's a relationship of consistent trial and error, commitment, determination, challenges."

"God, I sound like I'm in a board meeting!" I throw up my hands, conceding defeat.

"It's the truth, dammit." He loosens his tie again, this time more gruffly.

"Well why would this time be any different?" I fix him with a hard, doubting gaze. "You've tried and failed before, why should I expect you to actually, *truly* be more attentive now?"

"Jackie," he says, his eyebrows drawing together seriously. "Should we be having a separate conversation? Where are you taking this?"

It doesn't take a literature professor to read between these lines, but I've never told Andrew about my research into divorce law last year. And, honestly, I'm not even hinting at a divorce right now. I just want to know how the hell his supposed vow to be more attentive is really going to fix our problem. An apple will stay an apple; it won't suddenly become an orange just because you say it will.

"The only conversation I want to have with you," I say, "is a serious discussion about how we're going to *fix* our marriage. You say you'll be attentive, but *how*? There's the talk but no walk, and I just—just—I just can't do this, Andrew!" I throw up my hands again and make a sharp cry.

"Dressing you in designer gowns and drenching you in diamonds," he says, waving a hand at me. "That's a pretty damn big show of love...demonstration of how I feel about you."

"I won't lie," I say, nodding, "I love a designer bag and glitzy jewels as much as the next materialistic girl, but there's *more* than that in marriage, in a relationship, Andrew. There are other ways to deal with a problem. It's like—like—sometimes...you're just buying me off!" I point a finger at him. "You know, *Cosmo* says when your man starts to buy you expensive gifts all of a sudden it's because he's probably got some mistress on the side. Feeling all guilty."

"Dammit, Jackie." He begins to pace the room, rubbing the back of his neck. "I've been spoiling you rotten from the get-go. You honestly think I've been screwing around on you all this time?"

"No," I say honestly. "But what the hell do I know now? We're in a rut, and you're not willing to fix things."

"Yes I am!" he shouts, clenching his hands into fists. "Listen, baby doll. You learn to trust me, and I learn to pay more attention to you. That's our project. That's it! Everything'll work itself from there." He settles back in his chair. "You want something beyond that, go to the shrink I pay a fortune for you to see! I don't know how else to show you I'm committed."

"You want a way?" I say in a cocky tone. "I think you firing Nikki is a great start, maybe even scaling back your hours—"

"Nikki?"

"Yes, Nikki! She's a bitch to me, and I don't like how when I call your office she's all weird about saying you're not available and that you're gone somewhere, and I go to meet you there and you're *not* there... It's like she's playing a game with me. She's hiding something from me!"

"Dammit!" he yells. "Enough! I don't want to hear her name and insinuations of an affair in the same sentence one more time! Do you understand me?"

The combination of his loud, aggressive tone and the deeply creased wrinkles of confusion and frustration that cover his face startle me into momentary silence. Squeezing my lips tightly, I can only nod my head harshly.

"Thank you." His voice registers calm. "I'm sorry for shouting, love. I'm just sick and tired of hearing this nonsense. It's like you're so bored you have to concoct drama."

"Yeah, well, I wouldn't be so bored if you were around more."

"I told you," he says through a locked jaw, "I'm a busy man. If you are so bored then go to the spa, go shopping, go visit your girl-friends...your shrink! *Do* something, Jackie, instead of fretting about insanely."

I nod again, then meekly say, "So that's it? We're going to keep on trying? Trying to play on the same team? That's the solution?" My upper lip slowly curls in a mock-sneer.

Reaching for his iPad, then Scotch, he says, "Quitters never win, Jackie. Winners keep on trying."

"And the ones in between?"

He looks at me with a muddled expression.

"The ones in limbo," I say without much life. "The ones stuck in the middle trying to win, trying not to quit...to lose."

Andrew simpers as he takes a sip of Scotch. "We should go on a trip soon." He licks his lips. "Just you and me. You're right, we need to spend some time together and you're obviously bored." He takes another sip of Scotch. "A weekend getaway. Get away from this noise," waving his glass of Scotch about, "the fighting, the tension, the stress of every day." He sets his glass down and begins to fiddle with the iPad. "I've got a wide-open weekend coming up soon, so let's do something. Help us reconnect, calm down. What do you say?"

"Yeah," I say, voice small. "I guess."

"And, look." He smiles at me, and I subtly oblige. "Since we ignored Valentine's, why don't we go do something tonight?"

I want to ask who Andrew thinks he's fooling by saying that we'll keep on trying, that things will get better, that a weekend getaway will really be the answer. I want to tell him that I lie awake at night or wander about Pioneer Square second-guessing my decision to marry him. I want to say I fear we're on a path that's leading to nowhere. No matter how much we may love each other and no matter how many efforts are made—all futile—we both know our marriage is doomed, and neither of us can admit it to the other. All we're doing with bandaging up this chronic problem—taking a trip and not making honest and real steps to recovery—is borrowing time. I like the idea of a getaway with Andrew, but what happens afterwards, or even in the weeks leading up to our "romantic getaway"? How much longer will we let the cancer grow before it takes us?

Instead of telling him this, I suppress the urge to speak out, the urge to cry, the urge to question, and I nod and grin, as I always end up doing—letting the cancer fester and grow.

"That'd be nice," I say. I force myself to think that things will get better from now on, just like Andrew promises. This lie won't cure anything, but it's less painful than the truth...at least for now.

Tonight is the start of our new beginning, I will myself to think even as those pesky feelings of emptiness, loneliness, and helplessness that weigh heavy on my heart double in size.

"Let me get changed and I'll call us a table at Metro Grill." Andrew stands and heads into the bedroom. "And we'll plan something spectacular and romantic for a weekend," his distant voice sounds. "Just us, baby doll. Just us."

I'm not a quitter, I think optimistically. *But I'm not quite yet a winner.*

I lie down on the sofa and hug a plush pillow to my chest. "I'm somewhere in limbo," I whisper as I close my eyes, listening to the not-so-distant stream of water sound from the bathroom.

14

It's been about a month since Andrew and I had our serious discussion, deciding our marriage wasn't going to fix itself and we had to do *something* about it. Andrew's been doing an okay job at working on things. He answers more of my calls, but not all of them; we go out for dinner a couple nights a week, but haven't danced in forever; things are better, but we're still in limbo. We have plans of going to Bainbridge Island for that weekend getaway he's been wanting to do, in two weeks. Should be nice. Am I feeling a bit better? I suppose. Do I still think our marriage needs work? It needs something. Maybe more time? More commitment? More hard evidence that Andrew wants it to work out?

"Our weekend away will probably be really good for us," I say to the girls. "Andrew's probably right that we need some time away from all of the craziness of everyday life. But, you know me, up and down. One day I think this trip's great and the fix-all, the next I figure it's delaying the next inevitable blowout."

Lara and Claire nod their heads.

"Dr. Pierce said it'll probably be good, anyhow." I blow a puff of air to the side. "Sometimes, though," I lean forward in my seat on Robin's front room sofa, "I think it's just a cheap move to placate me again." I rest my elbows on my legs and clasp my hands together. "Take the wife off of the mantel, show her a fun time, and that'll keep her quiet for a while."

"Whatever happened to Hawaii?" Lara asks, her fingers rifling about the bowl of homemade Chex Mix. "Wasn't Andrew secretly planning something like that for you?"

"For Valentine's?" Claire queries.

"That was a guess," Sophie jumps in. "Snooping, were we, Jack?" She gives me a wink as she reaches for the snack mix.

"I don't know what that was," I say listlessly. "Forgot all about Hawaii until now. Thanks, Lara."

Lara tosses a mini pretzel at my head.

"Well, I'm glad you talked," Emily says as she makes funny faces to baby Phillip, who's lying on his back on the blue and white blanket Claire crocheted for him, snug between Lara and Emily. "It's the first of many talks, I'm sure." Emily eyes me scrutinizingly, and I shrug. "Step by step."

"Talking is always better than deathly silence," Sophie says.

"Definitely," Claire says. She sets down her crochet needle and patch of yellow yarn in her criss-crossed lap. "If I could tell you how many times Conner and I have had tiffs." She heaves a dramatic sigh and returns to her craft. "I mean, it doesn't matter if we're having yelling contests or turning cold shoulders, they're both nasty. But not bringing up a problem will get you nowhere. Just ask Lara."

"Puh-lease," Lara moans, tucking her hair behind her ears reservedly. She checks the backing of her pearl earrings. "I'm finally over Nathan *for good*—"

"And Jack's little gaffe?" Sophie cuts in.

"Yes," Lara says, looking at me. "Even Jack's foolish little gaffe with his car." She gently rubs Phillip's tummy as he begins to fuss. "Jackie was only standing up for a friend in the best—albeit *insane*—way she knows how. Anyhoo, I'm over Nathan." She caresses Phillip's head as Emily makes a soothing cooing sound to try to settle him.

Phillip's fussing only grows so Robin scoops him up. She situates him gently on her chest and shoulder, like a pro. She drapes a receiving blanket over him and lightly bounces in her seat as his mewling softens.

"The silence, the cold shoulders, that big void Nathan and I had," Lara says. "Not a recipe for a healthy relationship."

"So if you're through with Nathan," Robin says, "then maybe you're ready to get back into the game?" Her voice is thick with jest. If anyone would be happy to direct Lara to the dating podium, it'd certainly be matchmaking Claire...or even me. God, how fun would it be to go out to a club, play the wingman? Do some dancing, have some drinks, some fun?

"Between the bottles of wine, the chick flicks, and the suspenseful Koontz books," Lara says, "not to mention Sophie's scrumptious cupcakes. After all that, I'm *much* better. I'm ready for a new start!" She tosses back a sip of wine, then adds, "But that doesn't mean I'm ready for a new guy." She looks from me to Claire, then back to me. "I'd like to keep things calm for a while before I head back into the dating scene."

"Claire," Robin says, pointing at the crochet project. "Sorry to change the subject, girls, but Claire?"

Claire's transfixed by her project, surprisingly not jumping at the chance to suggest a blind date set-up for Lara. She raises her brows in response.

"Are you making Phillip *another* blanket?" Robin asks.

"Didn't you just make him that one?" Sophie gestures to the one on the floor.

"Actually," Claire drawls out.

"Whoa!" Emily says, jumping the gun. "*Actually* what?"

Robin nudges her glasses further up onto her nose and motions to Claire, whose fingers are working in rapid twists, turns, and threads. "Claire? Something you want to share?"

"Omigod!" I shriek, nearly knocking the Chex Mix out of the bowl. "Are you—?"

All eyes dart to Claire, who's still gaily working her yarn.

"Uhh," Sophie says, one hand on her hip. "This is the first time I'm finding out, Claire? Where's the BFF love?"

Claire just smiles.

"Seriously?" Sophie says, thunderstruck.

"Shit," Emily breathes, equally astonished. "Are you—?"

"Okay," Claire says, only slowing her crocheting pace, not stopping for even this kind of potential news. "No, it's not what you think. I'm not that crazy, making baby blankets before the baby."

"This from the girl who buys ovulation kits in bulk and has multiple pairs of newborn-sized shoes," Lara kids.

"I'm serious, girls," Claire says. "This *is* for Robin. I'd *love* for it to be for me, but," she shrugs, "Conner and I aren't headed down that road just yet." She pauses her crocheting. "I'd love to, and we've talked about seriously trying, but it's just talk right now."

I make a sputtering noise, then say, "Yeah, I know *all* about meaningless talks."

"It's not meaningless," Claire counters.

"So you and Conner are trying?" Sophie asks. "Or considering trying...soon?"

Claire squishes up her face, then says, "All right. We're trying as in I'm no longer on the pill."

"Whoa!" Emily whoops again. "That's huge news! Omigod!"

The rest of us look on in silence, eagerly awaiting more details of this juicy story. Claire continues, saying, "But Conner insists on still using protection." She heaves a very heavy sigh, her whole body shaking slightly. She sticks her needle in the large ball of yarn. "We'll have a better chance of conceiving if I've been off the pill for a few months. That's what all the books say, anyway."

"Your trusty homework," Lara says with a wink.

"And once Conner's ready then we'll, well..." One corner of Claire's mouth turns up in a half-smile. "We'll *really* try then."

"It'll happen when it happens," Sophie says cheerfully. "But that's so exciting!"

"It'll be really exciting when it's real," Claire says with round eyes. "For now our options are open and," she blushes, "it *is* really exciting just *thinking* about it! That it can really happen, and soon!"

"So is Conner ready or something?" Robin asks. "Almost ready?"

"That's a new fresh scoop of news, actually," Claire says, looking at Sophie, who obviously already knows, seeing how the two are exchanging wide grins. Not to mention, they're practically soul sisters.

"Conner's up for a promotion," Claire reveals. "It comes with a nice pay raise, and he's confident he'll get it. I mean," she holds one hand out and shakes her head, "the only way he *wouldn't* get it is if they go for an outside hire, and that's unlikely."

Sophie nods in agreement.

"So that means," Claire says, "in about a month or so Conner could become the new manager of the accounting department, and then we'll start *really* trying!" She squeals in delight and bounces her head from side to side. "With the job security and extra pay Conner said there's no question about it. We can really try!"

"That's wonderful," Robin says, starting to tear up slightly. She waves a hand at her face to cool down.

"Oh, Robin," Emily whines, embracing her in a side hug.

"It's still these hormones," Robin holds open her mouth and pants exaggeratedly. "Goodness, Claire, that's great news! I'm so happy for you. And how great is this? Me not being the only one with kids." She rubs at her eyes underneath her glasses. "You'll make a super mom, Claire."

"I just hope to be half the mom you are, Robin."

"I never imagined having two kids already. At twenty-eight!" Robin says. "Was focused on my career and then came Rose..." She sighs. "Now Phillip." She's glowing. "I wouldn't have it any other way, though. Being a mom really rocks. It's work, but it's rewarding."

"Oh, I can't wait," Claire says giddily.

"And you're really going part-time after your maternity leave?" Lara asks Robin. She takes a seat back on the sofa after folding Phillip's blue blanket.

Robin was toying with the idea of going part-time at her publishing house after Phillip was born, since Bobby's well-established there and Robin's already beyond busy keeping up with two kids. She says even with Rose in daycare while she's at work she still has to be punctual getting out of the office to pick Rose up on time, and sometimes her boss needs more than the usual eight-to-five.

"And having two in daycare full-time!" Robin declares. "No way. I'd be working just to pay for the care. Doesn't make any sense."

"I think it's a great decision," Emily says as she twists one of her freshly made cornrow braids in between two fingers. "The fact that your boss lets you opt for part-time, that's the perfect setup for you."

"Well," Robin says, "it comes with a demotion. I'll no longer be able to be a project manager, but Phillip and Rose are worth it."

"And Bobby's supportive?" Lara asks.

"Absolutely." Robin gives a shrug of contentment.

"That's important," Emily says. She nibbles on a handful of Chex Mix. "Finding a guy who understands you—understands what you want—and is supportive." She swallows, then smacks her lips. "Toughest thing in the world."

"But with Gatsby you're golden," Sophie sings, getting up and wandering towards the kitchen.

Sophie returns a second later with a fresh bottle of chilled rosé I brought along, the burp rag Robin asked for, as well as one of the many boxes of Chinese takeout I brought over to Robin earlier this evening. She's been so exhausted with becoming a new mommy the second time around I figured that while Sophie's got desserts and breakfast goodies covered, every now and then I can swing by with dinner.

"Delicious, by the way," Robin says to me as an aside in the conversation about Emily and Gatz. She gestures to the carton of fried rice. "You're the bestest, Jack."

"No prob," I say, criss-crossing my legs. "Least I can do to help out."

"He really is a fine catch, that Gatsby," Sophie says, topping off Robin's pink lemonade.

"Gatz is definitely a winner," Emily gushes, "that's for sure."

"So it's officially labeled a serious relationship now, Em?" Robin asks. "We know how silly you can be with *labels*." She prepares to nurse Phillip after taking a quick bite of fried rice.

"If me needing to clear my crap out of her place so that there's room for Gatz's stuff indicates seriousness," I say with a laugh, "then yeah."

"There's no need for Gatz to have much at my place," Emily says simply.

"Oh, yeah!" I smack my forehead. "Because when he's over he's immediately naked and you two go at it like—"

"Anyway," Emily says, laughing. "It's not like that."

"You mean you guys haven't even done it?" I ask, not able to buy into this.

"Of course we've 'done it,'" she says, making air quotes in jest at my choice of immature words. "I'm saying he's not moving in and replacing you, Jack." She licks the snack's spice from her fingers.

"How could anyone ever replace me?" I press fanned-out fingers to my chest and bat my lashes. "So is he good? Amazing in the sack?" Come on, a girl can't help but pry!

"Jackie!" Emily groans. "He's a creative and romantic artist; I'll let your imagination run wild with that."

The girls snicker as I push my tongue into my cheek, then make a clicking noise and say, "Definitely running wild."

"Anyway. Sometimes I'm at his place, sometimes he's at mine," Emily says breezily. "But this summer I think that's all going to change."

"Ohhh," Sophie groans. "Don't remind me of this wretched news. I'm already losing you in a couple days so you can go be a plumber in Africa."

In a few days Emily's going to leave for Zambia for an eight-week-long volunteer project in Africa, and if missing out on Robin's wedding isn't rough enough, she's also leaving Sophie shy a very handy helper at the café. Sophie says she'll cope somehow, but it won't be easy.

It definitely won't be easy losing Emily again—I'll say that much. You'd think I'd have gotten used to it by now, seeing how Emily's always wanderlusting somewhere. But every time that ratty old backpack of hers gets dusted off and a new luggage tag is attached, a new patch of another country's flag is ironed on, my heart aches, and I feel like I'm losing a large hunk of the security and comfort I have in life.

I know I've got Andrew, and he *is* getting a teensy-weensy bit better at being around for me, but Emily fills all those voids he can't, and then some. She gets me, loves me, and doesn't judge. That's not to say she doesn't tell me when she thinks I need to pull my head out of my ass, but she never makes me feel like shit. She never makes me feel like the exploited young girl who uses her wild and free-spirited personality to get past all the years of pain and unjust treatment. Knowing she's down the road, her door and heart open, ready with a box of tissue, a soft pillow, and a bunch of world-wise advice, is more comfort than any pair of Louboutins or expensive meal in Manhattan Andrew can offer.

"It's only two months, Sophie," Emily says calmly. "Gatz will be at the café the whole time, and when I return from Zambia I'll be back to help."

"Until you leave again," Sophie pouts as she pours herself a glass of rosé. "Oh, I'm not being fair," she quickly brushes off. "I'm just sad, that's all."

Lara pours herself a glass of rosé as well and says, "Where's it to next, Em?"

"You know how Gatz has been talking about wanting to study abroad?" Emily begins. She tucks her legs under herself and billows out her long, flowing, paisley skirt.

Gatz has been auditing classes at U Dub for fun for a while, but he's been wanting to go back to school, possibly to get a Masters or something. Evidently he's considered doing so abroad, which of course was music to Emily's ears. She's got her passport handy and ready to scan like I've got my Amex, MasterCard, Visa, Discover card, and the first card I ever qualified for on my own credit: Victoria's Secret.

"He's serious?" Robin asks, lightly rocking Phillip as she feeds him.

"Next term," Emily says, humbly curling up one side of her lips.

"Summer?" Lara says.

"The fall," Emily replies, tossing back more Chex Mix. "I don't get back from Zambia until May, and we're not going to leave Sophie empty handed so abruptly like that."

Sophie smiles weakly before taking another sip of wine. I know she's conflicted: glad that Emily and Gatz are working out and disappointed that she'll be losing one of her best friends to the travel bug, yet again, not to mention *two* sets of hands at the café!

"So that means..." I say, trying to remember if Emily told me they were thinking of mid- or late-summer. I admit that when she initially told me about their possible plans I was rather caught up in my drama with Andrew. I still had that nasty gash in my palm and was so damn depressed about the state of my marriage, even in spite of the talk Andrew and I had, that I kind of selfishly missed the details of her and Gatz's plans.

"July," Emily says. "We want to backpack and travel around for a while before he's got to start classes."

"Where are the classes?" Robin asks anxiously.

"Australia," I answer. I look at Emily. "Brisbane, right?"

"That's the plan," Emily says, a mixture of excitement and solemnity in her voice. "U Dub's got a sister school there—a good literature program for Gatz. And I'm researching volunteer opportunities there. There are quite a few options."

"Well," Lara says, "I think this is fandamntastic news, hon."

"Yeah," Sophie says. "I'm being selfish, but this *is* really good news, Em."

"Definitely," Robin and Claire say.

Emily looks at me with a sheepish grin.

"Well *obviously* I'm not elated that my bosom buddy is fleeing." I roll my eyes. "But if it's with some hot, artsy poet who can't keep his clothes on when he's at your place then I guess I understand."

Emily gives my shoulder a shove. "It's not like that, dork."

"Well why not?" Lara cackles. "Isn't that the fun of a serious relationship?"

"Yeah," Sophie gushes, "and getting to go travel together, running off, having fun, being so happy, so lucky... Having the time of your life! I envy you, Emily. Totally envy you."

I catch a glimpse of my sparkly wedding ring as I bring my glass to my lips and take a sip of the sweet wine.

Envy, I think as the wine settles on my tongue. *Like limbo, like life, it's a funny thing. When you think you have nothing, you have envy; when you think you have it all, the envy's still there—it's just a different kind of envy.*

15

The moist, salty air and light spray of the aquamarine water envelop me, sending me sailing along in a comfortingly euphoric state. The fresh and crisp breeze tickles my newly fake-n-bake tanned skin, bringing goosebumps to my bare forearms; it whips through the billowing white sails overhead and blows about Andrew's loosely fitted, white button-down. With my arms outstretched wide, I close my eyes against the bright afternoon glow the sun casts in slivers through whipped-cream clouds. I breathe in deeply, my nose tingling with delight as I take in the pleasant fragrances of coconut-scented tanning oil and hints of Andrew's Burberry for Men that wafts by just right, when the wind catches past him at the stern.

I peek open my eyes, my large Alexander McQueen, studded, cat-eye sunglasses providing some shade against the scintillating sunshine. I look behind me and instantly a smile plays my lips. Andrew's standing at the helm, one arm resting loosely on the large, wooden wheel, slowly inching it from one side to the other, keeping course as we cross the Puget Sound.

This has to be one of Andrew's best ideas yet—a sure-fire way to help get our marriage back on track—and a great way to pay me some long-overdue attention. I had some small reservations beforehand, thinking this was just another useless attempt at keeping things hot and interesting, but Andrew's trying—walking and not just talking. And besides, how could I say no to this luxury?

We used to go sailing when we were dating, Andrew somehow having found the time years ago in his busy schedule to take up the hobby. I was impressed when he revealed his nautical skills to me, but he just brushed it off saying it was something men in his position do, like golf—it makes for conversation, gives you something to do on that rare occasion you have vacation time, and you get to join a fancy-shmancy club that holds galas, benefit auctions, and apparently an annual cup race, all of which you get to enjoy *if* you manage to find the time away from the job that *gets* you into the sailing club to begin with.

I unfurl the corners of the large sunbathing towel I've laid out on the deck, fighting a losing battle against the wind that throttles our boat further across the water. I set the bottle of tanning oil on one corner of the towel, and my brand new navy blue and white, rubber-soled deck shoes on the other.

I take another peek at Andrew. He looks so sexy standing there at the helm, maneuvering the vessel like a pro. His shirt's top three buttons are undone, the sleeves rolled half-way up his arms, the cuffs of his khaki pants rolled up a couple of times, too. It's a rare moment my husband can take off the suit and the tie—escape the confines of his coiffed world. I like that I get to see him unplugged.

Adjusting the top of the too-adorable-for-words white, ruffled bikini I found during my shopping spree yesterday, I lean back on my elbows and take in the picturesque scenery surrounding me.

Bainbridge Island is not even ten miles off the waterfront of Seattle, and is a quiet place where a lot of Seattleites either retire or have their second, more relaxed home nestled among the tall vegetation and along the sandy, remote beaches. Some locals actually live here, too, and just commute via the ferry to the city, and, you know, considering Andrew's hellish work life, I don't think I'd mind relocating to a place like this if it meant keeping him home a couple days a week. "Looks like the ferry won't be arriving today, dear...guess you have to stay home..." I could picture that happening. Okay, not like that would *ever* happen for any reason, but the idea's nice enough. Keeping my husband hostage on an island...

Of course, I know after about a month it'd get old and I'd be dying for the city, the pulse, the life. Not to mention Andrew probably wouldn't know what to do with himself stranded on an island surrounded by nothing but nature, Mom and Pop shops with homemade crafts, American diners, and laidback cafés that close for siesta at two in the afternoon. Okay, we'd both go insane, but for a weekend getaway Bainbridge is the ideal location for some R&R—romance and a romp.

"Baby doll," Andrew calls out.

I peer back to see him stepping away from the wheel. He moves along the deck, adjusting cranks and pulling taut some ropes, just like a pro.

"You want to stand at the wheel for me?" he says. He pushes up his black, square-framed RayBans—a very sophisticated-looking pair—as he yanks hard on a rope.

"That's it," he says as I cautiously place both hands at the top of the wheel. "Just keep it steady for me while I work on the mainsail."

"Like this?" I ask, standing on my tiptoes and looking far over the large wheel of the beautiful wooden sailboat we've rented.

He flashes a quick look back and tells me I'm doing everything just right. "Keep it steady," he says.

I watch my towel flip a little in the wind in the near distance. Andrew moves further along the boat, pulling more ropes and fidgeting with different objects. I look down at the large wheel, paying careful attention not to move my hands a centimeter. *Got to stay the course.*

It can't have been a minute yet, though, and I'm already done with playing captain. I don't see how this hobby could be *that* much fun if you're the one having to steer it and all. Sailing is awesome if it means you get to lie on the deck, paint your toenails, page through the latest *Cosmo*, and I suppose carve a notch in your I-did-it-in-a-sailboat-on-the-open-seas belt. Sailing's a luxury hobby for a reason, obviously. But just standing here? And not even with a cocktail in hand?

I look down at the wheel again and frown. "Baby!" I shout through the cacophonous breeze. "Can we put this on, like, auto pilot or something?"

"What?" he bellows, still cranking and pulling.

Suddenly one of the sails begins to shrink, then turn a good ninety degrees. Our course starts to gently shift, and we can't be more than a half-mile from our docking point in Eagle Harbor.

Andrew pads his way over, his stark white soles making slippery, sucking noises against the misted deck. "What's that, baby?"

"Can I do something fun like the sails? Move them or something?"

He chuckles and rolls up the cuffs of his pants farther. "All right then." He slips a looped rope around the wheel and leads me towards the bulk of the sails. "We can do this quickly. First I'll give you a fast rundown on what each of these parts do."

"Okay," I draw out, not really wanting a Sailing 101 lesson, but what the hell?

"This here," he says, hunkering down low and pointing at a thick pole, "is the clew, right at the end of the mainsail here, this big one," pointing up at the massive, open sail, "and there's a clew at the opposite end, on the jib, which is that sail here," pointing at the smaller sail he just angled. "Opposite the clew are the tacks, and then we've got the boom here, the..." Blah-blah-blah so it goes.

My eyes kind of glaze over, and all I can do is stare at my husband and plaster on an amused smile. He's so excited about all this silly boat lingo it's kind of endearing. He hunkers down even lower and grabs hold of the mast (that much I know). Folding a hand across it, he looks at me, pulls his sunglasses atop his head, and says through a squinted grin, "Want to have a go around the bow and I'll explain how the shrouds and spreader work? Real quick?" He looks on at me with eager eyes.

"I think I was good with steering, come to think of it."

He smiles and leads me back to the wheel. "Then you can help steer us into the harbor, okay?" He slips his arms around my waist as I place my hands cautiously on the wheel.

"Like this?" I ask in a sugary tone, looking over my shoulder at my husband.

"Just like that," he whispers. "There you go..." He presses his lips tightly against my cheek, then nods forward. "That a girl. You're doing it."

A loud clap sounds overhead, and the sail—was it the mainsail?—billows open like a popcorn bag slowly beginning to rise in the heat.

"I'm doing it!" I say excitedly, bouncing lightly on the balls of my feet. "I'm steering us in like a regular Captain. Captain Jack!"

Andrew just keeps smiling, his arms wrapping tighter around me. He kisses the nape of my neck as I begin to take my steering duties much more seriously now that the sails seem to be talking back and the harbor's growing nearer.

"I love that we get to spend this time together," Andrew says softly. He moves one hand from around my waist to the top of my hand. "I love you, Jackie. I miss you. I miss us."

"I miss us, too." I press my body into his slightly and lean my head back onto his chest.

"This is how it's supposed to be, baby doll."

"I like this," I say, closing my eyes for a moment. "Just the two of us." I inhale and exhale deeply. "*Exactly* the way it's supposed to be."

I squint open my eyes and look up at him. His eyes, which were focused straight ahead at the harbor a second ago, are now locked with mine. An overwhelming sense of safety and security washes over me like a tidal wave as I get lost in his gaze. It's like he can read my mind, my soul—so intimately connected on so many levels. He doesn't have to say anything more, and neither do I. We connect. The moment is just right. And, right here and right now, *we* feel just right.

No need for words, but filled with an urgency to tell my husband the only thing on my mind, I break the speechless moment to tell him I love him. "I really do, Andrew," I say in a soft tone. "In spite of everything, I absolutely love you."

"I love *you*, baby," he says, the scruff of his weekend's whiskers tickling my cheek as he kisses me tenderly.

"I'm going to finish up mooring," Andrew says, tossing ropes and buoys about. "You can go on in and let them know what slip we're in."

"Huh?" I put on my big, floppy white hat and push back its red polk-dotted ribbon that's waving in the gentle shore breeze.

"Just head in," he says, "I'll be there in a sec."

I grab Bella's carrier, then cram my necessary travel goods into my Louis Vuitton Neverfull GM—magazines, a crumpled mess of the already-tested perfume samples that came with the magazines, tanning oil, cigarettes, cell phone, bubblegum, bottle of Evian, Red My Lips-colored nail polish, oh, and Bella's doggie treats and portable water dish.

"Hi, there, little lady," a white-haired and leather-skinned man behind the counter of the Bainbridge Wharf Marina greets as I walk through the wide-open door. "What can I do ya for?"

I remove my sunglasses and set my achingly heavy bag and Bella in her carrier on the nearest vacant table, a small, rickety-looking, old wooden thing in the quaint corner of the marina's café.

"My husband and I have a boat out there," I say, pointing towards the harbor.

"I reckon plenty o' people have boats out there," he says with a hearty chuckle, exchanging glances with the other leather-skinned man at his side.

"Yeah," I say, rolling with their teasing, "but how many have boats that are captained by Seattle's very own Captain Jack?" I flash them a toothy grin and wave at my salt-water-kissed face beneath the brim of my hat.

"You captained your boat, eh?" the white-haired man asks impressively.

"Yup, and never a lesson in my life. I don't know what's starboard, what's port, what's a mainhead or a jig." I take a lumbered seat in one of the creaky chairs. "But I pulled that bad boy in all by myself."

The two mens' eyes have grown large; they're speechless.

"Kind of bumped my way through," I say in a mock-serious tone, and now their eyes are larger, their mouths starting to form small Os. "But I don't think I scratched any other boats up too badly. Just a little nick here, nick there. Nothing a little nail polish can't cover up." I laugh in mirth.

"Dear god, woman," the white-haired man's buddy gasps.

"I'm pulling your leg," I say at last. "Although I'm sure I could captain that thing all by myself if I wanted to."

They laugh uneasily together, perhaps still trying to come down from an elevated state of panic.

"Sure, sure," the white-haired man says, rubbing at his beard. "You know you can take lessons if you're interested in that sort o' thing."

I peer inside at Bella, and her cheerful little tan and black head pops up. She licks at my Tiffany charm bracelet.

"Come here, baby," I say to Bella, scooping her out of her carrier and cuddling her close.

"Classes begin in the summer," one of the men says as I bury my face in Bella's soft fur. "Start in June, another in mid-July, some in late August, even, if weather permits, one or two in September. If you're interested."

"Thanks, boys," I say. "I'm much more the type of girl who likes to enjoy the *perks* of sailing, not sailing itself." I situate Bella in the crook of my arm and stroke her head gently as Andrew struts through the door.

He starts conducting whatever business is usually conducted at a marina, so I take the opportunity to give Bella a potty break.

The sun is fully shining down on the island now; I wouldn't have thought we'd have such glorious weather considering the windy ride across the Sound. There's barely a breeze in the air, the place doesn't look to be particularly popular with tourists right now, and the ferry is making its routine, sluggish way out of the harbor, on back to the bustling civilization of Seattle.

Bella sniffs delicately about the wild grass and purple and yellow flowers that dot the harbor's edge. A small flock of seagulls find solace on the fence posts and ropes, some on the cable lines that swoop up and down along the docks. There's a sweet fragrance in the air—the scent of spring about to arrive.

Bella trots off a short way farther along the lush patch of lawn, and I follow, breathing in and exhaling deeply, eyes closed for a moment as I say a silent thank you for *just* what my marriage needs.

"This is going to be a great weekend, Bella," I say with confidence. "Best. Weekend. Ever."

16

"Yes! Omigod," I gasp, clutching my chest. "My god." I blink long and hard, panting, trying to catch my breath.

"I'll take that as a, 'It was good for me,'" Andrew says with a smirk, rolling back over near me. He places a tender kiss on my jaw. "It was *definitely* good for me."

"A whole new meaning to 'don't come a knockin' when the boat's a rockin,'" I say, returning the kiss.

"I should get you out on the water more often." His voice is husky, sexy. He places more kisses along my jaw, hungrily moving them to my chin then to my lips. He gently bites at my lip. "I thought you had energy and were creative on *land*."

I roll over onto my stomach and push away the down pillow. "Shall we?" I say in a seductive voice as I reach for Andrew's cigar pouch.

"I know I've told you a million times already," I say once the cigar is finally lit, "but I really appreciate you taking the time for this."

"I can carve out a little time for my wife," he says with a wink.

I wince a little at his words, and respond with, "Well *taking* and *carving* out time isn't exactly what you should *have* to do when it comes to your wife…"

"Please, Jackie. Not here, not now."

"I'm not wanting to fight," I say hurriedly. "No, not at all." I take a small puff of the cigar and let the sweet smoke linger in my mouth and on down to my lungs for a contemplative moment. I exhale slowly and say, "I just want you to know how much I appreciate you following through on this...this *us* time. It means a lot. Thank you."

"You're welcome. Wish I could do it more often," he says while I take another puff before handing the cigar to him. "But see. What did I tell you?" He rubs with his pinky the top of my bare shoulder, then plants a sweet kiss on it. "A little work on both ends—me being more attentive, you being patient with me—and look!" He surveys the nook of a bedroom. "We're here, just the two of us, spending quality time together."

"No work," I point out.

"No work," he repeats. "Office is left to the office, and this weekend you have my complete and utter attention."

I sigh in satisfaction and snuggle up close to him. "My husband all for myself!" I give him a quick kiss on his lips before he brings the cigar to them. "We should do this again soon. Just us."

"The coming weeks are really busy for me, Jackie," he says in a steady note. He takes a long puff of the cigar. "But eventually..."

"More out-of-town business trips?" I readjust my pillow and rest my head down, curling up closer to Andrew. "Leaving the poor wife home alone? Again?"

"Singapore's coming up. At the end of next month." He sits up in the surprisingly comfortable and roomy bed and wraps the starched sheets loosely about his waist. "It's a really big deal, babe. I don't know when I'm going to have a peaceful weekend for a while." He blows a smoke cloud upwards, out of the opened hatch.

"I know, I know."

He takes another long puff, and his eyes narrow in a sophisticated way, as they usually do when he talks with a cigar in hand.

I take the cigar from him and take a puff myself. "You realize you're leaving me to go stag to Robin and Bobby's wedding?"

"You know I've had this trip cooking for a while now." He gives me an erudite expression. "It should come as no surprise to you that I won't be able to attend their wedding. We've talked about this, baby doll."

"So it's a for-sure thing?" I say, deadpan. "You're definitely out of the country then?"

"Meeting finalized, flights purchased last week." He examines the tip of the cigar before taking another puff.

I groan and sink further into the pillow.

"Let's enjoy now, Jackie baby," he says soothingly, focusing on his puff-puff-*puuuuff* technique.

"If I show you how I can be *even better* on the water than on land," I say with a scheming look in my eyes, "then can you arrange to go with me to the wedding?"

Andrew tosses his head back and lets out a low, smoky laugh. I love how much deeper his voice gets just after he's smoked a cigar. It's all growly and playful.

"I wish, darling," he says. He places the cigar in between my outstretched fingers. "You'll have a great time no matter. All your girlfriends there...you'll have such a fun time you won't even notice I'm not there." He brings a finger to my lower back and begins to trace my large butterfly tattoo. "I can even arrange to have a driver take you and bring you home, if you like." He kisses the small of my back, then continues tracing.

"I'll probably just crash with Lara," I say effortlessly. "Somethin' like that."

"Isn't she in Africa?"

"That's Emily, babe." I twirl the cigar in between my fingers and stare at its small embers.

I want to say, "Maybe I'll stay with her...all the way in Africa." I'm so annoyed at Andrew's upcoming absence. Yet again, he's leaving town on business. Just when I thought we were in for more romantic and intimate moments together, like now, when the office could be left at the damn office, when Jackie came first and that was that. Rather, I make a *hmph* sound and place the cigar between my lips, taking a long, slow, and deep pull, closing my eyes and trying to ingrain in my memory how good *now* feels.

Andrew and I have done everything you could imagine on Bainbridge Island this weekend. We had a relaxed breakfast on the boat's deck, cuddled together under a big fleece blanket, feeding each other strawberries and melon and toasting with mimosas. We've walked along the main drag, stopping in clothing stores, shoe stores, and a handful of antique and furniture shops. We even ducked into a Persian rug shop after I pleaded with Andrew to let me have a quick peek. He said the Persian we have in the office that he bought when he was in Istanbul is better and more authentic than anything we'd find in Washington. Sometimes he can be such a bore. All I wanted was to look and gawk at the variety of intricate patterns and use of color.

We took Bella for a fun frolic along the beach, and we even got to dig for tiny beach crabs. We had to throw them all back into the water, especially once Bella decided they were no longer objects of innocent curiosity but tiny chew toys.

Our weekend getaway has been fantastic—everything I could have imagined, maybe even more. For lunch we ducked into an old-school American diner where they cook your meal right in front of you. We got a spot front and center at the bar, and Andrew made manly conversation about what it's like to live on the island, manage a boat, that sort of thing. I eventually pulled out my ratted, lightly waterlogged copy of *Vogue* and got lost in the world of fashion.

Once during lunch, Andrew's cell phone rang, and I tried my hardest not to get into a tizzy. He'd said he'd set it to *Do Not Disturb* for our special weekend, but evidently that wasn't the case this afternoon. It was someone from the office wanting to discuss "very pressing business matters," but Andrew said he couldn't take the call because he didn't have any of the paperwork in front of him. Not because he was out of town, not because he was on vacation, not because he was away with his wife, and *not* because he said he wouldn't be bothered with business, but he said he couldn't manage the call because he didn't have his work in front of him! Can you believe that? Trust me, it took all the willpower I could summon to contain myself and not erupt into a screaming mess right then and there in front of everyone.

At least he couldn't take the call, anyhow.

And it *was* just one call.

"What shall we do for the rest of the day, baby doll?" Andrew asks, swinging my hand wildly as we stroll along the very quiet main street after a filling lunch. "More shopping? Look inside those ratty antique shops you like?" He flashes a purposefully cheesy grin. "Go out for a drink or walk along the beach? You name it. We don't have to leave the harbor until four."

I give a quick tug of the leash to keep Bella from eating a weed along the side of the road. "I honestly wouldn't mind lounging on the boat," I reply casually. "Just lying out in the sun." I look at him, covering my sunglasses-covered eyes. "You think the marina guys would frown upon me doing some topless sunbathing?"

"Oh," Andrew says with a throaty laugh, "I don't think they'd mind at all, and I sure as hell wouldn't." He spanks my jean-skirted rear and leaves his hand there, one thumb tucked in the pocket. "But their wives might."

I pull down the back strap of my bikini top and try to reapply some oil without making a mess of the deck or myself or my white suit. Honestly, topless sunbathing would be *so* much easier.

I take a sweeping glance around the harbor, searching for any possible peeping Toms. There doesn't appear to be anyone around. Would it be so bad if I just slipped this thing off? It's all in the name of tan lines, so that should be okay, right? I'll just lie here, face down...no harm.

Suddenly the sounds of children ring from behind. I investigate and take notice of a family of four boarding a sailboat a few slips over.

"Screw it," I say to myself, pulling my strap up higher and making sure it's fastened. If I don't get this oil properly applied I'm going to wind up like an oyster at a clam bake.

Where is *Andrew, anyway?* I survey the marina off in the distance, but there's no sign of my husband. It's been—I glance at my cell phone—over an hour since he left to grab some snacks, or a newspaper, or whatever it was he said he was off to get.

"That's it," I say, feeling my back itch with crispiness.

I make my way up the slight hill, curving its way from the dock to the marina, wobbling a bit in the new pink and yellow wedge espadrilles I got at the most darling boutique earlier today. The shoes didn't exactly fit when I tried them on, but they were so adorable I couldn't pass them up. I figured they'd just fit better once I wore them out of the store, but that is *so* not the case.

"Andrew?" I call, standing on wonky ankles, one hand gripping a bottle of tanning oil, the other clasping my big, floppy straw hat.

"Sir?" I look to the man behind the counter, the same white-haired, leather-skinned man I encountered yesterday, except today his partner isn't around.

"Glad to see someone's getting to use the sunshiney rays this afternoon," he says jovially.

I give a tight smile, then say, "Have you seen my husband? You know about way tall?" I raise a hand above my head, indicating five-foot-ten as best as possible. "Salt and pepper hair, kind of..." I wag my head. "Well, *older* than me." I roll my eyes. "Did he come by for snacks or a book or something a while ago?"

"Why, yes!" The man turns slowly. He gestures with a thumb behind and around the corner. "He'd be using the computers back there. We've got WiFi, if you're interested."

"Computers?" I say, aghast. I pull my sunglasses down my nose and stare at the bearer of shocking news.

"With WiFi, yes, ma'am," he says proudly, thumbs tucked behind his well-worn suspenders. "And since you're such a pretty lady, I'll give you the first fifteen minutes free, if ya like."

"What the fuck?" I breathe, stomping off towards the computer room.

"I 'spose I can go for thirty free," the man says.

I power around the corner, feeling like steam is shooting from my ears, out my head, my eyes. I'm like one of those cartoons about to explode! And it doesn't matter one iota that I'm fuming and looking like a crazy person, dressed in nothing but a tiny, somewhat see-through white bikini, oiled up like a sardine in a can, and wobbling on wedges that are slowly cutting off the blood supply to my toes.

"Andrew!" I shout, yanking my sunglasses off the instant I lay eyes on him, seated in front of a computer. "What the *hell* are you doing?"

17

"Oh, Lara, it was horrible. Absolutely horrible," I rasp, shaking my head harshly.

"Worst-vacation-ever horrible? Or just Jackie-wants-to-bitch horrible?" Lara says, impassive.

"Please," I hold up a hand. "Be real here."

Lara slips her maroon-lipsticked lips around a neon straw, taking a short sip of her Long Island Iced Tea. "You honestly had a horrible time?" she gets out quickly before I can stand back atop my soapbox. "Or are you only focusing on the horrible parts?"

"It was a *vacation,* Lara." I stir the naked toothpick around my martini briskly. "No parts of vacations should be horrible, kay?" I stick the toothpick in my mouth.

"Point taken." Lara takes another sip, this one slower, longer.

"Anyway," I say, sitting taller on the barstool. I return to my stirring. "There were some great parts—most of the time was really great, actually."

"See?"

"But!" I hold up the toothpick. "The horrible part was what made the whole thing snowball into what I think turned out to be a shitty vacation. Totally unfair."

I explain to Lara over a desperately needed Monday evening happy hour at House 206, a swanky bar downtown, all about what turned out to be my sour weekend on Bainbridge. I tell her how I caught Andrew sneaking email correspondences during our entire trip, even taking phone calls. So his cell phone rang once at lunch, and once more later that afternoon (which is probably why he sprinted off to the marina's WiFi hotspot—damn modern day technology).

It was his computer usage that really burned my short fuse to the nubbin, though. The fact that Andrew took over an *hour* of our vacation time in that marina, clicking about doing work-related crap, answering emails, even coordinating meetings for this week! And you know what? Turns out it wasn't the first time. The day we arrived, when I went to walk Bella, apparently that was the moment he discovered the stupid WiFi and, well... Is there no end to this madness called a career?

"So you see why I insisted on happy hour?" I say to Lara with wide eyes.

"Hey," she says, peppy. "This is like a thing now, huh? Happy hour to bitch about men. *Our thing*, I guess." She smiles and bends the tip of her straw in half. "Granted these sugar-filled calories," she gestures to our colorful drinks, "probably aren't going to help my *ass* get any smaller." She simpers.

"You're such a goober, Lara." I look at her ass. "Looks good to me. I'd tap that."

"Well, even though some of the vaca was a bust, at least you got some one-on-one time with Andrew, you know?" She gives an optimistic smile. "Got to reignite the sparks, rekindle the love, all that schmoozy stuff?"

"Oh, girl." I push aside my drained martini and lean in to her. "I read about these special tricks in *Cosmo*—last month's issue, if you're interested."

"Oh, right, because I have *soooo* much sex with my invisible boyfriend." She takes a pull on her cocktail.

"Anyway," I rush out, "it was an article with all these tips collected from hookers all over the world—such an enlightening read, let me tell you!" I lean a bit back and press my lips together.

"Can I get you ladies anything else?" the bartender, an attractive man with dark, wavy hair, hazel eyes, and strong hands, asks in a deep, guttural voice. He thumps the bar with his heavily ringed fingers. "Happy hour deals end in ten."

Lara looks down at her half-drunk tea, then gives me a questionable face.

I look down at my own drink, the glass empty, and consider calling it quits just to prove that I can stop if I want to. Last thing I want is to go home to Andrew, have him wince at smelling my breath, and accuse me of being some alcoholic. We're already not on the best of terms since we got home yesterday after a rather silent and awkward boat ride home. Giving him ammunition for a whole new battle is just *not* what I want to deal with tonight.

"Couldn't help but overhear your awful weekend," the bartender continues, his hazel eyes sparkling in the lilac and deep blue lighting of the modernly decorated bar. "Sounds like you girls could use another drink." One side of his mouth turns up into a sly grin. "Or maybe a *good* weekend."

I push my martini glass towards the edge of the bar and look at Lara. "I think I'll pass on the drink, really," I say smartly with a wink. "Though god knows I could *so* use a good sloshing right now. My husband's so dull sometimes."

"I'm good, thanks," Lara says in a dismissive way. She averts her eyes from the bartender to me, her lips pressed firmly together.

The bartender takes my glass, gives Lara a little nod, then gives me an indecipherable look as he moves along. I can't tell if he's giving me eyes that say he'll surprise us with a drink anyway? If he wants Lara's number maybe? Perhaps mine? Or if he's just practicing his smooth-talking moves before the evening crowd hits, when the bar will fill with the usual twenty-something, up-and-coming gentrified crowd.

"Anyway," I say to Lara. "Whatever. I'll go home tonight and Andrew'll probably already be in bed, asleep with his damn sleeping pills. God, isn't life *thrilling*? Aren't you *envious* of what I have?" I cackle in spite.

"Envious that you have a man who loves you?" She sniffs. "Yeah, that'd be a nice thing to have."

"Please. If he really loved me he wouldn't be racing to the office like he does. Second-best Jackie."

Lara's silent for a moment, looking at me with soft eyes. Finally she says, "So did you guys make up already or what?" She takes a short drink before pushing her glass away.

"Not really," I say with a sigh. "He was such a bore last night. He just took his Ambien and said he had a busy week ahead of him, then went to bed. I mean, granted I was totally POed over his whole 'I can't leave work for a single second' thing shtick. I might have been kind of unapproachable. But he promised he could take a break from the office. One simple weekend! It's like he can't help himself, Lara."

"For what it's worth," she says in a cautious yet direct tone, "take it from a woman who lives to work. When you get into that mode and it's churning project out here and meeting deadline there, Black-Berry glued to your hand and your next day's—next week's!—schedule zipping through your mind twenty-four-seven, you can really get your head lost. Work-life balance is tough when you've got a high-powered career."

"Then Andrew never should have gotten married if he wasn't willing to compromise," I say astutely.

"And," Lara says, holding up one manicured finger, "maybe you shouldn't have gotten married if you weren't willing to compromise."

I furrow my brow, taken aback by her words.

"Look," she says in a flurry, "I'm just saying it goes both ways. Give and take, yin and yang, takes two to tango." She waves a loose hand. "You know how it goes? I know Andrew's not being the husband he needs to be, but, in all honesty, Jackie, are *you* being the wife you need to be?"

"I'm going to a therapist," I say through a whine.

"And that's great."

"I know I've got a difficult past and demons to deal with. I know I'm *not* an easy person to get along with."

"Yet we all love our crazy Jackie. Although, seriously, a little crazy goes a long way." She gives me a playful shove.

"I try to keep busy," I say, "and I try not to dwell on Andrew being gone so much, busy so often..."

"Maybe..." Lara looks away from me and straight at her cocktail. "Maybe...you might want to consider getting a job? Or volunteering?"

"Lara, please." I wag my head indignantly. "I'm not the volunteering type and there's no point in me working. I'm too...emotionally worked up to even consider *applying* for something like that."

"Just a thought." She whips out her BlackBerry and clicks about for a few seconds. "You don't have to work just because you need the money. Look at Em. At Chad."

I sigh, plunking an elbow too harshly on the bar. I rub at the tingling spot, and the bartender reappears.

"We'll get the check, please," Lara says to him.

She turns to me and says, waving about her phone, "Not to add fuel to the down-on-careers fire, but I've got some take-home work to do." She sticks out her tongue and crinkles her nose. "It bites, but I've got to get going." She drops her phone back into her bag. "Maybe when you feel like you're back on top of the emotional wagon you can consider doing something to help keep your mind off your troubles."

I point at her half-drunk cocktail. "That could do it," I tease.

"Ha-ha." She pulls her discreet black wallet from her bag and is about to produce a credit card when I tell her I've got this one.

"You've always got this one, Jack."

"Hey, if I can't be happy that the husband's big-bucks-career keeps him tied up and away from me, the least I can do is enjoy the perks of being able to cover a BFF's tab."

"Cheers to that." She jingles the melting ice in her glass, imitating a toast. "Look, just try to see his side of things, hon." She puts her wallet away. "There's a reason you can cover these tabs, like you said. There's a reason you can live such a glamorous life."

"Trophy-wife-life," I say glumly. "Not as shiny as they make it out to be."

"Would you rather him make less money and work less? Maybe you *both* work? Claire and Conner...Robin and Bobby..."

"While they're happy in their relationships, that's not exactly what I had in mind."

"You're a lucky woman, Jack." Lara pats my hand, then hikes her bag onto her shoulder. "You're just a tad too spoiled and caught up in your drama-drams to realize it."

"I know," I grouse, having heard this time and again. "I'm working through shit, what can I say?"

"Keep it up. And keep the lines of communication open. Sounds like you guys are back to 'The Sound of Silence,' and that's not good."

The bartender sets the bill on the bar between us, and I snatch it up and say, "*Silence of the Lambs* is more like it." I snicker and pull a fifty from my wallet. "There's definitely a thick, heavy...*something*... between us. It's icky again, Lara. Probably headed downhill—*again!*"

Lara gives a sympathetic stroke to my cheek and tells me to keep on talking. "Don't give up."

"You know what the real problem is, Lara?" I tap an acrylic nail on my front teeth, and she raises an eyebrow in response. "I think he *is* having an affair," I say saliently. "Work can *not* be making him race to the computer like that on a measly overnight trip. No way."

"You'd be surprised how demanding the office can be."

"Come on, Lara." I glance at the bill and set the fifty on top of it. "After all Andrew and I've been through? With us having that heart-to-heart about him being more attentive, and he still can't give me the bare minimum of a weekend away?" I push the cash to the bartender and tell him I'll take only a ten in change. "Our marriage is on the line here, and he's playing Russian Roulette with it!"

"I wish I could say with certainty that Andrew is just a workaholic." Lara's voice turns low. "But after my recent deal with Nathan..."

"Exactly!" I slump my shoulders forward. "It's so pathetic, isn't it? I mean, what other explanation could there be for him being so obsessed with staying plugged in on vaca?" I sigh loudly. "He just *has* to be having an affair with Nikki! I've got to get to the bottom of this, Lara. Something's just not right."

Adjusting her bag on her shoulder, Lara shrugs lifelessly. "Well, if I can help, let me know." She abruptly holds up a finger and says, "You know. Not to encourage acting on insane emotions. I mean, you did totally key the hell out of my ex's car, and I still can't completely swallow that fact."

"BFF love," I say with a peppy pump of my fist.

She closes her eyes and waves the topic away with a swift wagging of her head. "But maybe...maybe if you were to just go over to Andrew's office, see for yourself what it's like when he's 'too busy to take your calls,' then maybe you'll feel better. I don't know. See that he really is busy, that there is no affair and..." She bites her bottom lip. "I don't want to encourage sneaky and dishonest behavior but...I don't know. Hell, we're grasping at straws at this point, right?"

"Right," I say, lackluster.

"I don't know. Just a thought. And it'd be a nice way to show him that you care, that you're thinking about him."

"Maybe you're right," I say with a forced half-grin. "Maybe if I went over there...took charge for once...saw for myself there wasn't anything to worry about..."

"Just keep your keys in your purse," Lara says, only half in jest. "Okay, I've got to go." She stands up and smooths out the light wrinkles in her power suit. "Thanks for another lovely date, Jackie. I'm sorry it was a bitch fest and couldn't be celebratory."

"My pleasure." I smooth out my own clothes, a simple black mini with a new pair of glittering gold Badgley Mischkas.

The bartender hands me a ten-dollar bill, and I smile and thank him. I quickly dart my eyes to Lara to see if maybe there's an opportunity for me to get her and this hunk of bartender meat out on a date, but she's already clicking on her conservative black pumps to the exit.

That girl, I think, hiking up my dress just a skosh, then clicking after her.

18

"Hi," I trill as I walk through the second set of doors of Jennings & Voigt, Andrew's firm.

Passing through general reception, I head straight to Andrew's area of the office, hoping Nikki's already out for lunch so I won't have to see her stupid face.

"Good afternoon," Nikki greets, somewhat unexpectedly. Her voice is like ice, her demeanor sub-zero. She's sitting here behind her large desk, posture perfect, her strawberry hair so finely set in large, swooping curls. Not one hair looks to be out of place. I scratch at my freshly trimmed inch-, maybe inch-and-a-half-length, bleached hair.

"Hi," I say, matching her saccharine greeting.

I appraise her some more, unable to ignore how slick and shiny her pink lips are, how thick her black, inky eyeliner forms faux-almond-shaped eyes, and how long and tarantula-like her heavily mascaraed eyelashes are.

"Yes? Can I help you?" Nikki says, those hair-leg-lashes fluttering in impatience.

I exhale loudly and scan the reception area. "I'm here for

Andrew." I hike my Gucci handbag up higher on my shoulder. "For lunch."

She looks at me, perplexed. She slowly blinks, exaggeratedly and annoyingly so. *If she blinks like this for much longer those spidery lashes will get tangled and she won't be able to open her eyes again,* I think. I stifle a childish giggle at the mental image as she begins to flip through a large datebook.

"I'm sorry, Jackie," she says in a crisp and grating voice—that nasally tone of hers. "I don't have you down." She takes a look at her iMac, scrolls the mouse, and with a slow headshake and painted smile, says, "No, he doesn't have you down for lunch today. He actually has a very important meeting this afternoon. A lot of prep before Singapore."

"Yeah, yeah," I pop a piece of Bubblicious in my mouth. "Always an important meeting."

"If you like I could schedule you in..." She consults the computer, then the datebook. "Would next Wednesday work? Looks like he's got a twenty-minute slot open for lunch then. I could pencil you in." She blinks slowly again, that fake smile still there.

"Look, Nikki," I say, feeling an acrid taste form in my mouth at the mention of her name, despite the sweetness of the bubblegum. "I'm Andrew's *wife*. I'm not *penciled in* for lunches with my husband. It's friggin' lunch. I'd like to see him."

Nikki's face grows long as I head towards the closed fog-glass door with my husband's name stenciled on.

"Excuse me!" Nikki calls out in fearful urgency.

"Oh." I spin on my heels. "And seriously, when I leave you a message for Andrew to call me back, I mean it. Okay? This game of cat and mouse is getting real old, real fast."

She looks perplexed—obviously her five brain cells are churning at the fastest pace they have in weeks. "I don't know what you're talking about," she gasps.

"Yeah, yeah." I blow a bubble. "Save it. I know Andrew's busy, but he can surely take a one-minute call from his wife now and then, kay?" I adjust my tight dress a tad, then place my hand on the cold, golden doorknob.

"He doesn't have time!" Nikki nearly shouts, standing from her desk. Her soft, practically perfect complexion is beginning to turn a violet-ruby color.

"I'll make it a quickie then," I say to her over my shoulder and with a wink. But before I can turn the knob the door swings wide open, pulling me forward and into the chest of my husband.

"Jackie," Andrew says in sheer shock. "What are you doing here?"

Nikki stomps over on her ridiculously long and Nylon-clad legs. "I'm sorry, Mr. Kittredge," she spits out, removing her headset. "I told her you were busy and—"

Andrew looks me up and down, a grin forming on his lips, and he holds a hand up to Nikki. "No," he says in that low voice of his. "I've actually got a minute, Nikki. This is all right."

I'm brewing with pride, filling up with "take that, bitch!" sense of self-satisfaction. I can't help but flash Nikki a quick look, one corner of my bottom lip between my teeth.

"All right," Nikki manages to say, her violet-ruby color abating slightly.

"Really," I say, slipping my hands under Andrew's double-breasted, pinstriped suit jacket and around his waist. "All I need is a minute." I pull Andrew closer, staking my claim, making it crystal clear to Nikki that Andrew's mine and I'm here, whether it's "scheduled" or not.

"I'm sorry," Nikki rushes out, looking to Andrew with apologetic eyes. She lightly pats down a soft wave of curls. "She wasn't scheduled, and I know how busy you are." She puts on her headset, amazingly not breaking one curl or setting a single hair out of place.

"That's not a problem, Nikki," Andrew says, giving her one of his charming smiles. "Thank you for trying so hard to keep my day free. I appreciate it."

"My pleasure," she says, and I swear she puffs her chest up a bit, as if to smite me.

I tighten my grip around Andrew's waist in jealous response and nudge him into his office. "Come on, honey," I drawl out in a sex-kitten kind of way. "We haven't got much time, you're so busy."

As Andrew and I inch our way into his office I catch Nikki's cold stare and give her a vacant look in return. Then, just as Andrew closes the door, putting up the wall between wife and possible-mistress, I raise one warning eyebrow—that expression that says to Nikki, "He's mine; back off, bitch."

"So, what brings your sexy self down here, baby doll?" Andrew asks as I strut in my best naughty girl walk to his desk. I prop myself up onto it, crossing my legs.

"Oh, you know," I sigh. I fling my handbag onto his large, leather desk chair behind me. "Running my errands, got my tan and sauna on, and now I'm looking for lunch with my husband." I kick off one espadrille. "But if you only have a few minutes I can think of an alternative to lunch." I kick off the other shoe.

He rubs at his clean-shaven jaw, unable to conceal a smile, as he says, "Now if there was ever a way to distract a man from work..."

I lean back on my palms, shoving aside whatever lie in my way—pens, papers, important contracts and million-dollar agreements, whatever.

"Come over here and I'll show you," I say in a seductive tone, beckoning him with a drawing finger.

Still rubbing at the side of his face, he looks at me with a sexy, sideways stare. I pull myself further back onto the desk, slightly parting my legs.

Andrew's eyes turn to slits, then grow wide, and wider. "Jackie!" he says, nearly shouting.

I toss my head back and give a guttural growl. "Andrew! Oh, Andrew!" I shout.

"Jackie," he says, voice much lower now. He charges over as I part my legs some more and sink further onto the desk.

"What the hell are you doing?" He pulls me upright by the waist, then he makes a motion for me to put my legs together.

"What?" I ask innocently, shaking off a Post-It that's stuck to my wrist.

"Where's your underwear?" He bristles.

I cast my eyes to my lap and giggle. "Well with only a few minutes to spare we can't be bothered with barriers, now can we?" I yank on his tie and bring him nearer me.

"Jackie." He briskly pulls back, adjusting his tie. I twirl a string of gum around my finger. "That's disgusting, running around town without underwear." He finishes adjusting his tie, his face pulled back in anger.

"*Disgusting?*" I gasp, totally taken aback. "Your *wife* is *disgusting?*" I can't believe my ears! I stick my gum onto a random piece of paper.

"You know what I mean," he says hurriedly. "You bend over in a little dress like that or something and you show the whole world your business!"

"Oh, Andrew! Don't be such a prude," I groan, tossing up my hands. "I don't get you." I point a finger sharply at him. "You know, when we were dating you *loved* when I did this." I motion down at my pantie-less self. "You never thought it *disgusting*. And what's with the sudden aversion to doing it on your desk? Do you know how many times we *used* to do it here?"

"I'm not here to drone on about the past and your problems, Jackie," he says curtly. "Or about how we used to have an amazing connection and now we're a boring married couple, yada-yada. I'm sick of hearing about it. I've got work to do, and I'd appreciate it if you let me get back to it."

I cross my arms over my chest and make a pouting but angry face. "Sorry that you *seemed* to be interested in what I had to offer. I came here trying to get sparks flying, trying to show that I love you, that I'm working at our marriage!" *And to see for myself that there isn't anything fishy going on with Nikki, I think, which I'm still as unsure as ever about.* But I don't need to tell Andrew this little piece of info.

"Don't get me wrong," he says, "I like it when you dress sexy like this. I like the unexpected visit." He touches my knee. "But come on,

143

I'm swamped and...well...that's a little gross. Grow up. This isn't sorority row anymore where acting slutty might be the cool thing to do."

"You jerk," I say, tightening my arms over my chest.

"Look," he rubs at his temples, "I appreciate you coming down here. Really, I do. But I'm busy." He touches my knee again, but this time I shake it off. "And I'm just looking out for you," he says, "wanting what's best. I don't like the idea of my wife running around town wearing a minidress and no panties. You're asking for trouble, baby doll."

"Yes," I say, angrily yanking my handbag from his chair. "I am asking for trouble." I crawl down from the desk, pulling free yet another Post-It, this one stuck to the back of my thigh. "Coming here was asking for trouble, and I'm sorry!" I shriek. I put on my espadrilles and sunglasses and look up at him, wearing the most proud and strong face I can conjure up.

"Baby doll." His voice is buttery smooth. "Don't let this upset your day."

He cautiously approaches me, one hand reaching out until it comes into contact with my small chin. He leans down and places a gentle and moist kiss on my lips. Then I feel a wandering hand ride up the back of my dress and cup my rear. "You just go on home and wait for me." He gives my rear a little smack. "Just like this."

I pull down my sunglasses and look him square in the eye. "You won't be home for hours," I state, point-blank.

He shrugs uncomfortably. "Yes, unfortunately."

"I can't stay cooped up in the house all day waiting for you, Andrew. I just can't!"

"Then go buy yourself some panties and, I don't know, go shopping." His phone begins to ring, and, without skipping a beat he pads immediately to his desk, brushing right on past me as if I'm not even here. "Let me answer this," he says, holding up a finger. "One second." He retrieves the phone.

"I don't know why I tried," I whisper to myself, thinking Lara's heart was in the right place, but this whole idea to come over to

Andrew's office unexpectedly is only stoking the fire that's become our marriage—one fight after another.

"Thank you, Nikki," Andrew says into the phone, his voice low and serious. He then gives a simple, two-beat chuckle, followed by, "All right, sure. Yes. Yes, I know. Okay." He glances up at me. "Yes. Please hold the call. I'll be with him in one second." He returns the phone to its cradle and looks at me imploringly.

"Look, baby," he begins, approaching me with open arms. "I wish I could spend time with you right now, but I can't. Maybe you can go make a spa day of it."

"I'll take care of my day, thank you," I say, pushing my sunglasses back up the bridge of my nose.

"You understand, don't you, baby?" he says as I'm about to pull open the door. "I'm so swamped what with Singapore and all—"

"No," I breathe out after a lengthy amount of dead air. "No, and I don't think I ever will understand, but what's it matter? It's Singapore today, something else tomorrow." I take a cigarette from my almost empty pack of Parliaments and blow him a quick kiss goodbye. "I love you, Andrew, but sometimes I really don't like you."

"Oh, Jackie."

"I'll see you at home tonight." I grip the doorknob tightly. "Whenever that will be."

"Sounds good, dear." He gives me a peck on the cheek. "Try and have a good day."

I can hear Nikki say to the person on the phone line that she'll "be happy to deliver the message to Mr. Kittredge" as I swing open the door and charge out. I guffaw loud enough for her *and* Andrew, who's now standing in his doorway, to hear.

"I'll try to be home at a decent hour," Andrew calls out, "but no promises, baby doll."

I wave a loose hand behind me, then light a cigarette. *No promises...broken promises...they're all the same*, I think bitterly as Nikki's voice instantaneously sounds. I can hear Andrew's door click shut as her nasally tone grates, "Jackie, you can't smoke in here."

I take a drag and strut on out of the office, giving Nikki the finger as I cross the threshold.

19

"Jack!" Sophie exclaims as I enter The Cup and the Cake. "You are a *life*saver! Thank you, thank you!"

"Couldn't coax Chad to come out and ride to your rescue?" I joke, not liking to miss a fun opportunity to tease Sophie about her one-time-fling a few summers back, in college, with Chad.

Sometimes I think Chad's got it bad for Sophie, what with him coming over to the café to help her out and all—it just seems odd that he'd want to spend his spare time helping a friend with whom he's always in spar-mode. When asked why, he just laughs and says he does it for the free baked goods.

"Ha-ha, you are hilarious, Jack." Sophie takes the brown paper bag of bananas and pears from me. "I *so* did not have time to get to the market this morning."

"All I've got is time, sister. Glad to help."

"I slept through my alarm...the stress with wedding season is here...I have *got* to make Robin's wedding cake absolute perfection!"

"Oh, chill," I say breezily. I follow her to the kitchen in the back. "You've got like two weeks."

"Eleven days, minus the hours ticking by as we speak." She sets the bag on a countertop and begins to scan over a pad of paper.

"Busy time, that's all. I love stress, I love the pressure, I love being busy," she says more to herself than me. "I can so do this."

"Hey, Gatz," I say with a wave, greeting the curly-haired, lanky guy who's got his hands in a bowl of mush, squeezing some kind of fruit—probably the few bananas Sophie still had on hand for the day's demanding menu.

"Hi, Jackie," he says with a sharp nod of the head.

"How's th—"

"Okay," Sophie cuts in, diverting my attention from Gatz. She hastily slips the pad of paper in her front apron pocket and gestures for me to follow back up front. "I've got orders to fill. Going up front." She charges forward.

"Later," I say to Gatz with a quick wave.

Sophie brings the pad back out once again and consults it. She pulls open the display case door under the countertop and carefully sets a pear and clove cupcake on a plate. "How's the marriage-fixing going?" she asks.

"Wouldn't know," I say languidly. "Andrew's in Singapore now."

She briskly closes the door then begins to flip some switches on the large, silver beast of an espresso machine.

"Oh, yeah!" She makes wide eyes for a second. "Forgot about that. Sorry, babe."

"I'm coping. I'm fine." I lean against the counter and play around with her tip jar. "Still seeing Dr. Pierce a few times a week. That counts for something, right?"

"That it does," she says as she swiftly prepares a handful of beverages. "Glad to see you're not too down about it."

"Manis and pedis always perk a girl up," I say, wiggling my freshly filled, neon-orange acrylics at her. "For a while."

She laughs and says, "You've got to stay determined and upbeat. It's a rough time, but you can get through it."

She pours helpings of steamed milk into three floral-decorated teacups. "When I was going through a really rough time in life, I had to remind myself ad nauseam that sometimes life serves you lemons," she says with candor, "and, as Claire says, you've got to try to make lemon cupcakes." She gives me a smile and peers over my shoulder. "And speaking of the positive ball of sunshine!"

I turn towards the door, and there's Claire.

"Hey, you!" Sophie exclaims cheerfully. "Day off? No hospital or house calls today?"

"Hey," I say to Claire, giving her a quick side-hug.

"Girls," Claire says, looking obviously dismayed. Her hair's in a messy ponytail, her wild curls shooting out like multiple antennae; her vintage t-shirt is all wrinkled; and, if I'm seeing things correctly, she forgot to apply mascara to one set of lashes.

"What is it?" I ask, searching her worried face for an immediate response.

"It's Conner," she says through a whimper.

"I'm calmer now," Claire mewls. "I think I'm over the initial shock."

"I'm not!" I declare, still just as flabbergasted as I was when Claire broke the news not ten minutes ago that Conner didn't get the promotion.

"Did he just find out?" Sophie asks in a mild manner. She runs her thumb methodically against a to-go box's edge.

"This morning," Claire says. "They've decided to go with an outside hire apparently." She pulls a napkin free from the dispenser near the register. "Said they weren't confident Conner could manage such a big and critical team." She blows her nose loudly. "Which is total BS, because he's worked there forever! I mean, how much is there to *know* about accounting, right?" Claire looks at us, dumb-founded.

"Don't ask me," I say, holding up two hands. "I don't even look at my credit card statements."

"So what's his game plan?" Sophie says, getting straight to business, getting those ducks lined up and a battle plan whipped up in traditional Sophie Style. "Is he going to stay on at his company? Is he going to look elsewhere? Was this a do-or-die deal, the promotion?"

Claire blows her nose again, then wipes at her moist eyes. She's barely shed any tears since she arrived, most of them probably shed earlier when she'd initially gotten the unfortunate news, maybe in her car ride over.

"Well," Claire squeaks out, balling up the used napkin, "it obviously would've been a nice thing. I mean, a *promotion* and a *pay raise.* God knows we could use it...and that he deserves it. Oh!" She beats her fist in as silent a way as possible on the countertop. "How could they do this to him? He's such a hard worker and loyal and always turning his monthly reports in on time!" She shakes her head sharply. "I don't understand. An outside hire!"

"Bullshit," I add in for girl-support and morale.

"And you know what this means now, right?" Claire says, thumping her knuckles on the counter, her voice climbing an octave.

"Conner's going to look for another job, isn't he?" I gasp.

"Well, maybe." Claire covers her face with her hands. "It also means the whole baby thing's put on the back burner." She abruptly pulls her hands down, revealing scared and sorrow-filled eyes. "I'm over the shock, okay. I am. And I only want what's best for my husband. Conner's happiness is what's important here. The baby can wait."

Sophie nods, and I follow suit.

"But I'm so frustrated," Claire wails, hands returning to her face. "How could they do this to him?" Her voice is muffled behind her hands. "He's such a hard worker."

"Girls," Sophie says, quickly casting about the café.

I rub Claire's back in slow, circular motions while she continues to lament.

"Girls," Sophie repeats, her voice stern and hushed. "I really sympathize with your plight, Claire, but—"

"It's so unfair," Claire cries, bringing her hands down to her mouth.

"Dear," Sophie says, her voice beseeching, "as much as I'd love to play Dr. Sophie right now, I've got some customers to tend to. It's not exactly a good time."

"It's never a good time for crap like this to happen," I say to Sophie, giving her an imploring look.

"Okay," she says over Claire's muttering and sniffles. "Take it in the back and I'll be there in a sec. I have something that maybe will cheer you up."

"Cupcakes?" Claire says, somehow exuding positivity and radiance.

Sophie only replies with a sly smile and a wink.

Claire proceeds to tell me about her latest conundrum in the solitude of the kitchen, where Gatz is stirring a concoction in an oversized bowl, eyebrows arching and face pulling tight or scrunching up every now and then, evidently honing in on the conversation.

"I knew it was a possibility," Claire tells me, squeezing tight her crumpled napkin. "I *knew* Conner might not get this promotion and then we'd be having a different conversation."

"About finding a new job?" I ask.

She nods in response.

"And that'd be a bad thing because..."

"Because—because—" She bites on her quivering bottom lip. "Oh, this sounds so selfish."

"Honey," I say with a smile, "I'm queen of selfish."

Gatz lets out a small but not-so-surreptitious chuckle.

"Heard that, saw that," I say, looking at him.

He recoils in his stance a tad, then says, "Sorry, but I can't help but overhear things if The Cup and the Cake is also used as the set of *Sex and the City*."

I playfully nudge Gatz's forearm as he churns the thick, pale batter. "You're a part of the fireside chat, voluntary or otherwise, so you have a two-bit piece of advice?"

Claire looks at Gatz, eyes and mouth drawn down.

Gatz contemplates the question a moment, not stopping his churning. Then he says, "Maybe this is just what Conner needs—a change of pace, so to speak. Our generation isn't keeping to the same stale job for forty-plus years like our parents and grandparents did, you know?" He stops stirring to push back a fallen curly lock from in front of his face. "Sounds like if this company doesn't appreciate him as much as they should, giving him the promo and all, then he ought-a skip out of there. You know?"

"I guess," Claire says, idly nudging around the flour that's scattered about the tabletop.

"That's how I'd see it, anyhow," he continues. "Like with this opportunity to study in Australia I've got." He dips a silver teaspoon into the batter. "I saw it as a chance to do something different, something new. I like what I do here, but that doesn't mean there isn't something else equally enjoyable or right for me." He hands the spoon to Claire and tells her to take a taste-test, that maybe it'll lift her spirits.

"He makes a good point," I say. "Em's the same way." I give Gatz a small smile. "She sees an opportunity—a new door—and she takes it. Maybe that's what this is for Conner. He just needs to...take it. Let go of his job and move on."

Claire finishes licking the spoon clean. "Yeah," she says resignedly. "I know *that'll* work out. He's a smart guy, and I have complete faith he'll find something great, no matter what."

"See!" I enthusiastically give her a clap on the shoulder.

"But it's the *baby*, too. I was hoping we wouldn't have to wait too much longer." She sets the spoon down, then flips it over, back and forth, letting it make a *ping-ping-ping* sound against the metal tabletop.

"You've got years to have babies," Gatz says breezily.

"I'm here," Sophie's voice appears exuberantly from behind. She makes her speedy way to the refrigerator. "And..." Two small saucers in hand, she closes the refrigerator door with a swing of her slim hip. "I come bearing my latest creation for you to sink your worries into!"

Suddenly a blue-glitter and white-iced cupcake appears before Claire, then before me. There's a miniature, white fondant fortune cookie propped on top in the center.

"I call it the Find a Friday Fortune," Sophie says proudly. "Now hurry and taste-test and let's get back to chit-chat. It's actually peaceful up there for a sec." She jumps up onto a barstool opposite us, right next to Gatz, who's now filling large, seemingly endless cupcake pans with the gooey batter.

Claire immediately begins to pull the light blue wrapper from the cupcake, and I take a swipe of the icing. *Mmm.* It's Sophie's vanilla bean special. Simple, but delicious.

"Go on," Sophie urges with a broad smile, gesturing for me to take a real bite.

So I do, biting right on in to the creamy sweetness, when— *What's that?* I pull back and peer at the bitten cake.

What the... I slowly pull out a thin strip of paper.

"Isn't that cool?" Sophie asks, eyes sparkling and hands clasped together in anticipation. "What do you think?"

I look to Claire, and she's licking her paper clean of icing and cake crumbles.

"It's..." I look sideways at the upside-down text of the small slip of what is obviously my fortune.

"It's ingenious, isn't it?" Sophie says.

I look at Claire once more, and she's trying to make out the text, too. I glance at Gatz, but he's paying full attention to his cupcake-making duties.

"Well?" Sophie presses.

I read my fortune aloud. "Today is your lucky day, so smile." I give Sophie a curious expression.

"And?" She's waiting on pins and needles for our opinions.

"Can I be frank?" I ask, the sticky paper in between my fingers, and... Yup. That's right. There's also a little bit in my mouth. I fish for the lost corner of paper and wince. "Sophie, babe. I think this is a terrible idea."

"It works for fortune cookies," Claire says sweetly. "But in cake?" She licks her fingers, then looks to be searching for a fragment of her own fortune.

"Ugh," Sophie groans. "No good, huh?"

"It works in something hard, like the cookie," I say, picking up on what Claire was saying. "But a soft and gooey cupcake..." I crinkle my nose.

"People won't expect that," Claire finishes for me. "We want to bite into the yumminess and softness of a cupcake. Paper just doesn't work in there, you know? Soggy with sogginess." She delivers the frank message with sincerity and her signature sweetness, never wanting to hurt a soul.

"That's what Gatz said," Sophie says, tossing a limp hand up.

Gatz just shrugs.

"It was worth a try," she says with a loud sigh. "Honestly! I don't know where my creativity has gone. I feel so—so—so stifled or something. I'm just workin' round the clock and I need something new. Something refreshing. Inspiration!"

"You know," I say, an idea coming to me, "it's a good thing you asked us to sample these before you went and made them a regular menu item. People could, like, *choke* on these things."

"Yeah," Claire says. "Imagine if I had a baby." Sophie and I share a brief deadpan glance. "It would choke on that and—"

"Okay! I get it," Sophie says. "Just trying to get your thoughts and offer up a bit of cheer. Besides, I already had to hear from Lara about how it could be a lawsuit waiting to happen with some unsuspecting ninny ordering and not knowing what they're in for."

"Oh, yeah," Claire says with a stern flatline motion of her hands. "You definitely don't want one of *those*." She shivers.

"Thanks anyway, girls." Sophie takes a swipe of frosting from Claire's cupcake. "Did the sugary sweetness help with your plight at least?"

"They work for me whenever I'm missing Em," Gatz says with a cheesy grin.

Claire holds out her cupcake to Sophie, who groans through a small bite.

"Between cheesy, romantic, head-over-heels-in-love, sappy boy here," Sophie says with a full mouth, thumbing at Gatz, "reminding me how unfair my love life is, not to mention him running on out of here with my only other super-fab worker, and then you, Claire, barging in with earth-shattering dilemma—oh! and worrying how I'll manage wedding season *and* the best wedding cake ever for Robin..." She makes a high-pitched sound. "I'm going to need a vacation." She takes a quick look at her watch.

"But first! Duty calls up front!" Sophie enthusiastically wipes her hands on her apron and licks her lips clean before bounding off the stool. "I'd love to girl talk it up more back here, but if I don't serve coffee and sell cakes I'm going to wind up on the street, Easy Bake Ovening my way back into the baking world."

20

Sophie had nothing to worry about. She delivered a positively scrumptious wedding cake for Robin and Bobby's wedding. It was beautiful, too. She called in a favor from one of her old coworkers, Oliver, a professional cake decorator. He piped dainty pink roses about the cake and made little beads that looked exactly like pearls, with the pearlescent sheen and all.

Like the wedding cake, the wedding was exquisite. The backyard affair was the perfect blend of homey, romantic, intimate, laid-back, and fun. I couldn't imagine a more ideal wedding for the two. Robin was absolutely gorgeous, and Rose made an adorable flower girl. Lara walked infant Phillip up the aisle, dressed in the smartest, tiniest suit. The ceremony was a really touching union of Robin and Bobby, and then Rose and Phillip were incorporated into the ceremony—sort of a marriage of the whole Holman clan. It was adorable and I cried an ocean of tears.

The teary exchange of vows and "family coming together" part were the only times I actually found myself thinking of Andrew, and missing him. Luckily Sophie was by my side, passing out tissues to me and to Claire, back and forth, stopping now and then to wipe away her own flood of emotion.

Aside from those sentimental moments, I honestly forgot about how Andrew wasn't around for Robin's wedding. In fact, I think I thought more about Emily and how much of a bummer it was that she was still in Africa and unable to come home in time for the event. What does it say when you miss your best friend more than your own husband?

Despite the dreariness that has overtaken my marriage, Robin's wedding was a brilliant shining light, and a ton of fun! As she and her new husband headed off for an extended weekend on San Juan Island, getting a much-needed tryst thanks to her sister watching the kids, the rest of the girls and the guys and I hit the town, after-party style. And you know what? If trips to the salon and the sauna, shopping sprees, and chats over cupcakes can't take my mind off of the things that plague me, a night of clubbing will. It always does.

"Any new guys on your radar?" I ask Lara, swaying my hips to the electric beat Re-Live has pumping through the speakers.

Re-Live is one of the hottest clubs in Capitol Hill, attracting mostly a queer crowd, but it doesn't matter if you're gay, straight, or have dismissed yourself of the romantic-partner scene altogether. Re-Live is high on energy and has some of Seattle's hottest DJs (not to mention quite a few hotties on the dance floor and working behind the bar). Honestly, I just don't come here enough. Em and I used to come here a lot in college, daring each other to see who could collect the most numbers from interested lesbians.

"Unfortunately, no," Lara says loudly over the thumping bass. She sashays in her slimming, mint-colored, silken dress, matching the soft color palette Robin had for her wedding.

Robin, like myself, didn't go with the whole traditional bridesmaid thing, and I think the girls and I were all okay with that, seeing how it felt like only yesterday we were all trying on a trousseau of bridesmaid dresses for Claire's wedding.

Lara, however, walking baby Phillip in the ceremony, was the closest thing Robin had to a bridesmaid or a maid of honor, so she found this really pretty dress. It's from the J. Crew wedding collection, so it's actually a really nice number for our after-party. It's not too obviously bridal, which could look either super corny during a night out or signal to all single males looking to get lucky within a two-mile radius that there's prime bridesmaid booty waiting to be tapped. Then again, that could be *just* the thing Lara needs...

"Unfortunately!" I say excitedly. "So it's now *unfortunate* that you're single, huh, Lara?"

Lara places her hands behind her head and sways heavier to the entrancing beat of the music. She's finally letting her hair down, ready to groove to the beat and have a night on the town.

"So it's time to sink your claws in a fresh piece of meat, then, right?" I press with a large, temptress-like smile.

Lara's dress clings to her curvy body and accentuates her long legs, and the mint color brings out the blueness of her eyes. It's a classy yet clingy dress, and that's a refreshing change from the usual pantsuits and ruffled button-downs.

"I don't want to go all carnivore on a man, Jack," Lara says with a laugh. She looks up at the ceiling, swaying.

Judging by her smooth moves, her fingers knotting in her hair, and the relaxed look in her eyes, it's evident she's had a drink or two, she's feeling sexy, and, if you ask me, she's ready for me to send the guy at two o'clock her way.

"I'm open to dating again, though," she says, rolling her shoulders as the music slows its tempo.

Bingo! I can't stop the growing smile from taking over my face as I lock eyes with the dark-haired, thick-chested, and square-jawed hottie at two o'clock.

I move closer to Lara and slowly slink my back up against hers. I move downwards on my five-inch leopard-print Louboutins. Her hips keep swaying as I slowly and rather seductively move up and down, trying to keep with her tempo.

"I want in," Claire squeals, prancing over with a cocktail in one hand and a party blower in the other. Seemingly making up for a bachelorette party she never had, Claire's got a neon purple boa draped loosely over the crooks of her arms. She blows the popper, its whirring noise inaudible over the club's music.

"Girl dancing!" she yells through a broad grin. She starts to move her voluptuous hips, her light blue taffeta dress moving brightly with her under the gentle but obvious flashes of the strobe lights that have just begun.

I place my hands on Claire's hips, leaning back on Lara, who's still moving seductively to the music, and I look at the dark-haired guy. This time I give a crooked smile as I tilt my head back and lean it against Lara's gently rocking shoulder.

"Woohoo!" Claire screeches. She shakes her booty at me, blows her popper again, then begins to dance ridiculously with her boa. "We've *got* to do this more!"

I notice out of the corner of my eye the dark-haired guy, his eyes trained on our little threesome, as he takes a slow drink of his cocktail before beginning to saunter out onto the dance floor.

I close my eyes and fall back further into Lara, then turn towards her, initiating a side dance together. Lara smiles, tossing her head about with more energy.

Quickly, I dart my eyes back at the approaching hottie. *Perfect,* I think. *Classic girl-on-girl dance move to get a guy's attention.*

I grab one of Lara's hands, and she motions for me to do a three-sixty around her.

There we go, I think, eyes back to the hottie who's closing in, taking one step at a time to the beat. *Come and cut in and then a slip of his hand in Lara's and instant hook up.*

I'm about to laugh out, "Get down with your bad self, Claire!" when I realize the tan, dark-haired, sinewy arms around me are not those of a short, soft-skinned, effervescent girl named Claire.

Instantly upon this realization, I entwine my fingers of one hand with the dark-haired guy's, and grab Lara's with my other. She leans forward, making a shaking motion with her shoulders, and pulls in closer. I take advantage of the moment and trade hands, slipping the guy's into Lara's, then give her a wink as I grab Claire by her taffeta-ed waist.

"Woohoo!" Claire bellows, jumping up and down, the cheap, itchy feathers of her boa brushing against my face.

As the music fades seamlessly from one track to the next, the strobe lights dimming down then finally shutting off, I retreat to an available bistro table with Claire.

"Did you see my moves out there?" she gasps, dropping exhaustedly into a chair.

"There's my dancing queen," Conner says, coming from nowhere and locking lips with Claire.

Chad appears at our table a second later, a sweating beer bottle in hand. "You two know how to heat up a dance floor," he says smugly.

"I know!" Claire enthuses, one hand gripping the back of Conner's neck, the other pulling the boa free from around her arms. She drapes the boa around Conner's neck and lets out a gleeful sigh.

"Should we all go heat up the floor a bit more?" Conner gives a sexy bite at the bottom of his lip and places his hands eagerly on Claire's hips.

Claire makes hungry eyes and leaps up, ever energetic when it comes to a night of dancing. "Let's do this!" She tosses me her party blower and grabs Conner roughly by the hand. "Come on, you two, get on out and join us!"

I look up at Chad. He's tapping a finger against his bottle with the tempo of the mid-key music, his head slightly bobbing in tune.

With a curious eyebrow raised, I grin through tightly pressed lips. "Well?"

With what seems to be some great deal of force, Chad turns his attention away from the bar, bringing his dark brown eyes to meet mine. "Huh?" he says with no expression. "What'd you say?"

I place the party blower between my lips, uncross my legs, and jump up. *Wheeee,* I can faintly hear the sound as the blower expands with an exhalation. "A dance?" I offer dryly.

"Uhh, sure." He takes a quick pull of his beer before setting it down and leading me to the dance floor, one hand loosely in the pocket of his black dress pants.

"Looks like my incognito setup for Lara is panning out just fine." I gesture across the way at the new duo as I move onto the dance floor with Chad. Lara's really working the floor, her hands wrapped around the dark-haired hottie, their bodies moving in unison.

"You organizing Operation Blind Date for Lara, now?" Chad asks, pulling me closer, but not too close, leaving about six inches of platonic distance between us.

Chad and I may have a history, but it's a brief one—a blip, if you will. It was so brief a fling sometimes I forget it even happened. Chad's been that dopey mutual friend for years as best buds with Conner, and I like to think our decade-long platonic relationship speaks louder volumes than a fleeting hour-or-so-long sexual encounter one summer a few years back.

It's not like either of us had ever considered hooking up again after our afternoon fling, anyhow. I'm kind of surprised at myself, actually, having hooked up with Chad. He's that good guy friend who's almost like a brother...the whole thing kind of sounds incestuous now that I look back on it, but hey! When you're alone, high, and horny, things happen. Maybe that's just another gritty detail for Dr. Pierce that I can add to the minestrone mix that's my life.

And, for what it's worth, I'm not the only girl here who shacked up with him one plastered night. Sometimes the girls and I get to kidding about how Chad's been that friend who's just there at a rather sexually convenient...or inconvenient...time. Anyway, what can you expect from a Pike frat boy, especially when there's loneliness and booze or dope in the picture? He's a nice guy and good friend, nothing more.

"I want Lara to find someone special," I tell Chad as I watch Lara dance. "She deserves to not have a total asswipe of a boyfriend. Definitely not someone who winds up as an asswipe of a husband!" I make a hearty groan.

Chad spins me, lightly placing a hand above the small of my back, the flight of the ruffles of my dress coming to a halt. He's keeping in beat with the music, but his focus is on the bar. He looks distracted.

"Maybe this club hottie is dating material, maybe just a quick romp," I say with a small giggle, drawing my head back to look up into Chad's eyes, his six-feet-plus height actually making me realize how grateful I am for Andrew's slightly shorter height.

Chad gives me another spin, almost robotic, and I push Andrew from my mind and give in to the music. Chad flashes a weak half-grin as his hand returns to my back and I sway and shake. "Maybe," he says simply.

"At least it looks like she's having a fun time." I glance over at Lara and her dancing partner once more. They've got their hands all over each other, and I can't fight the giddy and satisfied feeling that washes over me. "And we all deserve to find someone special after all," I say loudly. "You know?"

"Yeah," Chad replies in a distant sort of way. "We do."

He nods, then gives me another spin, this time making it a double one, causing me to laugh and hiccup, feeling that third cocktail slosh in my stomach and head. *Oh, I don't go dancing and clubbing enough*, I think as Chad spins and twirls me about the floor throughout the duration of the rest of the upbeat song.

"Phew!" I gasp through a half-trot, half-stumble.

"Nice work there, Jackie," Sophie says once I take a seat next to her at the pink-lit bar. I wipe at the sweat that's coating my forehead. "Lara and Joey Tribbiani over there." She stifles a laugh as she pulls on her cocktail.

"Hey," I say, looking back at the entwined couple as I catch my breath. "You've got something there..."

I swiftly turn back to the bar and rap my bright red nails against the metallic bar. "Lara needs it," I say.

A tall, lean, bleach-blonde twenty-something bartender struts up. "Hey there sweetie," I say with a bat of the lashes. "Do me a solid and give me an apple martini, please."

"Tab?" he asks by rote, rapidly shaking a cocktail mixer.

"Anderson," I say. "Jackie Anderson."

I can see Sophie twist her face in confusion.

"And you?" the bartender asks, gesturing to Sophie.

Sophie declines with a shake of her head and looks at me, expression still one of uncertainty.

"Anderson?" she finally spits out.

"Yeah." I act like there's nothing to discuss.

"Decided you're no longer married or something?" She wheels around on her barstool and faces me head-on.

"No bigs." I flick a wrist at her, it heavily dressed in a wide ring of Swarovski crystal wraps and bracelets Andrew got for me before he left for Singapore. He said it was a "because you'll miss me and I'm sorry for having to leave" gift. Whatever they're for, they look absolutely fabulous with my outfit, and the way they sparkle under the strobe lights and sprinkle about pink glitters against the bar! Fabulous!

"Jackie, I'll never get you," Sophie says vacantly. "So damn hot and cold."

"Taste that, sweetie," the bartender lisps as he sets the iridescent, green beverage in front of me.

"I'm a very complex creature," I say to Sophie in a mock-seductive tone.

"You revisiting the whole divorce thing?" She nurses the remains of her drink.

I take the cold martini in my hands. "Nah. Just makes me feel good sometimes to use my maiden name. Especially when I'm going stag at a wedding, at a bar."

I smack my lips and sing to the bartender, "Delish!" I offer Sophie a taste.

"You know," I continue. "Sometimes when I want to feel free and have fun and just *not* like a prisoner trophy wife." I simper and wink at the bartender. "It can feel good to pretend I'm single." I run some fingers through my short hair.

"And pretending you're single on the dance floor, too?" she queries in her oh-so-adult way.

I don't respond, instead sipping at my fruity drink.

"Please be careful, Jack." Sophie rests her bony hand on my bare arm. "I know things are rough with Andrew right now, but I don't want you to get hurt—even if you end up hurting yourself."

I laugh and look back at the dance floor. Claire and Conner are lip-locked, making out kind of grotesquely at the far corner of the floor. They say weddings make people horny, and apparently that buck doesn't stop with the single-and-looking-to-get-lucky crowd. Evidently married couples can be just as in love and ready to get some as the unattached. Well, *some* married couples I suppose.

I glance at my large, sparkling wedding ring, and Andrew's face comes into view. I said I didn't think about him much at all at the wedding, but I'm certainly making up for it here at Re-Live. And seeing couples out on the dance floor together only makes Andrew's face pull closer into view.

"I'm fine," I brush Sophie off, looking back to Claire and Conner, who are now moving off the dance floor towards a table. I glance over at Lara and her hookup. They're pulled close together. I search for Chad, who meandered off to the bathroom when I set out to join a single Sophie at the bar. Here he is now, dancing closely—grinding is more like it—with a long-haired brunette who's wearing ripped tights with cut-off jean shorts.

I turn back to Sophie. "Hey!" An idea pops into my head. "You want me to find you a dance partner?" I nudge my elbow jokingly at her side.

She laughs in her glass. "I'll pass."

"You know, here I'm thinking that Lara's the dry-on-love chick, but you're sitting here dating a cocktail."

"Jack, I'm fine."

"You can be fine, or you could be lucky." I wiggle my brows.

"I'll go with fine, thank you." She clears her throat before taking another short sip.

"Suit yourself. But you know?" I lean my head to the side, nearer her. "You could really do yourself a favor. Treat yourself to something fun. Let me help."

Sophie raises her almost empty cocktail and gently shakes it.

"What do you call this?" Her voice turns proud as she adds, "*And,* Gatz is running the café all morning tomorrow. This woman knows how to treat herself."

"Wow!" I'm impressed. Sophie is *actually* giving herself a break. A pathetically short one, but a break nonetheless.

"I'm not going in to the café until noon," she says, still proud, and I suppress the urge to roll my eyes.

"A treat's a treat, however brief, I guess." I pull myself farther onto my seat.

"Actually," she says, crossing her legs. She runs a fingertip along the rim of her glass. "I'm going to take a longer break."

Her words take me by surprise. Did she just say *break* and *longer* in the same sentence?

"I'm just feeling dried up a little," she continues. "All stale. No fresh, creative ideas, nothing exciting going on—"

"Join the club!" I quickly cut in, because I just have to seize the opportunity to point out the obvious. "See? Life isn't *always* a party or whatever you said. All lemon-y."

"That's not the same thing," she says. "I'm talking about actually doing something for myself, something that's *not* work-related."

"Yeah?"

"You know John's in London again?"

John, Sophie's brother, is an international lawyer at a fancy firm down in San Francisco. The kind of law he practices means he's often working both in California and overseas in England. Sophie visited him the last time he had a case over there, when she was studying in Paris. Right before she left for Zambia, Emily even encouraged Sophie to go over for another trip this summer, to give her that much-needed time away from all of the stress and monotony at home and the café. Sophie had said "maybe," then immediately went on and on about how she has a business to look after now and can't just take her ten days vaca like that, with nothing to really consider.

I'm with Emily on this one, though. Sophie just needs to choose a week or two, pack up her bags, and hit the road. Go visit John, maybe even zip back to Paris like she's been dreaming of, and, hey, maybe she'll get lucky with that Frenchie she used to see when she was living in Paris. Just have fun!

"I haven't seen John in ages," Sophie explains. "Not since Thanksgiving. And I've done some serious thinking about a trip, even mentioned it to my parents—"

"And?" I ask excitedly.

"I've decided I'm going to take one this summer," she says with a smile. "In June some time, when Emily's back and she and Gatz can help out at the café." She takes a quick sip. "And after I hire and train a new full-time replacement for Em and Gatz. My parents thought it was a great idea and gifted it...a kind of one-year-café-anniversary gift."

"Sophie!" I enthusiastically pat her arm. "That's great news!"

"I need to refresh," she breathes out. "Need to get out, get inspired, and, hell, like I said, do *something* for myself." She takes another sip of her drink.

"Paris, maybe?" I bite my lower lip in anticipation.

"Maybe..."

"Oh! Paris! So jealous."

"Ask Andrew to take you to Paris and I'm sure he will."

"Eh." I loosely wave a hand. "So!" I grin broadly. "London? Then maybe Paris?"

"Maybe." A small smile forms at her lips.

"Some French flings, maybe?"

She groans and gives me a discerning look.

"Okay, okay. I know. 'Grow up, Jackie.'"

That coy smile of Sophie's is still playing her lips when she says, "Hey, maybe," and she raises her glass to mine and toasts, saying, "To letting go of those lemons and makin' some cupcakes."

21

"Honey?" I ask as I emerge from the bathroom, clad in a black-lace La Perla teddy. "You already asleep?"

"Out like a light in a few," Andrew grumbles.

He's rolled onto his side, one arm propped under his folded pillow. He blinks a few times and blows a kiss my way.

"You and your damn sleeping pills." I spritz some Chanel Mademoiselle on my wrists and décolletage. "You've hardly been back in town and you're already back to your boring, busy routine."

With a flick of the bathroom light, I jump into bed, purposely moving rambunctiously so I might have one or two extra waking minutes with my husband.

Since Andrew returned home from Singapore a couple days ago I haven't had more than a minute to tell him all about Robin and Bobby's fabulous wedding. He's been so busy with "loose ends," as he calls them, to tie up with the big overseas deal, and I suppose I'm lucky I've been able to tell him one, maybe two, anecdotes about the wedding and my time while he was gone.

"Busy day at the office tomorrow," he says through a short yawn.

I roll my eyes as I fluff two pillows. I place both against the headboard and make a high-pitched sigh as I sink back, upright. "Well, if

I've only got a few fleeting seconds with you before you fall into a deep sleep, then I want to tell you more about Robin's wedding."

I turn towards him and nudge him—softly at first, then more aggressively when he doesn't respond. "Come on. Don't sleep just yet. *Please*. Can't you spare five short minutes? I'll make it quick. Promise."

"I'm really tired," he grumbles. "I'm sorry." He blindly worms a hand behind him, reaching back towards me and finally alighting on my leg to give it a few conciliatory pats. "Tell me more 'morrow."

I swallow hard and stare at the back of his head, his salt and pepper hair freshly cut and still coiffed, and frustration begins to brew. He had enough energy for the past half hour to sit here and toy with his iPad while I got ready for bed, yet now, once I'm here, it's light's out—no moment spared to reconnect, to be husband and wife.

"You really would have enjoyed it, Andrew," I whisper. "It was a really nice wedding."

A smile can't help but tug at my lips as I think back on how beautiful Robin looked, how truly happy and content she seemed. "It was really classy and well done, understated but sweet and—"

"Can you please shut off the light, doll?" Andrew interrupts. "It's past ten and I'm exhausted."

"You're really that exhausted?" I say in a small and dejected tone. I pull the comforter up tighter and tuck it snugly around my waist.

"Time change...big client...fine details..." he rambles in a sleepy haze. "Lights..."

I give a quick huff and cross my arms over my chest. "Oh, Andrew, just give your sleeping pills a second to kick in and then you won't give a crap about the lights."

I reach for my copy of *Home & Design Décor* on the nightstand and shake open to the middle of the magazine, conceding defeat. I stare at nothing in particular—simply something to do as I brood and eventually settle into one of my routine evenings: Jackie with her magazines, Andrew with his Ambien.

"You know," I say after some festering, "if you're not going to talk to me and you're always going to go to bed early, then I should just go out. Go do something." I look over at him and he doesn't make a sound, doesn't stir. "It's not like you'd even notice."

Suddenly he mumbles, "I love you, doll." He pats a hand in my general direction behind him, then lets it fall limp between us, the Ambien working its black magic. "G'night..."

"Goodnight," I mutter through a heavy sigh.

I move my empty gaze from the magazine to Andrew's hand.

My eyes fall to his wedding band, and I can't contain myself. I slowly shake my head, pick up his hand, and drop it in between his slumbering body and the edge of the bed, nearly letting it hang over into the dark, empty space.

"I just don't know how this is going to work," I say quietly to myself as I flip through the magazine's pages. My eyes fall on a spread featuring a gorgeous, aquamarine lap pool that's splayed across it, with a superficially bubbly couple sitting at the edge, toasting champagne under the moonlit night. I sniff at the thought of how *some* couples still have a spark.

Emily's been in town back from Zambia for three weeks already, but it feels like a lifetime. And that's a great thing! She's been around like old times and we've been getting to hang out a bunch. I have to make the most of my time with her, seeing how she and Gatz are officially leaving for the complete other side of the globe on the first of July.

I try not to think much about it, because then I get all dreary and mopey and want to pour myself a glass of JD or text Lara a hundred times asking if she wants to blow off work in lieu of the latest Ryan Gosling movie or something.

Getting to spend so much time with Emily takes my mind off of my Andrew woes, and my Nikki ones, too—which, sadly, are escalating a touch. Nowadays Andrew returns about ten percent of my calls, and I don't even call that much, so ten percent probably isn't even mathematically possible.

Lucky for me, since Andrew's so busy and spending heinous hours at the office lately, I just dash on over to Emily's. I even stay the night sometimes. Andrew's not very keen on me jetting over here, leaving him alone some nights, but what's the alternative? Watch him fall into an Ambien-induced sleep night-in, night-out? Fifty-something isn't exactly old, and he did marry a woman in her mid-twenties. So it shouldn't come as a surprise to him that I'd like to go out for drinks or dancing now and then, certainly stay up past ten some nights.

I don't know when or if things will get better between us, but for now I'm trying to enjoy Emily since she's in town. I'm trying to work through my issues and focus on the positives, like Dr. Pierce says I should. I'm going to therapy regularly; I've been bringing Robin takeout dinners a night or two a week to help her out. Even though she insists Phillip's not as exhausting to care for at three-and-a-half months old, she does appreciate the gesture (not to mention Bobby loves the gourmet takeout I find). I'm trying not to complain too much to Emily and the rest of the girls about the state of my marriage. I know my personality can be a bit too much to handle at times, but what are best girlfriends for if you can't run to them when you're having marital problems? Even so, I try not to bring it up *every* time we're together.

Of course, no matter how much I am honestly trying to stay upbeat and work on things, Dr. Pierce says I need to talk to Andrew, maybe even insist on couple's counseling.

I've given all that crap a go. All useless endeavors. Andrew simply refuses to go because *I'm* the one with the rough past, the one with the problems. If anyone needs therapy, it's the little trophy wife, not the mogul husband.

"Hey," Gatz says, ducking his wet head out of Emily's bedroom. "Em already head to work?"

I lightly moisten the end of the cigarette paper with my tongue and moan out an "uh huh."

"Shoot." He briskly towels dry his mane of brown curls. "Sophie wanted me to ask Em to swing by the market to get some things. And I remembered once she left."

"She still doesn't have her cell, huh?"

"They're programming it. I'm picking it up after class." He disappears from view.

Emily is the least technologically inclined person I know, and I love her for it. She doesn't give an ounce of care for Apple this or Bluetooth that. A television with cable? What for? A cell phone from this century? Who needs that? Front and back apartment doors that lock securely? "Who would ever want to steal from me?" she'll say.

Emily's carried around a beat-up old phone from circa 1998. When she went to Zambia she left the thing behind and on, and the battery drained all the way down so that it's now completely useless. I think it committed suicide, putting itself out of its outmoded misery, but the funny thing is that Emily doesn't care all that much. It took Gatz to go down to the AT&T store to get her a new phone.

"I'm running late for my final," Gatz says when he reappears a moment later, dressed in a wrinkled pair of brown, linen pants and a fitted white t-shirt that has *May the Forest Be with You* written boldly in green. "Would you do me a *huge* favor and pick up some stuff, Jackie? The list is on the coffee table."

"Just call me delivery girl," I say, happy that I've got something to fill my day before my hot stone massage and planned stroll through the air-conditioned cathedral of retail at the Westlake Center. I finish rolling the sixth and last cigarette. "I've got some yummy smokes for Em, anyhow."

Gatz washes down a hunk of muffin with a big gulp of orange juice. "Don't encourage her. I'm trying to get her to quit."

"She's a social smoker." I slip the cigarettes into my small Chanel clutch. "These three will last her weeks. I, on the other hand…"

Gatz slings his rugged brown messenger bag across his chest and marches for the front door. "So you don't mind?"

"An excuse to go to The Cup and the Cake and hang with Em… Sophie…do *something* with my day?" I cackle, tossing my head back in exaggerated mirth.

"Hey, you know if you're bored there are tons of clubs and stuff that meet regularly. Like hobby clubs and stuff..."

"Like your and Em's book club?" I pick up the latest book Emily's reading, perhaps for her book club. *Hidden Cities: Travels to the Secret Corners of the World's Great Metropolises* is the title, a book about urban exploration.

"Not necessarily a book club, but something...I don't know." Gatz pulls a hair tie from around his wrist and draws back his hair into a messy, stubby ponytail. "There are always volunteer gigs and clubs out there...part-time work, even."

"Heard it *all* before. I'm not a working girl, Gatz." I toss Emily's book aside. "I'll stick with picking things up for the café right now, thanks."

"Just sayin'," he says with a shrug. The door opens with a loud, grating squeak. "Tell Em I'll relieve her at noon. See ya."

I saunter from the fancy pull-out bed in Emily's living room and into the steam-filled bathroom, ready to begin my day.

Though my little market pick-up may not be much more than a simple favor—certainly nothing that qualifies as life-saving material—it really does feel good to be do something...anything.

22

I slowly suck the juice from the succulent strawberry, letting the sweet and fragrant fruit settle on my tongue a while before licking my lips clean and going in for another bite. Biting at the tiny remainder of fruit, nothing but the green palm-like leaves sticking out, I flip the page of the newest issue of *Seattle Socialite* that I picked up near Pike Place Market during my fruit run.

There's a fascinating article (with even more fascinating photos) of some millionaire's home over in the ritzy Queen Anne district, on the south slope, with sweeping views of Mt. Rainier and Elliott Bay. The breathtaking mansion has more than 16,000 square feet of living space, decked out with a wine cellar, a second kitchen, fireplaces in each of its seven bedrooms, and a lush, Tuscan-style garden, complete with a Koi pond, a lengthy veranda, and yet another fireplace.

If the design looks impressive, take a look at the décor! Marble inlay flooring accented with thick and vibrantly colored Persian rugs, gold fluted mirrors, tufted ottomans, vintage French chairs and chaise longues, and retro-Gothic styled shelves and sconces. It's a dream!

"Damn," I breathe, pulling the fraction of remaining strawberry flesh from my mouth. I run a finger over the shining chandelier that graces the ceiling of the master bath.

Feeling for another strawberry from the bowl, I scan over the text.

"Phew!" I exclaim when my eyes alight on the asking price of the dream house. Nearly choking on the bite of strawberry, I pop my head up and look over at Emily, who's icing cupcakes. "Six-point-two million! Can you imagine?"

"Fantasy mansions again?" Emily says from her workstation in the center of The Cup and the Cake's kitchen.

"Damn." I pick up another ruby red strawberry from the small bowl I prepared for myself from the massive basket I just brought in to the café. "I can't imagine spending that much on a home!"

Emily giggles. "You do realize your home isn't exactly a shack?" She thickly stirs a bowl of lavender-colored cupcake icing.

"Yeah, but it ain't six point two mill!" I exhale an astounded puff of air. "The décor, though, is what's really impressive! How much *fun* would it be to decorate a mansion that's—" I rapidly turn one page back, "sixteen thousand square feet? Now there's a design job!"

"So how's Andrew doing?" Emily asks out of nowhere. "You two doing well?"

"Uhh, he's working... I'm here," I stutter.

"Have you two even..." She pauses, stopping her stirring, "Have you talked at all? I mean," she resumes stirring, a hint of hesitancy in her voice, "you've stayed at my place two nights in a row, Jack, and, as to my knowledge, you two haven't chatted on the phone, you haven't gone back home..."

"Oh, Em," I say with a sigh. I close the magazine and lean an elbow on my crossed leg. "Welcome to my world. This is totally normal. Whatever. He's busy; so am I."

"Normal's one thing, but fine's another."

I brusquely wag my head and shake open the magazine. "I'm trying to work through things. I'm trying to repair my marriage, in case you haven't noticed."

"I haven't, really." Her voice is small, but the hesitancy that was in it is no longer a hint but a loud, cacophonous roar. "Doesn't repairing your marriage mean you need to be *involved* with your husband?" She scoops a large dollop of icing onto a naked white cupcake. "I just really think you should be home with Andrew tonight."

"What? Where's this coming from, Em? I thought you liked having me over."

"I do. I love having you over, don't get me wrong. I just don't think it's healthy that you're sleeping over when you've got a husband at home, alone, and you've got marriage problems. It's one thing when he's out of town—"

"It's not like he's even conscious when I'm there, Emily," I say dryly.

"It doesn't matter."

"You and Gatz want to get it on or something?" I laugh. "Want the apartment to yourself?"

"That's not the point."

I shrug.

"You being away all the time is not helpful for your marriage," she says, "and that's certainly not going to help your problems. Distance is probably only going to worsen them."

"Tell that to Andrew. He's gone when his job calls; why can't I be gone when my social life calls?"

"Jackie, listen to yourself. First it's distance with not talking, now physically. You complain of a failing marriage and—"

"And what makes you an expert on marriage, Em?" I shoot out. Frustrated, I slam my magazine down on the counter.

"I'm not claiming to be an expert on marriage." Her voice is soft, patient, and concerned. "I do know a thing or two about relationships, and about conflict...about working at something you want, you love."

"Well..."

"Look, when Andrew's away on business, I have no problem with you wanting to crash at my place. But one minute you complain about him not being home enough, the next, when he *is* home, you run off. It's like you don't know what you want!"

"Maybe I don't!" I say, nearly shouting.

"I don't want to argue, Jackie."

"For someone who doesn't want to argue you sure are making quite the accusations and doling out quite a bit of advice. Just mind your own business, Em."

"Jackie." She walks over and places a hand on my forearm. "I'm looking out for you; trying to help you. The way you ragged on about Andrew last night, the way you've been telling bartenders how miserable you are in your marriage..." She exhales loudly. "You're the one who's always said that that's a dangerous game to be playing —making yourself vulnerable like that and hurting Andrew behind his back."

"Yeah, yeah." I blink rapidly, trying to keep back the tears starting to sting. "I'm trying *not* to complain about Andrew so much, you know?"

"I know, I know," she soothes, rubbing my arm. "But then, on the other hand, Jack." She nudges my chin up and locks eyes with me. "Not to upset you, but on the other hand, you talk about how much you love Andrew, about how much you miss him—"

"Miss the way things *used* to be," I quickly clarify. "*Used* to be, Em. When I was the center of his world."

"I want what's best for you." She smiles weakly, then returns to the cupcakes. "You know that. That's all."

"I know." My voice is weak. I thumb at the magazine's corner. "I *don't* know what I want," I say with more urgency, "that's my problem. I'm not happy in my marriage, and I don't know how to fix it..." I bite my tongue as I prepare to say the next revealing and honest words. "...Maybe because a little part of me...*doesn't* want to fix it." I wag my head in exasperation and let some tears escape, however unwillingly. "I'm tired of trying, Emily."

"Oh, Jackie." She rushes back over and pulls me into a hug. "Don't say that. That's laziness talking."

She pulls back and I rub my hands over my face, moving one of my faux eyelashes out of place. I press at it and fight back more tears.

"If it makes you happy," I say, "and for the sake of trying to rekindle the sparks or fix my marriage or whatever, I'll go home tonight."

Emily's lips curl into a small grin as she says, "Good. Talk to him. Work through things. Don't give up, Jackie."

"When is enough enough, though?" I manage to ask the question that's been gnawing at me for months. When do you reach that final peak, if ever? That final valley?

Emily's cheeks puff out, then she exhales a long shot of air, her eyebrows raised high. "Damn," she mumbles. "That I don't know."

I sniffle and wipe away my tears.

"I think..." she begins cautiously, her hand loosely gripping the wooden spoon, "I think it happens when you find yourself wondering how things *could* be—when you find yourself picturing the two of you separated and then you're imagining what it'd be like *had* you stuck it out..." She nods. "Yeah, I think that when you find yourself wondering about how things *could* have been if they'd worked out, then you're really hoping that things *will* turn out. Sounds a little hokey, I suppose, or not really well thought-out..."

"It's something."

"That's it." She looks to me. "When there's still that *something* you're clinging to, hoping for, then I think, why the hell not stay and try and fight? Like with Gatz..." Immediately she begins to glow. "Zambia was rough at times. I didn't like that our relationship basically started out long-distance. I even began wondering what it'd be like if I *didn't* have him—if I'd let him go, how would life be? Basically, no matter the scenario, I always found myself unable to really let go.

"Like, if we were to break up, I know I would always wonder if there could've been something, and that's because I *want* there to be something. That feeling alone—that wanting him—and..." She begins to blush, grinning lips pressed tightly together. "...Since I love him, I could never fathom walking away."

"You love him?" It's the first time I've heard Emily say this.

"I love him. I do." Her blushing deepens, as does her smile. "I love Gatsby Carter, and life without him..." She pauses, looking across the room. "I could live life without him. I could. I'm a free-spirited type, you know?"

I laugh and tell her she's right about that much.

"But I don't *want* to live life without him," she states. Her eyes meet mine. "Given a choice, I'm always finding myself running in his direction, with him."

"Wow," I breathe. "We should all be so lucky, Em."

"Look in the mirror, babe." She returns to her icing duties, a peaceful and contemplative air about her, a cheerful beat to her movements. "You and Andrew have something, and it's up to you two to figure out if it's worth running to, or from."

"That's deep, Em."

"What can I say? I'm in love with a poet. He's rubbed off on me more than you'd think."

"Guess I should get going." I glance at my slim Cartier watch. "I have a massage in a bit and wanted to do some shopping." I leap from the counter and stuff the magazine in my Michael Kors snake-skin handbag, feeling slightly more upbeat.

"You just keep on trying, Jackie," Emily says. "Don't give up."

"Thanks." I pull my handbag onto my shoulder.

"And remember, so long as the love is there—that heat and that passion and that powerful urge to love and protect and be with and there for your partner—then everything else will kind of slip away into the background." She licks her finger clean of some icing. "And what doesn't slip away will become inconsequential, manageable. With love you can pretty much work through anything."

"Damn, that poet in Gatz really *is* rubbing off on you."

I check my phone for any missed calls or new text messages, but there's nothing, as I sadly expect.

"He'll call when he has time, I'm sure," she says, reading my mind.

"I called Nikki like two hours ago." I return the cell phone to my handbag. "I know she didn't deliver my message. Bitch."

"Don't concoct tall tales."

"They *could* be having an affair."

"Don't speculate." She sets a cupcake neatly on a tiered tray. "Operate."

"Yeah, well, I'm out of here," I say with a chuckle. "Someone's been smoking the shisha. Oh!" I quickly pull three of the self-rolled cigarettes out of my handbag. "Almost forgot. Especially made, with love."

She sticks one cigarette behind her heavily pierced ear and slips the other two in her back pocket. "Thanks. Have fun shopping and enjoy your massage. I'll see you tonight...?"

"Don't think so," I say in a peppy tone. "I think I've got a friend's," I lower my voice, "and a therapist's," returning my voice to a normal level, "advice to listen to. Andrew and I need to fix things and, well," I shrug and head towards the exit, "I kind of need to be home to do that."

23

"**B**aby doll!" Andrew exclaims a brief moment after I walk through our front door.

I set down my overnight bag. Atop the entry table, where I notice a vase of fresh fuchsia and white peonies, I toss my keys.

Right then, Andrew waltzes into view. He's cleanly shaven, his hair damp with that just-got-out-of-the-shower look, and he's wearing my favorite pair of lounge pants that he doesn't wear nearly as often as I'd like. The cream-colored, loosely fitted linen pants sway as he makes an upbeat strut towards me. He's clad in an equally loosely fitted baby blue button-down, the top couple buttons undone.

He wraps his arms tightly around my small frame, lifting me an inch or two off the ground. "How's my baby?" He gives the top of my head a hard kiss.

He sets me down, and I'm careful not to step on his bare feet with the new pair of four-inch, silver, peep-toe Jimmy Choos I scooped up during today's shopping spree.

"Damn, I missed you, Jackie. I miss you when you're gone at Lara's." Gripping my arms warmly, he pulls back and looks at me almost appraisingly. "I love you so much."

"Emily's," I say.

"Hmm?"

The butterflies rousing my stomach at high speeds on the drive home begin to settle some, Andrew's surprising pep throwing me off guard. I've been so nervous about talking to Andrew, about this heart-to-heart we've had a long time coming.

I breathe in deeply, shakily. "I've been at Emily's, but never mind." I swallow. "I missed you, too." My words come out huskier than I want.

"So!" he enthuses, taking me by the hand. "You've been enjoying your girl time?"

I nod succinctly as he leads me into the living room, to the sofa.

"Yeah. Been nice." I give him a vague smile.

This is not going to be easy, I think. *I don't know where to start. We've already had a "serious" talk, and look where that got you, Jackie. Broken glass, blood, shouted insults...*

"I'm glad you're having fun," he says.

How is this time going to be any different? I give him another vague smile, trying to summon the courage, beckon the right mood, to do what I know I need to do.

"But, I'll be honest. I really don't like it when you run off so much, baby doll." He pulls me tighter, and the scent of his rich after-shave and cologne are titillating. "I miss you when you're out with your friends, and I don't like sleeping alone."

"Now you know how I feel when you're out at work or off on business all the time." I crack a smile just to insert a dash of repose in what could quickly become a recipe for a fight.

"Well not tonight," he says in a low voice. He gives me a kiss on my cheek before pulling back and bounding towards the kitchen.

"Dinner and dancing? An old movie?" I ask curiously, my interest piqued. *If that's the case then maybe we don't need a talk after all... Maybe he's finally being proactive. Getting the hint? Demonstrating instead of just talking?* "Are we going out somewhere?" *Of course, I'm only delaying the inevitable.*

"Not exactly," Andrew says, monotone. He picks up two glasses of champagne. At first I think they're pink—my favorite—and a flip of excited, rather than nervous, butterflies flits about inside. Andrew's been thinking of me, thinking seriously about me, about us. It's not just the peonies and the champagne, but *pink* champagne! It's my favorite not because I prefer a rosé to a brut, but because of the charming way it brought Cary Grant and Deborah Kerr together in *An Affair to Remember*.

When I take the glass in hand, however, I realize the chilled beverage is not pink.

"But I've been doing some thinking," Andrew says, stepping near.

A befuddled expression on my face, I slowly bring the glass to my lips. *He's still trying... He's thinking about you, Jackie. You two have love and hope. It'll work out. Give it a chance.*

"Wait, wait," he rushes out. "We have to toast."

"To?" *To us? To working through things?*

He takes me by my free hand and proceeds back into the living room.

"I've been thinking about us," he says, stopping a short step from the expansive glass windows. "About our marriage."

The jittery butterflies return, and twice in just a few seconds I find myself resisting the urge to pull nervously on the bubbly.

"Yeah?" I get out, shakily.

"I haven't been as attentive to your needs as I should be."

I exhale in relief, having been somewhat worried that he was going to tell me he'd done some thinking about our marriage and decided he was going to leave me for Nikki, or that I needed to increase my therapy sessions, or put more into this marriage—as if our problematic wedge is somehow all *my* fault.

"I really want to make things work," he says, looking from my eyes to his glass.

"Yeah, actually—" I start, but Andrew cuts in.

"And I hear you loud and clear."

"You do?" I'm in shock. *He's actually gotten the hint? He's finally going to be proactive and do something about our failing marriage? I don't have to be the one to initiate this?*

"Absolutely!" His eyes meet mine again. They're filled with a childlike wonder, excitement, fervor.

"Great, because I've been talking to Dr. Pierce—"

"Great, great," he says with a round of nodding.

"And he says that we need to work through our problems together—"

"Exactly," he breathes.

"Really?" I look at him with a dumbfounded face. "We need to be honest and seriously listen to each other, Andrew. Things have *got* to change."

"Yes, yes."

"You put me as a priority and show me you *really* love me—be there for me—and I'll be patient with you so you can do that."

"That's just it!" he says jubilantly, pulling me near. "I *can* show you I really love you." He kisses my cheek.

"And," I say cautiously, "be there *emotionally* for me?"

"Yes, yes."

"I know I have a lot of my own insecurities and issues to work out," I pause to bite my bottom lip in an almost desperate kind of way, "but I'm working at it, at therapy."

"And I couldn't be prouder of you." He kisses my cheek again, giving my hand a firm squeeze. "Now come here." He leads me closer to the windows. "I want to show you something."

He pulls me tight as we look past Elliott Bay and out to Puget Sound, the last sliver of the setting sun glittering the surface of the cerulean water.

"Look out there." He points across the horizon.

"It's gorgeous."

"It's perfect."

"Yes, it is perfect. Beautiful." I look up at him, and a smile plays my lips as I get lost in this sweet and simple moment. He looks so happy, so content, and those nervous butterflies are gone. I'm feeling content, too, like Andrew and I really can work things out. I feel safe and at home.

"It's perfect for us." He pulls me closer, slipping a hand in his pocket. "Perfect to help us get over this marital rut. A sign that I really do love you."

"What do you mean?"

"Well..." A coy expression begins to cover his face. "I got to thinking about the old times—like how things were when we were first dating. What you reminisce about so often."

"Yeah?" I squeak out in excitement and curiosity.

"Minus the sail home, our time in Bainbridge together was magical," he waxes lyrical.

"Yes..." I don't know what he's getting at, but I'm mightily curious now.

"And my mind was spinning when I was out of town on business, thinking about what we *need*. Something to help bring us closer together, get those sparks going again, *prove* how much I love you." His eyes light up. "You're right! Things were exciting and big and fabulous and...why can't we still have that?"

"True." I cross one arm over my chest and grip tight the glass of champagne.

"I'm a man of considerable means, so I can show my wife *just* how much she means to me. I can't believe it's taken me so long to think of this."

"Okay..."

"I woke up this morning and the idea just came to me!" He looks back out the window. "See all this. This water, this beauty, this opportunity." He draws an invisible line along the horizon with his champagne glass.

I raise a quizzical eyebrow as he continues. "So," he says, "I went and bought you a boat."

I nearly choke on my spit, darting my head to the side. "You bought *me*...a boat?"

He nods sharply. "I'm bringing the adventure back into the relationship, baby doll! No need for couples therapy." He dangles two keys in front of me. "The perfect gift for the woman who," he chuckles, "has everything." He continues to dangle the keys. "Now does this tell you how much I love you?" He looks self-satisfied, as if he's successfully landed an impressive deal with a key Jennings & Voigt account.

"A boat?" I squeak, hardly able to believe what I'm hearing. "But...why?"

He laughs in bewilderment. "Why? Does a man *need* a reason to shower his wife with expensive gifts?" He laughs some more. "Look, I was thinking," he says, his tone evenly excited and earnest, "if things were amazing between us before—before all these arguments, back when we spent so much time together, had exciting dates and getaways and adventure..."

My mind starts to drift back to those beginning months of our relationship, losing my connection to the here and the now as Andrew rambles on in a flurry of excitement.

Things *were* really great back then, true, but Andrew was still just as committed to his work then as he is now. He just invited me to more of his out-of-town business trips; he squeezed in time for me between meetings and conferences; he actually made me a priority and didn't just talk about it. And, honestly, it was all new. Anything's exciting and breathtaking when it's new. Things can probably still be the same level of excitement and action years later, I suppose, but won't be as fulfilling because they're, well, *old*. What we need now isn't necessarily a recreation of the past but—but—I don't know what, and that's the problem. We just need something different... something new...we need a change. And this is not it.

Suddenly the bile is rising, the agitating butterflies are flooding my stomach again, and I'm feeling lightheaded. I place one hand on Andrew's arm in an attempt to steady myself. Andrew's voice regains my focus.

"We can have adventure! You can have your glamor!" I hear him exclaim as I shake myself back into the present. "It's all yours!" He raises higher the keys. "You can even name it. Brand-spankin' new; just bought it this morning."

I swallow and blink hard, trying to gather my bearings. "A boat..." I mutter as I slowly set my glass of champagne down.

Andrew's wearing a broad grin. "That's right!"

"And..." I swallow again, rubbing hard at both my temples. "And where are you going to find the time to, uh, *use* it?"

"Well when I find the time to use the boat it's there..." he carries on, as if the question is an absurd one to ask.

He brushes me off with a brisk shake of his head. "Details. Look, it's here, it's bought, it's for you, it's a declaration of my love. And, look." His voice is deep and insisting. "See this gift as that thing that will encourage me to *make* time for you." He hurriedly sets his champagne aside. "Actually *having* a sailboat is going to force me to make time to be with you. To go out and have those adventures together." He pauses, then adds, "*When* I can get out of the office, of course." He simpers.

"*Force* yourself to *make* time to be with me?" I gasp, thunderstruck by his choice of words.

"I don't mean it like that." He takes my hands in his.

"Andrew," I say, my voice small. I look at him imploringly. "I love you, but..."

"But what?" A pallor creeps onto his face. "Don't you like it? I mean, it's a hell of an expensive sailboat!"

"This isn't going to change anything." I swallow the persistent lump in my throat. "This isn't going to be a long-term solution. You can't throw money and material possessions at the problem."

"What?" he gasps, his brow knit together tightly, almost painfully. "Jackie, you know I've *always* given you the world—anything you want. Shoes, clothes, cars, trips, spa treatments, a home..." He wags his head in exasperation. "Now you, what?" He winces. "Don't *want* any of this?"

"Of course I like and appreciate everything." I press my lips tightly together, not sure where to go next. I thought I had this whole discussion planned out earlier. Surely I never could have seen this coming!

"We can see the world together," he says with urgency. He points out the window. "Together!"

"When you *make* the time! Because you're *forced!*" I pull away from him. "Andrew," I breathe out, "you just don't get it." I squeeze my eyes shut, trying to keep back the sudden surge of tears. "Running off on exotic trips and buying expensive things is running away from the problem. Throwing money at things doesn't solve anything. I'm talking about an *emotional* connection."

"Dammit, Jackie," he growls. "I don't understand you!" He rubs gruffly at his jaw. "You know, this would've been an answer to your problem in the beginning. I don't know what you want anymore!"

"Well..."

"Actually, I don't think *you* know what you want, babe." He rubs some more at his jaw. "I'm—I'm—I'm just confused. I don't know what to do!"

"Well buying a fucking boat wasn't the thing to do!" I cry, losing all of the nerve and calm I'd mustered for this evening's talk. "The idea is nice if you'd *actually* have time for it—for me!"

"But I can *make* time with this," he goes on imploringly, the veins in his neck beginning to bulge.

"No!" I stomp my foot in protestation. "It's just a bigger empty promise, Andrew. Another failure waiting to happen."

"Dammit, Jackie." He smacks a hand to his forehead.

"I'm not happy with *us,* and obviously all of the diamonds and money in the world—all the boats and fancy cars—aren't going to make that unhappiness go away. I have it all and I'm miserable, Andrew! Miserable...no emotional connection to my husband and..." I break down in tears. "I give up. I just don't know what more to do." I turn on my heels and begin to walk towards the kitchen.

"You're impossible," he wheezes. "*You* give up? *I* give up! What can I do, Jackie? I buy you a boat—"

"I don't want a fucking boat, Andrew! I want a marriage. A *real* marriage and a husband who actually cares!"

"Look around you, princess!" he yells, hands in the air. "I *do* care for you! What more do you *want* me to do?"

I wag my head in exhaustion and pull out a bottle of rum from the cupboard. "Whatever," I mutter. "I should've known you couldn't be reasonable."

"Me? Reasonable?" He throws his hands higher into the air. "Are you even *listening* to yourself? *I'm* the unreasonable one?"

"You go out and buy a sailboat like it's nothing!" I scream. "Who does that? That's insanity!"

"A proof of how much I love you." His voice is lower, slightly calmer.

"No." I shake my head harshly as I pour a glass of liquid courage. "A proof that you don't care, after all. It's easy to whip out the checkbook and '*fix*' things, but it's another to be there emotionally."

"Emotionally?" He strides over with brisk steps. "Be there emotionally? Look at yourself, baby doll."

I take a quick drink, then say, totally aghast, "Myself? Look at *myself?*"

"Yeah." He puts his hands on his hips, standing, cocky, on the opposite side of the kitchen's island. I uncomfortably bring the glass to my lips. "You," he says, pointing a finger at me, "are more emotionally invested in *yourself* than you are *me!* In *us!* You drown your troubles in your booze and cry to your therapist and run off to your friends, shop 'til you drop. *You* are emotionally checked out, Jackie. Shallow and selfish and spoiled and emotionally checked out." He gives me a scornful look. "I knew I married a pampered princess, but I didn't realize she'd fail to grow up at twenty-fucking-seven years old. Let go of the past, Jackie, and grow up already."

"Fuck you!" I scream, throwing the glass onto the floor. "Don't hit me where it hurts, you asshole!"

"Maybe that's what you finally need to hear, princess." He holds up his hands in surrender, shoving off all the blame onto me.

"You know what?" I spit, charging to the foyer. "I'm out of here."

"Good." He tails me closely.

"I'm going to Emily's. *She's* emotionally there for me." I grab my overnight bag.

"Good," he says, all full of himself. "Stay as long as you like."

"I will!" I scream, turning to face him. "And I may never come back."

"Oh, you'll come back," he says smugly. "When you want money and new shoes," he points at my high heels, "you'll come crawling back."

I slap him hard across his face. I'm surprised I actually did it, half-expecting him to grab and stop my hand in time before I made contact. Instead, now his cheek, once pale, is turning a twinge pink.

With one hand touching the assaulted cheek, he points to the door and says, "You're crazy, Jackie. All my spoiling you is only worsening the problem."

"You're an asshole!" I swing open the front door. "You know, if I'm such a money-grubbing whore then alarms should sound that I'm talking about *not* wanting shopping sprees and stupid *sailboats*. There's more to me than that, Andrew, and it's a damn shame you can't see that." I pull my overnight bag roughly onto my shoulder and step into the hallway.

"You talk about me walking the walk," he shouts after me. "Why not try taking your own advice, huh?"

"Screw you." I abruptly reach back into the apartment for my keys, then stomp out the door and on down the hallway.

"Jackie, wait." Andrew's voice, the low and almost caring tone, takes me by surprise. I stop in my tracks and turn to face him. "Look, I love you, Jackie." He sighs loudly, his shoulders sagging. "Please, let's not do this."

I'm flabbergasted. After what he's just said to me? Now he's remorseful? This is unbelievable!

"I'm sorry," he says. His blue eyes search mine apologetically. "Let's start this over. Please. Look, if you don't want the boat, I'll return it. I just don't want to lose you."

I sigh and shake my head, looking down into the depths of the hall. "Andrew," I say as I step nearer him, "you've been losing me for a long while. And I'm done. I'm not putting myself through this anymore. It's too painful."

"What are you saying?" Standing so helplessly in the doorway, he reaches an unwelcome hand forward and plants it softly on my shoulder.

"I'm going to Emily's for the night," I say easily.

"And then?" His sorrowful face now looks curious and discomposed.

"I don't know. I just don't want to be around you right now." I shrug off his touch.

"Fine." His face is now one of irritation. "Don't get yourself into trouble." He turns back into the house. "I'm taking a sleeping pill and going to bed early. If you call or lock yourself out or something, I won't hear you."

"I wouldn't dream of calling you, Andrew," I say spitefully, beginning to step down the hallway. "Like you'd even pick up."

"I'm serious, Jackie," he calls after me. "Don't do something stupid and hurt yourself."

"Like you care!" I wave a hand loosely behind me and stomp off towards the elevator. And I don't look back. I know he's watching me, the door not clicking closed. He's standing in the doorway and watching me walk off.

When the elevator arrives I step in and I still don't look back. Sometimes a girl's just got to let go and walk away without looking back. I gave it my best try, having a heart-to-heart with my husband, but I can't monologue my way through it.

I press the button for the lobby and ignore the warm tears that begin to trickle down my cheeks, slowly at first, then gaining speed with each floor I pass. The *ping-ping* sound of my descent acts as a bell calling forth the tears, ringing loud and clear that I'm falling further and further away from a happily ever after.

24

D r. Pierce hands me the tissue box, and I help myself to a handful. He's just suggested right now, halfway through our session, that I spend the next few days recouping from the huge fight Andrew I and had last week—time spent only thinking about positive solutions to the state of my marriage. If that means talking to Andrew, fine, but only so long as I offer up constructive and positive words.

In my defense, I did go home the second night after the big blowout, thanks to Emily's encouragement. She even walked me to my front door for moral support. She also offered to let me come back and stay at her place in the event Andrew and I were at each other's throats again.

Thanks to months of Dr. Pierce's advice, support from my girl-friends, and my gnawing conscience, I was able to return home to the scene of the crime just one night later. I love Andrew, no matter how much I feel like throwing in the towel. He's my husband. Walking away isn't going to be easy.

Unfortunately it didn't even matter, really, that I went back home, hence my return to Emily's shortly thereafter. When Andrew and I were in the same room, it was as if I wasn't there...as if he wasn't there. Andrew did his work, I read my magazines and watched television. Dinner was silent, there was the requisite kiss hello and goodnight, and a mumbled "I love you" from him, followed by a hollow shrug and lopsided grin from me, and, finally, the pill-enhanced sleep and the bone-chilling silence of the dark night. As if no big argument had ever happened, as if there was nothing to discuss. Just silence. Emptiness.

"An important note here, Jackie," Dr. Pierce says with a furrowed brow. "Remember?"

"Yeah?" I use the last of the bundle of tissues to wipe at the corners of my eyes.

"You are not to spend *any* time complaining about Andrew, revisiting your fight, or touching upon any negative thoughts or doing *anything*—anything at all—that will cause negative emotions to surface. You must continue to stay positive. Can you agree to do that?"

"That's, like, impossible!" I grouse.

"No, it's not."

"Whatever." I scratch my head, then glance at my watch. "Fine. No negativity. I'll try."

"It's for the best."

"But I'm not going back home again. I like it at Em's."

"That's fine for now. But stay positive."

"All right. I'll *try.*"

"Good."

"With Em around that shouldn't be a problem, actually." I smirk.

"Excellent." Dr. Pierce stands up and holds out his hand. "Then I wish you the best of luck, and I'll see you next week. You can do this, Jackie."

"You really should consider starting each day with yoga," Emily says, undoing one of her fuzzy cornrowed braids. "Or some meditation."

"Oh, no," I moan, unwrapping a stick of gum. "Next you'll suggest I go study Scientology."

"No, don't be silly."

"Me? Yoga? Emily, you know I don't like sweating outside of the sauna." I jut out my chin and bottom lip. "And sex, I suppose."

Emily laughs as she rubs free the base of her dissolved braid. She begins work on another. "You *do* check your horoscope each morning, right?"

"I may be blonde, and the bleach may have gotten to a few brain cells, but I'm not stupid. *Obviously* I check my horoscope when I get a chance." Truth is, it's been at least a week since I've checked the thing. I'm horribly overdue.

"Good," she says matter-of-factly. "Now just relax, like Dr. Pierce said, and give yourself some reflection time and stay away from dark energy and vibes."

"So I shouldn't watch this film with its vampires and demons?" I wiggle my eyebrows seductively.

"Hell no," she yelps. "It's a girls' night in. I'm kind of wondering why that movie isn't already on."

As is always the case, not ten minutes into the movie Em and I are chatting away, our voices drowning out whoever's on screen. But I like it this way. It's comfortable. It's fun. And it sure as hell beats being back home with Andrew for another silent evening.

"And I can't believe she found her so fast," I say to Emily with a mouthful of greasy pizza.

"I can." Emily smacks her lips after a long pull of her beer. "Capitol Hill's an awesome place to work. It's central, it's hip, the place is flooded with cupcakeries and eateries, clubs, cafés... And tons of college kids looking for summer jobs live all over there. Sophie definitely wasn't going to have trouble finding someone to man the station."

"Well, I'm glad she did." I wipe my fingers on a paper towel and take a slug of beer. "When's the new girl start, anyway?"

Sophie's hired a girl whom she calls "the perfect fit for The Cup and the Cake!" Her name's Evelyn, and she's going to be a junior at

U Dub. She's living in Seattle on her own over the summer for the first time, knocking some electives out in summer school. She's had some stints at Starbucks but is looking for a full-time job this summer. Sophie says she's really sweet and already a fan of the café. She's the ideal candidate to have on board for the short-staffed summer, and she'll certainly allow Sophie to get that much-needed time away in London and Paris in just one week! Oh, I'm so jealous of her upcoming trip!

"Evelyn's already started training," Emily says. "Training this week, starts next Monday."

Emily's new cell phone begins to ring loudly, evoking a shriek and a jump from her. "Oh no!" She waves her hands sporadically. "Help me, Jack."

I erupt in laughter, watching Emily's eyes grow round as her shiny new iPhone announces an incoming call.

"Em," I say, exasperated. I wipe my hands on the paper towel and tell her to just pick it up and answer the call, like any phone.

"No." She's shaking her head. "I hate that thing. Just answer it for me." She takes a large bite of pizza as the ringing continues.

"Em." I cock my head sideways and smile. "It's a phone, not a bomb."

"No." She points at her mouth and lazily shrugs. "Foo mouf, cad taaalk."

I roll my eyes and answer, "Emily the Goofball's phone."

"She still too frightened by this piece of modern day technology?" Gatz's cheerful voice replies.

"The girl has no problem going native and popping squats in the bush, elephants and lions ready to pounce," I say, "but she can't cope with having a cell phone that isn't a twenty-year-old brick."

Emily sticks out her tongue.

"Yeah," I tell Gatz. "Okay. Thanks."

"Sorry," Emily says after I hang up. She wipes her lips clean. "I don't know what Gatz was thinking getting me that thing. He knows me better than that." She fixes her cell phone with a steely gaze. "What'd he want, anyway?"

I retrieve my phone from my clutch, and sure enough the sound has been deactivated and I notice I have two missed calls and a text message, all from Lara.

"Lara's been trying to get a hold of me," I say, speed-dialing her number. "And she doesn't have your new number yet—"

"And knew you'd be here, figured she'd call Gatz," Emily finishes.

I nod as Lara's voice comes onto the line. "Jackie!" she says, practically yelling.

"What?" I meet drama head-on with drama. "You okay? You meet a guy?"

"I love how that's the first thing that pops into your head." She laughs. "No, but maybe tonight. You never know."

"What?" I tuck my fishnet-stocking clad legs into my chest. "You going out tonight? Oh! I want to go out! Em and I are staying in and watch—"

"No," Lara interrupts, her voice filled with urgency. "I've only got a second, so hold it."

"Yeah?"

"My boss is having me go in, last-minute, to some party, some function down at the Marriott."

"Okay..." I give Emily a dumbfounded look, and she just chomps down on her slice of pizza.

"A function for Jennings & Voigt," she says. "That's where Andrew works, isn't it?"

"Yeah. What on Earth are you guys doing having a party together?" I press the phone tighter to my ear.

"Apparently one of their subsidiaries is seeking new advertising representation, and we're up for the bid." Lara exhales loudly. "It's a big one. We're having a mix and mingle kind of thing. I don't know too many details yet since I've just been thrown in last-minute since Jeff in New Accounts ate some bad seafood."

I make a squished face in disgust.

"So anyway," Lara blurts, "I'm out the door, but I just wanted to tell you that I'll see Andrew tonight."

"Makes one of us," I say dryly, sipping at my beer.

"I wanted to let you know," she draws out, "and, if you wanted me to go in and, I don't know...help out with damage control or something? I don't know." She sounds both pressed for time and distraught. She clears her throat. "I don't want to get in between you and Andrew or anything, but if I can help in any way—"

I make a gagging face to Emily, and she looks on, clueless.

"Jack?" Lara says.

"Lara, Dr. Pierce told me to stay away from negativity. All I can think of you doing is telling Andrew how upset I am with him and how help—"

Emily pats my shoulder and gives me that warning look of hers.

"Anyway," I blurt out to Lara with a shake of the head. "Thanks but no thanks, girl."

"Just trying to help."

"So a party, huh?" I take a small bite of pizza.

"Nothing too exciting. Probably just a bunch of schmoozing and, hopefully, deal-making. It's supposedly a *really* big deal. Practically the whole Jennings & Voigt firm will be there."

"Probably that little skank, Nikki, too." I can't help myself, and Emily gives my shoulder a shove this time.

"Nikki'll be there?" Lara sounds surprised.

"Maybe." I look at Emily and decide to heed the advice of taking the positive path. "I don't know, Lara, and quite frankly I don't care. You have fun, and thanks for the offer to help."

"No problem. Well, say hi to Em for me, and you girls have fun. *So* wish I could ditch this party and join you."

Suddenly, I have a wonderful idea!

"Lara!" I shout. "Actually, you *can* do me a giant favor!" I toss the nibbled-on piece of pizza back into the box, and Emily scrunches her brow.

The instant I disconnect from the call Emily flips on the TV's mute button and turns her full attention to me. "Spill it. What's going on and, first, are you *crazy*? Asking Lara to *spy* on Andrew and Nikki?"

I give a devilish grin as I take a drink of beer.

"How exactly is this stint going to work if Andrew obviously knows Lara? Not exactly *Mission: Impossible* stuff, is it?"

"Emily," I say with a slow wag of my head. "She's not going to, like, actually *spy-spy* on Andrew. She's just going to keep an eye, *discretely*, on how he and Nikki interact."

"I don't think this is part of your negativity abstinence plan, honey," Emily says smartly.

"Oh, whatever. This is a favor from a friend."

"Lara's okay with this?" She looks slightly bewildered.

"She got cheated on by an asshole," I say, deadpan. "Been there, done that. *Obviously* she's okay with it." I pull a Bic lighter and two hand-rolled cigarettes from my clutch and hold one out to Emily. She takes it and sticks it behind her ear as best she can given her thick plumes of freshly unbraided and crimped hair.

"So how exactly is this going to work?" Emily asks.

"Like," I begin, "if Nikki's all sweet on him, or if he's gently touching her, the hand on the small of the back kind of thing?" Emily makes an *aha* expression. "Or, if they start banging it out in one of the hotel rooms or something," I say much too easily. I jump up and gesture to the back patio. "Shall we?" I wave the lighter.

Emily follows me out back into the crisp, refreshing night air and, as best of friends, we spend hours relaxing on her ratty loungers under the stars, gossiping, laughing, smoking. I'm doing exactly as the doctor ordered; no negative energy or vibes can ruin this perfectly fine evening.

25

D r. Pierce had suggested it was time I go home. I'd spent ample time reflecting and being positive and sorting things out in my head, and now it was time to return to the scene of the crime. No more of this home one minute, out the next.

"Your absence is evolving into avoidance, Jackie," he said during our session yesterday. He then droned on about how my trying to cope by "giving Andrew a taste of his own medicine," as I put it, was yet another method of avoidance. "You can't very well go on and bury your feelings, run from the pain, hoping it'll disappear into thin air by magic."

We'll see about that.

See, I've taken the good doctor's advice. I've gone home from time to time over the past two weeks, staying at Em's only every other night or so. I've engaged in small talk with my husband. I've tried to pretend that everything's all right and that mind-numbing small talk leading to rote sex on occasion is just the norm that has become my marriage.

Whenever Andrew and I do hint at getting down to a serious discussion, however, he brings up the damn boat and begins to shout about how he's confused and doesn't know what I want. I start to shout, then, and tell him that *I'm* confused and frustrated and alone and... Well, it's the same thing, over and over again. It's getting so old. I've pressed couple's therapy, like Dr. Pierce suggested I offer, but that just leads to more shouting, even a broken picture frame in Andrew's office. Another mishap the Kittredges will sweep under the rug...that Marta will be responsible for when taking out the day's garbage.

At least I've been kept pretty preoccupied at Emily's, which has helped keep my mind off my troubles at home. She's only going to be around for a short while more before she and Gatz are off to Australia. I'm going to miss her terribly when she's gone.

Actually, I don't know what I'll do with myself. Lara's busy at work, more so now that she's got this big deal with Jennings & Voigt. Evidently that went through, with flying colors. Lara was quick to share the good news via an ebullient text message, much in the same enthusiastic vein as when she'd texted me after the big corporate party to say that she definitely did *not* suspect Nikki or Andrew were having an affair. "It was strictly business at the party," she told me that same night. "I honest to god do not think they're having an affair."

Affair or not, it doesn't answer my marital woes.

Unfortunately, the hours upon hours of fun I've been able to have with Emily recently have gotten cut rather short. Sophie's in London right now, soon to be in Paris, so that means Emily and Gatz are pulling lots of hours at The Cup and the Cake, still helping out newbie Evelyn, and Chad, whenever he's around. Sometimes, when I'm super bored, I'll drive over to Capitol Hill and hang out with them—pinch at some muffins, help mix something, or just sit around and page through a magazine while they go about their work.

Tonight, though, Emily promised me a night out. She and Gatz have been wanting to go dancing, but with all the extra work and late nights at the café they haven't had a chance. She insisted I come along. Chad overheard our conversation during closing time, saying he'd be up for a night out, too. Then Evelyn piped in saying it sounded like fun. Eventually we found ourselves inviting as many of our friends as we could for a night on the town. And seeing how, whether Andrew and I are in a rut or not, I *am* his wife and privy to all things that come with that title, I sprang for a stretch limo and called dibs on ordering up the first round of drinks.

"Who's up for shots now?" I scream over the bass-heavy music of the club. I climb atop the aluminum stool, holding firm the edge of the bar for support. I've had a couple of cocktails already, not counting the glass of bubbly on the ride over.

"I've got the day off tomorrow," Chad shouts as he withdraws a tattered leather wallet from his back pocket. "You three," he points at Emily, Gatz, and Evelyn, "are the poor suckers working on a Saturday." Evelyn playfully nudges him in the shoulder before taking a petite pull of her cocktail, and he takes some cash from his wallet. "Order us up," he says to me, passing the cash my way. "On me."

"I'll do shots!" Lara says loudly. "I've got nothin' tomorrow." I pass the money to the bartender and order up three shots of the special of the night, some neon-blue-colored thing I think contains vodka. Lara vibrantly adds, "'Cept for a *date.*"

"Wha—" I gasp, the bartender yanking the bills from my grip.

Lara sits taller in her seat, a look of smart satisfaction coating her lips. "That's right." She crosses her legs. She's still wearing a pair of power suit pants but has dolled it up for the night out with a flowy magenta and black v-neck top. "I've got myself a date."

"A Claire setup?" Emily asks with a smile. She lets go of Gatz's hand as he heads to the end of the bar with Chad and Evelyn. Taking a seat next to me, she says, "Is she pawing around your love life again?"

"Nope." Lara takes one of the blue shots from the bartender.

"Was it Jackie?" Emily raises a quizzically playful brow as I take the second of three shots.

"Thanks," I say with a wink to the bartender. I look to Emily. "No, it wasn't my doing."

"Cheers!" Lara says, holding up her shot glass. I follow suit and we look down the bar to Chad, who now has the last shot.

"Cheers!" I yell, raising my glass higher and gesturing Chad's way. But he's too busy laughing with Evelyn and Gatz to notice. "Whatever." I look to the girls and clink my glass against Lara's, then against Emily's cocktail. "To Lara's hot date!"

"Phew," Lara winces as the burning sensation makes her face pucker up.

"So, spill it," I say as I wipe the back of my mouth. "Who's the lucky guy?"

"His name's Worth Rowlinson," she says, and she cannot hide that goofy grin that's spreading across her face.

"Sounds important," I say with a laugh. "Sounds rich."

"Met him at that business party," Lara goes on to explain. "The one with Jennings & Voigt."

"Ugh!" I slam the empty shot glass onto the bar and knock it a few times to get the bartender's attention. "That lame-o party?"

Emily gives me a remonstrative look as Lara says, "We got to talking about the caviar, over caviar," she blushes a little, "and just made some small talk and—"

"Hey," I say to the bartender who's just about to pass by. I clink the glass a few more times against the bar. "Hey, what's your name?"

"Blake."

"Blake, can I get another one here? Please?" I wave the glass in front of him.

"Sure thing," Blake says, returning the wink I passed his way earlier.

"And get my friend here another one," I point to Lara. "She's finally going to get laid. *So* happy for her!"

"Jackie!" Lara says, swatting my arm. She turns to Blake and says, "But, sure, I'll take another shot, please."

"On me!" I yank Lara's glass from her and hand it over to Blake. With another wink, Blake snags the glasses from me, his fingers grazing mine for a second longer than it would be had it been accidental and says, "Another specialty of the night"—a smirk with another wink—"on its way."

"Anyway," Lara says with a clearing of her throat. "As I was *saying.*" She shares a brief yet petulant look with Emily. "We weren't even talking business, Worth and I. We were totally getting along and having fun and were relaxed and—"

"Thank you," I say in a slurry way to Blake when he reappears with fresh shots. "I *so* need this. My friend here. She's getting lucky with some guy." I close my eyes and nod my head. "Some guy from Vennings & Joint, where my husband works."

I can feel Emily's fingers grip and tug lightly at my forearm, trying to bring me back to the conversation with Lara. I'm feeling lightheaded and kind of careless—actually the first time in a long while I've been able to completely let my hair down and have fun like this—so I ignore her, trying to shrug her off.

I lean further into the bar and tell the blonde, brown-eyed cutie on the other side, "Blake, my husband's an ass. Totally boring. He's like twice my age and if he in't sleeping, or workin', or bangin' his sec-tary, he is making...my...life...*miserable.*" I raise the glass up an inch or two, then whisper, "Here's to hope Lara's booty from that place in't a total *boooore.*"

"Jackie," Lara's low voice commands my attention as I knock back the next shot.

I set the glass down and turn in my seat, but not before saying to Blake, "Marriage blows."

"All righty," Emily sings, grabbing both my arms now. "How about we get our dance on, honey?" She nods enthusiastically, smiling her bright, wide smile. "Some dancing? I know how much you love to dance, Jack."

"Whatever," I mumble, rolling my head about. "Lara, I'm happy for you." I hiccup suddenly, then giggle at how fast my intoxication has hit me. "Just don't get maywied. Ever. Okay?" I hold up a finger. "No mahwidge. Kay?"

"Dear lord," Lara says as she wraps an arm around my waist. "Let's dance this off, okay?"

"No, I think she's fine," I hear a voice say. "We've got to go." A pause. "She won't pick up. Think she's hungover. I've left her a message."

I lift my head. Something's on top of it. I peel open my eyes and squint into the amber light, the stuffy air. I lift my head higher and slowly the pillow and blanket atop it fall away.

"Thanks, Claire," the voice—Emily's voice—says. "Just for a while. At least until she's all right or Lara can come over."

"What's going on?" I say once Emily says goodbye into the phone. I pull myself up into a seated position and look at Emily across the way, her lips pursed as she fidgets with the *disconnect* feature of her cell phone.

"Sunshine, you're up," she sings gaily. She tosses the phone into her patchwork hobo bag.

"What the hell happened last night?" I rub at my throbbing head. "I didn't drink tequila, did I?" I make a repetitive smacking sound with my tongue, detecting a great deal of dryness to my mouth. "You know tequila and I do bad things together?"

Emily leaps from her seat on her living room chair and dashes towards the kitchen. "Nope," she says, "but you had plenty other dangerous drinks. Lucky for you, Lara and I stopped you before you got too tanked to forget everything that happened."

"What *did* happen?" I pull a pillow into my chest and sink further into the sofa.

"Okay, maybe we didn't," Emily says with a worried face as she pops her head around the corner. "Anyway, it's all about recovery for you today. I'm making you a get-well drink, and Claire's on her way over to baby you until you sober up." I hear her rummage about in the kitchen—silverware, glasses, the refrigerator opening and closing. "Or at least not *as* hungover, dear god."

"I didn't..." I begin, scratching at my head as if it's going to bring back the memories of the night before. I wasn't so wasted that I really forgot what had happened. I'm just a bit groggy from the sleep and the drinks, obviously. I scratch harder, trying to summon the memories quicker.

"I didn't do anything stupid, did I?" I wrinkle my nose, worried about Emily's answer, but deep down certain that I didn't actually do something *that* incriminating. Maybe there was a tabletop dance, or perhaps an accidental flash of a boob, or maybe a drunk dial to Andrew, or Nikki, even.

"If you don't call kissing Chad something stupid," Emily says flatly.

Or that, I think.

"And?" I ask. "What happened?"

"Oh, it was nothing," she says easily, yet with confidence. "He knew you were sloshed. He was kind of sloshed too, in fact." She emerges from the kitchen with a tall glass of red liquid. "You were just excited on the dance floor, jumping up and down and screaming. You know?"

"Jackie-like," I say dryly.

"Exactly." She carefully hands me the beverage and tells me to drink up. "We were talking about Lara having a hot date, and you mentioned how Gatz and I were going home to shack up while you slept—passed out—on the sofa." She flashes a smile. "Your words, my dear, not mine."

I nod while sipping the peppery tomato juice.

"But we *did* take the opportunity since you were out like a light," she says, eliciting from me a snort into my juice.

She carries on, saying, "Anyway, you screamed a bunch of things at the club—Sophie getting it on in Paris, happily married Robin, happily married Claire...and then you got down on yourself. Chad said something about being single, too, and, well..." She holds a hand out to me. "You kissed him, but it was no biggie. Drunk Jackie stuff, I 'spose."

"God," I breathe in between hearty drinks.

"Evelyn sure had a gobsmacked look about her, though." She makes a *tsk*ing sound, then bounds up and towards the bedroom. "Don't know what that's about, but, anyway..."

She quickly throws her untamed mane of hair into a ponytail. "Gatz and I are headed to the café and Claire's coming over to nurse you back to health, kay?"

"I can take care of myself," I say through the glass.

"Last time I heard that, a stogie got a little too friendly with my futon." She opens her bedroom door. "Gatz? Ready in five?"

He mutters something about being chronically late as I set the half-drunk glass of juice on the coffee table.

"Chronically late, yeah, yeah," Emily says through a friendly sigh. "And be easy on Claire," she says to me. She looks briefly my way as she fills her bag with a bunch of crap.

"Be *easy* on her? What's up with Claire?"

"Ready!" Gatz says, emerging from the bedroom a second later, out of breath and head still quite wet.

"Hey there, party animal," he says to me with a goofy smile. He slings his messenger bag over his chest and snags one of the bright green apples from the fruit bowl. He tosses it up, takes a hearty bite, then says through a full mouth, "Feeling tip top?"

"Shut it," I groan, falling back onto the sofa. I pull the fuzzy blanket around me.

"Claire should be here any sec, but she can only hang out for a little while," Emily explains as she takes abrupt strides to the front door. She swings the creaky thing open. "She's pulling an extra shift at the hospital today—a hefty one, apparently—so she'll be by soon, but not for long. After that *please* take care of yourself. Call me or come by the café if you're bored. Kay, babe?"

I wave a loose hand. "Yeah, yeah."

Then, before I can ask again why I need to be easy on Claire, the sound of the creaky door slamming shut echoes throughout Emily's apartment, and she and Gatz rush past the living room window hand-in-hand.

When I can finally muster the stomach to stand, I drag myself to the bathroom, grabbing my white Chanel clutch on the way. Relieving my bladder, I rifle about for my cell phone, curious if Andrew called to check in on me. He knows that if I'm not home at night then I'm most likely with Emily. There's no need for him to call and check up. But, still, it'd be kind of nice if he did. Just to show the effort—prove that he cares.

As my fingers search about for my phone, a small note sticks itself to my bright red lacquered nails. I'm about to flick the note free when a bold letter 'B' stands out. Pulling the note free from my nail and turning it right side round, I immediately gasp.

"Crap," I whisper, clapping a hand to my mouth. That woozy feeling I had in my head, that nausea I could feel come the moment I even considered standing from the sofa, all rush forward like a tidal wave.

I'm anything but a total bore, the note reads. *"Call me—Blake,"* I read aloud. Then I scan over the seven digits.

"No good. Crap, crap, crap." I cram the note back into my clutch and am about to set it aside when I see my phone.

I swallow the visiting frog in my throat and touch the circular button on my phone. I squeeze my eyes shut right as the screen glows to life. I'm filled with such a mixture of emotions. I want Andrew to have called, yet I also don't want him to have.

I let out a loud, low moan and pry open one eye. Not a single missed call or text message.

"Phew," I breathe out in relief...and disappointment.

"No," I quickly blurt out when I look at the note again. "No. Everything's fine. Nothing happened."

I shove my phone back into my clutch and tear up the note into several tiny pieces. I drop them into the toilet when a cheerful and familiar voice rings out. "Jackie? Emily? Anyone home?"

"Claire!" I say happily, but a little too loudly. My head begins to throb more forcefully. "I'm in the bathroom!" I flush the toilet and watch the colorful confetti disappear, telling myself once more that everything is okay.

26

"You sure you're all right, Jack?" Claire asks, flipping through a stack of photos Emily had printed up from her trip to Zambia for Robin's project.

Robin's been making progress on getting a coffee table book published of Emily's photography from various trips to Africa. Things are moving a bit slower than Robin had hoped, what with now being part-time at her publishing house and having two little ones at home—she jokes it'll be ready by the time Emily gets back from Australia. Although, who knows how long that could end up being.

"Huh?" I ask, massaging my temples.

"You looked like you'd seen a ghost in the bathroom." Claire, dressed in dark blue scrubs, sets the thick stack of photos in her lap. "Major hangover?"

"Yeah," I reply loosely, thinking back to that incriminating note. I wasn't even flirting that much with the bartender. *Blake*, his name flashes through my mind. I groan at the thought of his name, at the fact that only minutes ago I had a come-on note from him and his phone number in my clutch. I lean back into the comfy sofa.

"Damn, Em's talented." Claire passes a photo my way, looking at them sweetens my sour mood, at least a little. It's of two young children from her village in Zambia, one looking so curiously on at the camera, eyes wide and filled with interest, the other, who's wearing a beautiful and ornate necklace of beads, has a bright smile and is pointing off into the distance.

The photo's in black and white—a great choice for this shot. Emily often asks my opinion of whether or not a certain photo should be black and white, maybe even sepia, or as-shot in color. I never know. She has her reasonings for each, and often it's a difficult choice. Here, the black and white perfectly captures the emotion and stillness as well as the underlying vibrancy and life.

"Well," Claire says with a high sigh. She sorts the photos into an even-edged pile and sets them on the coffee table. "I've got bucks to make, so off I go."

Turns out Claire's been putting in extra shifts at the hospital and grabbing any available rounds she can find as a caretaker. It's exhausting her. Evidently Conner's really unhappy at work, and things are on edge what with him not getting the promotion he was up for. She thinks he'll either quit abruptly or get fired if he doesn't find replacement work soon, the tension's so high.

Claire told me this morning that Conner's been putting in applications everywhere, but he's just not finding that stroke of luck he had straight out of college six years ago, when he landed the accounting gig he currently has.

Claire said if he doesn't end up finding a new job soon at least they'll have the income from her overtime to help stay afloat. But only for so long. He's already had three interviews, but nothing came of any of them. Not to mention, finding interviews is so difficult they've actually decided to start searching out of town! Claire insists it's just precautionary—they're still aggressively working on finding something in Seattle—but she says they have to do what they have to do.

And I have to do what I have to do now that Claire's left for work; Emily and Gatz are at the café; Lara's apparently still in dreamland, not having responded to my multiple text messages; and Robin's at a baby Gymboree class, whatever the hell that is. There's nothing else to do but try to deal with that suspicious and terrifying little note I found in my Chanel clutch.

Sophie, I type out an email on my cell phone. *I've sunk to a new low. Marriage is still a mess, I'm so lonely, Andrew's checked out, apparently—no calls, no care—and I went out last night. With Em and Lara.*

I stop writing my email for a second to ponder. Pieces of last night's events—events that ultimately led to the receiving of that note—rush forward. I recall that episode of verbal retching—words spilling all sloppily and shamefully together. I was telling this Blake guy how miserable I was in my marriage, and I was drinking. A lot. Flirting, too.

I've warned myself of this behavior before. It's dangerous. Any *Cosmo* reader *knows* that talking to another man about how discontent you are in your relationship with *your* man is an invitation for messages just like the one Blake left for me. Each complaint about Andrew I spewed was meant to help to fill the void, heal the wounds, make me feel the way Andrew used to make me feel.

"He must have stuck it to my receipt or my credit card," I say under my breath. Massaging at my left temple, I return to my email.

Ragged on Andrew to the bartender, I write to Sophie. *Total hottie. He left me his number and I was so wasted I never noticed. I'm such a horrible person, Sophie. The situations I get myself into... But I can't remember when I've been so unhappy.*

I look out the front room window; Emily's tacky, worn, and damaged mini-blinds are turned open to let in a full and shining morning sun.

Everyone has their someone, their something. All I have is my mess, I write.

I'm not sure where to go with this email next, so I set my phone aside again, and prop my bare feet on the coffee table and stare dead ahead.

Emily's stack of Zambia photos are still in their neat pile, just as Claire left them, except the black and white one is on its own, off to the side. I lean forward and pick it up. You can barely make out the huts or tents in the background, and some of those savanna-style trees.

I bring the photo nearer to examine more closely. The smile and the inquisitive looks on the two children are priceless. I want their joy, their curiosity. I lightly run my thumb around the outline of one of the enquiring faces, and then I get an idea. I can feel my own eyes, my own face, fill with joy and curiosity.

I, too, need something, Sophie, I abruptly write. My fingers are moving so fast across the screen, my excitement is almost too much to contain. *I want to come to Paris. I want to see you. I know it's last minute, and I know you're only there for a short time more, but I want to come! I need this. What do you say?*

I send my love and sign off, ending the email with a smiley face... and a grand feeling of hope and excitement.

Hey, wasn't it the classic Queen of the Screen who said Paris is always a good idea?

To say Sophie was less than understanding or sympathetic would be a gross understatement. It hadn't even been a full twenty-four hours before I got a reply, filled with panicked undertones.

I don't think this is the best idea you've ever had, Jackie, she'd written. *Does Andrew know? What would he say to you running off to Paris? And, yes, I am only here for a few more days.*

"She's just being controlling," I say to Emily at the café later that peaceful Sunday night.

The last of the few end-of-week evening customers have gone home, and now it's just the two of us, Evelyn, and Gatz. Gatz is in the front assisting Evelyn with closing down the cash register and tidying up, while Emily's washing pans and I'm picking the backs of my acrylics in between a quick and lackluster drying motion of the clean pans.

"Jackie," Emily says. "Your request is a little rushed and last-minute, don't you think?"

"Please. This from the woman who's motto is, 'Catch the wind of sails and fly away.'"

"Butchering Mark Twain there," she replies with a chuckle.

"You know what I mean. Besides," I blow at the back of a nail, "you're leaving me for Boston soon, and then who will I have to hang out and bug all the time? Everyone else is so damn busy. Lara's got *another* filled weekend, dating that Worth guy."

"I haven't seen my family in a while, Jack," Emily says succinctly. "Don't make it out like I'm running away from you. I'm going to be abroad for a long time. I need to visit. And it's only for a couple days."

"I know."

"And as for Lara, I'm happy for her. And you should be, too." She scrubs at a baking sheet. "She hasn't been this happy about a man in a very long time. She needs this."

"I know, I know," I say with a moan. "I *am*. But what's so wrong with me wanting to do a little something for myself? With wanting to see *a friend* who just so happens to be in the loveliest city on the planet?" I bat my lashes and draw out a small giggle from Emily.

"Well," she says in a sugary tone, "I think the bigger question you should be asking is *why* you're wanting to do this, Jack." She hands me the wet baking sheet. "*And*, why you're not even considering telling Andrew. I mean, the man worries about you going out to a bar five blocks from home, or over in 'freaky, hippie' Fremont to stay with me." She casts a goofy expression. "Don't you think he'd pop an artery over this?"

"Whatever," I say, loosely towel-drying the baking sheet. "I don't care, Emily. He obviously doesn't care that much about me."

I quickly snatch up my cell phone and wave it at her. "We rarely ever talk anymore. Nothing real, at least. Just questions like where the take-out menus are, or if he needs to feed Bella or take her for a walk." I exaggeratedly flutter my lashes. "He takes better care of my dog than me."

"Oh, Jack. Come on."

"At least I can count on him to take care of Bella when I'm out. *That's* something, right?" I scoff. "It's pathetic, Em."

"Andrew, like you, is putting space between you guys to keep the fights at bay," she says sagely. "He knows you two will probably trade zingers, at the very *least*, if he dares ask what you're doing, where you are." She rinses another sheet, turns off the water, and assists with the drying. "I do *not* like making judgments, but you two have a lot of shit to work out. Running off to Paris ain't gonna fix it. I've told you distance isn't going to work in the end."

"Please, Em," I whine. "I've already gotten shot down by Sophie, I'd really rather not have you make me feel lousy, too."

Besides, I think, *things are getting scary what with that come-on note from Blake and all. Maybe it really is best that I leave town for a while.* Even Sophie had said that my flirting with the bartender was a bad deal. Of course, it didn't exactly pave the way for an invitation to Paris, but still!

"You know I don't intend to make you feel lousy. I want what's best."

"Maybe what's best is that I go to Paris."

"Well..." She slows her drying. "I'd be calling the kettle black if I said running off on vacation or in search of an adventure wasn't *one* way to deal."

"So you think I should go?" My mood perks up.

"I didn't say that."

I cave my shoulders forward and squish my lips to the side. "If I told Andrew," I say, finally. "If I told him I wanted to go to Paris, to see a friend. Just a little vaca or something..."

Emily's back to drying at a rapid pace, but her attention is piqued. "Yes?"

"If he knew, and if I honestly went just to clear my head and have some fun...with a friend!" I quickly rush out the last part. "Then there'd be no harm, hah?" I set a dry dish down.

Emily shrugs and returns the collection of dry baking sheets to their shelf. "That's your call."

"Oh, Em." I lean against the cold wall.

"As for harm?" she says. "That usually comes after the fact."

"You don't know until you try," I say, tapping a finger to my chin. "Or, how about it's easier to ask for forgiveness than permission?"

"Erm, not *exactly* where I was going, but—"

"Come on!" I say enthusiastically. I jump from the countertop. "Finish up here so we can go home and watch a movie or somethin'. I've only got you for a little while, and I'm going to monopolize your time, especially since tomorrow I'm going home because I've got some schmoozing to do with Andrew."

"Oh?" Emily drapes the drying towel over the oven handle.

"I'm going to Paris, Em!"

27

"Hŏtel..." I dig through my Louis Vuitton Neverfull GM, rummaging over an empty bottle of water, an iPhone that's useless on this side of the Atlantic, and a hurriedly purchased copy of Lonely Planet's Paris guidebook, as well as a small French phrase book, both of which I snagged from Randy's travel section with hours to spare before my plane ride some twenty-odd hours ago. I move past the latest issue of *Vogue* I've already heavily dogeared during the long flight overseas, the sleep mask, ear plugs, and baggie of Ambien I popped out of Andrew's bottle during my rushed packing job—pills that, along with the the makeshift bed in first class, made for a truly splendid in-flight experience. Finally, as I dig through the endless tubes of lipstick, two packs of Parliaments, and some Bubblicious, I find what I'm looking for.

"Hŏtel..." I read from the piece of notebook paper I used to scrawl down all the info Sophie'd given me. "...St-Louis en..." I say to the cabbie, twisting my lips funnily as I prepare to say the last word.

But the cabbie beats me to it, thank god.

"*Hôtel St-Louis en l'Île, oui, oui,*" the cabbie says, holding open the back door of his Mercedes. "*S'il vous plaît.*"

"*Merci.*" I duck into the car and think how maybe *not* failing high school French two years in a row and barely making it through my required two terms at U Dub with 'C' averages would have proved helpful right about now.

But as the cabbie shifts the car into gear and whisks me and my three Louis Vuitton luggage pieces (two of which are empty, ready to be stuffed to the brim with authentic Parisian fashion finds) away from Charles de Gaulle and on my way to Hotel Saint wherever, I couldn't care less about languages learned or lost, classes barely passed or dropped, failing marriages or romantic relationships. I'm in Paris!

"*Merci*," I say to the cabbie, handing him the appropriate amount of rainbow-colored Euros once we arrive at my final destination.

As he heaves my luggage onto the curb at the entrance to a truly grand boutique-style hotel, muttering things I cannot discern to the hotel doorman, I stare up in awe at the pristine façade, a soothing taupe color.

Hôtel St-Louis en l'Île is on the poshest street on the quaint little island of *Île St-Louis* in the Seine. I know Sophie's parents are well-off, and I know they wanted to give her a special gift in celebration of making such a success of her café in just one year, but damn! If I thought the exterior was elegant, try the interior! Everything my eye can see in the lobby is polished to perfection, with both a homey, quaint charm to it, as well as a regal and distinguished air.

Before I can root about my handbag for the handy piece of paper with the room number written on it, I hear a chipper and familiar voice. "Jackie!"

I spin around and am immediately enveloped in a tight hug.

"Sophie!" I screech, hugging her just as tight and slightly spinning around in enthusiasm.

"My god, I can't believe you're here!" She pulls back to look me up and down. "This is going to be so much fun! I'm glad this worked out." She pulls me into another tight hug.

"I'm so glad you let me talk you into letting me come."

Sophie says something in choppy yet impressive French to the petite woman with the severe blonde bob at reception. She then turns back to me and says, "I'm glad you got Andrew to agree to let you come!" She gives my arm a friendly squeeze.

"Yeah, well," I begin as I hand over my passport to the outstretched hand of the receptionist. "It's a short few days but it's *so* what I need right now."

"You and me both," Sophie says. "I forgot how spoiled I was having Claire visit me last time I was here. Oh!" She claps exuberantly. "I'm just so happy you're here. Come on! I've got your days all planned out, girlfriend. It's going to be fantastic!"

"Of course you do, Sophie," I say with a laugh.

"We've got the whole day to do nothing but sightsee, Jackie!" Sophie proclaims, handing me a metro ticket. "I got you the tickets you'll need to ride the metro and RER. We can go anywhere."

"On your pre-approved list of places to see, of course?" I tease, slipping on my white Gucci sunglasses.

She, too, slips on her pair of oversized designer sunglasses, then shakes open a map. "It's such a gorgeous day; we should definitely visit the Arc de Triomphe, Eiffel Tower, lunch in the Tuileries..." She says these things so French-like.

"And shopping?" I wiggle my eyebrows.

"Shopping, eating, strolling...is there anything *else* to do in Paris?" She tosses out a Hollywoodesque laugh. "Come on! Notre Dame's just around the corner, over the bridge— Oh!" She springs up and down on the toes of her blush-colored ballet flats—definitely a new purchase, and a Lanvin one if I know my designers. "And there's the darlingest café on the way to the cathedral, the most gorgeous view over *Pont St-Louis*," Sophie waxes on. "Oh! And then you just *have* to have the clichéd but totally scrumptious and worth-every-bit-of-cliché Ladurée macarons! Omigod, I'm going to be the size of a whale before I leave gay *Pah-ree* behind next week!"

I take the map from her, fold it in quarters so the circled part indicating our hotel's location is in the center. I link my arm in

Sophie's and look up at her glowing face. "Notre Dame it is! And that café sounds like the *perfect* idea right about now. I need some caffeine."

"Excellent!" Sophie begins striding forward.

"And eventually we're hitting up the Champs-Élysées." I point down at her feet. "*So* getting me a pair of adorable ballet flats."

Still striding spiritedly and in wide lengths, which is causing me to double my speed thanks to my shorter legs and three-inch heels, Sophie gives me a sly grin. "Couldn't agree with you more, Jackie." She pats my arm. "Because there's this second pair I've been contemplating buying. I'm so doing it!"

Sophie was right. The café, Taverne Philippe, served me a simple but tasty *café au lait* that hit the spot. Then, since it was just a hop, skip, and a jump away, we wandered about the fragrant and colorful flower market that has apparently been around since the 1800s—the oldest market in the city! Sophie got a sprig of lavender for her hair, I a white rose for my vintage jacket lapel, all to feed the corny need to feel Parisian.

We walked arm-in-arm about the city, exhausting our feet (and our metro passes) for the duration of the morning and early afternoon. We rode to the highest level of the Eiffel Tower, walked silent and in awe under the chilly and inspiring vaulted transept of Notre Dame, and took photos of the Arc de Triomphe. We zig-zagged all about the city in whimsical fashion. It was like a girl's dream come true—no cares in the world and only fun to be had.

"Okay, how awesome is this?" I ask Sophie as I pop the cork of a bottle of rosé we were happily talked into buying at one of the many open-air markets we strolled by. The man who sold us the bottle insisted that on such a *jolie* summer day like this, a bottle of rosé *must* be enjoyed!

Sophie arranges the rounds of camembert and brie, the small jar of plum preserves, the freshly baked baguette, the tin of herbed olives, and the large, red, globe grapes—all delectable market finds—about a spread of napkins that create a makeshift miniature picnic blanket.

"This is the life, Jack," Sophie says, popping a grape into her mouth.

"Could you imagine living every day like this?" I say, looking around the lush green landscape.

Off to the far right is a large fountain. Children are crowded around, taking long sticks and poking about their wooden sailboats, a competition of sorts to see whose colorful sails will catch the tiniest of breezes this early afternoon, and ride it across the water the fastest.

To the left is a long, pristine line of well-manicured trees and shrubs where the occasional buggy-pushing mom, elderly couple arm-in-arm, or jogging tourist wearing an NYC or Stanford shirt enjoy some of the most famous gardens of the world—the Tuileries.

"I'm sure even the most passionate of Parisians don't live like this every day," Sophie says unequivocally. "I do have to remind myself that this is vacation."

"This could be my day *every* day!" I pull free a grape. "This is pure heaven!"

"Makes you forget everything, doesn't it?"

"Definitely." I tuck one leg into my chest, then take another grape. "No troubles, no worries—"

"No work."

"You so deserved this time off, Sophie," I say, watching her spread the slightly melted camembert on a torn-free piece of baguette. "You work your ass off at that café."

"It's still running, right?" She bites down on her lower lip, pausing her spreading motion. "Chad hasn't burned the place to the ground? Emily and Gatz haven't pushed forward their Australia trip? Evel—"

I can't suppress my laughter. Through a mouth full of grapes, I say, "Everything's fine, worry wart. Under control and doing well."

"And you?" Her question kind of takes me off guard.

"Me?"

"Yeah." She pours some rosé into two paper cups. "How are you and Andrew getting on? Things better?"

I take my cup, and before I can answer Sophie blurts out, "No more notes from up-to-no-good bartenders?"

"No," I groan, rolling my eyes. "And with Andrew..." I give a one-armed shrug. "...I wouldn't say things are *worse*. Not better, though."

"Jeez, I'm sorry, Jack."

"We're not really talking, but I guess that's better than fighting, right?"

"Yeah," she says with a smile.

"Andrew just doesn't get me." I pull my legs into a criss-cross position and lean forward, slowly turning the half-filled cup in my hands. "And I don't really get him, I guess."

"Not dancing to the same drummer's beat, or however that saying goes?"

"If only he'd be open to therapy with me..." I look off in the distance. "More action than just talk. Or just realize he can't constantly *buy* my love, *buy* my appeasement..."

"Well, we can thank him for buying you this trip to Paris." She holds up her cup of wine. "That doesn't sound like a completely doomed marriage to me."

I raise my cup to hers and she sings, "To Paris and happy endings!" We tap our cups together.

"To Paris," I say, looking at her sparkling and gleeful blue-green eyes. "Yeah, and happy endings," I add in a mumbling fashion.

It's worth a wish, or at least a toast, I think. *Happy endings...*

"How was London?" I say after we've polished off nearly all the market snacks. A picnic lunch in the Tuileries was, like Taverne Philippe, like the visits to the Eiffel Tower, Arc, and cathedral, like the entire idea for me to fly to Paris on a moment's notice, splendid. "I imagine fabulous, as well?"

"London's always fab," Sophie says. She flaps some baguette crumbs from her white, linen summer dress. "John was pretty busy, but we did do the requisite fish and chips together, Big Ben, Buckingham, and London Eye sightseeing...the usual."

"What fun," I say. "Like Paris, I don't know how anyone'd get work done if they lived in a city like London."

"Well," Sophie says saucily, "he's definitely finding *some* down time to have some fun."

"Oh?"

"While I was there he had two dates with someone named Jean." She winks.

"Your brother's a dating machine, isn't he?"

"Dating, yes. Unable to commit? That, too." She rolls her eyes and grabs some of the last grapes. "Not that I really care. I mean, it's his life," she says with a full mouth. "Our mother just keeps pestering me about settling down. Finding someone I can marry, pop babies out, that kind of thing." She swallows. "As if opening and running my own business isn't already something to be proud of, she's begging me to let her fulfill her grandmother duties."

I laugh and lean back on my elbows in the soft grass.

"I'm serious. I never pictured my mother to be the type to press about grandchildren, but I swear, if John doesn't get serious, then the buck's passed to me." She takes a small pull of wine. "Like my eggs are going to expire soon or something."

"You're twenty-eight," I gasp. "Hardly the age of expiration."

"Yeah, well," another pop of a grape, "whatcha gonna do?"

"So this Jean character? The real deal, you think?"

"Ha!" Sophie rolls her eyes again. "As real as the swimsuit model was, and the slue of attractive women he's dated. Time will only tell, my dear. Time will only tell."

I sigh and look up into the sea-blue sky. I close my eyes, and as I breathe in deeply I catch the faint aroma of lavender mixed with the buttery scent from a *boulangerie*.

"But if Jean's the one, then maybe she'll pull through and fill my mother's grandmotherly void," Sophie continues on in her rambling way. "My love life sure as hell is *not* very much of a love life." She sighs heavily. "Think I've had enough wine." She pours out the small amount that's in her cup.

"No romantic trysts since you've been here?" I pry, raising my eyebrows suggestively. "London lovers, maybe?"

"Please, Jack." She brushes the tops of her ballet flats. "I wouldn't call it nonexistent...but it's nothing romance-novel-worthy."

"Oh!" I exclaim. "Ha, ha! If it *isn't* nonexistent, then that means it's *somewhat* existent. Which means things just got a whole lot more interesting. I beg to differ that that *isn't* romance-novel-worthy, girl!"

She tilts her head to one side and gives me an impassive expression. "No," she says simply.

I let out a whistle. "You got lucky, didn't you?"

"Hardly call it luck."

"That Frenchie you were seeing last time you were here, was it?"

She pulls up some blades of grass and plays with them in her palm.

"Come on," I urge, flipping onto my stomach. "Sophie and the Frenchie hit it off again." I whistle again. I can sense the slightest of blushes as she fiddles more aggressively with the plucked blades.

"This is the epitome of girl time, and you're kidding me!" I'm flabbergasted. "You're *not* going to spill?"

"All right," she says in a coquettish way. "Henri—"

"That's it! Henri!"

"Henri and I..." She stops playing with the grass.

"Yes?"

"We've seen each other," she says, voice hesitant.

"And?"

"It's nothing serious."

"I don't care. It's something! Tell. Tell!"

She begins to play with the blades of pulled grass again. "It's nothing. He's seeing someone anyway."

"Oh, damn." My enthusiasm deflates immediately.

"Or...dating someone. I don't know. He's the kind of guy who has open relationships. Casual, you know?"

"*Ménage à trois!*" I sing through a throaty laugh. "Oh, shit, Sophie!"

"N-No," she stammers out. "Not like that. Well," she blushes harder, "okay *he* would go for that, but not me. No, no."

"When in Paris..." I sing, still laughing.

She closes her fist around the grass and shoots me a cautious look. "I told him I wasn't up for that. I'm the kind of girl where it's either a committed, one-on-one relationship—which, let's face it, is impossible to create given our locations."

I nod quickly.

"Or..." She returns to playing with the grass, dropping a piece, then two, back onto the lawn, "I'd consider a simple no-strings-attached kind of thing. No broken hearts allowed."

I raise one eyebrow inquisitively. "That means..." I wait for Sophie to fill the space, but when she doesn't, I blurt out, "You mean you guys had a threesome?"

"No, Jackie!" She winces. "No! What? Okay, you're crazy."

"Well then...*what?*" I eagerly await her response.

A grin breaks out on her face, and she gives a hard exhalation to the remaining blades in her palm.

"Sophie!" I lightly punch her thigh. "Tell me!"

"Paris is the City of Love...and opportunity. I'm on vacation." She pauses, looking over to the fountain and children. Her grin's weakened, but it's still obviously there. "You do the math, Jack."

28

My first night in Paris was spectacular! Sophie took me to this really energetic nightclub over in the Latin Quarter, where we danced with rounds of guys, some international students studying abroad, some locals looking to unwind, and even a couple of Spaniards on vacation who thought some smooth moves on the dance floor was the instant ticket to mine and Sophie's hearts...or at least our hotel rooms.

The dancing was fun, and afterwards Sophie and I made our way to the lively area near the Place de la Bastille. We ducked into a really fun and uniquely decorated wine bar where there were dozens of oak barrels stacked up and down the walls. Eventually we made our way back west and found a swanky rooftop bar a short walk from our hotel where wine and oysters were served atop hardback classical books, brought around by waiters with hairstyles and clothes circa the Golden Age. It was like something from a dream!

We laughed, we dined, we drank, we gossiped. We had all the fun two girls out in Paris could dream of having, and all that after a revving time wandering about this *rue* and that *rue*, hitting up the Louvre to catch a look at the Mona Lisa (and a few others Sophie really wanted to point out, but about which I couldn't care less), trekking to Sacré-Cœur, and taking an evening boat tour along the Seine, and watching the glittering Eiffel Tower sparkle in the sapphire, evening sky.

It was sightseeing Paris in a day, because today, my second and last full day in the City of Lights, is all about shopping! I mean, how can I be steps away from the birthplace of high French fashion and not introduce my credit cards to the homes of Hermès, Chanel, and Lancel?

To break up the monotony of designer labels and historic haute couture along the famous and glamorous Champs-Élysées, I have to be fair to Sophie and agree to duck into some *boulangeries* and *pâtisseries*, and the occasional café or chocolate and wine shop. She calls it "market research," but I tease that we should call all of the sampling and small purchases and finger-licking just what it is: a damn good excuse to stuff our faces with the finest food we've ever had the pleasure of eating.

Between each pastry-, macaron-, espresso-, and wine-tasting stop, we step inside top French fashion houses along the Triangle d'Or. Dreamy places like Chloé, where I can finger the bohemian dresses, and Louis Vuitton, where I can get lost in the intoxicating scent of leather and handbags (oh how beautifully the two go together). I'm in a shopper's paradise, getting lost in the land of Chanel, Dior, Lacroix, Givenchy, Hermès, JPG, YSL...oh heavens, just look at me!

I have carrier bags weighing me down, a brand new Lancel handbag hanging off one shoulder, a new pair of Dior aviators perched upon my head, and a pair of baby-blue Lanvin ballet flats on my feet, Sophie sporting her beloved new black and white polka-dotted pair. Hermès is around my neck in the form of a slate-colored scarf, Givenchy's on my wrist with dazzling rose gold and peach gems, I've got a box of assorted Ladurée macarons to snack on (and some to bring back to the girls), and even a pair of sharp-looking cufflinks for Andrew, compliments of a very successful spree at Cartier (where I also happened to find a dazzling teardrop necklace).

It isn't until I'm in the dressing room at Eres, trying on a sleek, black bathing suit, when I begin to worry that I've bought more than my third empty suitcase can hold.

"Sophie," I whine, glancing about the carrier bags and totes that cover the dressing room's floor. And this is only about half of them! The other half are out with Sophie.

"Yeah?"

"I think I might have gone overboard."

Sophie giggles, and I can hear her pad over.

"Yeah, overboard a little, maybe," I say, still surveying the pile of goods splayed about.

"Too many macarons and wine?" She titters, her head now peeking up over the dressing room door. "Can't fit into your size double-zero bathing suit?" Her fingers grab around the top of the door and she peers down. "Damn!" she gasps. "You look good."

"Thanks." I slowly pry open the door, and she peers her head through the crack. "But that's not what I mean."

"Buy it." She waves her hand up and down my body. "It was made for you."

I look back at myself in the mirror and sigh. "Yeah... There's a reason they're regarded as the finest suits in the world. They're *all* made for *somebody*."

This little black number is the most beautiful and form-fitting suit I've ever tried on. Eres cuts their suits to fit all shapes and sizes, and they don't miss a beat. Whatever you want and need, Eres has it and will hide it, cover it, flash it, make it perfect.

"You must get it," Sophie says, looking agog. "I wish I could splurge and get one."

"I'll buy you one," I say spiritedly. "Please let me buy you one!" I don't know why I hadn't thought of it before, but I've been using my credit cards—the ones Andrew says are practically limitless and at my disposal to make myself happy—to fill my closet (as if it wasn't already filled to the brim). Sophie's picked up a couple things along our shopping way, but I've got an easy fifty-pounds' worth of carrier bags and totes on her puny handful.

"Jack," she says, one hand on her hip. She pries the door open further. "Do you know what these things cost?"

"A small arm and a leg, yeah," I dismiss. "And worth every appendage."

"No. I won't let you."

"Come on! It'll be fun!" I give her pleading eyes. "Just throw my crap into a room, get yourself some pieces to try on, and let's have fun!"

"As if we aren't already on fun overload," she says with a smile, about to close the door. "Oh!"

"Yeah?"

She peeks her head back in. "What was that about going overboard? That suit looks smashing on you."

"Oh," I wave off with a flick of the wrist. "I was saying I think I went overboard with all the purchases I've made."

Sophie's eyes grow wide.

"But who cares, now? You're going to try some suits on and get yourself something Henri or whoever will drool over. It's all good."

Sophie rolls her wide eyes and pulls back out of the door. "Dear lord," she mutters. "You really shouldn't get me something, Jack."

"Oh, hush." I grab the door's golden handle. "Just go try things on and get something that really shows off those long legs and trim waist."

"You shouldn't."

"My mind's made up!" I make a motion with both hands to shoo her on her way.

"But if you're already worried you've gone overboard with—"

"No, no." I shoo some more. "What's a few more things, really? In the grand scheme? The main damage has already been done. Now this is just...what? Like residual profits."

Sophie's face twists. "Huh?"

"Pennies," I brush off. "It's Andrew's money, anyhow. He's loaded, won't even notice. And after the damage I've done on the Champs-Élysées what's a few suits at this point?"

Sophie sighs and begins to gather together the hill of carrier bags. "If you insist..."

"Besides," I say as I close the door, raising my voice so she can still hear me, "I haven't even touched their lingerie section yet!"

"*Désolé, Madam,*" the tall, thin lady at the registry says, holding out my American Express.

"Thank you," I say, taking the card and slipping it into my wallet. I look about for the pen, ready to sign. "I mean, *merci.*" I flash Sophie a toothy grin, seeking approval.

"*Désolé, Madam,*" the lady says again, arm still outstretched.

I give her a stupefied look as she says, "*Un moment.*"

"What's the problem?" Sophie asks.

"Your card did not go through," the lady says in even yet heavily accented tones. She clasps her hands together and stands stoic, waiting for a response.

"Your card," Sophie says. She looks to me and motions to my wallet.

"I thought I paid?" I look at Sophie with the same stupefied look.

"Your card did not go through," the lady repeats.

I hand back the American Express when Sophie says to give it another try.

"*Désolé, Madam.* Again, it did not go through."

"What?" In a flurried movement I open my wallet and pull out my Visa. "Here." I thrust it forward. "Try this one."

"Have you used this one yet?" Sophie asks, turning the American Express over in her hands.

"Please," I splutter, "I'm burning a hole through it."

"Maybe that's the problem, silly." Sophie gives me a goofy grin and slips the card in my wallet.

"*Désolé,*" the lady says, this time holding out the rejected Visa card.

"That one, too?" Sophie spews in bewilderment. "Maybe you didn't authorize that one to be used abroad."

I shake my head in denial, not yet at the point of nervousness. I still have a few more cards to try. "No, no," I say insistently. "I alerted my banks. Half of them are auto-enabled as it is, what with Andrew's overseas travels all the time." I pull out the MasterCard. "Here."

Sophie and I wait eagerly, silently.

"*Désolé, Madam,*" comes the familiar phrase after the card's run through the machine.

"Dammit!" I pull free my Discover card.

Again, Sophie and I wait eagerly, silently, and this time I'm actually sending up a silent prayer that it goes through. This has never happened before!

"*Non,*" the lady says.

"Try it again," I urge. "I've used the other three like crazy today. Maybe they're burned out. But this one *surely* must work."

I don't return the glance, too nervous to peel my eyes away from the card as it goes sliding through the machine, but I can feel Sophie looking at me.

"*Désolé, non.*"

"Fuck." My heart starts to race. I can feel the heat coming from behind as the next customer in line taps her foot lightly.

"Let's not get angry," Sophie whispers.

"Here!" I pull out my Diners Club card. "Try this one."

The lady looks at the card with a furrowed brow, then slowly shakes her head. "No, sorry. We don't take this card."

"Okay, no problem." Sophie pushes the Eres carrier bag filled with beautiful designer bathing suits and lingerie forward. "We're sorry for wasting your time, but I'm afraid we can't pay for these."

"Wait!" I say, a little more loudly than I wished. "Here!" I thrust forward nervously my second Visa card. "This one's my backup. If this baby doesn't work I don't know what will!"

I cross my fingers on my right hand and pull it tight against my back. I grip my wallet firmly with my other hand. I bite down on my lip and watch on in both fascination and fear. *Please work, please work.*

"*Déso—*"

"*Désolé*, yeah, yeah, I know," I say curtly. "Dammit."

Sophie quickly grabs my wallet, manages as best as possible the bulk of the carrier bags, and gestures towards the door. "*Merci beaucou, madam.* So sorry for your trouble. So sorry." She leans in and whispers in my ear, "Let's save the last shred of dignity we have and scram now!"

"I don't know how that's possible!" Sophie says, exasperated. "You've been using those cards all day, left and right." She pauses, stares straight ahead across the trafficked street, then says through a low chuckle, "Then again, that's probably exactly *why* this has happened."

She turns towards me in her seat on one end of the green wooden bench. "Jackie?" She situates herself a little more comfortably among the piles of carrier bags that fill the space between us, and spill out onto the ground near our new Lanvin-ed feet. "I know you spent a lot of money, but just how *much* did you spend? Maybe you do have a limit and you shot it through the roof."

I fix her with a blank stare, then blindly pull open the Ladurée box. "I once bought a one-of-a-kind L'Wren Scott gown, a Tiffany's bracelet, *three* designer bags, and rented a Ferrari for the weekend and dined at a five-star Michelin restaurant in the Hamptons on one card in less than twenty-four hours. Those plastics can take a beating." I pop a pistachio-flavored macaron—the whole thing—in my mouth.

"You and Andrew live on another planet," she breathes out. She stares down at the mess of consumerism that divides us.

"Macaron?" I offer, holding out the box.

She declines, then says, "I don't get it! Jack, you've said that's never happened before?"

"Nope. Never." I fish around for another tasty pistachio macaron, but when I spot an orange one I opt for that instead.

"Oh, no!" She grips my arm as I'm about to take a bite.

"Okay, okay." I lean forward and take a bite at the treat. "I know they're not intended to be eaten whole."

"No!" Sophie pushes her bangs back, her hand dramatically clasping the top of her head. "Why didn't we think of this sooner?"

"Hmm?" I take another nibble of the orange one, this time the bite significantly smaller than the previous, despite its mouth-watering taste. Now is certainly the time to indulge...in already-purchased, delectable sweets, that is.

"Theft!" Sophie exclaims. "Maybe someone's stolen your cards and your credit card companies have shut them down! That happened to me once, when there was odd activity going on with one of my cards." She scratches her head.

"And?" I chew more slowly, realizing that perhaps that's the reason behind the trouble. Although, if I'm completely, one hundred percent honest, I know that can't be the reason. See—

"It all got sorted out," Sophie continues. "I ordered some Italian espresso direct, and what with it being a new business card and all, and being international and—" She blinks rapidly. "Anyway, it all worked out once I explained and the hold was lifted. Look." She grips my arm, and I decide then to give up on eating another macaron. Besides, my stomach's starting to feel a little queasy.

"Let's go back to the hotel," she says. "We'll call up your banks and the card companies, and we'll get this all figured out. That'll make me feel a lot better." She scoffs. "That'll make *you* feel better! Come on." She begins to gather the carrier bags.

"Erm..." I stammer.

"Come on. Time's a-wastin'! The sooner we call and find out what's going on, the better."

"Sophie, wait." I try to reach for her hand, but she's moving so swiftly about, gathering all of the bags.

"Come on, I'll hail us a cab." She heaves some bags further up her forearm. "My treat, penniless Jackie," she teases.

"Sophie, wait!" This time my voice is louder and sterner.

She pauses and stares at me, expressionless.

"There's something I need to tell you."

I await a response, but she just keeps looking at me in silence.

"I think Andrew might have put a stop on my cards," I say. But I can't continue looking her in the eyes. What I'm about to say next will surely disappoint her, and I can't bear to watch.

"Why would he do a dumb thing like that?"

"Erm..." I twirl my thumbs around each other. "He doesn't... exactly..." I suck in a quick breath, then spew out, "know that I'm here."

29

"Could you *be* any more selfish?" Sophie yells, charging forward and at such a brisk pace I can't keep up. The scads of designer carrier bags aren't even weighing her down. I, on the other hand, am about to break with the weight of the bags at each harsh step I take along the street to our hotel.

When I broke the news of my secret escape to Paris, Sophie gasped, told me she couldn't speak, then hailed a cab. The whole ride was bone-chillingly silent, save for the French pop music bleating through the tinny cab speakers.

When I knew we weren't far from our hotel, I finally broke the silence, slicing it with a dull knife. "I'm sorry, Sophie," I said. "You just don't understand what it's like to be married to him. I'm miserable. I'm bored. He never would have let me come if I'd asked."

Sophie put up a cold, stiff hand in front of my face and told the cabbie to pull over right there, that instant. She'd be walking the rest of the way.

Of course, I couldn't just let her walk alone. Besides, who'd pay the fare? So I hopped out with her, and now here we are, making the grueling half-mile walk back to the hotel in the energy-depleting June heat, Dior and Chanel weighing us down.

"I can't believe you!" Sophie shouts.

"Sophie, let me explain!" I whine, trotting now. My new ballet flats were meant to be lightly broken in, not to perform the Iron Man.

"No!" She picks up her pace.

"*Sophieeeee.*"

Suddenly I find myself nearing her. I'm gaining on her. Has she slowed or...

She's stopped.

The carrier bags come to a crash around her feet, and she slowly turns around.

"Sophie?" I cautiously step forward.

"You know what?" She firmly plants her fists on her hips. "I don't have to listen to this, and I sure as hell don't have to carry this." She motions to the small mountain at her feet. "This is your mess, Jackie Kittredge, *you* clean it up! Be responsible for once in your life!"

"Sophie," I say in a hushed and taken-aback voice.

"No!" She shakes her head violently.

"I can't manage this all by myself." I take two steps closer.

"You managed to get into this all by yourself—not telling Andrew, not telling me about your little scheme to run off to Paris— you can now get yourself out of it!"

"Sophie," I heave. "I'm an adult, I can—"

"Then start acting like one!" She turns on her heels and begins to angrily charge forward, the bags left in her wake.

"I'm having a difficult time, Sophie!" The bags are painfully boring into my palms, but I continue to strut forward, stopping at the mess she's left behind.

"We *all* have difficult times, Jackie!" she shouts, turning back around to me. Her hands fly up into the air in exasperation. "Just let me walk home in peace. I can't be around you right now."

"But Sophie...this stuff. I can't manage this."

She spins back around, about to continue her solo walk to the hotel, when she says, "You'll survive! It's all shit you don't need, anyhow. It's probably good Andrew put a stop to the cards."

"Fine," I huff under my breath, bending down in a pathetic attempt to scoop up the abandoned merchandise. "I'll do it myself."

"Wait!" Sophie rushes over and scoops up one lone bag. "I'm taking this for my walk." She waves the Place de la Madeleine bag about. "I'm not letting these snacks go to waste."

Then, with a sharp glare sent my way and one final, "I can't believe you sometimes, Jackie!", she storms ahead, prying open the bag of gourmet chocolates.

I thought it best to give Sophie some breathing room, and I was so stunned over the blowout myself, so I took my time getting back to the hotel. Well, actually, the bags were so heavy and aplenty that I had no choice but to creep my way back home. But once I got there, I left everything in the lobby and, out of breath and sweating, asked reception to please take everything up to the room.

I then decided to lose myself on the Left Bank, going so far as the Luxembourg gardens. I figured the fresh air and lack of cash to rely on to take a cab home would do me some good, and the length of time I'd be away would surely lend a hand in helping Sophie calm down.

As I walk along the length of St. Michel, no carrier bags digging into my flesh, no credit cards or cash to access save for the lone five-Euro bill in my wallet, and with Paris's beautiful environs at my visual disposal, I get to thinking about what I've done. I suppose that's what a walk like this is good for.

A big part of me knows coming here unbeknownst to Andrew wasn't one of my better plans, no matter how great an idea Paris is. And I know that keeping that tidbit of info from Sophie (and all the girls, for that matter) was probably one of my more foolish moves. But I needed this. For me. I needed to do something that wasn't by the books, something that maybe, if I'd actually had the cash, would've done when I was unmarried, unattached. The fly the sails thing that Emily does!

Had I known that it would've sent me down this path, however, I don't know that I would've done it. Not really speaking with Andrew, fighting with Sophie—oh, and the disappointment I'll get from Emily... I don't keep secrets from Em, or Lara either. They tend to put up with my shenanigans a bit better than the rest of the girls, always willing to ride in on a white horse and save me when things inevitably go sour.

I know I have a way of making my friends' eyes roll and their faces go all pale when I reveal a less-than-stellar move I've made. Like with Claire that morning and how I didn't exactly divulge the whole Blake mishap; I don't want to share all of my secrets and stupid choices because, well... Dammit, I make so many of them, I fear eventually the girls will tell me they're good and done with me and my antics. Selfish Jackie, Spoiled Jackie, Doesn't Live in Reality Jackie. I wouldn't blame them, though. I know I can be a spoiled brat sometimes. I know I don't make things easy on them. It's who I am. I'm a difficult woman with a screwed up past, and while I know Dr. Pierce says, "That's not an excuse, Jackie," sometimes I feel like it is. Or it should be. At least until I can figure my life out...until I feel like I'm really healing...until I know where I'm supposed to be.

Returning from my lengthy stroll, daylight burned and a friendship slightly singed, if not burned, too, I cautiously set the room key down on the writing desk. I lean against the half of the balcony French door that's closed.

Not sure where to begin, I'm relieved when Sophie has the first word. "I'm sorry for acting ridiculous out there," she says quietly from her seat on the balcony. She's sitting out on our narrow balcony, on one of the two small metal bistro chairs that sit before a tiny table topped with red geraniums.

"I'm sorry for causing the trouble to begin with," I say meekly. I press my cheek to the glass of the door. The coolness of it feels good to my flushed, warm skin. "Sophie, I'm sorry for acting so stupid. *I* was the ridiculous one."

She takes a pull of her miniature-sized Perrier, and I can see the side of her mouth turn up in a small grin. "You were being you, Jackie."

I'm not sure how to react to this statement. I take a tentative step onto the balcony.

"You're wild, you shop, you want fun. That's you." She takes another brief drink. "But what I really don't like—"

I put my hand on the free chair and pause, giving her time to send me body language that says I'm either welcome to take the seat or better get my ass back inside. Judging by the return of her half-grin, I take a seat.

"What I don't like, Jackie," she looks me straight in the eyes, "is that you lied to me. You deliberately lied."

I look down at my lap and begin to carelessly pick at the backs of my nails.

"I said you should talk to Andrew," she says. "I said you shouldn't just catch a plane and run away from your troubles."

"I know," I say, eyes still locked on my hands.

"Why'd you lie? Don't you feel like you can be honest with me?"

"I don't want you disappointed in me, Sophie. I just wanted to do something on my own—just do it—and I didn't want to hear how I was being stupid."

"Oh, Jack."

"I'm serious. I do stupid stuff, and I knew you'd be upset with me if I told you I didn't tell Andrew. I knew you would insist that I talk to him before I came. And—and—well." I inhale deeply. "I just didn't want to deal. I wanted to just do what I wanted, period."

"Jackie." She sighs and swats away a fly that's buzzing about. "I'm sorry you feel that way. I don't want to harangue you."

"Eh." I flick my wrist. "Sometimes I need a good harangue'n."

"I bet Andrew's worried sick about you."

"Psh. Yeah, right."

"Look, I know you two are going through rough times." She places a gentle hand on my leg, and I look up. Her eyes are soft, welcoming, encouraging. "I believe Andrew loves you very much, and I can see it in your eyes that you love him, too."

I can feel tears begin to rise from deep within, wanting to flow up and show themselves.

"In the park, the gardens," she says. "During the picnic. I watched you. Those couples in the garden."

"The kids," I say with as much strength as I can muster. "I was watching the kids."

"Yeah, *and* you were watching the couples. The young couple kissing, the elderly couple taking their dog on a walk, those American newlywed tourists..."

I blink hard, fighting off the tears trying to push forward.

"You want that love; you miss Andrew." She grabs my hand. "You have a marriage that I can see in your eyes you want to fight for, that you don't want to lose." She squeezes my hand, and I blink long and hard. "No more lies. No more running."

"It's so hard, Sophie," I whimper. "It's so hard."

"I know it is." She squeezes my hand tighter, bouncing it on my leg. "But you have come so far in life. You've gone over leaps and hurdles that I've never seen *anyone* take on before. You're a tough woman."

I guffaw in jest, then quickly clamp my mouth shut as I feel the tears about to break through.

"You are!" She leans down and peers around, trying to meet my eyes. "You've come a long way, and I'm proud of you. Yes, you have got to really keep on growing up. It's a journey; don't stop it. But look at what you *have* done. You've made your way through college when it wasn't easy. You did what your parents said you never could do—and *went* to school! You kicked the pot and that short but *seriously* stupid blow stage." She rolls her eyes quickly. "You're no longer dating *horrible* guys; you've married a man who, as difficult as things may be right now, really does love you. You're in therapy and have been for a long time."

"A long time," I cut in. "Exactly. Tell ya somethin'?"

"Stop that. You know what I mean. Yes, you are full of drama, and yes, you are a bit self-consumed from time to time. But your heart is gold, and, Jack, seriously." She touches my chin and pulls my face back towards her. "Do you honestly think Robin, Lara, Emily, Claire, and I would be your friend for *ten* years if we didn't love the person —the soul—that you are? Truly?"

"You also kind of like me for my crazy drams, too, right?" I say in half-jest. "I do bring the party and entertainment to you?"

"In more ways than one," she says with a laugh. "You've just gotta keep up the race, Jackie."

"Oh, Sophie." I look upwards at the sky in a last-ditch effort to quash any possible tears. "You can be so corny, I love you."

"I'm serious, Jack. Stay strong and don't give up."

"No matter how bad it is?" I sniffle preemptively.

"It can always be worse." She cocks her head to the side. "It may be bad, but this isn't the worst. You can get through this."

"What do I do now?" I look down at my hands and feel the heat of oncoming tears sting my eyes. "Andrew's going to kill me for doing this."

"Well, the trip over here, the splurging..." She motions in the general direction of the Seine. "It's all water under Pont Neuf."

I give a short, loud shot of laughter. "You sure are cheesy, Sophie."

"That's why you love me."

"That and because of how awesome a friend you are to show me the best damn vacation of my life!" I wipe at my stinging eyes with the back of my hand.

"Minus the minor disaster at Eres," she points out with a twisted mouth.

"Yeah. *Faux pas*, guess you'd call it?"

"Major *faux pas*, hon." She claps my lap and leaps up. "Come on. It's your last night here, and I know you're not exactly looking forward to explaining yourself to Andrew tomorrow."

I groan, rubbing harder at my eyes.

"Come." She holds out her hand and wiggles her fingers. "Let's get dolled up and go out. It's our last night on the town and we are going to make a night of it."

30

I pull out my nearly empty pack of Parliaments and slap out a slim, refreshing cigarette. I haven't been on the ground at Sea-Tac Airport an hour yet, and I'm already sweating bullets—craving that sweet and calming nicotine fix—as I think about going home to Andrew.

Sophie was right; I was off my rocker for fleeing town unannounced. It isn't until now, after the fact of Paris, that I see where Emily was going with the whole "harm afterwards" thing. Andrew's just going to be livid the moment he sees me. He's going to be furious that I flew off and spent all this money.

I glance down at my collection of Louis Vuitton luggage and can't help but let a grin and small chuckle slip out. I did some serious retail damage on the Champs-Élysées and up and down the Triangle d'Or. The gift-giving Andrew would be proud; the I-want-my-wife-controlled-and-on-the-mantel Andrew will, well... I don't know what he'll do or think.

As the cab driver races into Downtown and approaches home, I muster up all the courage I can find. *Easier to ask for forgiveness than permission,* I repeat in my head.

I trail the doorman carrying my luggage, thinking that the length of the twelfth-floor hallway has doubled since I was last here. I catch myself keeping beat with my mental blabbering of *Easier to ask for forgiveness*— Step, step, step. *Than for permission*—Step, step, step. *Easier to*—

"Ma'am?" the doorman says.

I look up and stop abruptly in my tracks.

He's standing at my front door, hands folded behind him, and he's giving me an unreadable expression.

"Oh," I say with a shake of my head. "We're here."

"I hope you enjoyed your trip," he says. "Welcome home." Then he stalks off.

"Yeah," I huskily breathe out to myself. "Wish it could've lasted a lifetime."

I root about in my deep Neverfull handbag, searching for my keys. *Forgiveness, permission,* I think. I take my keys in a nearly sweating palm. *Forgiveness, permi*—

Then I come to. Why the hell should I be asking for forgiveness? Okay, okay, so I did do a bit of lying. I already got a ribbing from Sophie for that. But why should I, a grown woman, feel guilty and like I need to beg for forgiveness like a child?

This is ridiculous. Just suck it up, girl!

And without a further thought I open the front door and charge right in, forgetting all about my luggage.

"Andrew?" I call out in a cautious voice—small and innocent-sounding. "Darling? Are you home yet?"

It's Friday, approaching seven o'clock in the evening. It's really anyone's guess if he's home or not.

"Andrew?" I swallow and nervously reach my hand towards the small table where we usually deposit our keys upon arrival. "I'm home," I sing. "And—"

"Hello, Jackie." The voice is deep, commanding.

I drop my keys in surprise, and they miss the table, landing with a sharp clang against the marble floor.

"Andrew," I whisper. I look into his eyes—his empty blue eyes—

and I force out a smile. "I'm home." I attempt the same singsong voice, but this time it comes out wavering and off-pitch.

He's got both hands in his black suit pants pockets. He's still wearing his dress shirt and jacket, but his tie has been loosened. He pads forward a couple steps on bare feet. "Wherever have you been?"

Seriously? Does he not know? Or is he playing games?

"Oh!" He scratches slowly and dramatically at his five-o'clock-shadowed chin. "Why, yes! A little bird told me."

"A little bird?" I laugh in trepidation.

"Yes." His voice is eerily calm. He takes two steps closer, then halts. "A little bird. A little bird from very far away." His hand returns to his pocket, and he lifts his head higher. "And do you know what I thought when this little bird told me where you've been?"

I bite the tip of my tongue and lock my jaw. I refuse to respond, actually a tiny bit fearful of what will come next. Andrew's so stone-cold right now, his eyes conveying absolutely nothing, his words and tone biting like a venomous snake.

"I thought," he scratches his chin again and looks off to the side, "my wife—whom I *love* more than *anything*," his voice deepens angrily, "has run off to Paris like a spoiled princess and didn't even have the decency to consider asking, much less *telling* me of her plans."

He locks eyes with mine, and now I can see the rage, the disappointment, the frustration brewing within.

"Jackie." His tone makes a swift turn to cool lane, yet again. "I don't ask much of you. I give you the world. I don't even have a problem with the tens of thousands you've gone and spent." He scratches at the back of his head and approaches me slowly, steadily.

I can't think fast or straight enough, so all I do is stand still, eyes still on his.

"I love you, Jackie. I love you more than I think you will ever know." He sighs, looks off to the side a minute, scratches his head once more. "But there comes a time when a man simply cannot stay standing in a burning building."

I feel my brow wrinkle against my will. I'm trying so hard to stand stoic and silent.

He holds both hands up in impasse and looks back into my eyes. "I give up. I can't do this anymore."

There's a long, stuffy silence for a while. I don't know if I should break it or if Andrew will...or if maybe he'll break it with something other than words.

Then, he says, "Your bags are already packed; judging by the credit card activity you have more than enough to keep yourself on your feet, at least until you find yourself a job; and—and..." He shrugs and looks down at the ground, rubbing at the nape of his neck.

"Andrew," I whimper, hot tears suddenly streaming down my cheeks.

He doesn't look up. All he says in response is, "I need you to go, Jackie." His tone has raised an unsettled octave. I don't need to see his face, his eyes, to know he's crying. To know that I've pushed him over the emotional edge.

"But Andrew!" I cry. "You can't be serious!" I swallow fast, hard. "It was only Paris! A four-day trip! It's *nothing* compared to how often you leave me!"

He meets my eyes—they're glassy and red—and he says, "That's business! What you've done, Jackie." He clenches a fist so tightly his knuckles turn white. "What you've done is selfish, deceitful, and hurtful. It wasn't until I tracked down your card activity that I was able to find you. You had me worried sick." His fist releases, and he looks back down at the ground. "I love you so much. I am just so hurt that this is how you repay me."

"Repay you?" I blurt out loudly. "*You* love *me* so much? Some love you showed, Andrew, cutting me off from all my cards while I was over there!"

"I knew you were with a friend there. You weren't completely without."

"Oh, thanks!" I toss up my hands and take a sharp step forward.

"No." Andrew's hand reaches forward and grips me by the wrist.

"Ow! You're hurting me." I wince and look from my wrist to Andrew, then back and up again, insisting that he let go.

He weakens the grip, but he won't let go. "No. I said I've had enough. No more."

"What?" I shake my head briskly. "What the hell are you talking about?"

"You can't stay here, Jackie." He's so cool I want to scream, shove him, throw something!

"Like hell I can't!" I wail.

"Jackie." His voice is so calm it's spooky. With a ginger shove, holding onto my wrist, he moves me back a pace. "No. I just can't be with you right now."

"Over Paris?" I'm gobsmacked. He can't be serious.

"It's the trip, the secrecy, the immaturity, the lack of consideration, the tension whenever we're together."

"And *I'm* solely to blame for this?" I'm livid. This is preposterous!

"I'm at the end of my rope, babe." He makes a stiff upper lip. "I'm at the end of my rope. You say me buying your love won't work, yet you go out and spend a small fortune. I just don't understand."

"Fine!" I scream, yanking free from his grip. "You know, this is *so* typical! Wife goes away and does one little thing for herself—probably giving you quite the opportunity to shack up with your floozy of a secretary—and then I get the brunt of the anger, the frustration." I point a finger at him. "The hurt pride!"

"Leave now, Jackie," he growls. "I don't want to fight."

"Fight," I spit. "Fight! You don't want to *fight*? You kick me out of my home and you don't want to *fight*?" I shove him hard in his chest. "Well then fuck you, Andrew!"

Just then a high-pitched bark sounds from the living room, and I peer over his shoulder.

"Bella," I say. "She's *my* dog."

Andrew steps around the sofa, rifles about, then returns with Bella in her dog carrier and a tote full of her belongings, including her large, sleeping pillow. "Here," he says. "She's all ready to go."

"I can't believe this!"

He pulls open the front door and sets Bella and her things down beside my pile of luggage. "I'm sorry we have to do this, Jackie."

"What? That's it?" My mouth hangs open in sheer disbelief.

He doesn't respond. He just slips one hand in his pocket loosely, the other resting on the doorknob, and a very small teardrop is nestled in the corner of his left eye.

"Andrew." My lips are quivering. "Please." The tears course down my cheeks rapidly. "Please. Can't we talk? I'm sorry! Please."

He shakes his head slowly, then slips a hand behind my head. His lips press hotly and deeply against my forehead, and he whispers, "I'm sorry, Jackie. I can't."

"Andrew!" I shriek. "Andrew!" I stomp my feet.

He opens the door wider.

"Andrew!" I give as forceful a shove as I can at his chest, and to my surprise he doesn't fight back. He just stands there, saying, "I can't," over and over.

I rush over the threshold and angrily gather my bags. "Fine!" I scream in rage. "Fine! I should have known I married an asshole!" I heave Bella's carrier high up onto my shoulder. "If you're going to act like this, then I want a divorce!"

"You'll hear from my attorney, then," he says resolutely.

And with a slow close of the door, my husband puts the final nail in the coffin that is our marriage. No amount of my screaming, my angry words, the pain and suffering behind my cries force him to reopen that door, take me in his arms, and weep with me. And so I gather my last shred of strength and walk away.

31

I t's been two days and two nights. Two long days and two harrowing nights since *the Incident*. The Incident that surpasses all other fights. I've barely been able to get out of bed, my mind's so wrought and heart so heavy as the horrible words Andrew and I said to each other repeat themselves in a roaring monotony. I have no appetite, the foul taste of our goodbye is so unrelenting. I'm afraid to face the day. Afraid of what today will bring. Afraid of what tomorrow won't.

Heartbroken and lost, I turned to Emily. When she laid eyes on me at her doorstep—luggage, dog, and all—she not only didn't expect me to deliver the news that I'd been kicked to the curb, but she wasn't exactly too pleased with my random and ill-planned trip to Paris. She said she was disappointed in my choices and didn't appreciate my lies and wished I'd been honest with her—she would have listened, encouraged, and imparted some advice, whether or not she could have understood my situation.

Then, after I begged apologies, she just smiled, gave me a hug, and said in her usual welcoming way that her home is always my home. She'd help me out as best she could.

As evening number three descends upon the cramped one-bed,

one-bath Fremont apartment, Emily drags me out of her sofa bed and shoves me into the shower. I'm not kicking and screaming, but I am dragging my feet.

She insists I go out for dinner with her and Gatz tonight. "One of the last times before our big Aussie trip," she says. "And I leave for Boston the day after tomorrow, anyhow. Time is of the essence."

She turns on the shower. "Come on," she urges. "We won't go anywhere fancy, so you don't have to feel like you need to get dolled up. Quick rinse and let's go." She glances around the corner. "Although with all the loot you brought back it sure seems like you *can* really doll yourself up." She snickers playfully, then tugs at the hem of my oversized DeeGee Philanthropy Week t-shirt from sophomore year that I've been wearing for at least forty-eight hours. "My treat, let's go!"

Reluctantly, I raise my hands and she begins to pull the shirt over my head. With a face full of t-shirt, I loosely say, "It *has* to be your treat. I'm dead-ass broke, yet again. Surprise, surprise." Just when I thought marriage to a wealthy man would seal the deal on financial trouble, think again.

"Oh, hush," Emily says, tossing the shirt into the clothes hamper. "Come on. Scoot, scoot into the shower. No one likes a stinky girl. And we're wasting precious water."

"But if it's not a place to get dressed up for," I say as I lazily yank off my panties, "then why bother getting showered?" I wrinkle my nose, chagrined.

"I'll give you two reasons, but one's enough." She spins around and begins to shuffle things about her cupboards. "One, we've got an early day at the café tomorrow, which means it'll be tough enough to get your ass up and out of bed, much less shower. And two—"

"Wait!" I say as I finish unclasping my bra. "*I'm* going to the café?" My facial expression is now more lively, surprise written all over it. "With you? You're working and *I'm* going along?"

"That's right." She turns back around, a fresh, rolled bath towel in her hands.

"But I feel so sick, so sad."

"All the more reason for you to get your ass up and out of bed—to shower," she points the rolled towel in my direction, moving it up and down, "and pick yourself up."

"Three days hardly constitutes appropriate grieving length for a marriage that's gone down the tubes. I'm in mourning."

"Piece by piece," she says, ever so joyful.

"I can't just forget about what happened. Just—just—pick up the pieces—piece by piece..." This part I say in a mocking tone, "And move on."

"I'm not saying 'move on.' I'm saying take care of yourself as you work through this. Besides, I really think Andrew just needs some time to cool off. He doesn't seem like the kind of man who just up and calls it quits."

"It's been rough, *really* rough, for a long time, Em. I wouldn't put it past him."

"I bet anything, before you know it, you'll be back home and working through this for real." She shakes out the towel and drapes it over the empty towel rack. "I really can't believe your days as Mrs. Andrew Kittredge are completely over. I like to be a realist, but also an optimist. Don't wave your white flag just yet." She holds up a finger and blurts out, "Erm, white flag as in you come in peace and want to talk, yes, not conceding defeat."

"Emily, you didn't see Andrew that night. You didn't see the calm rage in those eyes. You didn't hear the finality in his words. You didn't feel the cold in the room..."

"Come on," she nods her head towards the running shower. "One day at a time. And tonight we're getting you out of that bed and out of this apartment." She roughly pulls the shower curtain open and gestures with a nod for me to get inside. "Dinner tonight, work tomorrow."

"Are you serious?"

She fixes me with a sobering gaze, then makes a clicking sound and thumbs at the shower. "Dead serious. I'm not leaving you here alone anymore to rot away and stew in your misery. Now move it."

"Fine." I step into the shower and begin to adjust the dials—

steaming hot, the only way to take a shower.

"Good girl."

I briskly peek my head around the curtain and say, "And for your information, I'm perfectly capable of being here by myself, thank you very much."

"This is no time to leave you unsupervised days on end," she says from the doorway. "You like to get yourself into trouble. What kind of friend would I be if I let you go down a destructive path, huh?"

"Oh, Em," I groan, pulling the curtain closed and stepping fully under the shower of hot water.

"Come on. Make it quick. Gatz and I are starving, and since you look like a Twizzler, I'm guessing you're starving, too."

"Wait!" I shout, spluttering out the water that's dripped down into my mouth.

Emily peeks her head around the curtain. "Yes, my dear?"

"What's the second reason?"

She looks confused.

"The second reason you feel the need to drag me into this shower?"

She makes an *aha* expression, and before dashing out of the bathroom says with a grin, "You stink."

"I'm here," I say in between slurps of the orange juice Emily poured for me. "Can you believe it? Up at the butt crack of dawn? In my condition? Drinking what *so* should be a mimosa." I kick my legs like a child would as they dangle from the high barstool in the kitchen of The Cup and the Cake and take another noisy sip.

"Honestly?" Sophie says. She twists her hair into a bun. "Yes. And good for Em for doing it."

"You're not still mad at me, are you, Sophie?"

I only talked to Sophie once, on the phone, since she got back from Paris the day after me. We apologized to each other—again—and insisted it was water under the bridge. She reiterated that she wasn't happy about what I'd done, nor how things turned out with Andrew, but that best friends with strong ties and long histories shouldn't let things tear them apart. "We've been through a lot over the years," she told me. "Friends don't give up on each other when the going gets tough."

I still feel guilty for lying about how I got to Paris; I hate that I deceived my friends. I've been feeling so lost lately, what with all of this Andrew stuff; I just don't know who I am or where I'm going or even what I want.

"No, Jackie," Sophie says with a quick flash of a grin. "Of course I'm not still mad at you. But I do think that you're in a fragile state right now, and getting some fresh air could do you some good. Emily's right; it's time to get out of your box." She pads hurriedly across the café's kitchen floor. "And when you're finished with your breakfast, maybe you can lend a hand?" Another quick grin, this one more insisting than courteous.

I let go of my straw and give Sophie a blank look.

"What?" she says as she pulls free some clean dishes from a cupboard. "Gatz has to leave early to close the deal on the sale of his car. I need the extra help."

"But—but—you mean, like...work here? I can't do anything," I splutter. "I'm really useless, horrible at jobs. You know that, Sophie."

"You're a decent dish-dryer! Look, I'll take your uselessness and make the most of it. It'll be good for both of us."

"Sophieeee."

"You can wash pans, fold napkins, sweep. Something simple."

"Can't you just make that new girl work more hours?"

"Evelyn?" Sophie kicks the cupboard closed with her heel.

"Or Chad. He can come over after work. Force some labor out of him." I giggle petulantly.

"Chad?" She sets the heavy stack of plates down on the counter and presses her lips tightly together. "Chad won't be working here anymore."

"Whoa. Why not?" I slurp at my juice. "This isn't exactly the time to be getting rid of staff, is it?"

"Jackie."

"And you're sure not considering hiring me on, because if you are—"

"Jackie."

I stop my slurping and raise my brows. "Hmm?"

"Chad's behavior is entirely inappropriate."

"Well Chad was *born* inappropriate," I say through a laugh. "I mean, it's *Chad.*" Greasy-haired, tattooed, rebellious, wannabe artist who's still, at twenty-seven, a frat boy at heart, enjoying the parties, girls, naughty jokes, and beer pong matches.

"That's not what I'm talking about." Sophie begins to pull handfuls of flatware from drawers. "He's a nice guy, and what he's done to help me out around here is really—is really—" She sets the forks down onto the counter with a clang. "He's been great. Annoying at times, as always, but great." She hurriedly tightens her bun, then scurries over to retrieve more flatware. "But I can't have him work here anymore."

"Hey, Sophie?" Gatz interrupts, his head popping around the corner. "Evelyn's here now. You want her working up front or helping back here?"

Sophie's shoulders heave upwards then down low as she exhales loudly. "Have her work up front until you're done cleaning the espresso machine, please."

"Got it!" Gatz slaps the wall twice before disappearing.

I drain the small remainder of orange juice. "So." I lean forward and poke Sophie in the arm. "What's up with the drams?"

She rolls her eyes. "It's Evelyn."

"Evelyn now? Sheesh. Is anyone good enough to work in your café?"

She gives me a stony look. "Emily and Gatz are wonderful workers," she says simply. She pokes me in the ribs and I let out a small yelp. "And I'm sure you would be, too, if you actually lifted a finger." She motions to the stack of pink napkins. "Here, help me roll these. Please." She taps at the pile of spoons.

"Fine," I say, picking up a napkin. "And the drams?"

She shakes her hands wildly and says in a flurry, "Chad and Evelyn are sleeping together."

"No!"

"Yes."

"Like, sleeping-sleeping? Or a one-night thing?"

Sophie groans loudly. "Ew, please. Gross! Don't paint a picture."

"How do you know this?"

"Emily. She told me Chad made it quite clear that he and Evelyn are an—an—" She crinkles her nose and makes a sick face.

"What?" I press.

"An item. They hooked up one night and now they're an item."

"We talking relationship?"

"I don't know!" She sends a napkin flying into the air and stomps back to the flatware drawer. "Emily just said it happened while I was in Paris, one thing led to another, and apparently they're an item. Chad and Evelyn. Evelyn and Chad. Eee. It's so weird."

"And this is a problem because..."

"Because they're employees! They shouldn't be sleeping together!"

I laugh loudly and toss aside the napkin. "Hello? Earth to Sophie. Are you *not* aware that Em and Gatz work together? That they're in L-O-V-E love?" I make kissing noises.

"That's different." She shuts the drawer with a swing of her hip. "Gatz is a good guy."

"I thought a second ago Chad was a good guy. A *nice* guy. He works here for free. I wouldn't even work here for money." I walk over to the nearby counter and jump up onto it. "No offense."

"It's not the same," she huffs. "And do you know what this means? Why I'm pissed?"

I lean over, neglecting my napkin-rolling duties, and pull from my bag the Parisian copy of *Vogue* I grabbed at Charles de Gaulle right before my return flight home. "Why? Why is Sophie Wharton pissed?"

"Because this is so typical Chad. He'll sleep with her, charm her, use her, and then he'll break her heart. Then *I'll* be left with two angry employees, and they'll both threaten to quit because they can't work together. Might us well cut off the weak duckling right away. Chad's got to go. Period."

"Sophie—"

"No." She's positively adamant, borderline livid. "I can't lose Evelyn. She's awesome around here and really getting the hang of things. Chad's expendable and he'll only cause trouble. He'll be all kissy-kissy around her and distract her and—no! I can't have it."

"Well, you're the boss." I casually flip past pages of gorgeous shoes and stunning gowns, all items I'll probably never be able to buy again.

"And the weirdest part..." Sophie prattles on. "Aside from the *whole thing* being frickin' weird. Sick."

"Mmmhmm?" I flip past more lovely pages, past words upon words I can't understand, aside from the occasional *"chic," "couture,"* and *"magnifique."*

"The weirdest part," Sophie says, "is when Emily told me about their little shack-up-affair. She was all hesitant and kind of weird about it."

"Probably because she knew you'd get in a tizzy over it. Firing the poor loser."

"Well, whatever. I'm letting Chad go. It's for the best."

I open my mouth, about to say something in jest—some snide remark about Chad, some joke about how he's dating Evelyn—when Sophie's words hit home. *I'm letting Chad go. It's for the best.*

"Come on," she says, gesturing to the napkins and flatware. "I could really use the help."

"Yeah." I set down my magazine, my eyes grazing past a gorgeous rose gold and peach champagne sapphire ring. "So could I," I'm about to mutter, but decide against it as I watch Sophie methodically and almost meditatively roll the flatware into neat little pink rolls, as if she's trying to package her anger and frustration and do just about anything to keep her mind off her troubles. I decide to try to do the same, but the emptiness that fills my heart, my gut, grows with each attempt at letting go.

32

"This is it!" Robin says with round, hazel eyes. "This is the moment you've been looking forward to for a *long* time, and the moment we've all been dreading."

"Ohhh," Emily whines, pouting with a thick lower lip. "Are you going to get all mushy on me?"

"Well," Robin shifts in her seat on Emily's luxurious sofa that's been my bed for going on two weeks now, "we all know how much you deserve this and want this...and need this. Of course we're happy for you, Emily, but I know I'm not alone in saying that I'm going to miss you like *crazy*."

Emily criss-crosses her legs and lays the flimsy folds of her tan cotton skirt over her knees. "At least it's not like Africa," she says optimistically. "I'm not going to the third world this time. Gatz and I will have our computers, we'll have internet, we can talk and Skype."

"Not all the time," Lara says pragmatically. "You two will be so busy, studying, volunteering, traveling, chasing wild dingos or something. Not to mention the time difference!"

We laugh and Emily says, "You're probably right. We are going to get to do some awesome backpacking around the country, and New

Zealand, too, before his classes start." She gets a dreamy look about her.

I know Emily intends to keep in touch, and she means well. It's not like she wants to run away and avoid us. Usually she's in such a remote part of the world that she finds it next to impossible to find a way to contact us. That's fine, I get it. But when her wanderlust calls, she answers, and if that means forgetting about that promised phone call or a very delayed email, so be it.

"I'll definitely try to do a better job at keeping in contact," Emily says determinedly. "Jack's going to be living at my place full time for a while." She pats my knee and gives me a smile. "At least until she and Andrew are back together. I'll have to check in to make sure this place hasn't gone up in flames."

"Oh, thank you," I say.

Emily claps my knee a few playful times. "I'm kidding."

"So how is the progress with that, Jack?" Claire asks. She hugs her knees into her chest and rocks on her position on the floor. She's still dressed in her scrubs, wearing no makeup and looking a bit tired and run down. She's still putting in heinous hours at the hospital and making extra patient rounds and house calls, Conner's career situation growing more precarious by the day.

Sophie told me the other day when I was at the café that Conner's already written up his two-week notice and is just waiting for the right time (and the nerve) to deliver it. Still no replacement job in sight, so it's obvious why he's been hesitant. But apparently his boss is throwing the crappy and small-time projects his way, paying all the attention and giving great, undeserved praise to the new outside hire. Conner used to be respected, but now it's as if he's old hat. I feel his pain. I still think Andrew's been quick to do away with me because he's ready to take that next step with Nikki.

"Jackie?" Claire asks, rubbing the corner of one sleepy eye. "How are things with Andrew going?"

Emily's hand instinctively goes out to my knee, and she begins to rub it.

"It's—" I start, but I don't know how to end. "It's—It's—" I look to Emily and give her a questioning glance.

"It's still...complicated?" Emily finishes for me, slowly.

Claire nods in understanding, or perhaps sympathy.

"You just need some time," Lara says. Her tone sounds assured.

"Yeah," Sophie pipes in. "I don't believe in much, but I do believe that time is the great healer of all wounds and suffering."

"Yup," Robin says. "You're still seeing Dr. Pierce, right?" She quickly checks her cell phone—something she does all the time when both children are not by her side.

I sniff and say, "For now. Who knows when Andrew will yank that rug from under me?"

"What do you mean?" Claire makes a puzzled face.

"Well," I sigh, "aside from my car and the clothes on my back, in my bags, and Bella, I don't really have anything anymore. My therapy sessions are on auto-bill, auto-pay and I just show up according to schedule, or sometimes last minute, thrown-in sessions... I never bother with payment. Andrew has all that taken care of."

"So you think he'd really cut you off like that?" Claire asks in a bothered tone. "I mean, that's like medication! You can't just take a patient off of their meds—you can't stop therapy cold turkey like that!"

"That'd be a jackass move," Sophie says sharply. "If he did that, Jack..."

"*I'd* key the douche's car," Lara says.

"See?" I say with a sly grin. "There's always a time and a place for keying cars, slashing tires..."

"You slashed Nathan's tires, too?" Robin gasps.

"No," I say. "Although if I'd had more time..." I glance to my right at Emily. "If I hadn't been coerced into *not* doling out justice, then I think that would've been the icing on the cake."

"Didn't you slash an ex's tires in college or something?" Claire says. She squints, trying to recall the memory I (and Lara) know all too well.

255

"Not exactly. My junior year..." Lara says with a roll of the eyes. "But thank god it wasn't slashing tires—"

"Or keying," Emily interrupts.

"It wasn't *that* bad, girls," I say in a brushed-off kind of way.

"It was *two* dates," Lara says. "I went on *two* dates with the guy and he stood me up on the third. Not quite an ex-boyfriend and certainly not a reason to go and paint his car windows with profanity."

"Profanity, proshmanity," I say.

"Spray-painting?" Robin says, agog. "You spray-painted his car?"

"Shoe polish," I correct. "That was before I learned how to *really* get revenge." I casually shrug. "That jerk hurt my friend's feelings, and he deserved to feel hurt, too! Besides, I also did the girls on campus a favor. Rumor had it on sorority row he wasn't packing much south of the border, so..."

"Oh, Jackie," Lara huffs. "Teensy-weensy or Guinness World Record-holder, you're crazy. He so didn't deserve that. Again, your heart is in the right place, your head not so much."

"Hey, you can't deny that you feel a *little* bit good about what I did to Nathan, though. Right?"

"I don't condone it, but...yes," Lara says with a weak smile, "I do feel good that saga's behind me."

"Exactly! *So* glad that asshole's done with," Claire says with a dusting of the hands for dramatic emphasis.

"Yeah. Lara's moving on to bigger and better fish to fry," I say.

"Mr. Sexy Businessman," Sophie sings.

"Worth," Robin says with a wink. "Worth is worth it, eh?"

Lara gives a disbelieving look to Robin. "You're a dork, but yes. Worth and I are doing great, dating a lot. Well, when our busy work schedules allow." We all nod in understanding. "But it's kind of refreshing to date someone who's in the same career boat—two nerdy MBAs who understand each other." She bashfully shakes her head. "We both work for demanding firms, have similar schedules, are dedicated to our careers. It's a good match, Worth and I, and of course there's a whole lot more we have in common." She smiles tightly. "I'm really happy with him and how things are going. He's so mature and driven and intelligent..."

"She's smitten," Claire says with a giggle.

"I hope it works out for you," Robin says. "Worth sounds fabulous, and I haven't seen you so happy in a long while."

"Yeah," Emily says. "When you were with Nathan those last few months..." She makes a sour face.

"Not happy," I finish for her.

"Definitely not as happy as you *should* be," Claire says. "Conner and I may have ten years on our relationship, and sometimes things can get routine and humdrum." She pushes behind her ear a thick blonde curl that's escaped from her ponytail. "But we make each other happy. The love is there, so the happiness, the contentment is there."

"Absolutely," Robin says. "A relationship like Claire's and Conner's, or mine and Bobby's... It's not really a gooey, butterflies-in-the-stomach-twenty-four-seven kind of thing like at the beginning." Claire nods, and Robin can't fight her smile, obviously thinking back on those first dates with Bobby. "But it's still love. The sparks are still there, they're just...different, I guess. *Good*, but different."

"That's how it is with Worth now," Lara says. "The gooey, sappy feeling, like at the beginning of good relationships." The balls of her cheeks begin to flush, but only very discreetly. "I just hope those magical sparks can evolve into something more." She looks down at her lap, and her voice drops an octave. "I'm ready for a lasting relationship, girls. Ready for that something more. I'm *always* on the unlucky side of love, I swear." She looks up and leans back into her seat with a sigh.

"But you can have that gooey feeling still," I say, feeling my upper lip curl just slightly. "I mean, come on girls. You're telling me you just *settle* for the end of the fun and the thrill and the *excitement*? The sparks?"

"It's not settling," Robin says insistently.

"That's what it sounds like to me."

"No," Emily says. "It's new love turning into..." She taps her chin thoughtfully. "I guess forever love. Sounds cheesy, huh?"

"Not everyday's a honeymoon," Robin says, "but that doesn't mean you love each other any less. In fact, I think it might even mean you love each other more."

"If you're expecting fireworks in your relationship every day of your life, then, well..." Emily says, and frowns a little. "I think you're setting yourself up for failure and disappointment. Life's what you make of it, and so is love, relationships. Hell, make fireworks every day, in any way, but don't expect to be riding Cloud Nine all the time."

In an unaware way Emily plays with her thick collection of bracelets and cuffs, and her eyes are searching the room as she speaks. "I mean, if we were *always* happy, then happiness wouldn't really exist, you know?" Her brow furrows slightly. "Or at the very least it wouldn't be anything special. It'd be that constant emotion, with nothing to contrast it, and if that was all we felt, we'd never really know what happiness felt like." She looks me in the eyes, imploringly. "You know?"

"Because there isn't any juxtaposition," Lara adds in.

"Exactly!" Emily snaps her fingers. "And happiness is just a state of mind, after all. There's so much more to life and love than selfish, personal happiness."

"Totally," Robin says. "Don't get me wrong, being happy in love is great, but there's more to it."

"Yeah, yeah," I say, suddenly overwhelmed with the walk down Philosophical Lane. Really, can't a girl just be honest and bitch about her relationship with her husband? Can't she say she wants to chase that excitement and passion, and that's how she wants to live her life? What's so wrong with that?

"I know I'm going to be far away," Emily says later that night after all the girls have gone home. Having a last get-together before Emily and Gatz leave for Australia tomorrow was as bittersweet a moment as they come. "I know I'm going to be busy and chatting won't be as easy as it is now."

I spread out the fleece blanket I've been using during the warm summer evenings onto the sofa-turned-bed. "I know," I say.

"But that doesn't mean I don't care about you, Jackie. I'm torn leaving right now, you know?"

I fluff my pillow and toss it at the head of the sofa as Emily tosses the second one—the "Andrew body" I've come to call it.

"I'm excited about my trip," she says, "and getting to travel with Gatz. It's a total dream. I'm looking forward to getting to do some volunteer work for the blind...and getting to help those troubled teens in the after-school program and... Oh, it's going to be amazing!" She looks completely smitten.

"But," she says as she sets down my "Andrew body pillow." "I'd be lying if I said I wasn't worried about you, Jackie." She takes a seat on the edge of the sofa. "I'm leaving at a vulnerable time for you right now, and I'm not happy about that. I have the confidence you'll pull through, but it doesn't erase the worry."

"I've been in worse ruts," I say encouragingly, also taking a seat.

"But not with Andrew."

"Yes, not with Andrew. You're right."

"Promise me you'll take care of yourself."

I chuckle quietly. "It's me, myself, and I with me, Em. I'll take care of myself."

She shrugs one arm, her head cocking to the side in agreement.

"I'll be fine," I insist. "I'll get through this. I don't know how, but somehow I'll manage."

"Call the girls, Dr. Pierce, me, email me, even call Andrew!"

I laugh loudly.

"I'm serious," she says. "You contact whoever you need to if you're in a really low place, okay? I probably won't be able to be in touch as often as I'd like, but there are plenty of people here for you. Okay?"

"Okay." I lie down on my side, propping my head under one hand.

"And do me a favor."

"Hmm?"

"Get out and do some good."

"Do some good? You mean feed starving orphans or something?"

She sniffles a laugh. "Do some good for you, for others... If you do good for others you're automatically doing a bit of good for yourself. It can make you feel really positive."

"Yeah, yeah, I've heard that before."

"But most importantly I want you to take care of yourself." She touches my bare shoulder. "I don't mean going to clubs and hitting the bottle and living up the single life. You're not exactly a single woman."

"Yeah, yeah."

"Have some fun, yes, but take care of yourself. Do something *real* for yourself. For your life. This mess with Andrew could be the single greatest thing to happen to you."

"Ha!" I throw my head down onto the pillow. "What sauce are you sipping, sister? Have you *looked* at my situation?" I shoot my head back up. "Have you taken a look at how screwed up my life and marriage are?"

"So your marriage is really on the rocks right now—"

"San Andreas Fault, is more like it!"

"Life isn't so bad, Jack." Her tone is stern. "Things are rough, yes, and I worry about you, yes, but you have a great group of friends. You have a therapist trying to help you. You *are* a strong person, deep down. You have youth, you have *life!*" She waves a hand about. "Life is the greatest gift we're all given."

"Here comes the hocus-pocus."

"Listen to me. Life is a gift. Don't squander it. It's short, gone in a flash. What's done is done."

"*That's* what I'm talking about!" I shriek, pulling myself up into a seated position. "Excitement! Thrills! Passion! *Fun!* Life is too short not to have fireworks in love!"

Emily sighs heavily. "Jackie, you're a handful, babe. A total handful."

"But I'm right." I cross my arms over my chest pridefully.

"I think it's time for bed." She looks at her bright yellow sports watch. "Gatz and I have a big day tomorrow, and I'm exhausted." She pulls herself up, flips off the radio, and saunters towards the bedroom where the low snores of Gatz can be heard, even through the slight cracks in the door.

"Emily," I quickly call out, whipping my head around to her.

"Yes?"

"Thank you."

"Oh, any time." She casually flicks her wrist. "*Mi casa es tu casa.*"

"No, not that."

"Huh?"

"Well, yes that. But, no." I pull myself up onto my knees and grip the side of the sofa with both hands. "Thank you for the talk, the encouragement. You're a wise girl. I'd be a fool to ignore you."

"Oh, Jack," she says in a gentle tone. "Wisdom comes with age and experience. I've got some experience, but at twenty-eight I'd hardly say I'm wise."

"I appreciate it, just the same. I don't know what I'd do without you."

"I love you." She tucks a thin braid behind her ear. "You get some sleep. I'll see you in the morning."

"Love you, too, Em." I slink back into the sofa, smoothing the black armrest meditatively.

As Emily disappears into the darkness of her bedroom, I continue to rub my fingers along the fine fabric of the bed. My mind wanders to those dangerous places it likes to wander, usually at solo times like these, late at night. I remember how painful the words were that Andrew said to me during *the Incident*. I think about how I miss him, despite the abruptness with which he kicked me out, shutting the door on everything that we had. I wonder when we'll see each other again—*if* we'll see each other again.

Then, as is always the case, when I bite down on my bottom,

quivering lip and consider the turning of these dreadful tables, I feel the familiar hot tears sting my eyes, run down my cheeks, and wet my pillow.

Sophie says time will heal, Emily tells me to be patient, Lara says it will get better... My best friends tell me I'll be all right, but why is it so hard to believe them? How can things get better when, as each trying day passes and each teary night keeps me awake, they seem to be getting worse?

33

D r. Pierce clicks his pen and scrawls something down in his leather bound notebook. He clears his throat aggressively a few times, then in his calm tone and even demeanor, says, "Three weeks it's been, correct?"

"Yup." I turn the ringer off of my cell phone and toss it limply into the new salmon-colored bohemian bag I got in the upper Marais in Paris—NoMa, as Sophie called it. "Three long weeks since I last saw or talked to my husband." I cross my legs. "Pathetic, huh?"

"No contact whatsoever?" Dr. Pierce looks up from his notebook for a moment. "Have you called him? Has he called you? An exchange of emails? Message passed through a mutual friend?"

"Ha!" I robustly shake my foot, clad in the new Lanvin ballet flat I scooped up in Paris. "Mutual friends? I don't think so. I've got my friends, and Andrew's got his business. His," I make a snooty face, "colleagues." I give an affected smile. "Although, he does have his stupid secretary. I'm sure they're able to have their torrid love affair now that Andrew's given me the boot."

"Jackie," Dr. Pierce says, his voice strong, demanding my attention, "we've been over this. It is unhealthy for you to continue to make assumptions that your husband is having an affair. A friend of yours said there was nothing between them." He looks down at his notebook and scratches the back of his ear in an unsettling way. "Not that I necessarily condone that kind of behavior—spying." He clears his throat loudly.

"But you have no evidence that this is the case—that they're having an affair," he presses on. "Do not borrow trouble, Jackie. This behavior will not help you." We lock eyes. "At all."

"I know," I say reluctantly. "My imagination goes wild now that I'm home alone, nothing to do."

"Staying at a friend's still?"

"Indefinitely, maybe." I uncross my legs, adjust my miniskirt, then cross my legs in the other direction. "Emily's out of town for the rest of the year, maybe two semesters. Who knows?" I breathe a hefty sigh. "But I get bored all the time, and my mind will concoct crazy scenarios." I rest my upper body weight on my elbows, resting on my knees, and I say in a low tone, "Like maybe Nikki's living with Andrew now. Moving all my stuff out, replacing me..."

"See, that's dangerous behavior." Dr. Pierce writes something down in his notebook. "You should be taking healing steps—steps to repair your relationship."

"What do you suggest I do?"

"You know I'm not here to tell you what to do."

"Ugh! Right! This again." I lift off of my knees and slam my back into the plush chaise. "Well, give me some therapeutic tips or something. Suggestions!"

He closes his notebook, pen in between the pages, and sets it aside. He makes a loud clap with his hands, rubs them together, and says in an energetic vein, "You're going to take your friend Emily's advice. Do something good. Something for yourself, yes, but not something—something—some—"

"I get it," I say sarcastically. "Not something selfish. Something good for me, but mainly good for someone else. So what do you suggest I do?"

"There are many things you can do to help you over this hurdle."

"Like a lobotomy." I chuckle at my attempt at levity.

"I stopped offering those services two years ago."

I slowly pull myself up out of my slumped position, not really sure if I heard the doctor correctly, when his mouth turns up into a wide grin.

"I can make jokes too, Jackie," he says with sharpness. "Come on. Get creative. You said one of your friends owns a café and that you help out sometimes—"

"I'm barely a help," I interrupt.

"Maybe you could...ask about employment options? Be there more often, get a routine down..."

Sophie did show Chad the door, and she is now short two sets of hands. I've only been over there a couple of times since Emily and Gatz left town and Chad was ousted. Each time it was pretty busy, and Sophie had zero time to chat. With only Evelyn to help her out, I saw Sophie go from regular-stressed-out-Sophie to over-the-top-mega-stress-mess-Sophie. I doubt she'll want me around more routinely.

"It's not exactly a welcoming atmosphere at The Cup and the Cake right now, Doc," I say with a worried expression. "Sophie's not really in a position to hear me complain, and I don't think she'll have the patience or time to offer up tips about how to help me get better."

Dr. Pierce reaches for his notebook, and as he pries it open, heaving a sigh, he says, "Jackie, I'm not suggesting you go to the café as a second set of therapy sessions. I'm talking about getting yourself a part-time job to keep your mind busy, keep your options open, have a greater sense of purpose. And, if I'm judging accurately, what with what happened in Paris, I take it you're going to need a financial resources soon."

"Please, Doc." I hold up a halting hand. "I'm not exactly *His Girl Friday*."

He looks on at me, slightly befuddled.

"I don't do work," I say insistently. "No offices, no bakeries, no cafés... Now, if Sophie had a clothing store or a designer boutique or something. Now then maybe I could help out, offer my fashion know-how."

"There's an idea!" Dr. Pierce enthusiastically sets down his pen. "How about you look into a job where you can utilize those skills, those talents? Where you can do something that'll help get you out of the house, help cure the boredom. Like your friend Emily said, you'd be doing something valuable for yourself *and* for someone needing the help."

"Doc." I laugh in mirth and adjust my miniskirt as I slip one foot underneath my rear. "Listen to me. I don't work. I don't know how. I'm helpless without Andrew! It's so pathetic." I cover my face with my hands in shame. "I've been fired from every job I've ever had," my muffled voice sounds from behind my hands. "It just won't work. Besides, I've got free rent, I don't really eat that much, and I've still got a car. I'll be fine."

"Until you need gasoline for the car." He looks at me with an expecting expression.

"I've got friends. Lara's well-off," I add simply. "She's always gotten me out of pickles. With Em's apartment so long as she's gone and doesn't mind—and she doesn't—and Lara who will lend me money if I really need it, I'll be fine. I can do this."

"I appreciate your positive approach and determined will." Dr. Pierce clears his throat and uncomfortably moves in his seat. "I have to level with you, however. You are either going to have a slamming wake-up call right now, or much later, and quite frankly it will be *much* harder if it's later."

"Wake-up call?"

"Eventually you're going to realize, Jackie, that you may just have to face the world on your own, without a husband. At least for a while, until you and your husband patch things up."

"*If* we do," I say bitterly.

"Precisely! *If.* And if you don't?" He looks exasperated. "If you don't, *that'll* be the *much* harder, slamming wake-up call that you won't like. Right now this situation is all very new to you, and you're feeling very out of sorts. But as time goes on, and if no reconciliation between you and Andrew is made, you may find yourself having to rely on your own efforts."

"I have good friends," I cut in.

"The best of friends can be supportive, but at some point you will have to stand on your own two feet. That's a fact of life, Jackie. Most everyone, barring some over-privileged elite, have to go through this experience."

"I *am* privileged. My husband is extremely wealthy—"

"And you've said it before." His face is drawn in a serious pose, his words sharp. "You and Andrew may not work things out, and then what? Best case in a divorce situation is you get a settlement to keep yourself comfortable, but in the meantime? Accounts frozen? Time on your hands to fritter away? *Think* about your options. The possibilities. *Think* about what you can do to help yourself. I'm your therapist and I'm here to help, but I can only counsel you. I can't force you to do anything."

"So you're saying I get a job?"

"That could be a good start."

"Yeah, well..." I say, my tone and intention empty.

"Employment will certainly help with your boredom, your depression," he says calmly. "You're still taking the Prozac?"

I nod, very grateful that the rather low dosage I've recently been prescribed is helping curb the pain, the rage, the depression.

"There's a very good reason to look into employment," Dr. Pierce says. "In the interim, waiting to hear from your husband's attorney about divorce, maybe a legal separation, or if you two make amends and you move back in, having some employment could help you out mentally, emotionally, *and* financially. *Please* seriously consider it."

"Fine."

He scribbles in his notebook and tells me he'll refill my prescription.

"And," he says, "though your finances are not really any of my business, I might as well point out..." He closes the notebook and looks at me with kind and sensitive eyes. "Your prescription, your therapy sessions... What happens when you can no longer afford those?"

Aggravated, I say, "Auto-pay, Doc. Therapy, medical expenses... As long as Andrew's still paying, just keep on charging."

I can't help but wonder, though, when Andrew will realize he's still footing the bill for my therapeutic help...and now my pills. When he does, what will I do then? Will Lara and Emily be there to help me when I fall, as they always have? Will even the best of friends eventually make me stand on my own two feet? I have no idea, and I hope to god I don't have to find out.

"All right, then," Dr. Pierce says. "I'll call in this prescription, and you'll maybe ask your friend about working at her café? Or finding a job in an area of interest?"

"Eh. I guess."

"Do you have a hobby or something you can spend your time with, say...for the rest of the afternoon? This upcoming weekend? Give yourself a goal..."

I blow out a long, hearty breath of air. "Hmmm."

"A project?"

"Actually, Doc," I blurt out as my mind wanders to Emily and her own similar advice. "I think I *can* do something with my time. Something good for someone else, too! I've been so caught up in my drams I totally forgot!"

Emily's left me some cash to play around with after I bugged her relentlessly for weeks about sprucing up her rather drab-looking apartment. I had such a blast getting to buy her some living room furniture last winter.

Since I'm living there now and always finding something to complain about in her tight and poorly decorated quarters, I've been wanting to take the sprucing up to the next level. Her place could definitely do with a new entertainment center. Hell, she could use some entertainment. Her bunny-ear solution for TV time is a joke, she has no proper console, her DVD player has a short, and don't get me started on the lighting in that place. It could really use some new furnishings and low light, a multiple-

268

setting feature for all of the lights in the apartment, in fact. Romantic for the bedroom, perfect for movie night in the living room, flattering in the bathroom when I'm applying my gobs of makeup.

Yes, Emily's place needs a major facelift, but as she says, she's never really there for too long—never in one place long enough to spend the time, energy, or money making it more than a temporary place to hang the camera, toss the backpack, and kick up her feet for a while.

After I begged and pleaded, saying it'd be something to perk me up given my sad state of affairs, Emily finally conceded. She left me a few hundred bucks in a mason jar atop the thick pile of silver bus change that's always filling half of the darned thing.

The day before she left for Australia she showed me the cash and told me to have fun and decorate modestly. "With *this* measly amount?" I asked, flabbergasted at the small budget. She just rolled her eyes, told me to get creative, stop complaining, and do something. And up until now I've completely forgotten about the golden opportunity!

"Decorating your friend's apartment would definitely be a great start, Jackie," Dr. Pierce says with a satisfied smile.

"Of course how I'll be able to afford anything great for so cheap!" I yank open my bag and withdraw my cell phone, half expecting to see that I have no service. I wave it at the doctor. "Shocked I even have a functioning phone still. Probably not for long, once Andrew forgets all about me and shacks up with Ni—"

"Jackie," Dr. Pierce says, warningly.

"Yeah, yeah," I brush off.

Noticing I don't have any missed calls, I drop the phone back in my colorful summer bag. "Session's almost up, Doc, and I'm pooped. I'm ready to call it early." I slip my bag on my shoulder. "If that's all right with you?"

"Whatever you want, Jackie." He claps his notebook shut, stands, and sets it on his desk. "Same time next week?"

"Sure." I stand up and smooth the back of my skirt. "So long as

Andrew's still paying." I cackle, and Dr. Pierce just looks at me like I'm half a step away from crazy.

"Good luck with the decorating." He takes long strides to the door. "I think that's a brilliant idea."

"Thanks. We'll see what pitiful magic I can do with the pennies I was left." I hike my heavy bag further up onto my shoulder. "It's so dumb, really. Em's a trust-fund kid, and she's *so* not materialistic. Probably doesn't even realize what furniture and redecorating a *whole* apartment costs."

"There's always that job to help pay..." Dr. Pierce looks at me with a stupid grin.

"Please, Doc." I step closer to the door. "One step at a time."

"All right," he says in a reassuring tone. "You take on your design project, stay positive, and if you need an emergency session, you have my number."

"Thanks."

"And remember," he says, his hand on the doorknob. "No concocting crazy theories about your husband's secretary. Don't borr—"

"Yeah, yeah. Don't borrow trouble." I roll my eyes. "Thanks, Doc."

"You said yourself a few sessions back you have no real reason to mistrust Andrew. You said your friend said there was nothing going on."

"Got it." I gesture to the door, ready to scram yesterday.

"All right." He opens the door. "I'll call in the prescription later this afternoon. Have a good weekend, Jackie."

34

D r. Pierce gave me the most brilliant idea! I can't believe it's taken me nearly the entire day to figure it out.

As soon as therapy ended, I drove back home to Emily's apartment and counted the cash she'd left for me. Minus the thirty-odd bucks in change, I had eight crisp one-hundred dollar bills. In terms of spare change, that's a hefty amount, but when it comes to redecorating an apartment...

I was immediately discouraged when I realized just how pitiful the sum was, so I tucked the cash back inside the mason jar and decided my decorating therapy would have to wait. Instead I popped in an old Cary Grant DVD that Emily still had lying around for me, and after a few tries the old machine sprang to life and I was happily taken back to a merrier age.

It was halfway through the film when it dawned on me: Dr. Pierce's brilliant idea about mutual friends and proving infidelity.

"I can't believe I didn't think of this earlier!" I exclaim to Bella, who's recently discovered just how comfy Emily's Euro-style loveseat is.

I leap from my spot on the sofa, the bed portion of it still out, blankets and sheets in a heap of a mess. I rush into the kitchen and pull my cell phone free from my handbag.

"*So* can't believe I didn't think of this before, honey," I say spiritedly to Bella.

"Lara?" I say as her voice comes across the line. "You out of work yet? You free to chat?"

———

Lara said I was insane, but she could commiserate with me. She'd been cheated on. She knew the road all too well. She knew it from both sides, in fact, not something she's particularly proud of, but something she always says she's growing from.

I really can't believe I hadn't thought of it sooner—what a grand idea! Lara's new boyfriend, Worth, works at Jennings & Voigt with Andrew. If anyone could have the closest interaction with Andrew and Nikki and all that went on in that office, it'd be him. The two don't exactly work in the same department, but Worth sees Andrew a hell of a lot more often than I do these days. He probably also sees or talks to Nikki on occasion. He *must* have the scoop on those two!

So when I went to Lara with the request that she ask Worth about what he'd observed between the two on an average, daily basis, she, on the one hand, thought I was insane (and probably rightfully so), and on the other couldn't blame me. She agreed, though rather reluctantly, to ask Worth if anything seemed peculiar between Andrew and Nikki.

"I don't know, Jackie," Lara says after fifteen minutes' worth of discussing the issue at her place early this Friday evening. She pulls an IZZE from her refrigerator, sets it on the counter, then pulls out another one, silently asking me with a questioning face if I want one.

I nod, telling her to go on and open one for me.

"I'll totally find out for you," she says, "but I can't just come outright and ask Worth if he thinks his coworker is having an affair. I mean, Worth and I haven't been dating that long. It'd be *way* weird."

"Do it for me. For your best friend," I plead.

She pops open the beverages and hands one to me. "I said I'd do it." She takes a quick swig. "I just have to be a little clandestine about it, that's all."

"Well, whatever," I say, taking a drink. "Whatever info you can get from him, I'd totally appreciate it."

Lara raises high one brow. "I suppose..."

"It isn't that big a deal, asking him. Just kind of hint at it, ask what mood Andrew's in. If he's all happy and stuff, then he's totally banging the whore. If he's miserable, then..." I can't hide my growing, lopsided grin. "Then that's kind of good, you know?"

"Have you heard *anything* from him? Not even any lawyers?" Lara scrunches her face in entreaty.

"Nope." I take a long pull of the bubbly, fruity drink. "It's better this way...for now at least. Give me time to figure things out. Get shit straight."

"So you're going to look for that job you and Dr. Pierce talked about?" She leans against her granite kitchen countertop, but not before unbuttoning her suit jacket and removing it, neatly setting it on the counter behind.

"I don't think so," I groan out in response, half-regretting having spilled the latest session to Lara. If I knew she'd play the employment card too...

"I talked to Sophie." *She what?* "A while ago, really," she says. "Robin and I both have, actually. Mentioned to Sophie that maybe she could give you some work. Dr. Pierce is right; it's a golden shot, really."

"No." I take my bottle and meander into the dining room. I take a seat at the wooden table, my chair inches away from the treadmill that's situated in a cramped way in the same room.

Lara follows me, her suit jacket in hand. "Sophie said okay. Only like one or two hours a day a couple days a week to get you started. See how things go."

"Uh-uh," I sound through a drink.

"It's responsibility, yes, but we all think it'd be good for you."

"I don't think so."

She sets her jacket on one arm of the treadmill. "Let's face it, Jack —you *are* going to need money. You *are* going to need do something. You've got all this time, no husband to come home to—"

"Thanks!" I say hotly. "Thanks a lot. Rub it in."

"You know I didn't mean it to sting." She takes a seat across from me.

She's right; I'm just upset with my situation. I'm angry with Andrew. How dare he put me in such a predicament!

"Look, if you're interested, Sophie said she'd be open to giving you some hours," Lara says.

"How courteous." I suppress the strong urge to roll my eyes or say some snide remark.

"I know she's the obsessive-controlling, Type-A girl and all, and working for her is probably some sort of nightmare for you."

I nod in agreement.

"But you could give it a shot. Maybe..."

"Maybe," I finally consent, but mostly just to put the topic to rest.

"Anyway!" I push my bottle into the center of the dining table, then trace the small line of condensation it's quickly made. "I can still work on Em's decorating as a project." Then I add in a mumbling way, "With the pennies I have."

"Yeeees," Lara draws out. "But that's not exactly a job. A hobby, yes!" She smiles broadly. "A good start."

"It's *something*."

"It *is* something." She pats my hand, then gives it a little squeeze. "I'll talk to Worth for you tomorrow."

"Tomorrow?" My face lights up.

"Yeah, we've got a date tomorrow. Going to Bainbridge Island. Some beach time."

My face falls at the mention of Bainbridge Island, as images of Andrew, sailing, our mostly happy time together, all flash by. "Good for you," I force myself to say, and in an equally forced tone of pleasure. "That's nice."

"Yeah, just a day trip, but a romantic one." She smiles gaily then takes another pull of her drink.

"So you'll ask him tomorrow?" I trace the remainder of the condensation line. "That's really great." I rub the dampness on my bare leg. "Don't know what *I'm* going to do all day and weekend by myself..."

Lara taps the tabletop a couple of times. "You said it yourself: Decorate Em's place." She stands and pushes the dining chair in. "Or go offer Sophie a helping hand."

I withdraw the second-to-last cigarette in my wrinkled pack of Parliaments and light up. Pioneer Square is comforting in the daytime, the red brick a cheerful color, the green of the trees vibrant, the chatter among friends and rustling of bags as shoppers duck in from antique shop to bookstore to novelty shop a familiar comfort.

At night it's even more magical. When the moon is large and golden, like tonight, and the sky is clear, the stars twinkle majestically, the brickwork has a warm, rustic charm to it. It's still very much like an old Hollywood film set, but one that's peacefully resting for its rote six, seven hours of sleep before the director, cast, and crew come flocking back. Lights, Camera, Action!

The moths and rare lightning bug flit by, ready for their own close-up with the golden, glowing lamps spotted about the square. The slightly misty air sweeps its roundabout way from the waterfront on through Downtown and turns this way and that about the hodgepodge of brick façades and candescent skyscrapers. Very little chatter, if any, can be heard throughout the square—mostly that of shopkeepers shutting down for the night or last-minute shoppers at one of the low-slung yet quaint used bookstores.

As I near the end of my cigarette, I catch sight of two people busily working inside one of the antique shops—the same antique shop, in fact, that had the darling hat box I had once admired. One of them looks to be on a ladder, the other holding something large and round above his head. The lighting from the shop spills out plentifully into the square, almost coaxing me to come in.

I rub out my cigarette and lightly jog over to the lively little shop.

"Hi, there," the middle-aged man holding up what turns out to be a large papier mâché globe says as soon as I enter. "Can we help you?"

"Are you still open?" I ask, looking behind me at the door, searching for a sign that might answer my question. I can't spot one.

"For a pretty lady like you, we're open a while more." He smiles and lowers the globe.

"We're still technically open for ten more minutes," the older man on the ladder says in a huffy way. "Have a look around, and if you see anything you like and can't reach," he gives one quick stomp to the ladder's step he's perched on, "now's the greatest time to ask." He chuckles at his sense of humor, and I thank them both, wandering around the cramped and dusty yet sweet-smelling shop.

When I left Lara's I hadn't intended on doing anything worthy. I thought I'd wander on home, try to tune in to something on the cable-less television, or maybe crack open one of Emily's few bottles of wine she has in her wine cabinet, maybe call it a night early. It's not like I'm swimming in cash to go out and hit the clubs or anything.

But instead I found myself in Pioneer Square, sitting on a bench all by my lonesome, enjoying the subtle summer evening—contemplating life, love, all the squeaks and troubles it's been causing me lately.

Sure, I've been meaning to get around to shopping for Emily's place, but her minimal budget isn't exactly inviting.

Then, when I thought I'd never get around to the project, I caught sight of Pioneer Square Antiques.

I finger a stack of green, leather bound books. *Gulliver's Travels,* one spine reads in gold. I twist my head to see the others: *Into the Looking Glass, Keats: Poetry and Prose,* and *To the Lighthouse.*

My eyes are averted to a Tiffany glass lamp in tangerine and forest green. The base looks tarnished by time, but nothing a quick polish couldn't fix up to a high gloss.

This place is such a treasure trove. I've stopped by on rare occasion in the past, but usually I just gawk through the windows. Like I've said, Andrew wouldn't dream of me hauling this "crap" into our modern home. It's just pretty stuff from a past and beautiful time, meant to be looked at, meant to be stored, peered at through glass, and simply admired from afar.

My eyes survey the room. I'm hungrily taking everything in, a feast for the eyes, and I stop at a large, wooden rocking horse. His mane was probably once the color of caramel, but now a thick layer of dust and the passing of time have turned it to a khaki hue. I touch the smooth, red seat—made to look just like a saddle. I run my hand up to the tail, also probably once vibrant but now colored by time, perhaps neglect.

"That's all hand-carved there," the middle-aged man says. He sticks his fingers, save for his thumbs, in his front pockets. "Dates back to the 1950s. Quality, sturdy piece, isn't it?"

"Yeah," I breathe, running my fingers back over the saddle.

"You have a little one? A son?"

I give a small laugh and say, "No. No, not me."

"Little brother, maybe?" He looks at me with a silly grin.

"No." I look back at the stack of books, shift upwards along the shelf stacked with China, knickknacks, sconces, and doilies, antique dolls, and lace curtains.

"It's a genuine find, and at just one-fifty."

"One-fifty?" I chuckle. "As in one hundred and fifty? A bit above my price range, but thanks." I glance about the room. *Probably can't afford anything, in all honesty...*

"Lend me a hand here, will ya?" the man on the ladder calls out to his coworker, and the middle-aged man rushes over and assists with the globe. "Dang thing just won't stay put."

I look up at the two men struggling with the delicate globe the size of a large beach ball, and an idea comes to mind. "Hey, uh, excuse me."

The middle-aged man looks to me.

"How much is that globe there?" I ask. "That's papier mâché, isn't it?"

"Yup." The middle-aged man takes the globe in his hands and brings it over to me. "Has a couple holes here." He turns it around gingerly, then gestures to Africa, turns again and points to the South Pole, and turns it a bit more, gesturing finally to a spot somewhere in Canada. "Couple of holes, like I said. But it sure has some charm, doesn't it?"

"I think the holes give it charm. How much?"

He looks up to the older man, who replies, "Twenty."

"Twenty bucks?" I ask.

"Twenty," he repeats.

The middle-aged man looks at me, a gleam in his eye. "Fifteen for the pretty lady."

"Aw, if we're always going to knock off a few for every pretty lady that comes on in, then—"

"Then we'd be doing the right nice thing, wouldn't we?" The man holds the globe out for me.

"Another steal of a deal today..." The older man's voice is deep and drawn out.

"Come on. It's an old globe."

"With holes," I point out.

"Which add the charm," the older man says smartly.

"Here. Fifteen. You can get this beautiful globe, and we can close up shop and call it a night."

"Deal," I say, handing him the twenty dollar bill Lara gave me tonight, telling me to fill the refrigerator with some substantial food. "This is too perfect for my friend; I just can't pass it up."

And with just five bucks to my name and a ratty old papier mâché globe high on charm carefully tucked under my arm, I'm happy as a lark as I bounce out of the shop and pass under the low awning of the storefronts along the square.

I'm just about out of the square when I notice the used bookstore at the corner. The lights are all off, save for a low window lamp shedding light on the front display, and there's a small sign posted in the corner. It reads, *Help Wanted, Part-Time, Inquire Inside.*

"Hmm," I say with a sniff, then continue my peppy walk out of the square to my awaiting car.

Maybe I will offer Sophie some help, I think. *Maybe some part-time work* will *be helpful.*

35

"Come on, pick up, pick up." I cross my fingers on one hand and eagerly grip my cell phone with the other. "Pick up, pick up." I consider disconnecting the call and just driving on over to Lara's place, but the needle of my gasoline gauge that's dangerously hovering over the 'E' warns me that it's best I stay put. "Dammit, Lara. Pick up!"

"Hello?" a groggy-sounding Lara answers.

"Finally! You do realize it's nearly noon?"

Even groggier now: "Jackie?"

"Who else?" Then, after glancing at my watch once more and considering her muzzy tone, I say, "Where were *you* last night?" I titter. "Having a *gooood* time?" I swing open the back patio door.

It's mid-July, and Seattle's having quite a hot summer. I love the season's welcoming sunshine and never want to miss a chance to don cute bikinis, wear chic sandals, and flash pretty pedicures, but sometimes too much summer sun is too much, especially when your bikinis are all at your soon-to-be-ex-husband's home and you haven't had a pedicure in several weeks.

I slip on my aviators and step outside, eager to enjoy the sun anyhow. The scorching heat of the patio pavement instantly begins to burn my soles. "Ow, ow!" I high-step it back inside to grab a pair of sandals from Paris.

"Jack," Lara grumbles into the phone. "What is it? What's going on?"

"It's hot outside." I reemerge on the patio, this time better equipped. "But such a beautiful day, really. What are you still doing in bed? It's gorge out. Super bad hangover or something?" I laugh some more at my teasing.

"No." Her voice is a raspy whisper now. "For your information, I had a date last night."

"Yes, and that's why I'm calling."

"Well, the date's not over yet."

"Ooooh."

"Jack, if nothing's on fire and you've got nothing to report but the weather, I'm going back to bed."

"No!" I lay an old and washed-out U Dub beach towel on one of the plastic lounge chairs Emily has on her patio. "I want the scoop. What did Worth say about Andrew?"

"Not right now. Let me wake up and get my day started and—"

"Just tell me quickly." I stretch out my legs, making sure I'm maxing out my sun space.

I've been taking peoples' advice and getting out of the apartment when I can. My moods are up and down, obviously Andrew's heavy on my mind, but I'm trying to get out. I haven't really found a job yet...haven't really started looking, actually. But I *am* getting out. And I did technically start the redecorating project with that globe I bought.

The trouble with getting out is, when you're low on cash there's a limit to how a girl can entertain herself. I tried to get my fake 'n bake on yesterday, bored out of my mind with nothing to do. It looks like I've really been letting myself go with the whole depressed-about-Andrew thing—my not-so-blonde roots are starting to show, my pixie haircut not exactly so pixie-ish anymore, and my lovely orange glow is—oh the humanity!—starting to fade away. I figured it was high time I pulled myself up and out of bed and get my glow back on. But when the girl at the salon told me that my tanning package had run out, I panicked.

"But isn't it on some auto pay or something?" I asked in a whirl of anxiety.

She blew a big bubble of gum, shook her head slowly and dramatically, and said, "Looks like the credit card was denied. Do you have another one we can use?"

Defeat. Flashback to Eres in Paris. If only Andrew had viewed my fake 'n bake sessions just as essential to my mental health and well-being as my therapy sessions with Dr. Pierce and put them on some auto-withdrawal from the bank, then I could be bronze and all coconut-scented right about now.

"Jackie," Lara whines in a high-pitched way over the phone. "My date's still kind of going on."

"Yeah?"

"Worth's still here." She whispers this part, as if it's something to be ashamed about.

"So!" I bark. "You can still talk. Where are you? Your place?"

"Yes," she says through a moan. "But please don't come racing over here. He's here and I'm tired—"

"Don't worry." I grab my bag from the second lounge chair where my feet are propped and root about in it. "I'm not going to come over and crash your love fest."

I'm looking for my cigarettes, but I can't find any. I dig deeper, pushing past way too many lipgloss tubes and lipsticks, a compact I forgot I had, scads of receipts and crumpled pieces of paper and notes. "I just want to know if you asked him." I give up my search and plunk my bag back down. "Ugh, I *so* need a pedicure," I say in a hushed tone.

"What? Jack, please, I'm going to go now."

"No," I say in a demanding way as I jump up. "Tell me quick—did you ask Worth about Nikki and Andrew?"

"*Yeeees.*" She sounds annoyed, drawing her speech out.

"And?" I duck inside the apartment and begin to go through Emily's kitchen drawers in search of any cigarettes or loose tobacco. Emily doesn't light up as often as I do—obviously doesn't need the sudden calm a good smoke provides when especially frazzled or anxious—but she usually has some loose-leaf tobacco or a spare pack of Marlboros or something lying about in the event she gets the social smoke craving.

"What'd he say?" I press Lara for information. "Is that slut screwing my husband? She is, isn't she?"

"Actually," Lara says, still whispering. "Worth he doesn't really interact with Andrew much. They don't work in the same department."

"Yeah, well, great! That *so* does not help me." I slam various drawers, growing frustrated as I come up empty one drawer after another.

"Worth said, though, that Andrew *does* seem preoccupied, lately."

"So he *does* see Andrew?" I stand upright, waiting on tenterhooks for the next piece of gossip. "And?"

"Well, *yes* they see each other," she says in an obvious manner. "Not all the time, but they do interact."

"Okay, okay."

"Andrew seems out of it, Worth said. Preoccupied, down, not himself. Like he's got something heavy on his mind."

"Okay..."

"Worth thinks it's the stress of the job or the big Cayman's thing they've been working on right now."

"Great!" I say ironically. I lean in a deflated way against the counter.

"Worth obviously doesn't know anything about your marriage details, Jackie. Not exactly office chat. It makes sense that he thinks it's just the demands of work."

"I guess..."

"Here's what I think, though. Just a sec." I can hear shuffling in the background, then muffled whispering. Lara's voice comes back on the line at last, this time at regular volume. "Okay, I didn't want to wake him. He's had a *long* week at the office and he needs some re—"

"Come on!" I screech. "Spill it! What do you think?"

"It's just my theory."

"I'll take it."

"If Andrew was really seeing Nikki, then he'd probably be all smiles, happy as a lark, running around the office all proud and stuff," she explains.

"Nice," I say, seeing where she's going with this. I return to my search for a smoke.

"But if he's as down and out as Worth says he is," she continues, "then maybe he really is just depressed as hell over your guys' fight. He's obviously distressed over your separation."

"That's great!" I yank open the last drawer and search madly.

"Jack," she says through an even-tempo laugh, "I wouldn't call that *great*."

"Oh, you know what I mean." Unable to find any cigarettes or tobacco, I pound my way out of the kitchen, frustrated and seriously craving a nicotine fix. "Lara? Can you lend me some cash?"

"Did you buy groceries with the cash I gave you?" Her tone is taking that maternal one she often has.

I smile and return to the patio. "Did one better than that. You'd be so proud." I tell her about the globe purchase I made with Emily in mind—my first piece of my project to spruce up the apartment.

"I'm glad you're doing something," she says. "You really should buy yourself some groceries, though. That's why I gave you that cash."

"Oh!" I say, suddenly remembering. "I'll just take it out of the mason jar money Em left. It's for apartment stuff, so she owes me for the globe."

"Not that I'm even awake yet and ready for a conversation." Lara yawns. "Have you given any more thought to working at The Cup and the Cake?"

"Actually," I say proudly, "I have, thank you very much. I'll give it a try, if Sophie'll have me."

"Oh, she will. Swamped to her eyeballs with work, and not enough people around to help."

"Don't know how long it'll last, but I *desperately* need cash to get some smokes and, oh—my tanning package!" I let out a loud, low groan. "Lara! I don't know what I'm going to do. I'm in dire need of a pedi," I catch sight of my fingernails, "mani-pedi, correction. I *so* need to be able to go out and pay a club fee, be able to buy myself a drink... You think it'd be kind of slutty to get a guy to buy me a drink now, don't you? I mean, I'm still technically married and all." I roll my eyes. "Who knows *when* Andrew'll send over that damn divorce lawyer."

"Jack," Lara interrupts. "If it's all right with you, I'm going to get back to bed."

I lean my head against the lounge chair and close my eyes. "Yeah, yeah. Sorry. You get back to your hottie boyfriend," I say in a jesting tone.

"He's not my boyfriend," she replies in earnest.

"Not yet he isn't."

"Whatever. I'm not jumping the gun and ruining this one. I really like him."

"Then hop back in bed, woman!"

The following day I stop by the gas station nearest Emily's apartment before leaving for The Cup and the Cake. I grab a fresh pack of Parliaments I'm in desperate need of and fuel up with what's left of the fifteen bucks Emily owed me before I head onto Aurora Ave for a slow, gas-conscious drive.

I'm still nervous about working with Sophie, even though when I talked to her yesterday she said she was more than ready for any help I would offer. She admitted she was worried how it'd be with me not exactly having much work experience and my working habits not being all that impressive—she doesn't want our employee-employer relationship to hinder our friendship.

I love Sophie, honest I do, but we have very different personalities, so I can understand. I like to get down with my wild self, have a blast, and not really bother with regrets or questions until after the damage has been done. Responsibility just isn't my thing.

Sophie, however, is so well put together. She's got her own business, for heaven's sake! She runs that thing like a well-oiled machine, and if one cupcake is too sweet, a scone too dry, she's all-hands-on-deck with damage control. The girl's got some serious integrity and major goals, and I love her for all her silly OCD antics, but working with that? *For* that? God help me.

But she needs the help, and I desperately need the money.

I keep telling myself the income is necessary, and as Lara and Dr. Pierce continue to remind me, and as Emily said in her email a few days back, the getting out of the apartment and doing some work will be really good for me. It's just the medicine I need (paired with the Prozac) to help me manage life sans Andrew.

"Hey," I say in a sugary voice as I enter the café. "Here's your new helper!" I spin three-sixty, my pink and white polka-dot sundress billowing around like an opening rose.

Sophie looks up from her job at the espresso machine and is glowing with delight. "Excellent!" She aggressively wipes it down. "I'll meet you in the back. Give me one sec."

As I head into the kitchen I pass Evelyn, the sweet, quiet, brown-haired girl who's been the only thing keeping Sophie from blowing her lid from too much stress.

"Welcome aboard," Evelyn says in her chipper voice. She pulls a notepad from her apron pocket, flashes me a white smile, and makes her way to the front of the café.

Evelyn is a nice enough girl, and she really knows how to help run the place. Soft-spoken and always seeming to say something positive or pleasant, nothing gets Evelyn's dander up. She's probably just the calm Sophie needs right about now.

I can also see why Chad would be interested in her. She's pretty, with her light dusting of freckles across her nose, gently tanned skin, blue-green eyes that would go with *any* color blouse—totally gorgeous. She's slender, on the short side, and has long, silky hair. Come to think of it, minus her stature, she could pass as Sophie's sister.

"All right," Sophie says to me a minute later. "Time to teach you the ropes!"

In record speed Sophie teaches me how to manage the basics of the kitchen. She shows me where all the dish-cleaning supplies are and how she prefers the pots and pans to be washed and put away. She shows me how to fold the take-away boxes; where to stock the delivery of dry goods—flour, sugar, and other things I've already forgotten—that will be coming in tomorrow morning, which I'll be helping with. She shows me where all the spices are and says they could use reorganization, an emphasis on the alphabetizing of them; I learn where the broom and mop are, as well as all of the necessary cleansers and sponges I'll apparently need when I clean the kitchen; and then I learn how to manage the ovens and timers and make sure things are taken out promptly and put in just as promptly.

When I ask when I'll get to do the slightly more fun stuff, like taking orders, making coffee, even trying my hand at baking a few things myself (not that I'm all that keen on the last one), Sophie just stares at me, face nearly white, and finally giggles.

"Oh, Jackie, honey," she says as she leads me to one of the large, stainless steel refrigerators. She hands me a big yellow sponge and a bottle of organic cleanser. "That's advanced stuff. Everyone starts with the jobs no one wants." She yanks open the refrigerator door. "But you *do* get to take on the job of cleaning this. Do this, and then we'll talk about the spices, kay?"

"But Sophie..." I watch her in dismay as she crosses the kitchen, heading back up to the front.

"Jack," she says, spinning on her heels. "You said you wanted to work, and I warned you it wouldn't be fun."

"I know," I whine. "But this?" I wave the cleanser and sponge about.

"Welcome to the workforce, babe." She smiles and turns around.

"Help yourself to the scones and fresh fruit set out on the corner table. I'll be up front if you need me."

I look at the refrigerator, the rather clean refrigerator, might I add. There doesn't seem to be anything needing cleaning. Okay, maybe I can organize some of the things inside, make all the labels face frontwards and stack the butter just so, put the milk cartons in neat rows, but only because that's Sophie's style. Honestly, the refrigerator looks fine.

I consider setting the sponge and cleanser aside and taking my first break of the morning. I mean, she *did* say I could help myself to some snacks.

As soon as Lara and Emily's voices sound in my head, their faces coming into view, all disappointed and warning, I think better of a premature break. I set down the cleaning products and begin to pull items from the top shelf of the refrigerator.

"This sucks," I huff. "This just totally sucks."

It's at this moment in time when I feel my anger and resentment towards Andrew boil and brew more intensely than I've felt in weeks.

What has happened to my life? I think, slamming down onto the counter a carton of milk, which, as would only be appropriate right now, bursts open and gushes a stream of liquid about the countertop, on down the cupboards and onto the floor.

36

I don't want to do it anymore, Em, I type on my computer.

I count my lucky stars that I chose to grab my laptop before I fled to Paris. Had I not, keeping in touch with Emily would be even more difficult a feat. Of course, I've only gotten a couple of emails from her since she left for Australia, since she and Gatz are traveling all over the country and New Zealand before his classes start next month.

I think Sophie's right, I type. *Our friendship could be damaged if I work with her. How the hell did you do it?*

I look at Bella, who's sitting snuggly on the sofa next to me. I give her head a pat.

It's not her or her demands, really, I type. *I guess it's just the work. It's so boring. Not at all what I pictured. I'm cleaning things! I've had a housekeeper for years. It's not my fault I no longer really know how to clean.*

I titter to myself, the irony of my words clicking. Emily would probably say I never knew how to clean, since I've always been kind of a slob. I survey the messy living room. It's not as bad as the bedroom, where clothes are kind of strewn about.

It is something to do, though, I return to the email. *And I appreciate*

Sophie wanting to help me. Evelyn's really stepping it up, though, and I think my cleaning's helping a bit, as dull as it is.

But dish-cleaning isn't exactly the best way for me to get my mind off of things. I think about Andrew every day, especially when I'm miserably working, sweating...cursing him for bringing me to this state. Then, oddly enough, I begin to miss him. I miss him a lot, Em. That sounds crazy, doesn't it? I'm convinced he's having an affair. He kicked me out of the house, I'm living like a peasant, and I actually miss him? I guess that's normal? I mean, I still love him.

I heave a sigh and cast about the living room once again. My eyes fall on the papier mâché globe atop the dining table, and my spirits raise slightly.

On a happier note, I started to redecorate your place, I type. *Okay, it's not much, and only one thing, but I think you'll like it. It's a great start. You didn't exactly leave me much money, so I'm doing my best.* I add in a smiley face, close the message with Xs and Os, and send the email.

As the rest of the week unfolds, one dish after another spick and span, oven-timers set and floors and countertops mostly clean of crumbs and spills, I'm rewarded with my first paycheck. I've been at The Cup and the Cake every day this week, and while the work isn't getting any more fun, it is at least getting me out of bed. It is giving me some sense of purpose, and that helps numb the ache the Prozac, sessions with Dr. Pierce, and girl talk can't.

However, when I see the total sum paid of my first paycheck, I'm completely thunderstruck.

How can this be? I think, clapping a hand to my forehead. I've been working so hard, and for two, three hours a day! One day even a full four-hour shift! I know Sophie pays a hint above minimum wage for my work, but *this?!*

Sputtering on fumes, the damn needle of my gasoline gauge permanently hovering over empty, I quickly speed-dial Lara from the car's dashboard.

"This is total bull!" I holler right when she picks up, answering in her business-tone, "Lara Kearns."

"Hey, Jackie," she says loosely as I slow at the yellow light. "What's up?"

"Total BS, Lara, that's what's up!" I come to a complete stop and throw the car into park.

Reaching for my handbag on the passenger's seat, I say, "I don't know why I even bother!" I find the fresh pack of cigarettes I bought this morning with just a little of Em's borrowed cash (I'll pay her back, I promise), and light up, my nerves instantly calming. "It's such a waste of my time!" I pull long and hard on the cigarette.

"Calm down. What's wrong?" Lara instructs.

"My job." I roll down the window and flick some ashes away. "I'm slaving away in there, and for what?" I pick up the pathetic excuse of a paycheck and scoff. "One hundred and sixty-four dollars? One week of work, and a hundred and sixty-four lousy bucks? I made more at that jazz bar!"

Lara sighs and says, "Where you worked many more hours. Even then I know you weren't making that much more."

"Ugh!"

It's true. Lara did have to pick up a couple of my bills, even when I was employed at the jazz bar years ago—the longest-standing job I ever held.

"This is just so pathetic," I seethe. I take a quick puff of my cigarette, then the bleating sound of the car's horn from behind startles me. "Damn." I throw my car into gear and accelerate forward. "This is just not going as planned, Lara."

She snickers. "It's been one week. You can't expect to earn enough to pay all your bills just like that."

"My lifestyle demands thousands a week, Lara." I flick more ashes out the window's crack. "I don't know how I'm ever going to adjust." I take a long, jagged drag.

"Your lifestyle's got to change then, babe. In fact, it already has. You're living at Emily's, you're working..."

"And you're depressing me further."

"Look." She sounds slightly nettled. "You off work now?"

"Yeah."

"I am, too. Swing on by, I'll give you some extra emergency cash, and then you can come meet Claire and me for drinks."

"Uh!" I turn down the blasting air conditioning and turn up the speakerphone volume. "You girls were planning on having drinks *without* me? So not cool!"

"Jackie. I do do things with the other girls, too, you know?"

"Yeah, well. Guess it's not like I could afford the drinks anyway. Damn." I place the cigarette in between my lips and check behind my left shoulder before I make my lane change.

"I'll be over in a flash. Give me a few. I can't exactly gun it everywhere on fumes." I exhale some smoke quickly and barely make the light. "I'd probably be better off on horseback."

"House 206," Lara says. "See you soon."

"It's the taxes," Claire says succinctly, looking at my pathetic excuse of a paycheck. She wrinkles her nose and hands it back. Leaning further into the bar, she lifts her chocolatini to her mouth. "The upside is that since you make so little you'll get tons of it back in your refund." She takes a small pull of the chocolate drink, then smacks her lips. "When you do your taxes next year, that is."

"Me? Taxes?" I laugh loudly. "Do you hear yourself, Claire?"

She shrugs. "Well everyone has to do their taxes."

"Andrew has a tax guy who manages that for us."

"When money's tight, times are tough," Claire says in a way that's a cross between helpful and self-pitying.

"Conner still dry on the job search?" I ask.

Lara says, "How's the search in Tacoma going?"

"Tacoma?" I gasp. "So you guys *are* serious about looking elsewhere?"

"Yes," Claire says in an obvious tone. "It sucks, but we don't exactly have a choice. There's been a rumor floating around that Conner's position is going to 'expire,'" she makes air quotes, then lazily pulls on her cocktail, "and if the firm does that—totally gets rid of his title and position—then he can't take legal action or contest or anything. It's like...absolved or something like that. I don't know all the correct legal jargon, but basically he's screwed."

"*If* the rumors are true," Lara says.

"Shit." I wag my head in disbelief. "So Tacoma, hah?"

"Yeah." Claire's eyes are transfixed on her half-drunk cocktail. "Spokane, Portland, and LA, too."

"You're going to go that far?" I start to feel a twinge beleaguered.

Claire isn't exactly my bosom buddy, but I still can't picture her leaving Seattle and our group of girlfriends.

Suddenly, a churning starts in the pit of my stomach. So much change, so much adjustment. I rub at the aching area, then take a long slog of my dry martini.

"We're doing what we have to," Claire says. "For now I'm just trying to hold my head up high, work a ton of heinous hours, and deal. I mean," she simpers, "what more can a girl do, right? You've got to play the hand you're dealt."

"Psh," I say into my nearly drained drink. "I say just leave the card table, or play a whole new hand." I can see Lara make a disagreeing face. "Some people cheat, too," I throw in for levity. "*Cheat* the cards you're dealt." I think about Nikki. Her stupid whored-red hair, that plastered smile, the likely fact that she's screwing my husband, no matter what Worth says.

"Please stop with this, Jack," Lara says. "There's no evidence, so stop."

"You've outright asked Andrew, haven't you?" Claire says. "Asked him if he's having an affair?"

I tell her yes, and she says, wearing a flabbergasted look, "Then you're in the clear! You think he'd lie to you about that?"

Lara laughs oddly, like a devilish antagonist in a Hitchcock film right before he sends the final blow with the gun, the knife, the surprise attack. "All men are born liars," she says sulkily. "I figure a third of those continue to be liars throughout their life, the other third actually learn how to tell the truth and become decent enough human beings, and the final third become even better liars." She throws back a drink of her wine spritzer. "But that's just the cynical view of a thirty-one-year-old woman who's found anything *but* true love. Burned too many times."

"But Worth?" Claire says peppily, encouragingly. "Worth is one of the good one-thirds, right?" She pauses, then adds, "Not that I really agree with the whole math you're doing. Women can be just as bad, just as deceitful as men."

Lara makes a ho-hum motion with her head. "True. I know I sound like a depressed and bitter woman."

"Just a tad," I kid.

"But I'm not. And I don't have a reason to be one right now, really. Things with Worth are good." She looks to each of us. "Really great, in fact."

"*Buuut?*" I pry.

"But I'm just worried it won't last." She brings her glass to her lips and before taking a sip hesitates for a second. "Eventually what is 'really great,' like with Nathan, will turn into, well..." She holds out a flat, upright palm. "Not the greatest track record, you know?" She takes a big gulp.

"You've got to push past that cynicism, girl," Claire says. She crosses her dark-blue-jean-clad legs and turns on her barstool towards us. "If you're in that state of mind that your relationship will fail, it might. All the magazines say that self-fulfilled prophecy plays a big role in early relationships."

"That's true," I say in a wise tone. "If you give off the bad relaysh vibes—the cynicism—then maybe you'll get it back."

"I guess you're right," Lara says. "I *don't* want to lose this good thing I've got going with Worth. I really like him, and I'm just—just —scared, that's all."

Both Claire and I instantly bring a comforting hand to Lara's back. "I'm sure it'll work out," Claire says.

"Yeah," I say. "And if not, there will be someone else just as great, even better!"

Lara smiles, a weak smile, but a smile nevertheless. "You girls are sweet. I just really hope this one's the real deal. I'm fighting my feelings that I really want it to work out, because it's just *amazing!* Because...if it ends up failing it'll be that much harder to get over, you know?"

"You don't have to tell me about it," I say in a mock-jovial tone, returning to my martini. "I know *all* about trying to get over a love that you don't really want to get over."

"Has Andrew..." Claire says cautiously, slowly. "Has he brought..." She pauses for a second. "Has he sent divorce papers?"

It's the question that's often asked, the question I'm always dwelling on.

I'm surprised myself that Andrew hasn't served me the papers yet. I've seen all those chick flicks where the women are thrown off balance with an unexpected packet of divorce documents shoved in their hands, or where they're thinking their on-the-rocks marriage is starting to look up, then *Wham!* They get that dreaded call from the law offices of Hedid, Cheatonyou, and Nowhewantsout.

"Maybe he does want to give your marriage a chance," Lara says.

"Or he's just too busy having fun with Nikki." I roll my eyes and wait for the girls to commiserate with me, but they don't. I shrug and take a sip.

"If we want to talk cynicism, Jack," Lara says. "Let's not talk me and Worth. Let's talk you and Andrew with the Nikki thing. I told you I don't think anything's going on; Worth said nothing's going on. And, in fact, there's nothing you should be worrying about now anyway!" She makes a surprised face.

"What do you mean?"

"Worth said Andrew just left for the Cayman Islands yesterday."

"Whoopitee doo-dah for him. Sun, sand, and surf. Don't rub it in."

"He's out of town on business, far away from Nikki."

"Not far enough."

"*And!*" Lara looks pleased with herself. "Nikki's out of town, too."

"She isn't!" The possibility is too much to bear. "Please don't say—"

"Calm down," Lara soothes, abating the blindsiding tension

that's caused both mine and Claire's faces to look completely gobs-macked and overcome with fear. "Nikki's out of town on *vacation*."

"So she's on vacation?" I say. "He's out of town on business? That hardly proves anything."

"On the contrary! Don't you think if they were having an affair Andrew would take this opportunity of a resort getaway to take his floozy with him?"

Lara has a point. A really good point, in fact.

"I...guess..." I say slowly.

"Exactly." Lara waves the bartender down and asks for a refill for all of us, on her. "Oh!" She digs through her handbag and hands me an envelope. "Before I forget. And *please* buy some groceries this time."

I stick the envelope of cash in my handbag and thank her.

"Anyway, I don't know of a better opportunity for a cheating husband to make a major move on his mistress," Lara says. "I think Andrew's being honest in telling you he's not having an affair with her."

"Well..." I zip my handbag closed.

"Oh, and here's an even bigger sign for you." Lara casually rests some well-manicured fingers on the top of her nearly empty glass. "Andrew's in the Caymans, and Nikki's on vaca in *Hawaii*. Hawaii of all places! Two über romantic places, and neither one of them are together, I me—"

"Hawaii?" I say in a daze. My eyes are fixed dead ahead at nothing in particular—I can't really see anything clearly.

"Yeah," Lara says cheerily.

"Jeez, Hawaii would be so nice right now," Claire in a dreamy way. "Some day Conner and I are going to get our finances in order—he'll get a job, and we can take a nice va—"

I feel for my handbag, mouth agape and eyes still staring straight ahead. "I gotta go," I stutter.

The bartender appears with refilled drinks as I stand.

"What? Now?" Claire asks in suspense. "But I never have free time to go out. And our drinks just arrived!"

"Jackie, what's wrong?" Lara tries to meet my gaze.

"Andrew's not being so honest after all," I manage to get out.

"What?" Lara furrows her brow.

"He may or may not be honest with me about having an affair." I blink a few times, snapping myself somewhat to, and look from Claire to Lara. "But he's *definitely* not being honest about where he is."

"He's not in the Caymans?" Claire looks befuddled.

"You think Nikki's in the Caymans?" Lara shakes her head in disbelief. "No way. Worth said Hawaii—"

"No." I pull my handbag closer to my body and take one step away from the bar. "I think Nikki's in Hawaii. And I think Andrew's there, too."

"Jackie, wait!" Lara calls out after me as I make a hurried flight for the exit. "Where are you going? What are you doing?"

"I'm going home!" I say loudly. "I'm going to get the rest of my stuff."

"Jackie," Claire whines, leaping from her barstool. Her arms are akimbo, her head cocked to one side. "What are you talking about?"

"I'm taking what's rightfully mine, girls!" I fling the door open. "Besides, Andrew's going to need the closet space so Bitch Nikki can move on in when they get back from their romantic getaway!"

37

W holly and implicitly beside myself, I withdraw the ring of keys from my handbag and bring a shaking hand to the front doorknob of what I used to call home. *I can't believe him! I can't believe he'd actually do this!*

The instant Lara had said *Hawaii* the image of Andrew's laptop that one night around Valentine's came into view. His search for flights to Hawaii...

Oh the nerve! How could he do this to me? To us?

Sure, the possibility of him shacking up with Nikki has been ever-present in my mind. Sure, I've been obsessing about it, and unnaturally so, as Dr. Pierce is quick to remind. But when I'm faced with the actual *proof*—the *evidence* that he and Nikki have something going on!

"Damn him," I curse under my breath as my nervous fingers press the key to the lock.

What the—

I press the key harder against the lock, but only a fraction of it goes in.

"What the hell?" I check to see if I have the right key. I do. I try again, but no further progress.

"The asshole!" I look up at the door and take a step back. "He fucking changed the locks!"

Just then a fury, an overwhelming rage I can't contain, races through my body, burns my blood, and I lunge for the door. I slam my body against it as hard as I can, feeling myself bruise on impact. "You bastard!" I scream as I pound my fist against the thick door.

In the midst of my screaming and pounding I feel the vibration of my cell phone in my handbag. My rage is interrupted by an incoming call from Lara.

I pull out the phone, its ringer accidentally turned off yet again. "What?" I curtly answer. "Now is *not* a good time!"

"Where are you and what is going on?" Lara demands. "You're not that buzzed from one drink, are you? And you're driving and—"

"Not now, Lara." I throw my handbag to the floor and give the door a good kick. "I'm at home."

"Already?"

"Not Em's home. *My* home. Well...Andrew's home, more like it. The bastard!"

"Calm down," she soothes. "What are you doing there?"

"I told you! I came to get my stuff and..." I begin to explain the whole mess.

After a few more kicks to the door just for the hell of it and one more pound of my fist (which I'm now regretting as the tender flesh is turning a soft shade of plum), I wind up slinking down onto the floor, head resting against the wall.

I tell Lara all about the Hawaii coincidence and how it just had to be the case: Andrew bought tickets to Hawaii—tickets for himself and Nikki. There was no Cayman Islands trip. And as for Worth detecting Andrew not being himself—it isn't because of me. That's a bunch of bullshit. Andrew and Nikki are having an affair, period. No ifs, ands, or buts.

"Well," Lara finally says after I've divulged everything, tears staining my cheeks, "if that's the case, then maybe *you* should serve *him* the divorce papers."

"Yeah!" I scoff. "And where am I going to get the money for that, Lara? Huh?"

"I could help."

"No." I state adamantly. "Not at all." The idea of my best friend footing the bill so I could get a divorce... It's preposterous. It's depressing. Besides, I honestly can't even consider divorcing Andrew right now. It's all too much to swallow. I may have toyed around with the idea of divorcing Andrew when I was lonely and miserable, but toying is a whole lot different than actually serving papers. There's looking into something, then there's the action, the investment.

"I'm not ready," I say in a low voice. "I'm not ready to talk about divorce, Lara."

"Not that I want to push for it or condone it," Lara says. "I don't want that for you, hon. Divorce is a bitch."

"Tell me about it!" I hear Claire pipe in in the background.

Claire's been through the ringer with the big 'D' with her parents, and I sure as hell don't need a reminder how damaging it can be.

"But you don't have children to consider," Lara says, ever the pragmatist. "If you're going to get divorced, doing it before you have children is better."

"Please, Lara," I sigh, rubbing at my eyelids, which by now are runny with mascara. "Children will never be in the picture. Andrew doesn't want them, I don't want them. That's besides the point."

"Look, I think *any* big decision made right now is a rash idea."

"Definitely," I hear Claire say.

"Claire and I are coming over to make sure you take care of yourself, okay?"

"No," I whine. I rub at my eyes some more, then at my cheeks, trying to clean off the mess of makeup. "I'm fine. I think I want to be alone right now." I gather my stuff and stand. "Thanks, though."

"Jackie, I don't like the idea of you being alone," Lara sounds leery.

"I'm *fine!* Really, I just want to be by myself."

"*Jackie? Wanting* to be alone?" Lara sighs. "I find that hard to believe."

"Things change, Lara." I chuckle emptily. "Please. Just let me figure this out for myself right now."

Reluctant, she eventually gives in and tells me to call her if I need anything at all, whether a shoulder to cry on or the number and deposit for a good attorney.

"And if I don't hear from you by noon tomorrow," Lara says before we close, "then I'm sending someone over there to check on you."

"You too busy?" I begin the walk down the long, quiet twelfth-floor hallway. "Office work on a Saturday?"

"Worth," she says, and I swear I can sense her blushing. "If you want me over, though, then—"

"No," I say quickly, "you have your date." I press the down arrow, calling up the elevator. "Something special planned?"

"We're actually going to the lake." Her voice sounds modest, hesitant, even.

"Good for you," I force myself to say, but I can't help but feel the tiniest bit envious. I'm happy for Lara, really I am. It's good she finally has some action going on in the bedroom, but what about me? I'm married, for god's sake! I can't even get *into* my bedroom!

The elevator pings loudly, the doors roll open, and I step inside, glum.

"May make an overnight trip out of it," Lara adds. I know she says it to be honest, to share her exciting news, to divulge fun tidbits of info that all girlfriends relish, but I can't help but take it as an extra sting to the wound.

"Well I'm going to go, Lara," I say as the elevator doors close behind me. "I've got some thinking to do...an apartment to clean before the rats move in. Fun stuff like that. I'll call you tomorrow to let you know I haven't killed myself."

"Jackie." Lara's tone is thick with severity. "Claire and I can turn around right now and meet you."

"I'm *fine*," I emphasize. "I'm just in my own sour mood. Being locked out and getting confirmation that your husband's a cheating asshole all in one evening is a bit of a load to swallow."

"Understood."

I step out of the elevator and click across the marble-floor foyer on the lone pair of black high heels I still have—a new pair of Louboutins I got with Sophie in Paris. "Love-ya-mean-it," I say lazily. "I've gotta run."

Then Lara and I hang up, and as I approach the swinging entrance doors of the luxurious townhouse complex—the place I used to call home and may never see again—the deskman waves and calls out with a grin, "Have a nice evening, Mrs. Kittredge."

The final sting to the open, burning wound.

I deserve them.

They're gorgeous and were made for me.

Last night, right after I left the townhouse in a state of rage and disbelief, I was on my way home, to Emily's apartment, maneuvering my way through Downtown, when I passed by Nordstrom and had an instant craving. I'd glanced over at my opened handbag, the corner of Lara's envelope of cash sticking out, and I had a very good, very naughty, very deserved idea.

"Gorgeous," I gasp, turning my feet to the left, the right, admiring the new aubergine- and lime-green-colored peep-toe Marc Jacobs heels. They're the perfect summertime and summer-turning-to-fall shoes, and they look even more perfect with my fresh pedicure.

In such a state of shock yesterday (and having a sudden wad of cash), I went all out on myself. I got my nails done, touched up my roots, got a trim, picked up these pretty shoes, and even had enough money left over to buy a bottle of Merlot, a cigar, various fashion and design magazines, and just about a full tank of gas. If Lara asked where all the money went—if I bought groceries—I'd tell her that wine and cigars are staples, they're practically groceries. I mean, I have a job now and all. I can pay for whatever I see fit.

I twist from side to side once again, smiling at the reflection in the bedroom mirror. I was born for these shoes.

"Hello?" I can hear a far-off voice call out. "Hello? Jackie?"

I make my way to the living room, heels clicking merrily along. I peek through the front window's mini-blinds. "Robin?" I say in surprise.

"What are you doing here?" I ask as I let her in. She's got a brown paper sack in one hand, and Rose's hand in the other, the little girl looking up at me with a big smile and two blonde pigtails tied off with tiny pink scrunchies.

"Good!" Robin exasperates. "You're alive!"

"You're awive!" Rose says, clapping.

I follow Robin into the kitchen. "Of course I'm alive," I say. "Why wouldn't I be?"

Robin yanks open the refrigerator and gives me a petulant look.

"What?" I ask defensively.

"Do the words, 'Call Lara before noon' ring a bell?" She begins to move items from her brown sack to the refrigerator. "Escape your mind, did it?" She's holding a half-gallon of mint chocolate chip ice cream.

"Oops," I say with a crooked smile. I gesture to the ice cream. "That's for me, I take it?"

"No," she laughs. "I was out getting some groceries when Lara called to see if I could check on you. Said she couldn't reach you on your cell."

"Damn thing," I mumble, looking over at it across the way on the kitchen counter.

"Language," Robin sings.

"Oops again." I look down at Rose hoping she didn't hear me, she's too caught up in the various magnets covering the refrigerator. They're souvenirs from all over the world, which Emily's picked up along the way.

"Thanks for checking on me," I say, watching as Robin hurriedly unloads her refrigerables.

"It's fine. I was in the area." She closes the refrigerator door. "I just wish you'd remember things like this, Jack."

"I don't need to be checked in on. I'm not a child." I fold the empty brown paper sack.

"You act like a child sometimes."

"Hey. If you came here to attack me..."

She rushes out an apology. "That came out wrong. Anyway, Lara told me what happened at the townhouse, and I'm really sorry."

"Yeah, well..." I help Rose with a large magnet too high to reach —a croissant with *Paris, France* written on it—and I can't help but give an affected smile.

Robin and I head into the living room, leaving Rose to play with the magnets. She's got a good number of them removed, lining them up along the kitchen floor.

Achieving comfortable seats on the sofa, Robin leans her head against the plush back. "What do you think you're going to do?"

I give a one-shouldered shrug. "I don't know. I really don't know."

The thing is, as much as I want to consider Hawaii proof of Andrew's infidelity, there's still an infinitesimal possibility that it's nothing more than a coincidence. And I can't end my marriage because of a coincidence, a hunch. I haven't even honestly considered calling it quits based on the loneliness and negligence and fights. Sure, we've got our problems, but when you push past the hurt and the bitterness and the depression, there's still that hope that everything will turn out right. There's still that flicker, that gleam, of hope—a chance—that we can right this wrong, just like we've done time and again. So things have never really been this bad before. We could work through it, couldn't we?

But the one thing I swore to myself I'd never allow in a marriage would be infidelity. I know what an affair does to couples, to families, to friends, to lives. It's a poison that will linger forever. Whenever arguments arise, there will always be that dagger to throw, that poison that will resurface, and it'll make it a hell of a lot harder to overcome even the simplest and smallest of obstacles with something as large and dark and looming as an affair hanging overhead.

No, my marriage could maybe survive the rough times—Andrew could eventually snap out of it and come racing back to me, telling me he's sorry and that it's time to make a fresh start, that we can go to couple's therapy and really work through our troubles, for real this time. But not now that he's cheating, now that he's sealed the deal with the affair. The tiny hope of a happy ending I've held onto these few weeks is fading; the only shred of hope I'm desperately clinging to now remains because of love. I still love my husband. I either let go of the pain, the fear, the worry, the anger, and hope for a reconciliation, or I let go of the love, the hope, the promise, the chance for a future, and I move on. Stuck somewhere in the vast void that is limbo, I don't know what to let go of.

But talking to Robin is refreshing, even despite my plan to spend the day alone, just like last night. She offered some helpful advice this afternoon, even saying I could always join her and Sophie at yoga class if I wanted. Which reminded me that Emily had encouraged I try meditation class, or at least be diligent in reading my daily horoscope, both pieces of advice I've ignored.

"Well, if there's anything else I can do to help," Robin says some time later.

She grabs her handbag and recollects her sack of groceries. She calls Rose over as she approaches the front door. "I'm not exactly free a lot of the time," she says to me. "Kids always keeping me busy." She rubs Rose's head, and the little girl holds up two handfuls of magnets.

"Ook at what I found. Aren't dey pwetty?" Rose says, showing off her collection.

"Oh, honey." Robin holds out her hand. "Give me those. Those are Aunt Emily's. You can't take them."

After a soft round of pouting and whining, Rose sets the magnets down on the loveseat.

"Hey," Robin says, gesturing to the top of the bookshelf across the room. "That new?"

"The globe?" I say. "Yeah, first and only thing I've gotten to get this place redecorated."

"Well what are you waiting for, girl?" She takes Rose's hand in hers and opens the front door. "That's a neat piece, and I can't think of a better way to help you get your mind off of Andrew right now.'"

Problem is, *I* could think of a better way to get my mind off of Andrew. Still feeling like I wanted to be alone, with resurfaced and ever-gnawing anxieties about my situation and the precariousness of it all, I grabbed some cash from Emily's mason jar and jumped in my Mercedes.

It was too early to go to the clubs, and going to the bars at that hour meant small talk with bartenders, which would get me into serious trouble. Or I'd get stuck talking to old geezers or drunks. So I did the next best thing and dropped by the corner liquor store three blocks over and grabbed a few things. I had already drunk the bottle of Merlot last night, and figured, judging by the way I was feeling at midday and assuming the pain wouldn't subside much any time soon, I was headed for a similar night tonight. I was in need of a restock.

Like always, though, drinking to the bottom of the bottle and grousing to myself and my dog only do so much good, if any. Sure, the emotional pain begins to feel numb, and I can't really think straight or form any intelligible word past a mumble or a *whoop*, so I guess knocking a few back does *some* good.

It's the hours later, though, that really bite. When the headache surges forward; when the backs of my eyes feel like anvils have been dropped on them; when the white noise becomes so loud I feel like my ears are going to burst and bleed; when the feelings and the issues that plague me begin to come back into view, however fuzzy... that's when I either wish I'd never have touched the drink, or when I wish the bottom wouldn't have come so soon.

I've drunk my resources dry, and now I'm in the middle of my bedroom, scratching my heavy head, wondering where I went wrong in life.

38

I'm not sure what day it is, much less what time. My mouth feels dry, my head massive, and my eyes crusted over with sleep. With one eye tightly squinted shut, the other barely pried open, I yawn and stretch one arm over my head. I make a high-pitched yelp as I conclude my yawn. Bella appears from nowhere, leaping up onto the messy bed and settling near my pillow.

"Hey, darling," I say, groggy. I pet her just as another yawn escapes my lips. "Damn. I think mommy's reached her limit." I rub at my eyes and make a mental note to lay off the alcohol for a while, weekend or no weekend. The way my head feels right now, I think a month ought to do it.

I grab my cell phone and wait a second before the numbers are no longer fuzzy. *10.49*, it reads. *Monday.*

"Oh no!" I cry once the reality of the time settles in. "Bella!" I look to my little Yorkie, as if she can talk to me or understands. "Do you know what time it is? What day?" I clap both hands to the top of my pounding head. "I'm late! Oh shit! I'm late!"

So that's another one for the ol' career book.

I strolled into The Cup and the Cake over two hours late that morning and Sophie had nearly had an epileptic fit. I noticed, a few hours too late, that she called me, even texted a few times first asking where I was, then if I was okay, then telling me I'd better have a good excuse or else. Unfortunately, I didn't have a good excuse for my tardiness, at least not one she was willing to hear a second time much less buy into.

I told you, I'm just no good at jobs. I screw them all up!

"You were doing so well," Sophie said once I finally arrived at the café, still a bit disoriented, but luckily my fresh visit to the salon resulted in hair that looked effortlessly fantastic. "I can't believe you'd blow off work like this! Second week on the job, Jackie!"

I weeped into the blueberry-lemon scone that eventually became Sophie's peace offering after she ripped me a new one.

As for my job? "Can I keep it?" I asked in a timid voice.

"Sheesh!" she cried, throwing her hands up and sounding just like Ricky Ricardo after a foolish Lucy stunt. "You're kidding me, right, Jack?"

I gave a lazy shrug, stuffed a piece of tasty scone in my mouth, and said, "Sowwy I asked."

It was a disaster. A total disaster. I'm so embarrassed and upset with myself, and Sophie. I know I'm far from Employee-of-the-Month, but how could she do this to me? After all I've been through, couldn't she have cut me a little slack? The fact that I'm dead-ass broke, the little nasty part where my husband has left me and run off to the Hawaiian islands with his secretary... Where's the pity? The sympathy? The warning and second chance?

It's only a few days after the fact of my firing, when I have nothing to do and not a cent to my name, that I'm beginning to really ask these questions. So Sophie was upset about my sleeping in. I came in, however late, and I offered to help, even though I wasn't too fond of working there to begin with. I tried, I showed effort, I did all those things Dr. Pierce and the girls tell me I should do, and look at me now! I'm back in the unemployment line, running through Emily's mason jar of cash faster than my marriage turned itself upside down.

After I finish typing out a hasty email to Emily, catching her up on the problems at home and begging her to email me back some time this century, I decide to give Robin a call. I know I've been a bit abrasive and kind of under the weather, locked away and hiding from the world this weekend, but she did say if there was anything I needed...

"Robin?" I say hurriedly as her friendly voice comes on the line. "Is this a bad time?"

"One child screaming at the top of his lungs for lunch, the other on a sugar high and jumping all over the furniture," she says with an exhausted sigh. "No, it's as good a time as ever."

"Great. Okay, I hate to ask and bug, but I could so use a favor right now."

There's a bit of dead air before Robin says, "I heard about what happened at the café, and I'm really sorry."

"Yeah, well. It wouldn't have worked out in the long run, I'm sure. Sophie's too perfect, and I'm a mess." I laugh pathetically to myself. "Whatever. I'd really rather not talk about it."

"You know Sophie doesn't mean any ill will towards your friendship," Robin says in assured tones. "She's just thinking business-wise here."

"Yeah, yeah. I'm fine. Let's just put it behind us." I sigh loudly. "Of course, I still think I could have been given a second chance—"

"Rose, please stop that right now," Robin calls off, voice sounding distant, yet booming. "Rose! I'm going to count to three. One. Please listen. Two... I'll call Daddy. Thr—" Her voice returns to a normal volume now. "Okay, crisis averted," she says to me. "For now, at least." She half sighs, half laughs. "Sorry. You were saying?"

"Robin, I need some help. Need to get back on my feet."

"Okay, I get it. You want me to talk to Sophie for you? Ask her to give you your job back, a second chance?"

"No." I wince. "No, no, no. Thanks, but no."

"So what?"

"Can I borrow some money? Just a little bit?"

"Jackie." She exhales loudly.

"Look, I can pay you back when I get a job."

"You're looking for another job?"

"Well...not exactly."

"Jackie."

"Listen, Robin, please." I scratch at my worry-creased forehead. "I'm just about down to the change in Em's jar."

"Huh?"

I shake my head, deciding against divulging the information she doesn't really need to know—the money that was intended for decoration and not gasoline and groceries...and the mani/pedis, tanning salon packages, wine and cigarettes, a magazine or rented movie here and there. Oh, and the two pairs of shoes and couple of shimmery tops I couldn't help myself from buying at the mall.

I want to cry out, "I need help! I've practically stolen from my best friend and I don't know what to do!" But, instead, I pipe out, "I'm broke, Robin. I really need some money."

"If you need some food, I'll bring some groceries by," she offers.

"Sophie sent me home with all sorts of sweets. I'm good."

"Jackie—"

"Look." I clear my throat in a discomfited way. It's always so much easier to ask for money from Lara. She's always been there for me with a spare twenty, a quick transfer of funds to cover a bill. "All I need is a little bit to help me for a few days." I pause, waiting for Robin to say something, anything. When she doesn't, I continue. "A little to tide me over until my next job. I'll find one! Promise!"

"Jackie." Her voice is calm and crisp. "I understand your predicament right now, really I do, but Bobby and I are working on a tight budget. We have two kids, I've gone part-time, there are the part-time daycare costs... I can't, and even if I could..." She pauses. "I know where you're at right now. You're depressed, you're lonely, you're having a rough time—"

"Yes, thanks for the reminder."

"And you're between a rock and a hard place."

"Tell me about it." *Yes,* I think, *she feels my pain, understands, and now the sympathy? Sympathy money?*

"I've been there," she says. "It sucks. Not in the same exact position with a husband possibly cheating and—"

"*Is* cheating, Robin. I know I'm not one hundred percent certain, but there *is* evidence. He's just *got* to be cheating!" I say this with such vindication and force. Though there's still that small glimmer of hope that Andrew has stayed faithful, the glimmer is waning. I feel more and more proof-positive with each passing day—each day that goes by without a word from Andrew—that I've lost my husband to another woman.

"I've been in that tough spot," Robin carries on, "single and pregnant and needing my friends to lean on. Emotionally, physically...financially."

So you understand! I think, starting to feel relief.

"You were all there for me, in one way or another. In whatever way each of you could offer, could afford," she explains. "You did what you thought was best for me, and you have over time, even after Rose was born. Sometimes I didn't agree with the choices or couldn't see the other side or got frustrated with things when they didn't go my way. I mean, we *all* want things to go our way, as we planned, you know?" She laughs softly. "But that's not the way of life, and I had to accept the things I didn't like and live with it. Make the most out of it! I had to step up and grow up."

I can sense where this conversation is headed, and I'm not exactly pleased. I pick the back of my pink, freshly polished acrylic and blubber out a loud sigh.

"That's where you are now, too, Jackie. It's time for you to step up." Robin's interrupted by some loud banging and screaming in the background.

"Look, doll, I've got to run. Rose is playing the pied piper, and I'm trying to feed Phillip and get him to sleep, and it's just—I've got to go."

"But Robin."

"I love you, Jack, and if you need some food or a shoulder to cry on, I'll try my best to get on over there. You're welcome here, too, you know?" Then she shouts out, "Rose, do not hit the windows with the spoon. Argh!"

A rush back to the phone, voice lowered but still just as frazzled: "I've really got to run, Jack. Later."

"Doctor, things are bad," are the first words out of my mouth during one of my routine mid-afternoon sessions with Dr. Pierce.

"You and Andrew talking?" he says as he takes his seat.

I toss my Louis Vuitton Neverfull handbag to the foot of the chaise longue and sigh melodramatically. I lie down, drape one arm over my eyes, and say, "I wish, Doc. Then I wouldn't have any money troubles. You know, if I had money I could so do this single woman thing on my own. I bet you *anything*."

"You have nothing to wager, let's not place bets," he kids, but his joke doesn't get a laugh.

Instead, I just shake my head and say, "I'm serious. You know, the only reason I flew home from Paris and ran home was because I had money troubles. I loved leaving town. I loved leaving Andrew behind and making him worry, getting to do my own thing without having to check in." I dart my head up and look Dr. Pierce square in the eyes. "Make *him* feel what it's like—shoe on the other foot! Things just got all shot to hell." I plunk my head back down, arm returning to cover my face.

"So you're still battling the hostility with Andrew and the last discussion you had?"

"Of course I'm still battling hostility!" I nearly shout, aghast. "And the last *discussion*? It was a disaster! It was the last *fight*." I bite the tip of my tongue, lock my jaw. "It was the last *anything*, Doctor. I try to forget about it and just move on, wait for the divorce or whatever's next."

"So what are the things that are bad?'"

I look at Dr. Pierce, my face contorted into an expression of bewilderment. "Doctor, are you *listening* to me? Things that are bad? My life! My whole life's bad!"

"You came in saying things are bad. Anything in particular? Anything...new?"

"I'm just in a bind with finances, and I asked a friend to help and she said no." I rub at my face. "Added stress, lost my job, marriage looks like it's over..."

"Your marriage is going through a tough time, and your finances aren't in order," he says cautiously. "You're stressed. These things are rough, yes, but these things are not your entire life, Jackie. They do not define you."

"Oh, Doctor," I groan. "These things are a *huge* part of life!"

"Yes—"

"Things are bad because I need to get back on my feet, but every time I try I fall down. I'm just so over this phase of my life. I'm ready for my marriage to be back to the way it was." I drape my arm over my face again. "Listen to me! I can't believe what I'm saying. I just didn't realize how good the bad was. What I wouldn't *give* to have my old life back."

"Jackie, you were very miserable back then."

"Not as miserable as I am now!" I say, shooting my head up once more. "Look at me! I'm practically catatonic!"

Dr. Pierce lets a half-grin slip through. "Jackie, the point is not to regress, the point is to *pro*gress. We're moving forward here. Wanting things to be...bad, but less bad...isn't going to make matters better. Are you still taking your prescription?"

"Yes."

"And you're not having more than one drink a day, right?"

"Yes."

Dead air, waiting for me to clarify.

"Yes to you're right," I rush out. "No to I'm not having more than one drink a day."

"And there are days, back-to-back, where you don't have a single drink at all?"

"Yes. Yes, there are times when I'm completely sober for days at a time. Ugh!" I pause, then splutter out, "So I have a little slip-up now and then, go on a little bender. Who doesn't?"

"These slip-ups aren't what we'd call...routine?"

"No," I say honestly. "Trust me, there've been times in my past where I'd party hard five, six days a week." I simper, thinking back on my dangerous days when getting to do a line of coke or being the designated girl one frat house or another elected to do body shots off of were my greatest priorities of the week. "I'm *fine*."

"This is better." He adjusts his navy tie. "What about the job search? Any progress on that?"

"Lara topped me up," I say simply, "when Robin couldn't. I can manage for another week or two without a problem. Of course I'm sure she'll start to get peeved or ask prying questions when I keep coming to her with my hand held out. I just am really living on pennies, Doctor, car chugging on fumes."

Dr. Pierce clears his throat in a purposefully apparent way. "Things can't be that bad, can they, Jackie?"

I meet his eyes.

"This is a safe place," he says. "You can be honest. Are you being truthful with me?"

"What?" I stare at him with a vacant expression.

He gestures to my handbag. "Nice nails, nice purse. I'm not here to cast judgment, I'm here to help, and if finances are a trouble, perhaps it's time we shift the discussion towards priorities."

"Hey!" I hold up a hand. "That bag's not new, for your information. Had it for years. As for the nails." I look down at the fill job I recently got. I give a weak grin and slip my hands under my thighs. "Cheap. A cheap fill job."

"Jackie."

"I need to look decent for job interviews!" I spew out the first thing that comes to mind—not a half-bad excuse.

"I told you," I say, tone calm now. "I've got enough to scrape by with Lara helping me. I'm fine. It's just *bad* because I'm not rolling in it like I used to when I was with Andrew. There were *some* fab perks to that marriage. Now on my own it's just... Well, it sucks."

"You know what I've said about this before," he says with precision, "and you know I have the same thing to say today."

Here we go again. Dr. Pierce thinks I should buckle down and get a job, any job, even one that requires flipping hamburgers or cold-calling. "Anything that is consistent and requires responsibility," he says.

"Same time next week?" I ask, perturbed at the deadbeat session today that's at last come to a close. I fling open the door.

"Same time next week," Dr. Pierce says as he scribbles in his notebook.

39

I'm on my way to Sophie's this hot August night for a much-needed girls' night Claire insisted on. At first we'd planned to meet at Claire's home, but when Sophie heard Chad was due to swing by to pick up Conner and go out to some pub to watch a game, she insisted we have girls' night at her place, dead-set on avoiding him.

I'm fine with it seeing how Claire's Madison Park home is clear across town. My car is back down to the 'E' mark, so driving straight down Aurora Ave at a slow and steady pace to Sophie's apartment in Belltown is fine by me.

I'm less than five minutes away when my cell phone notifies me of the email I've been waiting an eternity for, and I can't help myself.

"Emily!" I shriek excitedly, nearly swerving into the lane of oncoming traffic when I see *Saunders, Emily* pop up on the screen.

I safely pull to the side of the road. Grabbing my phone, I begin to eagerly read Emily's message, not a second to wait.

Hi, Jackie! It is so good to hear from you!! I miss you too! Travels in Australia and New Zealand have been nothing short of amazing. The wildlife is spectacular, the landscapes brilliant, the company fantastic!

Gatz is a natural-born traveller, and I couldn't think of anyone more perfect to wander with.

I'm sorry things at home aren't going well. If I were with you I'd pinch your cheek and tell you, 'Chin up!' I wish I could give you a big hug right now and tell you everything will be all right. Well, how's this? Everything <u>will</u> be all right! Even though you can be totally zany and make some insane choices, your aura is a bright one. You're special, Jack, and Andrew knows that. He's got his load to figure out right now, and so do you. Take this time to do something big, something wonderful, something important.

And as for Sophie firing you, she probably did it because she loves you. That café's got a lot of mysteries and intrigue about it. It's got a funny relationship with love, and I bet Sophie's just doing what the café gods are telling her is best. (Yes, I think the Maori tribes I've been reading up on are having a wonderfully infectious effect on me.)

Hang in there, kid. I'll try to Skype you in the next couple of weeks. We're going backpacking in Byron Bay for a bit, and I anticipate I'll be getting caught up in some crazy-awesome photography and surfing (taking it up, BTW). Sorry in advance for not keeping in better touch!

I love you and miss you. Take care and keep that chin up!

PS: I read the horoscopes today and yours says that someone or something is going to intimidate you and make you feel like you need to escape. (No, I don't think it's referring to Paris you crazy girl!!) Advice of the stars says this person or thing is just what you need in order to do what you have to. The opportunity is there, but it's disguised. Rest assured, it says that once you gain the confidence to face the intimidation, you can carry on your journey safely. Pretty cool, hah? Appropriate? I think so.

Well, safe journeys to you, my BFF, and wish me the same. Hello and hugs to all the girls, hi from Gatz.

XO,

Emily

"I'm serious!" Sophie says in a no-laughing-matter kind of way, even though she's fighting off a fit of laughter herself. "It was not funny. It was so awkward and humiliating."

Claire and Robin are howling, Lara can't stop her covering-the-mouth chuckling, and I can see the whole sordid thing right now, clear as day, and the laughter just won't subside.

Sophie giggles at last, the humor of the ordeal no longer lost on her. She reaches for her glass of Riesling. "So in retrospect it's kind of funny, okay," she admits. "But at the time it was just downright horrible. Totally embarrassing, girls!"

"It's Chad, Sophie," Lara says with a large smile. "How embarrassing could it really be? I mean, maybe if he was a total stranger or something—"

"Or even if he wasn't," Robin says. "Like if it were Gatz."

Sophie groans as she sets her wine glass down on the coffee table.

"So what'd you do?" Lara asks.

"Well I didn't stick around to watch, that's what I *didn't* do!" Sophie looks appalled.

A roar of laughter erupts loudly again.

"They weren't like..." I pause, purse my lips, and survey the room. I then look to Sophie and say, "They weren't like...doing it, were they?" Sophie's face goes long. "Or about to?"

"Oh, no! Ew!" Sophie writhes in discomfort.

"You think they would?" Claire asks with hungry eyes. "Omigod, how gross, but how sexy." She shakes her hips.

"Claire," Sophie says with a straight face, "there's nothing sexy about Chad, a *former* employee," Lara and I share a roll of the eyes, "and Evelyn, an *employee,* doing the hanky-panky in *my* café!"

"Oh, come on," I say, unable to restrain myself. "You've got to admit there's at least *some* sexiness to hanky-panky in a forbidden place."

"Oh, yes, I forget that laundry rooms are perfectly acceptable places to get lucky," Sophie says smugly, arms crossed.

"Oh!" Lara cries. "That's right! The dorms, your freshman year? Jackie, I can't believe you didn't get caught."

Sophie laughs and holds up two fingers. "Okay, that makes *two* for the laundry room," she says, obviously referencing that *one* time —that *one* really stupid, high-out-of-my-mind time—when Chad and I did it in the laundry room at his parents' house years ago. "Jackie, I love ya, hon, but you're obviously not the most unbiased of people in this situation."

"Conner and I've done it in the men's locker room at the pool," Claire snickers. "Sophomore year, U Dub pool."

"Okay!" I say, clapping my hands. "Let's all share the most risqué places we've ever done it!"

Sophie groans and rolls her eyes, trying to hide her embarrassment and flushing cheeks behind her wine glass. She takes a long, slow pull.

"Okay," Robin says eagerly. She rolls up the cuffs of her capri jeans some, then props herself higher up on her the small loveseat with one leg tucked underneath her. "I've got one for ya!" She fans at her face with what looks like a metro map of Paris, which she snagged from under Sophie's coffee table.

"A hot and heavy session, was it?" Claire kids.

"It's hot in here," Sophie says, eagerly leaping forward to leave the titillating discussion. She goes to adjust the air conditioning when Robin says, "Okay. So it was with Bobby."

"Obviously," Lara says with a sugary smile.

"And it was on our honeymoon."

"Ooooh," I coo. "Fresh naughtiness."

"We were hiking, and, well, one thing led to another and we did it right there off of the hiking trail." She pulls her shoulders up and giggles like a schoolgirl. "Not exactly crazy-risqué, but—"

"Bold," Sophie says. "Definitely bold."

"And you?" Robin says, looking at Sophie. "Where's your craziest place?"

Sophie nervously laughs as she settles back into her comfortable position on the sofa. "Paris is definitely meant for lovers," she says in a singsong way. "Couples making out left and right."

"So true," I interject.

"Even though I have no love life to talk about," Sophie waxes on, "that French guy, Henri, and I did give it a go in some daring places." She's blushing again.

"When?" I blurt out. "This year? Before I showed up?"

Deeper blushing, then, "Okay, we did hook up a couple times this summer."

Oooohs and *Ahhhs* fill the cramped living room.

"But that first summer." Sophie pauses for a lengthy moment, pressing her lips together tightly, ready to let us in on her naughty little secret.

"Tell already!" I cry at last.

"It was a crazy-fun summer!" Sophie bursts. "There was the bathroom at this wine bar over in the Latin Quarter. Victor Hugo Caveau or something like that. A classy, artsy place that was totally defiled." She smiles fiendishly. "There was the attempt in the Tuileries, but that totally failed. A hot make-out session, though. Then the really romantic time in the gardens of Versaille."

"The Palace of Versaille?" Claire says.

"The place is gigantic," Sophie says. "Those gardens? The chances that someone would have seen us were so slim. It was perfect."

"Was this when *I* was in Paris with you, Sophie?" Claire makes a curious face. "When *we* went to Versaille together?"

Sophie brings her glass of wine to her lips, and before taking a drink says, "No, this was another time. Before you and Conner came over."

"Well you should've told me!" Claire lightly smacks her on the leg. "Conner and I *love* doing it in forbidden places. Oh, and how romantic would that have been?" Claire presses her hands to her heart. "We were just engaged, on vacation together in romantic Paris, a romp in the gardens..."

Sophie laughs and says, "Minus the brambles and the damp grass and the bugs...and the heat...it was pretty romantic."

"Well now that my mind is filled with pornographic images,"

Lara says teasingly. "You want to finish up this ode to love and tell us what happened with Chad and Evelyn finally?" She motions to Sophie.

"It was closing time," Sophie says, "and it was just me and Evelyn —as always. I've *really* got to get myself another employee, you know? I've been thinking of hiring on another person, but part-time is all I can afford."

"Back to the subject," Claire sings.

"Well, anyway, I stepped outside to take out the trash," Sophie proceeds, "and Evelyn was in the back finishing up the cleaning. Chad pulled up in the parking lot. Said hi, kept it simple and sweet."

"I am so glad there's no lingering animosity over him dating a coworker," Claire cuts in.

"Yeah, well," Sophie flicks a wrist, "he's not working for me anymore, so...whatever. He's always getting under my skin anyway. I just need to remember to apply the anti-itching cream now and then."

"The story!" I press.

"Anyway, he was picking up Evelyn. I got to sweeping the front walk, then I noticed the front window was all dirty..." She takes a quick pull of her wine, finishing off the glass. "I guess my lengthy cleaning period outside was an open invitation for Chad to just feel up Evelyn. I walked in and he had her on the countertop, hands under her shirt, they're making out, she's moaning..." Sophie shivers. "Too much detail."

"Fun!" I say, hanging on each word.

The girls all give me a quirky expression.

"What?" I say in a high voice. "I've been without for months."

"Anyway," Sophie says, "it was totally awkward and unacceptable and just wrong. Not in my café, thank you very much."

"But in the Louvre or the Tuileries?" I say with a chortle.

"Or Café Victor Hugo," Lara adds.

"Yeah, yeah." Sophie criss-crosses her legs, dressed in a pair of black yoga pants. "When I walked in I made my presence announced, and they were, well, honestly, they were more embarrassed than I was. Chad just kind of skulked off, and Evelyn apologized a zillion times. Begged me not to fire her. Poor thing. Think she's scared of me or something."

"The wrath of Sophie," I say with a cock of the head.

She pokes me in the ribs. "You know I still love you."

"What a story," Lara says with a sigh. "What were they thinking? I mean, they *knew* you were there!"

"It's that risk of getting caught that can be fun," Claire says with a sneaky grin. "That's half the fun of it, really. The rest is that mad pull you have for each other, that attraction—"

"That love," Robin adds dreamily.

"Yeah."

"Hey," Robin says. She looks to Lara. "What about you? You never shared your most tawdry encounter."

"Ha!" Lara sounds. "How about countless times in my office, on my desk?"

"Aww, yes," Robin says, head tilted back. "That illicit affair."

"Actually," Lara says. A grin tugs at one corner of her mouth. "Worth and I have a weekend getaway coming up. He's taking me to his cabin up in the mountains." She clicks her tongue seductively. "Romantic setting, just the two of us..."

Claire claps and shrieks, "Lara, you *so* have to do it in the woods! Right, Robin?"

"It can be fun," Robin says. "Just find a boulder or something to prop yourself up. Keep you off the pine needles and stuff."

We all laugh as Claire says, "Or if there's an area with a stream or lake or something, a random pool of water. Conner and I once did it in this pond when we were visiting my family down in Oregon. A-ma-zing!"

"Okay," Sophie says, holding up the bottle of Riesling. "Think we've either had enough for tonight or we're topping up and moving on to other topics of convo."

We opt for the latter, even though I think Claire could have been just as happy continuing the chatter about all the unique places she and Conner have consummated their love.

I'll admit that it makes me a teensy bit jealous, them having a successful and happy marriage, loving each other. But what makes me more jealous is Lara and Worth. They have that new and exciting passion—what Andrew and I used to have. Andrew and I never really had what Conner and Claire have—a long-time relationship where the routine is actually still fun and fulfilling. I mean, Conner and Claire have their own rough patches, as all couples do, and I wouldn't really want to be in their shoes right now what with Conner having just turned in his two-week notice. Things are going to get even tighter and probably tense, and there's that very real possibility that the replacement job Conner's searching for will be outside Seattle.

Lara and Worth, though...things seem perfect. They're happy, they're having fun, they're not lonely...

"So what does this mean?" Robin says once Claire delivers her news—the reason she insisted on this last-minute planned girls' night.

"It means," Claire says, playing with the hem of her bright pink tank top, "that things have been taken to the next level. Conner's got interviews lined up with two different firms in Seattle next week, which is great. He's also got a telephone interview with a firm in Spokane, for a really well-paid and high-up position in the accounting department, actually. It pays better than the two he's looking at in town. And he's got some feelers out in LA, too."

"Oh no," Sophie grumbles. "You're moving?"

"Nothing's for sure yet, Sophie," Claire reassures. "The possibility is there, though."

"Do you even want to move?" I ask.

"Of course I don't want to!" Claire looks thunderstruck. "I love Seattle, I love my job, I love being near you girls—our lives are here!"

"So why move?" I pick up the bottle of lime-flavored mineral water and fill my wine glass with it. I've already had two glasses of

Riesling, and I'm trying my best to follow Dr. Pierce's advice. I can have some fun now and then, but I can't turn to the bottle every time there's a reason to celebrate or, much worse, sulk.

"Because," Claire says, still wearing that thunderstruck look, "my husband's career is at stake, and it's what I, as his partner, his wife, should do. Being supportive and understanding comes with the territory of marriage."

"If you had a career move to make, I'm sure Conner would do the same for you," Robin says.

"Exactly." Claire looks from Robin to me. "It's not cut and dry all the time, Jack. Trust me, I wish it was. I wish Conner could've sucked it up and made the most of the job he had. Or, heck, it'd be nice if he could've been promoted like he was *supposed* to be." She hugs a grey throw pillow to her chest. "But life doesn't always turn out the way you thought. And I've got to take it in stride. Can't freak out over every thing that doesn't go my way."

I casually shrug it off and drink my water.

"Spokane's nice," Lara says. "And it's not *that* far."

"Not like LA," Sophie says sadly.

"I didn't want to sour the mood," Claire says. "I wanted you all to know, though. Wanted to let you know of the possibility..."

"It'll all work out," Robin says perkily. She rubs her hands together. "Maybe unexpectedly, but things will work out just fine."

"It's true," Lara says. "Did I think the guy who talked about the difference between Beluga and Sevruga caviar would have swept me off my feet and be taking me on out-of-town trips?" She smiles broadly.

"Girl," Sophie says, "you are *so* hung up on this guy. It's great. I'm happy for you. But you're *so* hung up." Sophie pans around the room. "Look at Lara, girls. She's got her glow back, moving on, shacking up."

"All right, all right," Lara says with a halting hand motion. "I know, I'm droning on. Sorry."

"No!" Claire says. "*Some* of us need to have happy stories to share."

"Yeah," Sophie says. "And it's about damn time it was you, Lara."

Lara looks down at her lap, smiling, then catches my gaze. I'm happy for Lara, really I am. But that big green monster is rumbling around inside of me, and I'm fighting it the best I can, trying my hardest to put on a painted smile and tell Lara, "Yeah, good for you."

40

I tried. Really, I tried.

I tried so hard to fight that green monster known as Envy, but it just wouldn't leave me the hell alone. Throughout the rest of girls' night I kept spontaneously thinking about Lara and Worth and how she was having the time of her life with a romantic, rich, and caring man. She was happy, she had a glow about her, and I was on the other side of the fence, watching on in envy.

I emailed Emily about my feelings as soon as I got home that night. I don't know when I'll hear from her again, and probably by the time I do the green monster will have packed his bags and moved on to his next victim. I can only hope.

As a last ditch effort to ward the monster away I had actually stopped Lara on her way to the car after girls' night and asked if she thought it was at all strange that she was dating someone who worked with Andrew. She made a funny expression, wagged her head, then spluttered out, "Why would that be weird?"

I explained that I just thought it'd be odd, seeing how Worth worked with Andrew (closely or not), if things ended up working out for the two of them, and Andrew and I didn't. "I don't know," I replied to Lara. "I just think maybe it could bring some unnecessary tension."

She just laughed it off, got into her car, and told me I was being silly.

The time had come, though, when I just couldn't take it anymore. I couldn't shake the thought from my mind that Lara and Worth were together, happy, and Andrew and I were not. If Worth were anyone else, if he didn't work with Andrew, I don't think I'd be as bothered.

But the fact that Worth is always in such close proximity to Andrew and dating my best friend just makes me feel like Lara is, in some roundabout way, condoning Andrew's behavior. Dr. Pierce said this sounded absurd and was a perfect example of me borrowing trouble.

But there's something to this idea, don't you think? Lara, and Worth, too, know things aren't exactly copacetic between Andrew and me. I'm sure Worth struts into Andrew's office now and then, all chipper and ready to chat about business, knowing all too well that Lara's BFF is still hung out to dry thanks to his asshole coworker. And Worth probably claps Andrew on the back in a jolly old sport kind of way, too, and Andrew probably returns the favor, chuckling and pretending everything's just peachy. Lara, in the meantime, stands back with a goofy grin and pitter-patter heart while I slowly drown.

Dr. Pierce told me self-pity wouldn't get me anywhere, nor would the trouble I was concocting. So I did the best thing I could imagine doing. I didn't drown my sorrows in bottomless glasses of rum; I didn't hit the clubs and make myself feel good by counting the numbers I could collect from horny bar hoppers; I didn't cry into my pillow night after night. I got into my car, despite the eleventh hour on a Tuesday night, and drove to Lara's.

"Jackie?" Lara gasps as she answers the door, dressed in a pair of black Soffe shorts and a Mt. Rainier t-shirt. "Are you okay?"

She takes off her wire-rimmed reading glasses and looks behind me, surveying the parking lot. "It's so late." Slight panic is in her eyes. She opens the door farther. "What are you doing out at this hour? Everything all right?"

"Is Worth here?" I ask as I come inside. I cram my hands nervously into my pants pockets.

"No. Why?"

I clear my throat as Lara turns on a second small living room lamp. "Look," I start, "it's late, and I know you probably have a busy day ahead of you at the office tomorrow." Judging by the sheaf of papers splayed about the coffee table and floor, highlighters and pens and pencils, too, she probably not only has a busy day tomorrow but hasn't quite finished the busy day today.

"What is it?" Lara looks worried now. She hops right to it, quicker than I am, and ushers me to the sofa. "This looks like it'll need tea." She moves towards the kitchen, grabbing her green mug from atop a stack of papers.

"No," I say. I take a seat nearby Lara's cat BeeBee. "I'm good, thanks."

"Well, I'm due for a refill," she says from the kitchen. "The office is really laying the deadline on hard for me. I feel like I'm working around the clock."

"Seems like you are." I pick up a loose paper that's colored with yellow highlighter and red pen. It's chock-full of numbers, running up and down tidy columns, with handwritten notes like *Consult previous year's #s* and *Pre-Rebrand* and *Post-Rebrand*. I shake my head and set the paper back down as Lara returns, walking carefully so as not to spill her warm refill.

"It's just exhausting," she says. "I love the pressure and challenge, but it's like the pressure's been building week after week." She snickers. "No end in sight."

She attempts a sip but pulls back when she realizes her tea is too hot to drink. "Anyhoo." She shakes her head. "You're obviously not here to chat about my workload. What's up?"

"Oh..." I drift, not sure how to say this. "I've just been doing some thinking. Some thinking about...relationships." I try to tread upon the subject with care. I don't want to insult or upset Lara, but I want to be honest about my feelings.

"Andrew?" She squints in disappointment. "You still thinking about Andrew and Nikki?"

"Sometimes," I say honestly. "Sometimes I think there's still a chance for us. Maybe whenever I see Andrew and talk to him again, I can ask straight out. Ask him about Hawaii... I don't know." I scratch at my head. "Put all the cards on the table and tell him to be honest. I mean, we'll probably be getting a divorce anyhow, right?"

Lara only shrugs in response.

"But it's not just Nikki and Andrew," I say in a small and tired voice. "Not just my marriage, but relationships with friends..." Lara nods. "Relationships friends have..." I begin to stroke BeeBee's soft fur, something to help keep my nerves from unraveling and making me lose the gall to do what I came here to do. "I've been pretty lonely, feeling pretty empty, you know?" Lara nods some more. "I'm still trying to figure this all out, Lara, and find my place and all."

"Mmmhmm," she sounds through a cautious sip of tea.

"I need the support, you know?"

"You have all our support, Jackie. We're all busy and have lives of our own, but that doesn't mean we don't support you."

"Yeah, well—"

"I mean," she gestures to her paperwork, "you can obviously see I'm in over my head with work these days. I can't always answer my phone..."

"It's not just that."

"Okay."

"It's—it's—" I can't bring myself to say it.

"Hey, how's this?" Lara puts on a cheerful face. "Once this big deal with Jennings & Voigt is finished then how about you and I go away for a weekend somewhere? My treat! Girls' spa weekend or something."

I force out a weak smile in response.

"And if it's any consolation, I'm not trying to be a rockstar and undertake all this work on my own." She gestures again to the paperwork. "Worth, on the other end, is working around the clock, too, and it's just so much!" She holds out a stiff, flat hand to emphasize her point. "It's just work here, work there, deadline here, deadline there. He's stressed, I'm—"

"I can't!" I erupt. "I just can't! Lara, I can't hear it anymore."

"Sorry." Her face twists in apology. "Worth says I have a tendency to run on about work, especially in situations where—"

"That!" I shriek, eyes wide. "Worth this, Worth that. Worth with work, Worth on romantic dates!"

Her face slowly falls, her shoulders sag, and she's speechless.

"I'm sorry, Lara, but I can't handle it. I'm going to just say what I came here to say." I take in a deep breath and exhale loudly and slowly, gripping the edge of the sofa for support. "I don't like you dating Worth."

"Wh-what?"

"I'm glad you're happy and have found romance, Lara." I fix my eyes on my kneecaps. "But I don't like that it's with someone that close to Andrew."

"I can't believe I'm hearing this."

"I already told you I wasn't comfortable with you dating him."

"Yeah," she shakily laughs out. "As in, 'it's weird,' but not as in 'I don't like it.' Jackie, I've finally found someone who really makes me happy...who gets me...who clicks with me!" I slowly meet her gaze. "And I'd hardly call Worth and Andrew buddies. They work for the same firm—so what?"

"You dating Worth is like saying you approve of what Andrew's doing to me." There. I said it. It feels good to have gotten it off my chest. However, what I've just said also makes me feel like total crap. Like the world's worst friend.

"What?" Lara's shocked, utterly shocked. "How could you *think* that?"

"I don't know!" I raise my hands in puzzlement. "It's how I feel."

"How could you feel that way? You know I love you, Jackie. I would *never* take Andrew's side. You're my *best* friend!" She shakes her head aggressively. "How? How could you feel this way?"

"I can't help the way I feel or what I think, Lara!" I form fists and pound one into the plush sofa cushion. BeeBee sits upright, alert. "I just don't think it's very supportive of you to be seeing someone like Worth. It's just—just—it's just selfish!"

As I say this last word, Lara's face drops. A long, awkward silence ensues, and as she picks her jaw up off the floor, I squeak out, "I don't want you to date him anymore, Lara. It hurts me too much."

"It hurts you to see me *happy*?" she says slowly.

I nod quickly.

"It hurts you—*you!*—to see me finally happy?"

"Yes, dammit!" I shout. "Is it so much for me to ask that you not sleep with the guy who works with my cheating husband, huh?"

"You're out of your mind, Jackie." She sets her mug of tea down and briskly pushes her loose strands of highlighted hair behind her ears. "*You* are the selfish one. This is absurd. You've taken selfish to a whole new level! I can't believe this is happening. I can't believe you're *saying* these things!"

"I wanted to be honest." My tone registers to a more normal volume. "I screwed the honesty pooch in Paris with Sophie, with Em, hell, with Andrew." My voice begins to quake. "This Worth thing's been eating me up lately, and...it just feels good to tell you how I honestly feel." I feel my fists sweat. I unclench them, but then my hands begin to shake, so I form fists once again. "I hope you'll understand."

"Understand?" Her eyes grow round. "Sorry, but I don't understand. And I can't help you here."

"So you're just going to, what?" I spit. "Keep on seeing him? No matter how much it hurts me?"

"My relationship with Worth isn't about you, Jackie. Get over it. Get over yourself!"

"It *is* about me!" My volume is raised again, my blood pressure beginning to join it. "You're sleeping with a guy who—"

"A guy who has nothing to do with your screwed up marriage!"

I wince. "Some friend you are."

"No." Lara claps both hands against her bare legs. "No! Don't turn this around, Jackie. Some friend *you* are to come and tell me to sacrifice my happiness because you're, what? Upset that I'm happy and you're not? That I'm in a good place right now and you're, for *once* in your picture-perfect richie, spoiled life *not?*"

"For once?" I gasp in bewilderment. "For *once?* You know the life I've led, Lara. You know the shit I've seen, the hell I've gone through! Don't make me out to be a spoiled princess all my life!"

"Fine, fair enough." She holds up a hand. "A spoiled little brat for the past couple years, then. That sound fair? That sound about right?" She stands. "I'm *sorry* you're having a difficult time and I'm *sorry* things aren't shaping up sooner. Maybe if you start putting your best foot forward and actually act like an adult things will start to look rosier sooner!"

"Look, I came to say what I came to say, and obviously you're not taking it well." I pick up my handbag. "So much for honesty."

"No. You're not going to come over here, threaten me, and turn this into some self-deprecation gimmick. Uh-uh."

"If you're only going to insult me and tell me how *greeeat* it is to be with Worth, backstabbing me, then I'm out of here!"

"You're jealous, aren't you, Jackie?" Her voice is low, collected, on the edge of reservation. "Jealous of me and Worth?"

I hate that word. Jealousy sounds as evil and gnawing as it is. But Lara's right: I want what she has right now.

"Yeah," I say. "I have nothing and you have it all. I'm jealous."

"You don't have nothing, Jackie." She takes a step closer to me. "You have me, the girls." She gently touches my arm. "And things with Andrew may still turn out. That whole Nikki thing may just be—"

"No," I stop her mid-sentence. "No, I don't have Andrew. He's left me." Tears instantly spring forth. "I don't really even have you or the girls. Not really."

"What?"

"Not really, when you look at history and how everyone else was catered to when they had their breakdown moments over the years."

"What are you talking about?" She backs up, hands on her hips.

"Look!" I cry, wiping away some tears with the back of my hand. "Robin gets knocked up, and you come *rushing* to be her savior. She moves in with you," I sweep my hand around the room, "she practically replaces me as your best friend—"

"Oh, Jackie."

"Then Claire. She's got the drama with her big ol' wedding and the whole world comes rushing to her aid! Bridezilla gets all the help from her bridesmaids, even your own mother comes in to help!"

"Jackie."

"Emily needs to find true love. Let's play blind date! Let's all pitch in to make her life better!" I feel my gut churn sharply at this one a bit, hating thinking negatively about Emily. "Okay, so maybe it's not the same, but still! Everyone was onboard to pitch in to help her. Then we've got Sophie!" I wave my hands about dramatically. "The things we *all* do for that girl with her damn café! And then you! *You!* You shack up with a married man!" The little color that's in Lara's face begins to fade. "You go and do the most *whorish* thing a girl could do and you steal a married man away from his wife. And we all rush to support your sorry ass!"

"I didn't steal anyone, Jackie. You take that back!"

"No! I won't take back anything I said! It's true. All you girls are kissy-kissy with each other, and when it comes to pathetic Jackie— wrong side of the tracks Jackie or slutty party girl Jackie—it's, 'We'd love to help, but we're just too busy.' Or it's, 'Grow up and, oh, I guess you're just getting what you deserve.'"

"No one's ever said that!"

"You don't have to. I know that's what you're thinking."

"Then you're judgment's way off. In fact, if that's what your instinct is really telling you, then you're probably all wrong about Andrew. There's no affair. You're just creating drama because you need it. You have nothing in life right now, and you need something to bitch about!"

"Take that back!"

"No! In fact," Lara purses her lips, "I will take *something* back."

"Seeing Worth. You'll stop that?"

She juts out her bottom lip. "Uh-uh." She takes a step nearer and looks me squarely in the eyes. "I take back that part about Andrew and taking his side."

I gasp in horror. "You wouldn't?"

"I would never take the side of the man who was cheating on you," she says, voice barely above a whisper. "But I *would* take the side of the man who decided he'd had enough with a spoiled, selfish, immature brat who didn't know what she had until it was taken away. You want to know why Andrew left?" She steps even closer. "You want the answer that'll help with those sleepless nights, wondering why your marriage is down the drain? It's you, Jackie. You drove him away."

"Screw you." I throw my handbag over my shoulder and charge for the door.

"Let me guess," she says in that same calm and unnerving voice. "This is how it all played out last time you saw him?"

"I came here to be honest with you, Lara!" I shout, my hand gripping the doorknob tightly.

"And *I'm* only being honest with *you*, Jackie." She crosses her arms over her chest. "Sometimes the truth hurts."

I yank open the door and am greeted with a stiflingly warm air. "Yeah, yeah. Trying to take the moral high ground. Steer the lost friend onto the right path, tell me I'm destructive. Why? Because you're *sooo* good at making choices?"

"Because I'm not!" she shouts back. "Because I know what it's like to make rash judgments and choices—to be totally blinded by irrational emotions that you ruin the *good* and *meaningful* relationships in your life. We're all trying to help you, Jackie. All us girls."

"Yeah, whatever."

"Have you ever thought for a moment that love and support and help come in different forms, for different people, different situations?"

"Spare me the psychobabble bullshit, Lara, please." I hold up a hand and step outside. "And if you're referring to the money you give me, don't worry! I won't be back asking for more."

"I won't be giving you any more. I'm at fault, too, Jack. I've been feeding this behavior by giving you a hand out left and right all these years." She sighs. "But not anymore. Now it's time to set things straight and for good. I haven't been doing you any favors whatsoever."

"Whatever." I throw up my hands. "I won't be a burden to you anymore."

"You were never a burden!" She strides up to me quickly and I take a step back. "That's the thing. You just don't get it! You don't see it! Wake up, will you?"

"I don't get what, Lara? That I'm a hopeless mess? That, uh, I don't know how difficult marriage can be? That I don't know what it's like to fall on hard times? That I don't know what it's like to have parents who couldn't give a crap about you? Who *resent* you ever being born?" The hot tears return. "You think I don't know what it's like to barely skid by in school? To be made the talk of the sorority house, the campus slut? That I don't know what it's like to worry every single day that her friends are going to abandon her like her husband because she's so fucking damaged? You think I don't know what it's like to have someone who *promised*, forever and always, to be there for you to just up leave? To give up, let go, move on, and *leave?!*"

I'm wailing, my vision completely blurred by the flood of tears. "You think I don't know what it's like to feel alone and empty and like a total failure...a failure no one loves, locked out..."

Suddenly Lara envelopes me in the tightest of embraces, her face buried in my neck. "Shhh, Jackie. Don't say these things. Don't." She rubs my back and tries to soothe me.

"I hurt so bad, Lara," I cry and murmur, and with each sob she pulls me tight, with each wail she whispers that everything will be okay, and then when the tears have stopped and the pain feels like it's carved a hollow notch in my stomach, I try to compose myself and tell Lara I have to go.

"Jackie, forgive me," Lara says. "I—"

But I don't let her finish. I hold up a hand, sniffle, and begin my walk back to my car. "You're not the one who needs to ask to be forgiven, Lara."

"Jackie. Jackie wait."

I look at her once more before I walk off towards my car. "I need to go now, Lara."

"But—"

"I'll be fine. Honest. I just really need to go now."

41

I rub my temples, futile efforts at getting rid of the pain that's still there thanks to the tequila shooters and the fifth dirty martini—the bar's tempting and evil deal of One Free After Four.

"You feeling all right?" Dr. Pierce queries, probably knowing exactly why I'm struck ill with the world's worst headache.

"I went out last night," I admit, ashamed. "Got tanked."

Dr. Pierce breaks out his leather bound notebook and pen and tells me to explain why I felt the need to go out on a Wednesday night instead of working on the job search. He asks if I was trying to run from my depression or numb the pain. He hasn't heard the half of it yet.

"Oh, Doc," I groan miserably.

"I don't like you mixing heavy drinking with your prescription."

"Oh, I don't take my Prozac when I go out."

He scratches at the bridge of his nose. "Jackie, the prescription doesn't work like that. It stays in your system, it's routine, and we're talking an anti-depressant paired with a depressant."

"Oh, please," I lean back into the chaise. "I beg to differ. Alcohol makes you feel good."

"Then brings you crashing down."

"So you're saying people on Prozac can never," I scrunch my brow, "drink? Ever?"

"No, but we're talking anti-depressants with a *heavy* amount of depressants. Binge drinking, Jackie."

"Doc, honestly, I've been limiting myself. *One* drink, two max for social occasions. Impressive, eh?" I flash him a toothy grin, but instantly, as my cheeks tighten, my head starts to throb heavily. "Ohhh," I moan. I massage my temples some more.

"Two? Max?" he asks, straightforward.

"Okay, okay. *And* the rare instance when I have *way* past my two-drink max. *Rare!*"

"Why'd you go out?" he presses. "Did you *want* to go out and drink? Did you feel like you *needed* to? What was the reason?"

"Doc, sometimes a girl just needs to get out and party, you know?" I glance at him and he's sitting there upright, pen in hand, the notebook balanced atop his knee, legs crossed. "Don't you ever get out of your shell and have a bit of fun?"

"Please answer the question, Jackie."

"Ugh. Yes, I *wanted* to go out. Did I think I'd get tanked?" I pause to ponder the question. It's so obvious it's almost comical. Okay, it's far from comical. It's downright sad, depressing as hell, and I hate to admit it.

But I do.

"I had a fight with Lara," I admit. "With one of my best friends."

"Okay," Dr. Pierce says, sitting up taller in his seat, "now we're getting somewhere. What was the fight about?"

I try my best to regurgitate the awful events of the night before last. I explained Lara's side, my side, the clash, and how rotten it made me feel afterwards. Lara had texted me not long after I'd gotten home after the fight, asking if I was positive I would be okay alone. She'd texted twice the following day, too, and once this morning, today's text saying that she would like to see me and talk...whenever I'm ready. I'm just not ready yet. I don't even know where to start.

"So why do you think you went out?" Dr. Pierce asks. "Was it an attempt to stamp out the pain after the fight with Lara?" He raises an inquisitive eyebrow. "And why not that same night, right after the fight? Why wait a day?"

"I thought I'd try to sleep it off," I reply plaintively.

"Good move." He writes in his notebook.

"But when I woke up the next morning, I felt just as bad. Worse, even."

"And that's when you hit the bars?"

"Three o'clock, Doc. Three frickin' o'clock." Massaging one temple, I shake my head ashamedly. "Pathetic, isn't it? Started at three and went on for...I don't know how long. Past midnight?"

"So where do you think you went wrong?"

"Huh?"

"You said earlier in the session you feel sorry about what happened, feel badly. What move instigated this feeling? Where did you go wrong?"

I blow out a puff of air. "Oh, let's see, I don't know." I clap my hands. "Going over to Lara's to begin with!"

"Really?"

I give it a second thought. "No. No, not really..."

I cast my eyes to my lap and fold my hands. I wait in silence.

When Dr. Pierce doesn't speak, I finally continue. "I had something to say to her...and I had to say it." I suck in a deep breath. "It hurt like hell, and then I said a bunch of horrible things afterwards," I blurt out rapidly. "Things I didn't really mean, Doctor."

"Okay."

"I never should have gone out drinking, to the bars, the club."

"The club?"

"Oh yes. The club."

"And?"

"And I need to find better ways to cope with my anger...my depression...my frustration..." I look him in the eyes when he pauses his writing. "My loneliness."

"Okay. Let's talk about what you said to Lara."

"I don't want to rehash it all. Please."

He waves one hand. "No, no. No word-for-word revisiting here. You told her you were jealous of the relationship she has with your husband's coworker..."

I sink down into the chaise, head propped on one end, high-heeled feet on the other. I slip one arm under my head and shut my eyes as I reply with despondency, "The big green monster, yup."

"Why do you think that is?"

"Why do *you* think, Doc? Do we always have to play Twenty Questions where I'm always the contestant?"

"You come to me for therapy, Jackie," he says pensively. "I'll ask the questions."

"Well, I suppose it's because..." I wriggle my lips from side to side, pondering the question, the possibilities...

Unable—or unwilling—to come up with anything, I meet Dr. Pierce's gaze. Perhaps he'll say something in this widening silence.

Not a thing.

"Okay," I say at last. "I don't know. M-m-maybe because Lara's happy...and I'm not."

"All right."

"She's having a successful relationship and I'm not."

"Okay."

"I guess I could go on and on about how *jealous* I am, but then I guess you can break out the Kleenex, let me feel all down on myself again." I roughly cross my arms over my chest.

"Here's a thought. Let's shift this for a second." He sets his notebook aside. "You have other friends than Lara, yes?" He snaps his fingers. "Emily..." Racking his brain. "Claire..."

I fill him in on the rest of the girls.

"All right," he says, "you have all these other friends, all of whom are in relationships, yes?"

"Eh, mostly," I say, thinking about poor Sophie. "One of them who isn't, but she could if she weren't so hung up on her business."

"Okay, let's look at this." Dr. Pierce leans forward, arms on thighs.

"You have other friends in relationships, and are you jealous of them?"

I wince. "No. I mean, I may get pissed that Robin spends most of her time with her husband and kids, or that Claire's married, which means she has to make compromises, possibly move away because of her husband, but...no." I wince some more. "No, I'm not jealous of them. Not like I feel with Lara, Doctor. Not at all."

"So then is it Lara, or is it the man she's with?"

"I told you I don't like that Worth works with Andrew. That's no new revelation."

"And why do you think it bothers you so much that your best friend is dating the man who works with your husband?"

"Haven't you been listening to what I've been saying?" I'm becoming irritated. How much do I—erm, Andrew—pay this guy?

"Jackie, please answer the question."

"Ugh! Because it's like Lara condones Andrew's cheating." I shoot upright in the chaise.

"His alleged cheating."

"Yeah, whatever." I roll my eyes. "It's like she condones him leaving me. Like she's taking his side. I mean, say Andrew and I do divorce. How awkward will that be, then? Right?"

"I think you're blowing this out of proportion, Jackie." Dr. Pierce hunkers further down, elbows digging into his legs.

"Enlighten me, please, Doc."

"You took Lara's experience of infidelity and self-manifested it, if you will."

"And I'm probably spot-on with that, right?"

He holds up a hand, gesturing to allow me to let him finish. "Is it a possibility that Lara's success with this relationship is a self-manifestation of the relationship you had, or maybe want, with Andrew? They work for the same firm, both wealthy, and, as you say, Lara's wrapped up in the newness and excitement..."

"Yes. Lara has what I want." Again, not rocket science here.

"That you want with Andrew."

"That I *had* with Andrew, yes!"

"That...you...*want*...with...Andrew?"

"That I had, that I want, *yes!*"

"That you want *now* with Andrew?"

"Dear god," I cry, tossing up my hands, then quickly dropping them in my lap. "What are you trying to get at, Dr. Pierce? That I still love my husband? That I wish things weren't as they were? Give me a new piece of meat to chew on, will you? Tell me something I don't already know!"

"Okay, different angle." He leans back in his seat. "Where is this envy, this frustration, this anger coming from? And before you say the separation, the fight with Lara, the jealousy, take a moment, breathe in and out, relax, and say what you're feeling, deep down."

"I'm feeling a lot of things." I try to breathe in and out at a relaxed pace, as the doctor instructed.

"Relax and think."

I bite on my bottom lip and stare long and hard at the Oriental rug. I try to get lost in its patterns and swirls, like I'm caught up in a therapeutic trance.

But the question of what I'm feeling begins to tear through the swirly patterns, through the peace and sudden relaxation. I don't feel the pounding in my head anymore, but rather a tingling numbness. Dr. Pierce's question tears through, deeper and deeper, until the answer begins to appear.

And then the answer tears harder, the swirly carpet patterns disappearing entirely, the numbness fleeing, the words on the tip of my tongue.

"Jackie?"

Tears gently begin to fill the rims of my eyes, and I allow myself to whimper out the answer, the feeling, the greatest feeling, the only feeling that means anything to me right now and ever since I returned home from Paris. "Oh, Doctor," I cry. "I miss my husband so much. I want him back."

Like magic, a box of tissues is pushed in front of me, and the words come spilling on out. "I'm lonely not just because I'm locking myself away in Em's apartment." I wipe at my tears. "I'm lonely not just because I don't have anything in life—no job, friends all with lives of their own." I wipe at the fresh tears and blow my nose. "And I know I can be such a brat to them sometimes. I mean, they come over and help me and take care of me the best they can. I know that. I *know* that!" I give a loud and hard sniffle in. "I don't want to act like this, hurting them and ruining the dearest relationships I have. They're all I have, Doc!" I wail into the moist tissue. "I don't know what to do at this point. I'm so lost."

Eventually, after a period of hard crying and pitiful sobs, I carry on, blowing my nose and dabbing at my tears in between every few sentences.

"I'm depressed my marriage has fallen apart, and I hate being broke, and I don't like this feeling of vulnerability and responsibility and—and—and I hate it! I hate this change, I hate the person I've become—so needy and clingy and demanding and—and—you know!" I point a finger at Dr. Pierce. "You know, Lara's right! She was right!" I wipe at my cheeks. "I drove Andrew off. It's no wonder my friends are exhausted by me. It's no wonder Robin doesn't want to give me money. No wonder Sophie took the first chance she got to fire me. It's no wonder—it's—" I stop in my tracks and stare into Dr. Pierce's eyes.

"Yes?"

"It's no wonder Andrew left me." I stick my tongue in cheek and look off to the side. "It's no wonder he left me," I repeat in utter disbelief. I slowly shake my head, coming to a horrid but honest revelation. "It's no wonder he cheated on me."

"Let's not jump the gun, Jackie. Excuses for cheating now...let's not get into that hot water. You and Andrew are going through a rough patch. You're separated. He might be having an affair, but you don't know. Cheating is not an excuse here."

"It's no wonder though, Doctor," I say, voice a hair above a whisper. "I'm a bitch. I looked in the mirror this morning and you know what I saw?"

"What?"

"Nothing. Absolutely nothing."

He patiently waits for me to expound on my statement.

"I'm empty and I feel empty because I'm so self-consumed, so selfish, so jealous and not understanding..."

I kick off my high heels and tuck my legs tightly to my chest. "Lara's right that I need to buck up and become responsible. I've lived it rough before, but I've managed. I can't always throw out the excuse for my behavior on having a bad home life or stupid choices or a failing marriage."

"This is excellent, Jackie," Dr. Pierce cuts in with a warm smile. "This is a very good breakthrough."

"Hey, that's what five dirty martinis and a couple of tequila shooters can do," I say through a chuckle, and he gives me a sideways glance.

"I can't explain it, but I feel like—like—like I see these things more clearly now."

"Breakthroughs happen at some point," he says with ease.

"Low points," I say with insistence. "Low points happen. I mean, how much lower can I sink, right? Until I find a new way to fix things?"

I pause to collect my thoughts, but I'm feeling dry. "The answers are clear," I say, "but I don't exactly know what to do about them."

"What do you mean?"

"Like," I set one bare foot on the floor, "how do I try to grow up and be that bigger person?" I draw my tucked leg even closer to my chest. "How do I try to become more understanding and less selfish and," I snort, "not such a pain in the ass to everyone? Drama queen on the loose! I mean, Doc, I've lost Andrew...probably for good...and now Lara's hanging by a thread..."

Dr. Pierce smiles as the alarm indicating the close of our session chimes. He turns it off and says, "That first step's been taken. Congratulations."

"Huh?"

"Coming to terms with the truth, the facts. You acknowledge you have things you need to work on, and now you're ready to try. Even being honest with Lara—though that didn't turn out so well—was a step in the right direction."

"But it's the talk afterwards with her that's going to be the real step...the real tough part."

"One step at a time, Jackie. One step at a time."

42

The sun's still shining, casting a warm, orange glow over the brick square, feeding the last of its daylight to the ivy that stretches around the windows and up the old buildings that house the various antique shops and bookstores. There aren't many people in Pioneer Square, probably on account of school coming back into session. Everyone's either out shopping for school supplies or spending their waning summer moments of freedom on the water, the beach. Oh, how I remember those days.

The occasional flock of pigeons swoops down to pick at a discarded hamburger bun or a half-eaten corn dog. Two bums rifle through a garbage can off in the distant corner. The very faint and plinky sound of a violin or fiddle is played a street or two over.

I consider taking one of the few remaining cigarettes from my pack, but think better of it when I realize that after this pack I'll be down to paying for its replacement with a handful of borrowed bus quarters.

I've run, like an irresponsible child, through all the money my friends have lent, and I don't exactly know where to turn next. I can't very well run to Lara and ask her to top me up. I mean, she said her giving me handouts wasn't doing me any favors, and she's, in all honesty, probably right.

Besides, I need to go over and have a heart-to-heart with her. I need to do some begging, pleading, and groveling, but not for money. Not this time.

I set my large Miu Miu handbag on my lap, pigeon-toe my feet, and stare at the line of quaint shops across the square. When my eyes run across the antique shop where I bought Emily's globe, my heart sinks. Here one of my best and most loyal friends in the world entrusted to me the responsibility to redecorate her apartment, and what have I done? I've pissed it away. Aside from the charming globe, I've squandered nearly every cent of her redecorating funds. I've wasted a month-and-a-half doing absolutely nothing but sulking and causing trouble, with a few shoddy half-attempts at doing something meaningful, and now I'm really stuck between that rock and a hard place Robin was talking about.

With not much daylight to burn, I half-heartedly gather my handbag and saunter across the redbrick square, kicking loose pebbles when the opportunities arise.

I'm about to turn the corner and exit, ready to head back home to either give Lara a call or root about the internet for job listings, when I look up and into the window of the low-slung bookstore. Its front display looks like it's gotten a makeover, books I don't recall seeing last time now front and center. One thing, however, that remains the same, is the handwritten sign in the corner, advertising *Help Wanted*.

Immediately, with a grin tugging at my mouth, I decide to enter the shop.

It's quiet inside, save for the very light tunes of Cole Porter playing in the portable CD player set up behind the register counter. The air is a little musty, like any library or used bookstore. It isn't an off-putting odor, but kind of comforting, actually. Even to someone who hasn't spent more than a few hours of her life in a library, and who doesn't really read that many books, I can certainly appreciate and find the tranquility in the scent of used books and old paper.

As I pick up a ratty Seattle guidebook—it looks as if it's at least fifty years old, beyond outdated—a friendly, male voice says from behind, "Hi there. Can I help you?"

I'm about to say, by rote, "I'm just looking, thanks," as I usually do when I shop, unless I'm at Kate Spade knowing *exactly* the pair of next season's peep-toes I want to pre-order.

"Actually," I say instead. I look over to where the voice is coming from, just on the other side of the large table in the center of the shop. "The sign in the window," I point at it, "*Help Wanted.*"

"Yes." The stout man, hair white as Santa's beard, puts one hand in a pocket of his olive-green corduroy trousers, and sort of balances himself with the other, guiding himself towards me with the aid of the table's ledge. "You looking for a job, dear?"

"Am I ever!" I gasp.

I can't believe I hadn't thought of this before. Here I've been fretting about finding a job that I desperately need ever since my blowout with Lara, and certainly all this afternoon after my ground-breaking session with Dr. Pierce, and this bookstore's been looking for help the whole while. I even saw the sign and didn't even consider the option!

I pan quickly around the small store filled to the brim with books. Surely this place would consider hiring me. I mean, how hard could this job be? Sure, I've failed some jobs that even an amoeba could take on, but I've got to give this a shot.

"Have you ever worked in a bookstore before? A library?" the stout man asks.

"Err, no," I say slowly. "But I'm a U Dub graduate." My voice turns prideful. "Studied at the library there." I can count on one hand the number of times I actually did that, but quantity isn't really relevant right now.

"U Dub..." The stout man looks up at the ceiling fondly. "We've had a couple of University of Washington students work here."

"Well I'm graduated, degree and all," I say in my most charming voice. I need to put my selling face on. If I could work here, that'd be an instant paycheck, and I wouldn't have to be bothered with those dull job searches.

"Communications," I add with a bright smile. "Like books, kind of—communicating a message." I know, I'm totally grasping at straws.

"You know this is only a part-time job?" He turns and shuffles to the register counter. "We're talking a couple days a week, few hours a day when you do come in. Mostly afternoons, some evenings."

He starts to fiddle with some papers. "The doctor says I need my rest, and this ain't exactly the Mediterranean, so I can't just close up shop and get some shut-eye for a few hours mid-day." He chuckles and makes his shaky way back towards me, a piece of paper in hand.

I step sprightly forward, saving him the extra sluggish steps that look to pain him.

"Here you are." He holds out the paper with a shaking hand. "Application. It's nothing fancy. Very straightforward stuff." He looks at me with ocean-blue eyes, wrinkles drawn all around in deep lines. "Legal hogwash I've got to do—standard—when hiring on help."

"Thanks!" I look at the application. It's been prepared on a type-writer and only asks for the very basic of information, such as name, address, phone number, date of birth, social security number, that kind of stuff, with two sections that require a more lengthy, thought-out response. *About You* is one of them, and I'm not sure what to make of that. I haven't seen many applications in my day, but I've never come across this kind of an open-ended and broad question.

"'*Your favorite book,*'" I read aloud the second question, then flash him a smile. "Thanks for the application. I'll get this filled out right away."

"Heck," the man says with a chortle, "I need to hire someone ASAP, and you look like a sweet, reliable young lady." He squints and moves in closer. "You are reliable, aren't you?"

"I won't come in a minute late," I say up front. "I'll do my very best, and I'll take whatever you'll pay me."

He grins, then says, "Favorite book?"

I glance down at the paper and bite the inside of my cheek. Of all the questions in the world, he has to ask this one. *This* one has to be on the application!

Well, you are in a bookstore, Jackie, I think. *What'd you expect?*

I'm about to blurt out *Tender Is the Night,* a book that I recall seeing on Emily's dresser the other day, but then I decide to tell the truth. Emily is always saying the truth is the best policy, and given my current state of affairs, I could use a dose of honesty.

"Actually, Mr...."

"Call me Tom." He extends his wrinkled and calloused hand. "Tom Hodge."

"Nice to meet you, Tom. I'm Jackie. Jackie..." I pause for a second. "It's Jackie Kittredge."

"So, Jackie, what's your favorite book? Of all time?"

"Actually, Tom, I'm not much of a reader. I don't read many books."

To my surprise, his face doesn't change much.

"I read magazines," I say hurriedly. "Give me a fashion magazine, or an interior design magazine, or even one on architecture, and I'll gobble it up." I nervously hold the application in both hands.

"You want to work in a bookstore, and you don't read many books?" His face is still blank.

I nod dolefully, wishing this spontaneous move wasn't taking such a dive.

I set the application down on top of a pile of old hardbacks. "I'm sorry I wasted your time, Tom," I say. "I guess it is a little silly of me asking for a job in a bookstore when I don't read any books."

I hold out my hand for a farewell shake. "Thank you for your time, though. I won't bother you anymore."

Tom's face folds into a small smile, then the smile begins to grow and grow, until he breaks into hearty laughter.

"I never went to college," he says. "I failed high school Algebra and barely squeaked by basic mathematics. I have no formal education in business or economics, and yet, here I am, running a bookstore—the *same* location, *same* store for over forty years!"

He picks up the application and thrusts it back into my hands.

"I'm just a romantic at heart with a passion for books. Who says you need a fancy business degree to run a shop?"

He pauses and makes a long, yet comical, face. "Of course, the shop isn't exactly turning major profits right now, but coming off that recession takes time." He winks, then adds, "And who says you need to devour books to work in a bookstore? If you're interested, I'm interested."

My eyes light up, and I can't help but blurt out, "Really? So you'll consider me for the job?"

"I could use some youth around here," he says, hobbling back to the register. "Someone quicker on their feet, sharper in the ol' noggin." He taps his forehead.

"Like I said, I need to take care of myself. Diabetes." He taps his heart. "Double bypass few years back, too. The ol' ticker needs to rest."

He squints a wink and pushes a pen forward on the heavily scratched wooden register counter. "You fill this out right here, right now. I'll talk to my Shirley—she's my wife." He says this with an endearing smile. "If she gives me the okay and you're free on Saturday, we'll start the training."

"Thank you!" I cry, eagerly grabbing the pen.

"Now it is just part-time...and pay isn't going to make you rich," he cautions.

"No, that's fine!"

"I've been looking for help for a long time now, but no one seems to want to work in an old bookstore for so few hours, so little pay..."

"Tom, this is something I think I could really use right now."

He grins and gestures to the application. "All righty, then."

"Thank you so much!" I fervently begin to fill out the application. "Oh, Tom, I need this job so badly. Thank you. Thank you!"

43

"You're here!" Lara and Sophie exclaim as I enter The Cup and the Cake.

Toting Bella in her carrier, I walk over to the table the girls are hunched over near the front counter.

"Haven't seen you in a while," Sophie says. "Glad you had this little idea."

I've been wanting to talk to Lara and apologize. Things aren't awkward between us—we're just too good of friends, I think, for things to really ever come to that. I mean, in a way we kind of hugged it out and made up straight away afterwards, but my conscience says that wasn't enough. I owe her more than that.

I called Lara this morning, and she said she was planning on spending her lunch break at the café and that I should meet her down there. The fact that Sophie would be around, too, was kind of the cherry on top. I could talk to Claire and Robin later, and I could email Emily hoping she'd respond soon. But getting to talk to any of my friends about my news, especially getting the chance to apologize to Lara, couldn't be put on the back burner a second longer.

"Yeah, well..." I say somewhat timidly.

Sophie pulls a seat open and helps me situate Bella's carrier on the floor. I scoop her up and set her in my lap.

"Can I get you something?" Sophie asks. "Evelyn and I just finished baking the most scrumptious strawberry-lime cupcakes, with a hint of coconut sprinkled on top."

"Delicious," Lara says, slapping a hip. "These puppies won't be thanking me, but it was worth it."

I decline the nice offer and tell Lara—Sophie too, in fact—that there's something I've been needing to say, something I've been needing to say to all the girls, actually, but Lara specifically.

"I've got some good news," I say with bright eyes.

Sophie's eyes grow the size of the saucers resting on the table. "Andrew!" She claps a hand to her open mouth.

"I wish." I pull Bella tight for comfort. "No, I've been doing some thinking, been going to therapy." I shrug in a small, cutesy way. "Had my," making air quotes, "'breakthrough,' and, well... My life needs some major changes."

"Changes?" Lara looks confused. "Aren't you going through enough change as it is?"

"They're all the wrong ones...for the wrong reasons."

Sophie makes an *aha* face and tells me to go on.

So I do. I tell them everything Dr. Pierce and I talked about—about the need to be honest, the realization that I must do some growing up, about how I should examine why things ended with Andrew the way they did and what *I* can do to either fix things or at least be better prepared for relationships in my future. I'm not quite ready to even consider a relationship with anyone but Andrew. He's still my husband, and there's still that glimmer of hope that we'll get back together...be able to work things out. But if I'm going to be able to do what I need to—to get my life in order—the right tools and mindset are a requirement. I can't very well go back into the scary cave, fight the same fights, and expect different results.

"Girls, I'm really sorry," I say, looking them each in the eyes. "I'm sorry for being so self-absorbed and moping about my problems, acting like an insane bitch."

Sophie just laughs, flicking her wrist nonchalantly.

"I'm serious," I persist. "I mean, I've complained about being lonely, about being bored, and then I go and lock myself away in Em's apartment, avoid life, whine about my state of affairs…"

Lara gives an acceding nod of the head.

"And then when I'm not locked away I'm not exactly treating my friends very nicely," I say. "I'm really trying to work on things now. And not just with therapy. It's kind of all baby steps, but it's a start!"

"Jackie," Sophie says, folding her hands. "Yes, you're a handful. Yes, you're our complicated little friend. But we love you; we want to be there for you and help you."

"But I haven't been the easiest person to get along with…the easiest person for you to help."

Sophie, too, gives an agreeable nod.

"I can just get so angry and over-the-top and dramatic and—" I sigh. "I can't say I'll change overnight, and to some degree I am who I am, but there's room for *major* improvement." I pet Bella between the ears. "I'm trying to grow up…trying to figure crap out. Trying not to be so…angry."

"Anger's perfectly normal," Lara says sagely. "And in your position, I'm pretty sure any woman would be upset." She leans one arm on the table. "It's all right to be angry," she fixes me with a hard gaze, "so long as you keep it in check and aren't going around keying cars every time you get a little pissed off."

Sophie giggles like a schoolgirl, and Lara presses on. "You can be angry at the people who have hurt you in your past—that's your cross to bear. But you can't take your pain and frustration out on the people who *do* love you and care for you."

Pressing my lips together tightly, still petting Bella, my gaze falls to the center of the table. What Lara's saying is spot-on, and I can't help but feel a bit emotional about it.

Picking up on my sensitivity, Lara reaches out for my hand and squeezes it. "We won't give up on you, Jackie, but you can't give up on us…on yourself. We're a team."

"Yeah, a team," Sophie tosses in cheerfully.

"Thanks, girls," I say. I dab at the faint tears in the corners of my eyes. "I don't know what I'd do without you."

Lara raps on the table. "Enough tears for a while, eh? Tell us about these changes!" She shoots me a sympathetic look.

"Yes," I say, pulling myself together. "Changes! Big ones, girls!"

They both look on with bated breath.

"Guess what I've got?" I say, singsong. But before I give them a chance to guess I splutter out, "A job! I got a job!"

"You got a job?" Lara says, astounded.

"Yup!" I ruffle Bella's soft hair. "Jackie Kittredge got herself an honest to goodness job!"

"Congratulations!" Sophie says in high spirits. "Where is it? High-fashion clothing store? A jeweler's?"

"A used bookstore," I say. The looks of shock on their faces is priceless.

"Whoa," Sophie sounds.

"Yeah. I saw the *Help Wanted* sign and went in and asked for an application yesterday. Then today I got the call that tomorrow's my first day. Training day!"

"Wow," Lara says with a smile. "I'm so proud of you, Jackie. That's not a baby step; that's a *huge* step!"

"Yeah, well." I look at my nails, the growth at the bases are really screaming for a fill job. "I'm kind of falling apart. Need to get things back in shape." I pull a taut face and wave my hand-in-need-of-a-mani at them.

Lara turns her head to the side in a desultory way. "Jackie..."

"More than that," I insist. "I need to grow up and start paying my own bills. Well, the ones that I can reasonably afford, like food, gas, eventually my cell phone when Andrew pulls the plug on that." I flutter my lashes.

"Still no word from the divorce attorney?" Sophie asks.

Lara: "Or Andrew?"

"Nope." I drum my nails on the table. "Peculiar, isn't it?" I shrug it off. "I just figure he's too busy to deal. I'm not going to borrow trouble dwelling on it."

"Good for you," Lara says.

"It's either that or he's too busy banging Nikki 'til kingdom come."

Lara rolls her eyes and tells me I'm ridiculous.

"So, yeah!" I place Bella in her carrier. "I've got a job a couple days a week, going to be able to pay for some living expenses—"

"I'm so proud," Sophie praises.

"And, yes, I desperately need money to get my nails filled."

Lara gives me a gentle shove in the shoulder. "Some things don't change, do they, Jackie?" She stands and begins to gather her dishes. "Glad you're riding the employment train."

"Me too!" I watch as Lara sets her dishes on the counter, then deposits some bills into the tip jar.

"I also need some major cash to pay Emily back," I add.

"Oh the decorating dough!" Lara sings on her way back to the table.

"The good thing is Em's not coming home for months, possibly a whole year, so I can certainly pinch pennies and save and decorate while she's gone."

"Wow!" Sophie looks impressed. She leans back in her seat and crosses her thin arms over her aproned chest. "Who is this woman? I don't recognize her. Talking *budgeting*? *Saving*?"

"Pennies!" Lara blurts.

"Hey, now." I sheepishly pat down my hair. "You girls make it sound like I'm hell on wheels."

"No, no," Lara says.

"I know I've been way selfish," I say. "It's obvious it's why it's gotten me where I am. Even though," I hold up a finger, "things aren't *that* bad. I mean, I've had it *way* worse before."

Lara and Sophie nod in unison.

"But things won't get better or change if I don't do something about it. Isn't that the definition of insanity? Same thing over and again and expecting different results?"

"Not every day will be great, though," Sophie says pragmatically. "Sometimes you can try and try your hardest, thinking you're at your end working so much, trying so hard, and things still don't seem to look up—*trust me!*"

"That's true," Lara says, voice soft and understanding.

"It took me *a while* to get my café off the ground and running; and my love life's been a joke for years! You can give it gas, and sometimes it's just not enough. But don't give up."

"I know." I take a long blink, inhaling slowly and exhaling twice as slow. "Things won't *always* go my way, no matter how hard I try."

"Very true," Lara repeats.

"And not every day will be a party," I say.

"Nope," Sophie says with a curt shake of the head.

"But life's only going to be what I make of it," I say. "Like Emily said, life's a brief gift. What we do with it is what matters. How it reacts, well..."

"Not to change the subject," Sophie says, "especially such a moving one, but have you heard from the girl?"

I tell her no, and Sophie rolls her eyes, saying how it's bad enough that Emily's off exploring another country, but adding in Gatz, a partner in crime she's head-over-heels for, only doubles the delay of a response.

"Hey," I say, looking on the bright side. "Em's making something of life. Her choices may be kind of inconvenient to her friends, but..."

"Got to give it to her," Lara says. "She does know how to make the most out of anything." She meets my eyes and pats my hand. "And it looks like you are, too, Jack. I'm really, really happy for you." She picks up her black leather attaché case. "I hate to call the lunch break over, but the spreadsheets won't manage themselves."

Before Lara can get into her smart Audi and drive back to work, I chase her down in the parking lot.

"Lara, wait," I say, approaching her car.

"Yeah?"

"I owe you an apology."

"Oh, Jackie," she waves off. "You apologized in there. Don't worry."

"No—"

"There's nothing to worry about. We both said things we're sorry about." She sets her attaché case inside the car.

"I said some hurtful things I didn't mean," I carry on anyhow. "And I wanted to apologize about what I said about you and Worth. I was awful to you, and you're right; I have no business telling you who you should and should not date."

"Actually..." She shuts her car door and ambles over to me. "You do."

"I do?" I crease my forehead.

"Mmmhmm. If I was dating an asshole, or some man I *shouldn't* be dating," she winks, "then I'd hope as a friend—no, I'd *expect* as a *best* friend—that you'd give me a piece of your mind. Set me straight. Not that I'd listen, necessarily."

I laugh and tell her probably not.

"But Worth's not that kind of guy," she says, gripping me gently by the shoulders. "He's different. This could actually work. And I'm happy."

"As you should be, Lara."

She pulls me in for a hug. "I apologize for hurting you. We both said some stupid things."

"Can you forgive me?" I ask when she pulls back from the embrace.

"I already have, silly. Can you forgive me?"

"Of course!" I wag my head as if it's a no-brainer. "And about all that embarrassing money I've been borrowing—"

She holds up a hand and ducks inside her car. "Nope. Not a word about it."

"I'll pay you back."

"You've got Em to pay back, which, by the way, I don't think she'd really care, but it's the thought that matters."

"It's the principle," I say. "What I've done is childish, and she never deserved it." I put a hand on the top of her car door and bend down a tad. "Let me do the same for you."

"How's this?" she says after hemming and hawing for a second.

"After you've been working a while and are on your feet and have the time and cash, you host a girls' night."

"Yeah?" I say with a sly turn of the head.

She laughs and starts her car. "Yup. And, of course, if you need me to bring anything, just ask."

I shut the car door, and as she rolls down her window, I kid, "Like if I ask you to foot the bill on the food and drinks?"

"Ha-ha," she says with a wave goodbye.

As she pulls out of the lot and turns onto the street, I look down at Bella, give her fluffy head a rub, and say, "Come on. Tomorrow's mommy's first day at work, and she needs to pick out her outfit!"

44

Training went better than I could have imagined! No one got hurt, books didn't go missing, the cash register didn't lock itself shut, no customers were scared off. In fact, I even made my first sale! All by myself! Well, just about by myself. Tom showed me how to calculate the sales tax and manually add it in the old school cash register, and he had to remind me to include a store bookmark with the purchase, but other than that I completed the entire sale by myself!

The job doesn't seem to be all that difficult, really. Aside from making sure I've got the calculations accurate and taking the time to make sure I'm thinking alphabetically most of the day, I can totally handle this job. I might have even been born for it!

Okay, not so fast. The pay isn't so great, but at least it's better than what I was earning at The Cup and the Cake, and it doesn't require antibacterial spray and sponges. I do have to deal with a bit of dust, and reorganizing books upon endless books can cause a bit of vertigo.

But Tom is a sweetheart, and I feel really good that I'm getting to help someone out who's in need. Usually Tom'll be there for the first hour I come in, then he'll head home for his nap, and a couple hours later he joins me for another half-hour or so before I take off my brown and forest green apron, imprinted with *Hodge's Bookstore* in the center. Tom's an affable old man, and we've had some fun conversations. Usually he likes to chat about his son, William, or his wife, Shirley, sometimes about his favorite books and how "timeless those ol' classics are!" Sometimes I'll share tidbits about life, my girl-friends, sometimes Andrew, about how salmon is the new black and how different lace patterns and certain colors should never be mixed, unless we're talking couture here.

I usually take lunch at the store and page through old books. I've even found a couple of *Vogue*s from the eighties and a giant stack of some vintage ones. They're a bit steep in price for me to cough up some paycheck money and race them on home, but Tom doesn't mind me poring over them during lunch.

One of the best parts of the job is that I'm only a few doors down from that really neat antique shop, Pioneer Square Antiques, where I bought Emily's globe. I restrain myself from ducking in every day, because, let's face it, I would *so* spend my entire paycheck, week-in and week-out, at that place. I'm kind of on a first-name basis with the shop owner now. Al's even willing to give me a ten percent discount on anything I purchase at his shop—a "fellow shopkeeper" discount, he calls it. He offered it to me after he asked why I came in three, four times a week and mostly gawked, only picking up a little knick-knack here and there.

"You know," he said, "we don't get new shipments of goods in that often. What you poked around yesterday is just the same old stuff."

"I know," I breathed out, caught up in the euphoria of how grand it was to be surrounded by so many lovely trinkets with so much potential—everything with an Old World charm.

I told Al his collections were *ideal* for the way I picture deco-rating Em's place, but that cash flow isn't what it used to be, hence my window shopping.

Then, with my new special discount, I bought a faux gold filigree lamp with stained glass that very afternoon, the second and absolutely stunning piece toward's Em's revitalization project. Slowly but surely that old apartment is going to look fabulous!

"Jackie?" Tom asks during my last hour of work for the week.

"Yup?" I peer over the stack of books I pulled from the shelf and set out on the large table in the center of the store.

"I know you're not scheduled to come in tomorrow."

"Uh-huh."

"I was kind of hoping to call it a half-day, take Shirley over to Bremerton or maybe Bainbridge." He shakily places a heavy hardback near my stack.

"Friday's are usually pretty quiet days round here," he says. "And summer's really winding down."

I pull myself up and dust off the backs of my skinny jeans.

"If you're comfortable closing the shop," he says, "and if you wouldn't mind working tomorrow, would you be interested? I'll pay you time-and-a-half."

Tomorrow I had plans on catching a matinee with Robin. It feels like ages since I've seen her, and she said it'd been forever since she did anything outside of the house other than work at the office or attend baby Gymboree.

I'd called up the rest of the girls, in fact, Robin included, after I'd apologized to Lara and Sophie at the café and filled them in on my attempt to piece my life back together. All the girls said they were proud of me and happy, Claire insisting I do something to celebrate. I told her all about the girls' night that I'm planning on hosting... once I save up and get things in order. Robin said we should spring for a movie and lunch out, but now that Tom needs the extra help... and he's offering extra pay.

The old Jackie would tell Tom where to stick it, and probably even turn in her keys and apron. Two weeks at one job would be two weeks longer than most jobs I've had.

The new Jackie, though, the Jackie who's really trying to grow up and put on her big girl pants, says, "Sure thing, Tom. I've closed up once before; I can do it again."

"I'm not spoiling any fancy plans or parties you've got going?" he asks, smoothing his white hair into place as he scoots on over to the shelf, a thin paperback in one hand.

"No worries." I offer to take the book from him, then shelve it an arm's stretch up. "You enjoy time with Shirley."

"You been over to the islands this summer yet?" He removes a book from a lower shelf, runs a finger over a few adjacent spines, then shelves the book properly.

"I went with my husband, Andrew." I feel a tiny frog forming in my throat. "Early summer."

"Beautiful there, isn't it? Bremerton?"

"Bainbridge."

He nods, taking a seat on the stepladder, but not before hoisting up his pants in that funny old man way. "You seen your husband lately?"

Tom and I've broached the subject of Andrew and our separation. I don't like to talk too much about it, reserving all of those personal run-on moments for Dr. Pierce and the girls, but I have mentioned him now and then. I shared that we were separated, that we haven't seen each other or spoken in two months.

"No," I reply sadly. "No, not yet."

"Well what's he waiting for?" He claps a thigh. "You're just about the prettiest lady I've ever seen." He leans forward. "'Cept for Shirley, of course. She's a real looker, that gal!"

Shirley, the real looker of a gal, will, on occasion, come to the shop when I'm around, but usually she's here to help Tom open and close, or when he's just too beat to come in at all. We don't chat too much, not like Tom and I, but she's certainly done her share of letting me know how ready she is for their son William to finish up his divorce details and get on back to the store to relieve "his old geezers of parents" from the hard work.

Apparently William had been integral in manning the shop up until his soon-to-be-ex-wife decided to put him through the ringer with a surprise sting of infidelity, then demanded a share of Hodge's Bookstore in her alimony package. I commiserated with Shirley, letting her use me as a sounding board, which is what I could tell she needed, even telling her things can tend to career out of control when separation or divorce is on the table. Eventually things would look up, I encouraged her.

Tom stands from the stepladder, and it makes a loud screeching sound. "I think that husband of yours ought to get himself straightened up and come on over," Tom says with a sweet look in his blue eyes. "He oughta take you in his arms and say he's sorry."

"Oh, I've got plenty of sorry-saying to do myself," I tell him matter-of-factly as I shelve a book by Mark Twain.

"You? Aww, no."

"Oh, Tom, I'm a handful. My husband may put up a good fight, but I know how to win a round myself." I give him a smile and motion for him to let me handle this, to get back to his reading and enjoy the down time he's got while I'm still on the clock.

"I can't believe we haven't come by here, yet!" Robin says, pushing her two-seater stroller through the narrow passageway to the back of Hodge's Bookstore.

"Look at Aunt Jackie," she says to Rose, who's happily captivated by the book she brought in with her, a colorful one that lights up and makes noises. "Aunt Jackie's gone out and gotten herself a job. Just like a big girl."

"Ha, ha, ha." I give Robin a hug. "You're a comedian, Robin." I peek into the rear of the stroller where I catch the chubby-cheeked face of baby Phillip.

Robin pulls back one of the many blankets Claire crocheted for him and rubs his tummy gently. He begins to suck on his pacifier rapidly, his eyes shut in what looks like a knocked-out, peaceful slumber.

"He's gotten so big!" I gasp through a whisper. "Do kids really grow this fast? I don't see him for a short bit, and then, bam! All grown up. A big boy."

"I'm a big girl," Rose says, peering around to the back of the stroller. "I'm going to be fwee dis year." She tries to hold up her three middle fingers.

"Try it like Aunt Emily taught you," Robin tells her. "Remember?"

"Oh yeah." Rose smacks her forehead with her small hands. "I'm going to be fweeee." As she says *three* she holds up her thumb, index, and middle finger.

"There you go," Robin says with a light clap so as not to disturb Phillip. She looks at me with a stupefied expression. "Em said that's how the kiddos in Europe do it, and probably practically the rest of the globe." She holds up three fingers, just like Rose. "So much easier, right?"

I've never considered it, but as I test it out for myself I realize sage Emily has a valid point.

"So, you don't close up just yet, do you?" Robin asks as she surveys the small shop.

"Tom said I could be flexible with the closing time, but I said I'd stay around until two."

"Very responsible, girl." Robin makes a *tsk*ing sound.

"Come on," I say, grabbing the index cards I've been using as I take inventory of the horror and sci-fi books. "I haven't made drastic changes. It's just a job."

"I'm teasin'." She picks up a book and flips it over to read the back. "I'm glad the job's working out for you."

"Mommy, I wanna cupcake," Rose says. She pulls one leg out of the stroller.

"Uh, she's escaping," I point out, standing on my tiptoes and leaning over the counter. I spy Rose pulling out her second leg.

"Rosie," Robin says, eyes still glued to the book, "we'll have cupcakes as soon as Claire gets here, once Aunt Jackie closes shop."

"When's dat?" She's now standing next to the stroller, her book at her side. It's still blinking red and blue lights and singing some lullaby.

"Hey-o!" Claire chimes vibrantly, striding into the store.

"Claire!" Rose shouts, running into her arms.

"Rose!" Claire scoops her up. "How's my favoritest girl ever?"

"Mommy said I can have a cupcake when you get here." She begins to play with the stethoscope around Claire's neck. Ever the observant and intelligent little girl, Rose presses the round portion of the scope to Claire's chest. "Cough," she demands. "Now bweave."

Claire laughs and explains how she should probably take back "this expensive little tool, whose replacement I won't be able to afford."

"How's life, Claire?" I ask, putting the index cards away in their wooden box.

Claire walks up to me, and Robin joins, two books now in her hand. Claire hoists Rose further up onto her hip and answers morosely, "All right."

"What now?" Robin asks, face twisted in worry. "Rough day at work?"

"Work's fine."

"Conner?" I guess.

Claire nods. "The LA firm he interviewed with, on the phone? Well, they're asking to meet in person."

"That's great news!" Robin says energetically, then her face twists back into that worried way. "Or not. You mean? So it's *more* than a possibility?"

"Likelihood," Claire says, glum. "I don't know, and I'm not going to freak out just yet. It is only a second interview, not an offer." She shakes her head briskly. "Jeez, listen to me. *Only* a second interview. It's the first second interview he's had. They're going to hire him; I just know it."

"That's great," Robin says, "*and* that's bad."

"Totally." Claire sets Rose down. "Then to make matters worse, one of the Washington firms he applied to said no, and the other we still haven't heard from. They could at least have the decency to tell him no."

"Bastards," I mutter, quickly clamping a hand to my mouth as I remember Robin's no-cursing rule around the kids.

"Agreed," Claire says. "Spokane we still haven't heard... I mean, at least Conner's family is in LA."

"But you hate LA," I point out, even though I know it's not exactly helpful.

"Yeah, well." Claire tosses her hands up. "What am I going to do? I'm working around the clock as it is trying to keep us afloat, and Conner's going mad without a job. He's either job-searching like a maniac or he's depressed, playing video games with Chad on the weekends—the last thing I like to come home to after a long extra shift!"

"It's still important he strike a work-life balance, Claire," Robin offers kindly. "Obviously he should be working in overdrive searching for a job. You're going above and beyond here. But the job market's difficult right now."

"Tell me about it." I knock on the countertop. "Look at me. I have a degree and I'm working in a used bookstore." The girls are silent, and I catch their drift. "Okay, not exactly the same thing. Maybe if I ever actually *used* my degree then I'd have a résumé." I chuckle. "Robin's right. Conner's working hard. He'll find something."

"I'm glad he can get rid of some steam hanging out with Chad," Claire says. "It's so tough to see him like this, saying he feels all useless and stuff."

"Come on," Robin says, looking at her watch. "Nearly two o'clock. Let's help Jackie close up shop and then get our cupcakes on." She sets the two books on the counter. "And I'll take these, please."

I read the titles aloud, "*Steamy Nights in Argentina* and *The Cheese Connoisseur's Guide*. Interesting choices."

Claire giggles, looking relieved to have gotten rid of some steam of her own—and I bet she's thankful for the comical change in topic.

"Planning on doing some wining and dining and hot love-making south of the border or something?" Claire picks up the romance novel.

"Research," Robin says she pulls out her wallet.

Claire laughs some more. "You can't be serious? Research? For what? How to put the moves on Bobby?" More laughter, belly-aching now. "With cheese?"

Robin stacks one book on the other, the rather risqué cover of the romance novel now hidden. "I like cheese, and I want to broaden our horizons beyond cheddar and mozzarella. So sue me."

"Still doesn't explain the Fifty Shade of Something or Other," I titter.

"Research," Robin says as I calculate the books' prices. "I'm working on an entirely different type of book cover at work right now, and I'm stumped. This might be the spark of inspiration I need right now."

"Nice save," Claire teases as she fastens Rose in the stroller. "You don't mind if I go push them around out in the square while you guys close up?" A sorrowful expression begins to coat Claire's sweet, peaches and cream face. I know how badly she wants a baby of her own, and right now is the worst time in the world for her and Conner to even consider growing their family.

But, like with all things, life's what you make out of it and sometimes you're just given a 'no' or a 'wait,' and while it can totally suck waiting or dealing with the denial, eventually the 'yes' to something will come your way, and, well, everything will turn out some way, somehow. It just has to.

45

Just when I thought Emily had dropped off the edge of the Earth, I finally got a return email from her. As expected, she and Gatz are having the time of their lives. School's in session, so he's got his nose in the books, Em says. But that's no problem for her, because she's been volunteering at a center for the blind. She said that it's a whole new world of volunteer work.

I've started reading about Helen Keller and her life and work, she wrote. *Amazing! Just think of this! How do you describe the grass to a child who's never been able to see? You can give them a blade of it or let them squish their bare toes in it, but when you tell them it's green, what then? How do you define color when you can't taste it or smell it, feel it or visualize it?*

I can't imagine the challenges Emily faces each day she goes to work with these children in need, but I know if anyone's up for the job and able to make a profound impact, it's her.

My response email was a little on the short side, and I didn't exactly mention the whole I-spent-all-your-money-on-foolish-things situation. I want to be honest, but I'm not stupid. I don't want to disappoint Emily, and I'm working hard at paying her back, putting almost all of my money earned at Hodge's Bookstore inside her mason jar.

I did fill her in on my new job, how I had some great ideas brewing for her redecorating, and that my sessions with Dr. Pierce are going well and I'm making progress, even if I'm still down about my marriage and Andrew and I are still not on speaking terms.

As I closed the concise email with a long line of Xs and Os, I couldn't help but laugh to myself at how that can so often be the case: When you're down in the dumps and feeling sorry for yourself, you can drone on and on in an email...that shoulder-to-cry-on kind of thing. When you're feeling good and like you've got a handle on things, you don't spend much time writing about how fab things are turning out.

Perhaps that's why Emily's tough to get a hold of when she's traveling. Sure, her connection to the internet or a computer may be spotty, but I can see now how when she's excited about a project and caught up in the moment, when she has a goal or a busy agenda to go after, taking the time to slow down and regurgitate the news can take a bit of effort.

"Come on, Bella!" I say in a spirited tone after I close my laptop. I leap from the sofa, eager to tackle my own goals, in particular a certain project I've recently been inspired to take on.

Throwing open Emily's bedroom closet doors, I'm met with a rainbow explosion of clothes and accessories.

Damn, I think, biting the side of my lip. *When Emily said I had a few too many things over here still, she wasn't kidding around.*

The craziest thing is that I've been living here for, what? More than two months, and it's only now that I really take the time to stop and look at the disaster that has become the closet, the dresser drawers—the entire bedroom, for that matter.

My clothes are all over the place, crammed into each closet shelf I share with Emily (although it looks like I've taken over); taking up a good half of the hanging space; almost every pair of shoes lined on the bottom of the closet floor belonging to, you guessed it, me; dresser drawers spewing out tank tops, halter tops, and pairs of jeans, leggings, and the occasional skirt—all mine. The bed has a few articles of clothing atop it, and what's under it I don't want to know.

My luggage pieces from Paris are still only halfway unpacked, pried open, with bras, necklaces, and scarves draped over the corners. The place is, in one word, a pigsty. It's embarrassing, and I can't remember the last time it ever looked so bad. On the bright side, I'd done so much shopping in Paris and had evidently left so much at Em's place beforehand that not being able to access my wardrobe at home thanks to Andrew locking me out was obviously not such a problem. I mean, sure I could so use some love from the Valentino, Versace, and even random summer-fun H&M and Forever Twenty-One buys that are locked up back home, but I really can't complain. I've certainly got enough to get by.

I decide to tackle the disastrous room one corner at a time. That's how Tom taught me to organize the un-shelved books at the store. In fact, it was all that organizing down there that's inspired me to turn in my Saturday plans of treating myself to a martini at House 206 (for working so hard and feeling so good) and getting to work on tidying this place up. Dr. Pierce would be proud, I think.

It's damn tempting to not snag twenty bucks from the mason jar and run down to a bar or club and do a little celebrating at finally earning a paycheck, finally feeling like I'm making some progress post-Andrew. (And trust me, I've been *very* tempted.)

But think how much better I'll feel by cleaning up this place? Knocking back a party drink and getting it on on the dance floor would make me feel good right then and there, but afterwards? I'd come home to a still-messy bedroom, and I'd eventually regret having wasted the twenty that would better serve Emily than my party habit.

My fingers alight on something spiky under the bed, and I peer below, gripping it and yanking it free. It's one of my favorite Balenciaga heels—bright yellow and silver-studded. I search for its match, then hold them both up at eye level.

"Beautiful," I whisper. I stand and race over to the full-length mirror.

Okay, I think once I slip them on. *These shoes deserve to go out to a club or a bar. They have no business staying closeted or, worse, stuffed under a bed.*

As I twist and turn my ankles, gawking at how gorgeous the brightly colored high heels are, I pretend to hold up a martini with one hand and press my hand to my chest with the other.

"Why, yes, they're pre-release," I say imaginatively. "Aren't they to die for?" I fake a sip of martini. "Oh, yes, darling, I would *love* to go away to the Hamptons with you next weekend. With my husband? Oh, why yes, Andrew will definitely block out a whole luxurious weekend. Dinner, dancing, luxurious parties." I fake another sip, then do an enthusiastic twirl, skip, and twirl, and then—

"Ow!" I shriek, instantly gripping my ankle. I hop up and down on an unsteady high-heeled foot.

Kicking off both heels, I rub at the ankle that went all wonky on me for some reason. The pain's brief, dissipating almost entirely now, but then a new kind of pain surfaces.

"Oh, no!" I pick up one of the shoes. I can feel my heart break. The shoe's long, skinny, four-inch heel is hanging on by a thread, snapped straight in half. "Son of a bitch."

Inspecting it with a long face, I decide it's not so bad after all. This happened once before with a pair of Manolos, and I just went out and bought a replacement pair—an even better pair, which I'd thought unimaginable.

I begin to root about one of my larger designer handbags, withdraw my wallet, pull open the bill pocket, and that's when the reality dawns on me.

I glance at the useless row of credit cards before dropping the wallet back into the dark deepness. I crinkle my nose. "Well that just blows chunks."

I cast back at the broken shoe—the broken dream. *Oh, how easy things used to be.*

For a brief moment I tabulate the amount I've saved up from

working at the bookstore. I then consider the cost of a cheaper replacement pair of heels over at Nordstrom or Macy's. It'd be tight, but I could definitely find a dashing replacement pair, borderline knockoffs, for under a hundred. Easily. And now would be the best time to snag up such a colorful pair! Summer's rolling on out, which means the fall line is already on the front shelves, beautifully glittering in the shop windows, enticing me to buy...

I look at the shoes again and thumb gingerly at the cracked line.

Surely I can find a great replacement pair. Even if I can't afford the new line, some summer stuff will still be up for grabs, and probably at bargain-basement prices!

My stomach begins to do delightful flips, and I'm about to get lost in the euphoria that is shopping. Then that small, logical, practical, although not very familiar side pokes its head around the corner. It tells me that one lost pair of heels, no matter how beautiful and flashy, is not a big deal. There is no real need to go out and replace them.

I thumb at the cracked line some more, each brush over the edgy break making my heart feel a touch heavier, my face grow a little longer.

As if on cue, Bella barks and grabs my attention.

"What is it, girl?"

She yaps some more, then trots up to me, tiny tail wagging playfully.

"You're right," I say with a resigned sigh. I place the heels on top of the recently cleaned dresser. "I've got more important things to take care of." I give a small, friendly pat to the spiky toes of the high heels. "You served me well."

About a half-hour later, the bedroom slowly losing its look of a walk-in closet devastated by a grenade, I get a brilliant idea. No, it has nothing to do with finding a way to buy a replacement pair of Balenciagas, although it is inspired by the gaffe.

The fact is, I have a ton of clothes. Even without access to my closet full of treasures back home, I have more than I need right here at Em's. It's really too much if we get right down to it. What's more, I haven't even worn some of this stuff since I moved in. Granted, a lot of it is more suitable for dance clubs and nights out on the town—certainly not wholesome bookstore attire.

Don't get me wrong, I'm the last woman who's going to throw on a baggy pair of jeans, a floppy old t-shirt, and call myself dressed for the day. There's still plenty of fashion to have and flair to flaunt wherever you work. But five-inch stilettos, sequined boobie shirts (as Emily calls them), and tight, hip-hugging pants aren't exactly appropriate for each and every occasion.

I have scads of minis and flimsy dresses, so many fishnet stockings, chic hats and fascinators, and pearled accessories. And don't even get me started on the leather handbags and designer clutches! The patterned silk shawls and neckties, too! I have at least five high-quality scarves from Hermès and Chanel lying about here. I love them all—I love all of this stuff. But do I really need it all? Given my predicament, do I really need *five* luxury scarves? Do I really need to switch out my handbags every few days? Is it necessary to have three pairs of red heels, each one just a shade or two lighter than the others?

It's in the middle of all this questioning, in the middle of stacks and piles of sorted clothes and accessories, my broken heels staring at me, that I get a brilliant idea!

"You're *what?*" Lara bellows into the phone.

"It's such a clever idea, isn't it?" I cradle the cell phone in the crook of my shoulder as I tie off the second to last large plastic sack. It's bursting at the seams with clothes and accessories and shoes I've decided I no longer need.

"B-but Jack," Lara stutters. "Are you sure you're not thinking irrationally? Is now really the time to get rid of the *only* clothes you have?"

"I'll be fine." I heave the heavy sack to the front door and pile it among the other three. "And when I need new clothes, I can go get some more—some *reasonably* priced clothes, of course."

"Have you been drinking?"

"What? No. Although I am *so* overdue for happy hour."

"Is it that time of the month? Are you down and depressed more than usual?"

"What?" I wince. "No, no. Nothing like that."

"Okay..." she draws out curiously.

"I figure at some damn point Andrew will send his dumb divorce lawyer over. When that happens, I'll be able to access my wardrobe again, and I'll be fine," I say breezily. "What good will all my clothes do in Andrew's hands, anyway? I'll *obviously* get them back in the settlement." I switch the phone to my other shoulder.

"Or you'll get your clothes back when Andrew realizes how much he loves you," Lara says optimistically. "He'll come racing over, demanding you back."

I chuckle. "Yeah, that'd be the better option, but I'm trying to be realistic."

"Well," she says through a sigh, "are you eBaying the stuff or what?"

"No, too much work. I don't want to spend the time, don't have the patience." I tie off the last sack. "I don't even know how to work all that stuff. It's fine. There's this place nearby that will buy back lightly used clothing and accessories, and they really look for high-end stuff." I wipe my moist brow with my forearm. "It'll be some nice extra cash."

"Wow. I'm impressed, Jackie."

"Eh, it's no biggie. It'll help me from letting Em's bedroom turn into a mess again, and I could *so* use the instant cash."

"Let me help you out some," she offers in a gentle yet insisting tone. "I'm proud of how you're really getting on so well. Let me lend you some cash, as a gift. You don't have to go and sell everything you own."

"It's not everything... You really think I'd sell *all* my stuff?" I cackle loudly, and she tells me I'm right.

"I appreciate the offer," I say, "but unless I'm in really dire straights—like starving and out of smokes—I won't take you up on your offer."

"All right..."

"Besides," I say as I drop the last of the sacks by the front door. I dust off my hands and grip the phone. "This way I'll be completely finished with paying Emily back, and I'll be able to get her place redecorated. *Finally!*"

"Nice."

"And maybe I can snag some new fall-season heels..."

"Jackie."

"A girl can dream! Anyway, the minimal budget Em left me will mean I'm working with my hands tied." I dive onto the sofa and flip on the TV. "She loved the furniture I bought for her last year." I give a proud thump to the luxe sofa. "They cost a small fortune, so she obviously can't expect these kinds of wonders again."

"Emily won't care; you know that."

"I know, but I still want to fix her place up nice. I'll just have to do it on a budget." I flip the channel to HGTV. "Like all these designing-on-a-dime TV shows. I can do that, too."

"Erm...like on PBS? I didn't know they had shows like that."

"HGTV, Lara. *Such* a helpful channel."

"Since when did Emily have cable?"

"Oh, yeah, that..." I rub at an eyebrow.

"You spent money on a cable package?"

"I'm selling my clothes," I quickly point out. "Being responsible, getting some extra cash, and I *am* working. I'm *trying*, Lara. Really, I am."

"Jackie," she says through a high-pitched sigh.

"You upset?"

"No, you're just a character."

"I promise; I'm getting this clothes money and putting it towards the apartment. And I've obviously got to cover the cable bill. You know this is like the first actual bill that I've had in a long time?"

"Someone who's *not* covering your exorbitant credit card bills for you?" she says with an ironic laugh.

"Exactly. It sounds superfluous, but this cable bill makes me feel responsible. And!" I hurriedly add. "It *is* for research. HGTV, Lara. Come on."

"All right. Well, if you change your mind and want to hang out tomorrow, you know where to find me."

"You and Worth not have a *roomaaaantic* date planned? No saucy rendezvous?" I titter.

"He's out of town on biz." She adds this part in cautiously, "With Andrew."

My mind immediately flips to images of Andrew, carry-on piece packed, jacket strung over one arm, briefcase in hand, out the door and away on business.

"I didn't think Worth traveled that much for business," I say at last. "So what is it? Caymans? Singapore?"

"A relatively new LA account," she says. "It's turning out to be more work than Jennings & Voigt thought, so Worth's over there. The client's a real hard-hitter, he says." Lara sighs heavily. "Anyhoo, like I said, if you change your mind about your organizing and design-on-a-dime shopping plans, let me know. Or if you want company."

"Will do." I pat the sofa next to me, and Bella jumps up, prancing straight into my lap.

"Oh, and one more thing," she adds hastily. "You wouldn't by any chance have that Prada wallet in the to-go pile, would you?"

"The little black one with the silver hardware?"

"That's the one."

"Sorry, babe," I say with a small, sneaky grin. "That one's a keeper."

"Bummer. Okay, never mind. Talk to you later!"

46

"Al said you came in to his shop yesterday and nearly cleaned him out," Tom says with a smile. "Antiques flying so fast out of there."

"I wouldn't say *cleaned* out," I reply as I run a dry dust cloth over the books along a high shelf.

"You needed help carrying all the stuff out to your car," Tom exclaims, laughing. "*Three* trips!"

I crane my head around, gripping the side of the sturdy wooden bookshelf. "Two-and-a-half, kind of."

"Two-and-a-half trips?" Tom gives a silly look. "Now how does that work?"

Returning to my dusting, I say, "It's for a good cause."

"Oh yeah? Good for old Al, I can say."

"I'm redecorating a friend's apartment." I carefully step down from the ladder on my new pair of bargain-basement black and white polka-dotted peep-toes. I couldn't help myself as I drove past Macy's with some newfound cash in hand yesterday.

I move the ladder over a skosh, then climb back atop it and continue with the first set of my Monday afternoon chores at Hodge's Bookstore.

"Awfully generous of you," Tom says.

"Wouldn't go that far." I give an extra hard scrub to a particularly dirty book spine. "My friend gave me a budget, and I'm working with it to get the job done."

"Aha, so like one of those fancy interior designers or something or other, huh?"

"Something like that. I'd hardly call myself a designer, but it's enjoyable."

Yesterday, while I didn't exactly clean out Al's antique shop next door, I did just about empty Em's replenished jar over there. After a very successful deposit of my used designer wares, I took my wad of cash and headed out to make some progress on Emily's project (with a slight shoe-shopping detour along the way).

As tempting as it was to abruptly turn my car down Pine or 6th Ave and go on a total shopping spree like I used to back when I had a credit card to my name, I ignored the urge, fought the temptation, and forced myself to keep on driving, all the way to Pioneer Square. (Although in addition to Macy's I did get weak and make a small stop near the waterfront for a strawberry smoothie, a pack of Parliaments, and a copy of *Seattle Socialite*. Oh, and a quick look at the back of the day's newspaper to check my horoscope. *Today's your day, grab the bull by the horns and live like there's no tomorrow!* it read. How fabulous is that, right?)

It was at Pioneer Square Antiques where I got almost everything I thought I'd need for a full-on apartment makeover. It felt exhilarating not just to do some shopping once again but to do something for someone else. You know, the feeling of helping others is kind of addictive. So long as I'm not cleaning out latrines in Africa or slogging it at the YWCA with epidemics of lice cropping up, this giving-back and selflessness thing feels pretty good. I see why Emily's such a fan. Helping out keeps me busy, I'm doing some good, and in turn it makes me happy. And talk about killing the boredom! I'm finding that the busier I am the less focused I am on my problems.

"Hey, uh, Jackie?" Tom asks later in the afternoon. His voice sounds a little unsettled, almost nervous, maybe confused.

"Yeah?" I peer around the doorway of the small back room where we keep the new stock that's not yet inventoried.

"Can I bother you for a second?"

"Shoot." I put another tick-mark on the index card labeled *Romance, A-C.*

Tom appears in the doorway, hands in his pockets and eyes trained on the floor.

"What's up?" I ask. I pull out the index card for *Romance, D-F.* "Did I screw up the alphabetizing again?" I roll my eyes. "I'm dyslexic with it sometimes, I swear."

"No, no." He shakes his head, eyes still focused on the floor. "Nothing like that. It's about William."

"Oh?"

"His divorce should be finalized in the next couple of weeks, maybe sooner than we expect," Tom explains.

He slowly lifts his head, and our eyes meet—his filled with a twinge of gloom, mine with enquiry. "William will be taking things over, as you know. I'm really much too old for this all the time." He gives a forced chortle. "William says he's planning on diving right in, getting things organized, and really getting this place off the ground running."

"Oh?" I've known this conversation was headed my way sooner rather than later, but I honestly didn't expect it so soon. I've started to really get the hang of things around here, and it all comes almost second nature to me, minus the occasional alphabetizing flub-ups.

"I've talked to him about you," Tom goes on. "I told William what a great worker you are and how helpful you've been."

"Thanks."

He leans against the doorframe. "He's made it pretty clear, though, that it's the bottom line that matters." He clenches his fist and pumps it up and down. He then holds out his hand flat and says, "Bottom line. We're not making much profit around here, and William wants to turn that around."

"Yeah?"

"Can't say that I blame him." He returns his hand to his pocket.

"He has a daughter, high school age, and he wants her to have some work experience, get that résumé polished up and all that jazz."

"I see."

"He wants her to help out around here, volunteer, intern, or something or other. He says there's just not any money on the books to pay an extra set of hands, especially since she'll be doing it for free."

"Ahhh," I say, trying to fight sounding as disappointed as I am.

"The rent's going up next quarter, life's not getting any cheaper." He clears his throat loudly. "I told William you're not working many hours, anyway, but he says the point of hiring on extra help was to help take the pressure off of me...and what with the summer season over and the slower months of the year now...William's coming back full-time..."

"I get it," I say sweetly. "Don't worry about me, Tom." It's evident my words are calming Tom's nerves, judging by the release of his deeper-than-usual wrinkles around his eyes, cheeks, and brow. "This experience has been *great*, and we both knew it was only temporary. It'll give me a huge leg-up when I find something else."

"Really?" He looks at me with those warm eyes of his.

"Absolutely!" I force myself to smile as I stand, setting the index card down on the upturned wooden crate I've fashioned as my inventory desk. "I'll hate to leave, but I understand. I'd rather see this place succeed than drive itself into the ground just to keep silly ol' me around."

He smiles and waves a hand. "Now, now, Jackie," he says as I slip out of the room.

He follows me into the front of the store. "Hey, you're not going anywhere just yet, now," he says. "We've got lots of inventory, and William's not back yet."

"I know," I say through a laugh from behind the cash register. "You're not going to get rid of me that easily."

I ring up a sale for the price of two of the vintage *Vogue*s, and Tom asks what I'm doing.

"I've been saving to pick up something here," I explain. "Something I've had my eye on for a while."

"Now, Jackie, I'm not asking for sympathy sales." He makes his way over to me.

"And I'm not making sympathy purchases." I insert the cash into the register and close the drawer. It makes its high-pitched *cha-chiiing-ping* sound as it shuts. "You have some rare magazines I want, and there's no arguing about it. A regular sale."

And without an argument more, and with no time to dwell on what it'll be like when my employment ends at Hodge's Bookstore, I continue with the rest of the day's chores, quipping, laughing, and even swapping a few jokes with Tom along the way.

Tonight and all day tomorrow, since I've got the day free, I'm pulling out all the stops for Emily's apartment project! On the way home from work I even picked up some paint supplies as well as a large bucket of taupe-colored paint and a small one of black to make some borders. I dropped by an arts, crafts, and decorating store for some Mod Podge so I could get to work on refinishing the damaged frames I found at a garage sale this weekend.

While I was picking up the Mod Podge, I found a bin of deeply discounted knickknacks, including some miniature luggage pieces with *Bon Voyage* etched on them; a nicked lamp that matches the antique, time-worn color scheme I have planned; some chipped vases; and even an old-school, 1950s-era airplane about the size of a shoe, made completely out of wire.

The following morning, with everything I can think of (and afford) stacked up in Emily's cramped kitchen, I crank up the ancient CD player Emily's had since college and begin my painting project. I start in the living room and work my way through the small dining room and on into the bedroom, running through CD after CD, none of which are from this century.

Emily's walls are a dirtied eggshell color that just need a little refresh, and taupe will do the trick. It's understated and will work with anything, especially for the antique, Old World-style travel and geography theme I've got going.

It's difficult not to make it too kitschy with a bunch of knick-knacks that, when on overkill, can look like a big pile of clutter. I think I've got a handle on it, though. If poring over endless magazines and blogs and even DIY-design TV shows counts for anything, surely Emily's apartment will look spectacular when I'm done with it!

In the middle of U2's foot-stomping song "Pride," I barely make out the ringer of my cell phone.

"Just a minute!" I shout, dashing out of the bedroom and into the freshly painted living room, roller brush in hand. "Coming!"

I've been expecting a call from Claire today, and I can't miss it. Sophie told me at the café today over breakfast (because my refrigerator and cupboards are practically empty) that any time today Conner will find out if he got the job in LA. Spokane still hasn't got in touch, and the Seattle position sadly said no flat out, so all of the cards are in the LA pot. If Conner's offered the job, he and Claire are moving.

I'm obviously conflicted. I know how horrible it can be needing a job and not being able to find one, especially for Conner, who's looking for a real and serious career. The thought of Claire not being in Seattle, though!

I take a fleeting look at the caller ID before I pick up. It's Lara.

"Have you heard anything yet?" I burst out with my greeting, hoping she's gotten the news from Claire already.

"Have *you* heard, that's the question," Lara says.

"No, I haven't heard. Have you? Come on, is it what we thought?"

"Erm...what are you talking about, Jack?"

"Claire!" I knit my brow in confusion. "Conner! Did he get the job in LA or not?"

"Oh."

"He did, didn't he?" I clap a hand to my forehead. "Oh, no..."

"I don't know about that," she says. "I haven't heard from Claire yet."

I exhale. "I'm on pins and needles!"

"Well, if it's bad news, then enjoy the prolonging of the news," she says with a half-laugh.

"Yeah." I return to the bedroom and proceed with the last portion of my painting job. "So, wait." I stop rolling the brush in the paint. "What's with the 'have you heard?' business then?"

"That's why I'm calling. I have some news I have to tell you. Brace yourself."

I don't like her choice of words or her cautioning tone.

"Oh no!" I say the first thing that comes to mind. "Did you and Worth break up?"

"What? No."

"Well, not break up, break up." I roll my eyes at how complicated it is with Lara. She's still insisting that she and Worth are just seeing each other. No need to label anything just yet. "I mean like a falling out?" I clarify. "I know you're not actually boyfriend-girlfriend, but—"

"Oh, we are!" she says excitedly.

"Since when?" I'm shocked.

"I *guess* we made it official...if you want to get all cheesy. We talked about it this past weekend."

"I thought he was out of town?"

"He is. But there's still such a thing as telephones."

I smile, thinking how rarely Andrew would call me when out of town, and if so how it was usually just to say that he'd arrived safely.

"Congratulations, Lara." I drop the roller brush in the paint pan, neglecting it entirely now. I am genuinely happy for her, although a very small part of me wishes that I was the one with the we're-an-item news.

"We were just talking," Lara explains. "He made me jealous—he's all lying on the beach and stuff when he's not working...so unfair."

"Totally." I slide open a window to get a fresh breeze going, as the paint fumes are growing thicker.

"We were talking, and then somehow the topic veered to our status, and, well... It is what it is. I've got myself a boyfriend." She lets out a slight squeal of delight.

"That's great, Lara. So that's the big news, eh? Definitely worth call—"

"No."

"No?"

"Worth's out of town."

"Yes."

"With Andrew."

"Yes, I know."

"And guess who's no longer in Seattle?"

I consider the possibilities for a second, when suddenly it dawns on me. "No!" I gasp. "She *isn't*?" That skanky Bitch Nikki can*not* be in LA with Andrew! That's impossible!

"That's right," Lara says. "Nikki's relocated to the East Coast. New York. Can you believe it?"

"Wait, huh?" I rub the side of my head, totally vexed and confused. "We're talking Nikki, right? Bitch Nikki?"

"The one and only," Lara sings. I love the way she rallies to my cause. Having only known my side of the story, and not knowing Nikki at all, she's there like a supportive BFF agreeing that Nikki is no ordinary woman. She's Nikki with a capital 'B.'

Her delivery of the news, though, is poorly executed.

"W-w-wait a minute," I stammer. "Nikki? Andrew's stupid secretary, Nikki?"

"Yup."

"She's not in Seattle?"

"Nope."

"And she's not in LA?"

"God, no." Lara sounds like her face is drawn up into a twist. "Where'd you go and get *that* idea?"

"Uhh, let's see. 'Guess who's not in Kansas anymore, Jackie?'" I use a valley-girl voice. "You make it sound like she's not here but over *there,* with Andrew and Worth and the beaches and—"

"Oh, yeah, you're right," she rushes out. "Eek. So, sorry, Jack. My bad."

"Who cares now!" I cry. "This is awesome! *Awesome!*"

"I know, right?"

"Okay, dish, dish. What the hell happened?"

Once I realized there was no need to pull out what little hair I have on my head, and once I realized I didn't need to give in to the toxic paint fumes and die a lonely death, paralyzed by the confirmation that my husband was shacking up with the world's biggest bimbo, I got back to my painting. I gave Em's bedroom walls the dazzle they needed, being super productive and multi-tasking, too. I gossiped like the best of gossip queens with the cell phone on speaker as I painted.

So this is how it went down. Turns out Worth needed something from Andrew's office for their business deal and called up the secretary's line, assuming Nikki would take the call. When an unfamiliar voice answered, Worth asked Andrew what happened to Nikki. Andrew told him—all nonchalantly, Worth had told Lara—that there was a better job opportunity for her with a firm Jennings & Voigt used to do a lot of business with, over in New York. So he gave a reference and off she went on her merry little way.

I honestly can't believe it! Andrew's wretched secretary is actually gone? Not just out of his office, no longer working for him, but out of the city...the state! Clear across the country, even!

"So you know what this means, don't you?" Lara says.

"Yeah! The Wicked Witch of the West is movin' to the East Side!"

"More than that. It means Andrew's *definitely* not having an affair with her."

"Erm...what makes you say that?"

I admit, her theory is exciting and I so want to believe it, but *why* does she think this?

"Here's how I see it. Follow me." Lara sounds exuberant, almost as if she's putting together the pieces of the He Loves Me, He Loves

Me Not puzzle of her own love life. "There's no way she's having an affair with him. Andrew's the one who was used as a reference for the New York position, and Worth says he even pulled a few strings to get the deal made. There is no way in hell a man who's having an affair would sweep the mistress right out from under him and send her thousands of miles away."

"You paint a horribly vivid picture," I say in a teasing tone.

"Seriously. Hear me out. You know that is *not* the action of a man with a mistress."

"Unless..." I say, giving Negative Nancy her soapbox. "...If they had a fight and couldn't be around each other anymore...or what if *she* was two-timing *him!*" Oh, the possibilities suddenly seem manifold!

"Or!" I add loudly. "Yeah! That's it! They fight, they can't possibly work together anymore, so he gets rid of her. Or he's jealous and angry about her two-timing him, so he sends her away. Or—"

"Jackie," Lara cuts me off, her voice sharp, severe. "You're being ridiculous. Listen to yourself. Don't you see? This is simpler than you're making it out to be."

"How so?"

"You guys have been separated for a long time. Too long. There's *still* no divorce lawyer, there's lots of time for him to dwell on your marriage, enough time for him to realize he can't live without you and misses you like crazy." She stops herself. "Men take a while to realize these things sometimes; it's a defect in their genetic make-up. I'm trying to get used to it."

We share a laugh, then I say, "Okay, so this theory of yours..."

"It's not a theory," she states. "I think it's fact. Andrew's realized he can't live without you, so he does the best thing he can do to make amends—aside from knocking on your door and carrying you away."

"Oh, yeah," I say with a heavy roll of my eyes. "Now we're not theorizing! God, we've moved way past theorizing and now we're fantasizing!"

"Think about it! I know I'm kind of on Cloud Nine right now

what with Worth and I being a couple and all, but think about it! I bet you anything Andrew will be calling you or knocking on your door in one, two, three days tops."

"You think?" A flurry of glee begins to spread throughout my body. I'm unable to mask my smile.

"I really think so, and I don't think it's just the Cloud Nine high talking. I really think, especially since you have *yet* to hear from a divorce lawyer, that things are going to turn around. You told him you wanted Nikki gone."

"Yeah, well, he was pretty adamant about not letting her go." My flurry of glee starts to be quelled ever so slightly. "That's why I don't understand why he decided to get rid of her all of a sudden. You know?"

"You were adamant about having the world take care of you. Now look at you! Miss self-sufficient. Things change, babe."

She has a point. Maybe not the best seeing how I'm *barely* self-sufficient, especially with a job about to come to a close, but she makes a point, nevertheless.

"Listen," she goes on, "I have *got* to get back to work, but I just had to share this news with you. I really think it's positive, and, hell, if anything it should be pretty darn good confirmation that your husband is *not* having an affair."

"That's one possibility."

"The *only* one. I love ya. I've got to go."

When we disconnect I force Negative Nancy away, as hard as she tries to stand in front of me and shout out all of the wretched possibilities. I force myself to consider Lara's theory...perhaps Lara's facts.

As I pick up the brush and continue my painting, letting the actual possibility of a rekindling of a relationship with Andrew sink in, I begin to feel the glee return.

I turn up the volume of the CD, the infectious and upbeat song "Sweetest Thing" reverberating throughout the room. And I think, as the paint makes its way around the apartment, that today is shaping up to be a pretty fab day. I knew it'd be a good day, but I had no idea it could be *this* good!

47

As is so often the case, I spoke too soon. I was having a grand time finishing up the painting when Claire called with the news. LA had called, and Conner didn't get the job. Spokane had called back, too, and he had gotten the job.

It was the most bittersweet moment I'd felt in a long time. It surpassed the bittersweet feeling of getting the final word that I was going to be let go at Hodge's Bookstore by the end of the week.

I hate to leave behind the brief yet enjoyable time I've had at the bookstore—leave behind the easy chats with Tom and the jokes and laughs, leave behind the place that took a chance on a girl in need with a pathetic excuse of a résumé, a place that's helped me through a rough time.

While I hate to leave all that behind, Claire's news is the bittersweet kind you wish with your whole body and soul never happened. I know it's probably unfathomable that six best girlfriends could really all stay in the same college town all these years. Most girlfriends are lucky if they have any time at all together once they graduate. Usually careers are found in other cities, opportunities take some out of state.

Rarely do you meet six close friends who all have the fortune of living a few blocks or a few miles away from one another. Even with sails-in-the-wind Emily with her wanderlust, she's still got her roots planted in her college town.

Claire says Conner's new job starts October first, and they'll be moving mid-September. I had to do a doubletake at the calendar when Claire told me this. I realized that's only two, maybe three weeks away. Through shared tears she said they didn't want to move so soon, or at all, obviously, but they need to search for housing and get settled and, well, as she babbled my mind kind of started to wander.

I don't like change very much, least of all the kind that means you're short a friend, a shoulder to cry on, a supportive hand, someone with whom to gossip and laugh, to share goofy stories and just swing by a certain café for a cup of tea and a cupcake.

With just a short time left before Claire would be packing up her bags, I realized I now have an even shorter amount of time to put together that girls' night I promised Lara.

Emily's apartment is nearly finished. I've spent most of the afternoon refurbishing frames and rifling through Emily's box of random photographs. Robin had brought back the originals of some of the African photos she had borrowed for use at the publishing house as she works on Emily's photography book. Seeing the photos lying there on the dining table I immediately knew I wanted to hang up that fabulous black and white photograph of the two young children smiling.

I filled the rest of the dozen or so frames with some more photos of Emily's travels—Europe, Asia, more of Africa, and a really gorgeous one she took of the ice sheets in Patagonia. Then I framed one of her and Gatz, taken over at Gas Works Park one blue-skied spring day in Seattle. I found a couple of the two of us from right when she got back from Ghana the second time around. We were at a club and both of us looked like anything but half our best.

I rifled about some more through a box labeled *Misc. Photos* and stumbled upon some old college ones. I laughed out loud when I found one from my sophomore year when we first met. God, what was I thinking with that hideous nose ring? And what was Emily thinking with that purple hair? I laughed a second time when I recalled that she had purple hair, yet again, not that long ago.

Then, as I'm about to put away the box and pore through a photo album, I find the perfect photo I've been looking to insert into the last empty frame. It was taken nearly ten years ago, when all six of us girls were college kids. We were at Bumbershoot, this big arts and cultural festival that happens once a year at Seattle Center, and we had had a ton of fun that day. All of us were wearing broad smiles, arms around each other's waists or shoulders.

I can picture the moment right now. I can smell the funnel cakes; I can hear the folk music blend in with the rock music; and I can feel Emily's arm squeeze my waist tightly, Lara's hand hanging lazily and warmly over my shoulder, her head resting against mine. I can even hear Emily say her usual, "Cheeeese," as she does when a goofy photo's being taken of her. More than anything, though, I can feel the sheer joy I remember being filled with that day—the comfort in knowing that I had five of the best girlfriends a girl could ever ask for.

I walk over to the empty frame and slip this photo inside, smoothing back the bent upper right corner and never minding the few wrinkles that time's given the photo. I flip the frame over before tightening the backing and I smile—that same goofy grin I'm wearing in the picture.

"Right where you belong," I say, admiring the photo, holding it out.

I look at Claire's bright-eyed and rosey-cheeked smile, the side of her head pressed tightly to Sophie's, her hand clenching Robin's arm. "Right where you belong."

The apartment redecoration is complete, and girls' night is here! I had a great last day at the bookstore, and Tom and Shirley were so sweet. They made me a cake and gave me a goodbye gift: the rest of the vintage *Vogues*! I was happy it wasn't a blubbery, sentimental last day. I wasn't up for that. I just wanted to thank the Hodges for taking a chance on me and helping me out when I needed it most. The bookstore is going to be in better hands with tenacious William, and I'll be all right. I'll find something else to keep me busy and fill my pockets. As Emily always says, "When one door closes, a window opens." Or something like that.

Besides, until I find that next job I know Lara will have my back if I really need the help. Although, I'm curious to see how long I can go before I bring myself to ask her. I'm sure I'll have a new job in no time...or maybe, just maybe, Lara's theory about Andrew will come true, and then I won't have to worry about finding a new job!

Whenever I do consider Andrew coming around, though, my stomach does flips and I really wonder how on earth we'll get back on our feet. Where would we begin? How do you heal something so broken?

Then, when I start to worry about finding ways to move forward in our marriage, even actually considering driving home and talking to Andrew, I remind myself that I'm just borrowing trouble, inventing problems. Right now Andrew still has me locked out of his life, and I'm still trying to carry on on my own. Until that reconciliation day—*if* that day—comes, I'll just have to keep on forging forward. I'll have to keep on hoping for the best, as the girls and Dr. Pierce consistently encourage.

So forging forward is exactly what I'm doing! I'm hosting girls' night tonight, and Lara's come over early to help with the preparation, bringing with her two sacks of groceries she insisted on picking up.

"You really did a fantastic job on redecorating, Jack," Lara says, removing the cork from the bottle of white wine she brought over.

"Thanks. To be honest, I didn't think it'd be all that possible, what with the small budget and all." I stick the last finger sandwich with a toothpick. "Not to mention I've had a hard time holding back from splurging." I pull at the hem of my new baby-blue and pale yellow v-neck Ralph Lauren sweater—a sweater that was not on sale and just may set me back a month on my cable bill. Luckily, with the apartment renovation pretty much finished, no longer in need of watching every DIY show, I can probably kiss cable and its bill goodbye soon.

"Jackie," Lara says in a warning tone.

"But! When you put your mind to something, it's pretty darn amazing what you can accomplish. I've *barely* splurged. Seriously. And look at the apartment!"

Lara gives me a smile and proceeds to open a bottle of red.

I saunter into the living room and set out the plate of sandwiches on the new coffee table. Well, it's new as in it's never been here before, but it's just three old crates, like I used in the bookstore's inventory room, all nailed together and smoothed out with some sandpaper. They still have some of the old stamping on them —from some kind of soda or beer company. To make the top of the table level I just took two old checkerboards, trimmed them to size, and nailed them down. Then, to give it an antiqued look, I sloshed some coffee all over the makeshift table, patted the liquid dry, and let the stain set. The table isn't anything that'd make it in any of my fancy design magazines, but something you'd see on an HGTV DIY show. It's a piece that adds to the eclectic feel I have going with the apartment. It pairs well with the swanky furniture, and mixes in with all of the new antique-y stuff and some of Emily's older existing antique pieces, like her wine cabinet. I can't think of anyone more eclectic than Emily; the apartment has her name written all over it.

"You've accomplished a lot," Lara says. She's got four wine glass stems situated between her fingers. I rush to assist her and we arrange them on the small table.

"The paint makes it look like I've done more than I have, I think," I say matter-of-factly.

"No, I mean everything. The apartment, the job, this girls' night. Look." She points at the sandwich plate. "You made finger sandwiches, with *toothpicks!*"

"Presentation is everything."

"I know I've already said it and I don't want to make you feel like you were so low before, what with me talking you up constantly."

I grab a knife and a grapefruit and begin slicing. "I love being talked up." I blow her a kiss.

"I'm just really proud of you, I want you to know that." She takes a slice of grapefruit from me and cuts it in half. "You know what would be the icing on the cake?"

My mind on thoughts of things to be proud of, improvements in my life, the way things are going... I reply with, "If Andrew swept me off my feet?" I giggle unsettlingly.

"Oh." Lara's voice is empty.

I turn to look at her, grapefruit juice running down my hands.

"I was talking about dessert," she says, pulling a tight face. "The icing on the cake would be Sophie bringing dessert."

"Aaaaand fail," I say with a throaty laugh.

"Haven't heard from him yet?" Lara sounds like she's afraid to say anything about the matter.

I shrug and continue with my slicing. "Not yet, but I'm still hoping."

"Keep hoping, honey. You're on the uphill slope right now. I really believe things are going to keep looking up."

"And if they don't?" I dare to ask, not really knowing if there is an answer for this hypothetical.

"Then *you* keep on looking up."

Suddenly a series of pounding sounds from the front door.

"I'm coming!" I cry, rapidly wiping my hands on the kitchen towel. I fly to the living room, and there's Claire standing arms akimbo in front of the large windows.

"What's this?" I can hear her shout. She points at the window and makes circles. "*Love* it!"

"Hey, girls!" I say, the rest of the gang charging in as soon as I open the door.

"Omigod!" Claire shrieks. "The window! I love that you got rid of those hideous old mini-blinds." She shivers. "They were god-awful."

Getting rid of the mini-blinds was one of the first things I did.

The simple and inexpensive Roman blinds I got at a garage sale that looked like it was selling everything-IKEA are the perfect replacement.

Once the door clicks closed Sophie gasps and says, "Wow! It doesn't make that horrid squeaking sound anymore." She points to the door.

"Oh, yeah," I say with a flick of the wrist, dismissing the easy fix to the grating noise the front door always made. "Turns out all it needed is something called WB-30."

Sophie gives me a questioning look, and when I simply shrug in response she just laughs, saying, "Oh, Jackie. I love ya."

"Wow!" Robin breathes as she slowly enters the living room. Her head's moving up and down and all around as she takes in the unfamiliar surroundings.

"Pretty fab, eh?" I make a sweeping arm motion, showing off the place.

"Fab?" Sophie says as she lets her handbag slide off her shoulder. "This is remarkable!"

"Emily's going to freak!" Claire says. "Freak out in such a good way. You totally did this place well, Jack. It doesn't even look like the same apartment."

"Amazing, hah?" Lara says, striding up behind me.

"Uh," Claire says, "when you come visit me in Spokane, you're *so* decorating my place."

"Oh, no," I whine, putting on my pouty face.

"Yeah, yeah," Sophie waves off. "I've already cried my allotted tears for the day. Let's not get the jump on tomorrow's allotment so soon."

Claire gives Sophie an apologetic expression and rubs her arm. "Sorry for mentioning it."

Robin, coming from behind Claire and Sophie, gives them a collective hug. "Come on, girlies, let's not get sappy yet. Wine first, tour second, gossip-fest and all that, and *then* the sappiness."

"I didn't know you had this in you," Sophie compliments a second later as she inspects the bookshelf. I completely reorganized it and spruced it up with some knickknacks and framed pictures. "You have an eye for the pricey stuff, but this—this—" She spins around.

"It's a lot of do-it-yourself, seeing how I had to stick to a budget," I say.

"But it's fabulous!" Sophie gushes.

"Come on," I say, waving them all further in. "Grab yourself a glass of wine; we've got some touring to do."

48

"All this for a few hundred bucks?" Robin asks, bewildered. She gawks at the bedroom with its freshly painted walls, one of which has a large section dedicated to a collection of framed photos. They're arranged in an off-kilter way, but one that still makes your eyes follow them down and up, left to right, kind of like following a story. I chose to display a series of landscape photos here that Emily had taken when she was backpacking in South America. I recognized Machu Picchu in the bunch, but the rest of them were just as foreign to me as the African collection I hung in the living room, the collection of mountainscapes I arranged above the dining table, the beach photos I put together in the bathroom and on through the hallway.

I tried not to go too crazy with the photos, cluttering things up. I wanted to strike that Zen balance I know Emily's big on. But Emily's life is a giant passport chock-full of stamps, with brilliant photos to show for her travels. I couldn't pass on the opportunity to look at redecorating her apartment as a chance to take a trip around the world. Anyone who walks in will feel like they're being transported around the globe.

Maybe when Emily's home again and she's thinking of jetting off somewhere, she'll take a look around here, feel comforted by all of the beautiful places, and feel right at home...at least for a while more...and willing to stick around a bit.

"It looks really nice, Jackie," Claire says, giving me a high five. "You've got a knack for this kind of thing."

"And check this out," I say, pointing at the small, round table next to the bed. I tap on the glass. "A watercolor painting Robin did."

"Omigod." Robin rushes over. "I painted that years ago!"

"Back in college," Lara says, leaning over my shoulder. "I remember you working on that, Robin."

"Wow," Robin says. "Em still has this?"

Spreading across the expanse of the small tabletop underneath the glass, I stretched out the watercolor I found in a desk drawer. It was signed, *Robin S.*, and I just had to display it. The painted bird in flight, zipping between two craggy tree branches in a winter forest, reminded me of Emily and her penchant to fly free. Maybe that's why Robin painted it for her.

I was unsure of how to hang the painting and didn't want to damage it, but when I saw the boring old top of the bedside table Em's had for years, I knew just what to do!

"You've got some talent, Jack," Robin says. She surveys the bedroom again. Pointing up at the ceiling, she makes a puzzled face. "Wait. What's that?" She twists and turns her head, straining her neck and squinting to figure out what's taped to the ceiling.

"Oh, a reminder," I say casually. I look up. "I have them in each room, actually, by each ceiling lamp."

"What is it?" Sophie squints, trying to see for herself.

"They're pictures I've cut out from magazines. Pictures of lighting fixtures I'd like to put up at some point."

Lara whistles. "Damn, girl. You really *did* go all out."

"Ha! Going all out would mean getting those fixtures *actually* in and not just having pictures taped up there."

I jump on the bed and scoot up against the headrest. Grabbing a throw pillow and tucking it to my chest, I say, "I'm not completely done with redecorating, but the budget's tired and I didn't exactly know how to change a lightbulb, much less an entire fixture. Eventually I'll get them done."

Sophie moves across the room, towards the closet. "Wow!" She turns her head back and gives me a look of surprise. "You really organized this place, Jack! Closet, too?"

The rest of the girls move over to gawk at the rather impressive closet project.

"Took a giant day," I reply, "and a lot of determination. But you'd be surprised what you can do when you want to keep your mind off your troubles."

"That's what I've been saying," Sophie says. "If you have a hobby or a job, you'll be surprised at how little time you have left to contemplate problems...or anything else, half the time."

Claire wags her head, which is still buried in the closet. "Totally," she says. "Work, work, work, avoid the problems." She's rummaging about, pulling out hung up shirts and dresses, *oooing* and *ahhing* at the ones she fancies.

"You know, you work so hard and so many hours you end up forgetting *all* about," Claire spins around, a peach-colored tank top pressed to her chest, "how your husband's been in desperate need of a job."

She looks at the shirt fondly for a brief moment before returning it. "Then he suddenly up and tells you he's moving you out of town, and since you're still working so hard and *so* many hours," she spins back around, this time holding up a sleek, black tank-blouse, "you almost work yourself into a tizzy forgetting all about the major life changes."

She drops the tank-blouse to her side and squeezes her mouth into a fish-face-pucker. "Then you stop for a second, for a breather, and you realize the problems haven't gone away. They're just waiting for you." She heaves a sigh, shoulders drooping.

"Your news bites, Claire," I say as I bring the pillow tighter to my chest. "Majorly bites."

"Got news for you, hon," Lara says to Claire as she plops down on the bed beside me. "There's no amount of work or busy-ness that can keep your mind off of major life troubles. At some point you just cannot avoid them anymore."

"Beg to differ," I say in a high voice. "My life troubles are *huge*. H-U-G-E *huge!* And I've been getting on fine keeping myself busy."

"Yes, but the problems are still there."

I make a one-armed shrug and in a cavalier tone say, "Yeah, well...so..."

"Don't get me wrong," Lara rushes out in a calm way. "It's important to keep on moving on with life, doing your own thing even when you feel like there's no point or that no matter what you do things will never look up."

Sophie gives a mirthless smile. "It's what we women do best," she says, looking at Claire. "Times get tough, we just slog on somehow."

"Eventually we get a grip," Robin says in a soft yet upbeat tone from her position on the floor, arms outstretched behind her in support. "Just remember to remain tethered to reality while you're working through the tough stuff. You're moving, Claire, and there's nothing we can do about it. The more you fight it, the harder it'll be to adjust."

"I know," Claire whines. She thumbs the dry-cleaner's hanger of the tank-blouse.

"But Jackie does have a point," Lara continues. "Look at her! She's been on crap-overload this summer, and she's pulling herself up by her bootstraps. She's got a tough reality, but she's working through it."

"Trying," I say with a small smile.

"Yeah, but she's still got hope that her troubles will go away," Claire points out. "There's still hope," her eyes meet mine, "you and Andrew will get back together. That hope's got to help you keep on going. With me it's 'I'm moving to Spokane, and that's that!' It's so depressing." She casts her eyes down, and Sophie wraps her arms around her. "I'm up and down with it. Happy for Conner...for us... but *so* sad to leave."

"Look at how you worked through not getting to have a baby right away," Sophie says to Claire in an encouraging tone. "You thought your world was going to end if Conner didn't hop on board that ship." Robin, Lara, and I share a light laugh. "You worked through that just fine." Sophie rubs a hand up and down Claire's back. "Right?"

"I guess." A faint smile forms on Claire's lips. "I still want a baby, you know?"

"Don't we ever," Robin teases. "You know that cream blanket you made for Phillip makes *four*?"

Claire can't suppress a giggle. "I admit, I kind of made that in hopes Conner would spot it and reconsider trying for a baby."

"Oh, the motives." Robin leans back on her elbows.

"Face the music," Sophie says to Claire. "Things are a-changin', and that might be tough, but it's nothing you can't handle."

"I guess so," Claire says in a small voice. "I just wish Conner could have found a job *here*."

We all nod in understanding.

"We'll come visit," Lara says. "And you can *always* come here."

Claire scrunches the tank-blouse in her hands, eyes on the floor, and she shakes her head quickly. "Not all the time," she squeaks out.

"No," Lara says, "not all the time. That's true."

"It'll be a great change," Sophie says. I look at her with a befuddled expression. This coming from the girl who sees Claire as a sister? If anyone's going to be torn up over Claire leaving, it'll be Sophie, hands down. To be frank, I don't know how she'll get on without her BFF. Claire's the girl who knows Sophie cover to back, who can actually tolerate her bossiness and quirks and dominating nature more than the rest of us ever could fathom. I pity Sophie, because I completely understand. Each time Emily leaves town or whenever Lara's too busy at her office to come and hang out, I know that gnawing pang of loneliness. I wouldn't wish it on my worst enemy (except for maybe Nikki).

I rest my chin on the pillow tucked into my chest and sigh as the chatter turns to a cacophony, as it usually does when the conversation gets going and everyone's putting in their two cents, their laughter, their takes on the story.

Thinking about how Claire will be moving shortly, I remind myself that Sophie, like myself, will be fine, because she has a great support system. She may not have her partner in crime, but she knows she's still got a top team. She has Robin, Lara, and I, and Emily when she's in town, to pop on by that café of hers or swing by her apartment whenever she needs us. And Claire may no longer have us down the street, but like Emily, she knows she can always give us a call, drop an email, or plan a visit.

"Everything will be fine," Robin says. She stands up and takes a seat on the edge of the bed next to Lara, then pulls out her cell phone.

"We'll make the most out of it," Lara says.

"That's what Em would say," I say with a small smile.

"Girls," Robin says in a melodic way, "I've got some fun news." She keeps her eyes locked to her screen. "Bobby just texted. He says that it looks like Phillip's first tooth is coming in!" She looks around at us, face aglow. "My baby's growing up so fast!" She fakes a sniffle, then says, "Goodness, the teething stage."

"That's a rough one," Lara says, knowing all too well the pains of having a teething baby in the house.

"And!" Robin sings. "Bobby also says Em's coffee table book, draft one, has been approved, and we're looking at a holiday-season release!" she yelps, slipping her phone back inside her jeans pocket.

"Emily's going to flip," I say.

"Publishing that book has taken longer than I expected," Robin says, twisting her lips to the side. "Better late than never, though."

"Absolutely!" I say. "Never too late to do something fab."

"Omigod," Sophie breathes out from the closet. I peer over Lara's shoulder to see what she's got. "*These* are fab." Sophie's holding out my pair of broken Balenciagas. Actually, I should say my pair of *refurbished* Balenciagas. "These aren't new, are they?"

All eyes are on me, and I dramatically groan out, "Yes, I'm dead-ass broke and I'm going and buying five-hundred-dollar shoes."

I pull myself from the bed and walk over to Sophie. "These are an old pair." I take the refurbished yellow shoes from her. "I broke a heel, and so..." I wave around the pump-like shoes, proudly showing them off. "I wasn't going to let them go to waste."

"They're amazing." Sophie fingers the new pump heels.

"What'd you do?" Claire takes one of the shoes.

"Pretty simple, actually." I toss the other to Robin so she and Lara can take a look at my handiwork. "One heel snapped in half, so I took a saw to the other and...voila! It took a while to get the height to match." I snicker, thinking back on that desperate evening when I really hated seeing those yellow beauties lying next to the trashcan. "That's why they're both sawed down so much. But pretty neat, hah? Instant pumps."

"Wow," Robin says, passing the shoe to Lara. "When you're in a bind and desperate for designer clothes, you don't mess around. The old Jackie would certainly go and buy a new pair."

"Erm..." I pan about the room. "I kind of did, but that's besides the point."

"Designer shoes on *your* budget?" Robin's eyes are wide.

"No, no, no. Basement deals. You really think spoiled Jackie's going to make a complete one-eighty?"

Robin makes a *psh* sound and tells me she's just happy I'm getting my priorities in order, putting everyday necessities and BFF's apartment redecorating ahead of Dolce and Gabbana.

"Speaking of designer clothes..." I open the bottom of the dresser drawer.

"Oh no," Sophie groans. "You did damage *elsewhere* in addition to the basement, didn't you? I mean, that's totally your business, but Jackie, I know you're happy you're doing better and your sessions with Dr. Pierce are going well and you're—"

"Shut up and look," I say, yanking free a plastic sack from the organized but still packed dresser drawer.

The room becomes silent in an instant, save for the rustling of the sack and my huffing and puffing as I pull it free and root about inside.

"Ta-da!" I cry as I withdraw a pastel pink and purple, silk Chanel scarf. "How's this for some good news, Claire?" I send the beautiful accessory her way, its supple material flittering through the air as she catches it, her eyes and mouth wide open.

"For me?" Claire fingers the gorgeous material.

"Yup," I say. "You didn't think I'd sell *everything,* now did you, girls?" I wink and proceed to pull out one item I kept aside for each of the girls amidst my mad cleaning spree. The gold and coral cuff and matching earrings that Sophie's complimented time and again; the Burberry umbrella and matching tote I'm sure Robin will get more use out of than I will; the leather bound journal—an impulse buy in the hopes of becoming the journaling type—for Emily, which I slip into her underwear drawer.

"And for you, my dear Lara," I say, pulling out the last item.

"The Prada wallet!" she cries, clapping her hands to her mouth. "You doll, you!"

I hand her the beloved wallet I've been secretly keeping for her once I got the idea to sell some of my things.

I know it sounds crazy, but gift-giving feels better than any shopping spree I've ever had. I've given gifts before, and elaborate ones like these and never-before-used ones, too, but come on—it's not exactly difficult to whip out the plastic and have Andrew pay for whatever it is I feel like buying.

Right now, though, it's different. It's a different feeling...a really good and satisfying feeling...to give a gift when you can't afford it, when you could selfishly choose to keep or sell them instead of giving them away. And, let's face it, I'm not really in the position to be giving away what few assets I do possess. But Dr. Pierce and I have been talking about embracing the changes in my life by adding a few more to the lot. It sounds kind of absurd, I know, but instead of fighting change, why not embrace it? Why not give it a run for its money?

Things with Andrew are obviously beyond my control, and I couldn't really do much about being let go at Hodge's Bookstore, but I *can* take control of my life and happiness in some ways.

So here's one way. Fixing Em's apartment is another. Searching for that new job or realizing that Claire moving away isn't the end of the world are other ways, too. Keeping myself busy so I don't pout about my troubles or go on a bender is definitely another way.

And, if I can be so bold, letting Andrew go is one more way. Letting that pain and that worry go, letting myself cling on to that hope of reconciliation while still staying 'tethered to reality,' as Robin says, getting on with my life newly independent and all, is just another way of taking control of my life...of my future...of my happiness. It's me moving from limbo and onto the winning path.

"Come on," I say to the girls, standing up and tossing the empty plastic sack behind me. "Enough gooey emotion here." I make my way to the door. "We've got perfectly good wine and snacks out there—"

"And finger sandwiches with toothpicks," Lara says cheerfully.

"That's right." I wave the girls to follow me back into the living room. "All this and so little time. Come on, let's get our girls' night started!"

49

"Lara could be right," Robin says as she sweeps together the crumbs that the pastel-colored macarons have left behind on the new coffee table. "I don't want to raise your hopes and then have them crushed, but I bet that's exactly what happened." She drops the crumbs onto the plate that once contained at least a dozen of Sophie's delicious macarons.

Sophie hasn't offered macarons at the café lately. She says they're a lot of work, and it seems the moment she's scraped up enough energy to make a batch she blinks and, just like that, they're all sold out. It almost isn't worth it, because she can't keep up.

Also, other than Gatz, she hasn't been able to find someone who knows how to make the difficult dessert. She's tried to teach Evelyn, but Sophie just ends up dealing with such a mess she's nearly given up, creating the petite desserts only when the spirit calls (or a certain someone demands a specific dessert at girls' night).

Lara told Sophie she should really jump on marketing the macarons if they're selling so quickly—they could even become more popular than her cupcakes! Sophie said she'd consider it, but tonight's batch—a plate full of rose-, orange-, and strawberry-flavored treats—would be the last for a while. "Until someone with experience working in a French *boulangerie* or *pâtisserie* is willing to work for me for pennies," Sophie said, "I'm going to have to stick to cupcakes and croissants."

We all agreed Sophie should churn out the colorful cookies somehow. The strawberry macarons were amazing, and the orange would be a popular seller for sure, especially in the summertime, because biting into one is like biting into an orange creamsicle. The rose-flavored ones we all agreed would be a big craze if she started filling her display case with them. Eating them is like smelling a rose and eating a sweet, fluffy cupcake at the same time. Delectable!

"You really think that's exactly what happened?" I ask Robin, eyeing her, then Lara, as I finish my rose-flavored treat.

"You girls already know what I think," Lara says, hands raised. She licks clean macaron filling from her thumb.

"Look at it this way," Claire says sprightly. "You and Andrew have been separated for decades!"

"Three months," I correct in a low tone.

"Like I said, *decades!* He's probably finally realizing you're pissed, still standing firm with wanting that Nikki girl gone." Claire crosses her arms over her perky chest, the biggest look of cheer of the evening covering her face. "He's figured out you're not coming back so long as she's around."

"Or that he dare not return, running to you, with her still working for him," Sophie says judiciously. She begins to tap her chin. "Or, and don't get worked up over this, he could have had an affair with her—"

"Oh, Sophie!" Robin says loudly, one hand flying to her hip. She shifts in her seat on the sofa. "Sophie, don't take that side!"

"*Or!*" Sophie raises the pitch of her voice. "He could have had an affair, and now he's realized his tragic mistake and is doing all he can to fix it."

"Covering up his tracks is more like it," I sneer.

Sophie heaves a heavy breath, eyes on me.

"What?" I take a pull on my Chardonnay. "So long as we're exploring all the options."

"Look, I think we've talked the issue to death," Lara says. "Jack, hang in there. I really think things will work themselves out some way, some time."

"They have to," Claire adds in. "What with all the pep talks we've given and advice we've dispensed. I feel it." She pats a fist to her heart. "I feel it, right here. Things are going to change."

"Yeah," Robin says, "and until that situation works itself out, focus on getting that new job. That'll surely take your mind off of things."

"Totally," Claire says.

"I wonder what I should do next?" I look to each of them.

"What about that antique shop next to the bookstore?" Robin offers with a pointed finger my way.

I shrug. "Asked Al. He said he thought it best I not work around all that temptation." I chuckle. "Anyway, he said if Hodge's thought finances were tight, then Al's place was experiencing the crash of thirty-nine all over again."

"Twenty-Nine," Sophie swiftly corrects with a quick grin.

"Rent's going up there, too," I continue, "so everyone's cutting back." I take a slow sip of wine.

"Bummer," Robin mutters. "I suppose you don't have mad macaron-making skills you're keeping secret from us, huh?" She picks up the empty dessert plate and scampers to the kitchen.

"Don't hold out on me, girl," Sophie kids.

"Hey, how are things with just Evelyn, anyway?" Robin asks Sophie as she disappears around the corner. "You still thinking of hiring on extra help?"

"Oliver!" Claire says abruptly. "He's French. He's a baker. He makes wedding cakes!" In a flurry she sets her wine glass down and turns to Sophie. "I bet *he* knows how to make macarons! Oliver would be perfect! Why didn't we think of this before?"

"Oliver?" Sophie laughs.

"Yeah! You know? Oliver..." Claire presses. "Your old coworker? From Katie's Kitchen? He's still baking and catering there, isn't he?"

"As far as I know," Sophie replies with ease. "But, Claire, I wouldn't just need a macaron-helper. I'm talking an extra set of hands, period. Macarons are a bonus."

"And he could do that and *so* much more! Come on, you know I've mentioned before that hiring him would be awesome," Claire enthuses. "You already know him, so that's just a bonus. You know how he works, he's reliable, blah-blah-blah. Come on!"

"Yes..." Sophie slowly rocks her head from side to side. "Don't think I haven't considered it. Seriously, I have. But it comes down to the ol' budget." She clicks her tongue against the roof of her mouth.

"Sounds like he could be your ideal employee, Sophie," I say.

She rubs her fingers together. "Like you, Jack, it all comes down to what we can afford. Honestly, I just don't have that wiggle room with my cash flow right now."

Then, a sparkle comes to her eyes. "But..." she sings, "that doesn't mean it'll always be that way. If my math's right—and my dad's done a little research and checked the figures—I should be able to consider hiring on more help next year." She raises her glass. "But until then..."

"Cheers to figuring shit out," I say. Sophie and I clink glasses.

"Hey," Robin says, reemerging from the kitchen, a dishtowel in her hands.

"Hmmm?" I say as I take a drink.

"Did you make this backsplash?" She points a thumb behind her. "The awesome mirror backsplash?"

"Yup."

"I thought that was always there," Claire says, scratching her head of blonde curls.

"Nope," I say.

"Em's never had a backsplash," Lara says, getting up from the sofa and walking over to Robin.

"Take a look at it!" Robin leads Lara into the kitchen.

"Have you Picasso'd it in there or what?" Sophie says.

"That's awesome," Claire says once she lays eyes on it.

"You did that?" Sophie points at the backsplash made of a shattered mirror.

"Yup," I say proudly. "I found a busted mirror and thought it'd look neat all broken up." I walk over to the backsplash and run my fingers over it.

I saw a piece of art in the *Seattle Socialite* that was a giant canvas with hundreds of glued pieces of a broken mirror. It sparkled in the light and shimmered everywhere. It was brilliant!

Then, one bored afternoon when I was sitting atop the counters in Em's kitchen, staring at the ugly wall above the stove, the idea for a backsplash came to me. So one busted mirror and a tub of grout later...

"You really went all out," Robin says, touching the mirror pieces.

"Yeah." I lean against the counter and begin to play with the edge of the drying towel Robin discarded. "I kind of wish I had this redecorating job to do *after* I lost my job at the bookstore. Would so keep me busy." I toss the towel aside and push away from the counter. "But whatcha gonna do, right?"

I pull open the drawer where Emily keeps her matches. "Excuse me girls. I'm going to light up for a bit out back. Welcome to join me." I snag a book of matches from the drawer and take a new pack of Parliaments from my handbag.

"Wait a minute!" Claire says in an enthusiastic tone. "Wait just a minute, Jackie!"

"Claire, please," I say with a thin stick between my lips. "I know you're a healthcare pro and all, but I'm not going to listen to a lecture about—"

"No, silly!" She races up to me as I slide open the back patio door. "I have a great idea!"

I take the unlit cigarette from my lips and glance from Robin, to Lara, to Sophie. I raise an inquisitive brow. "A great idea? The last time you had a great idea—"

Claire charges into the living room, hands dancing wildly around the room. "Look around here, Jack!"

I cast about. "Yeah, I'm looking." I return the cigarette to my lips and strike a match.

"Your design skills!"

I step one foot out onto the back patio, cup a hand around my cigarette, and light up.

Claire looks like she's going to burst from excitement. "Turn them into a business!" she shrieks. "Take your hobby and make it your job!"

———

"Claire," Sophie says, "I thought the blind date idea for Em was a terrific idea. This is borderline genius!"

"Why thank you," Claire says with a pleased face.

"I'm sure if *you* had been the victim of Operation Blind Date, Sophie," I say candidly, "you wouldn't be so keen to think this is a genius idea."

"Come on, Jack," Robin says exuberantly. "You know this is not a bad idea."

"It's not *not* bad," Claire retorts. "It's good! It's great!"

"It's got possibilities," Lara says with a sharp nod, her tongue gliding over her teeth. "It's definitely worth exploring." She hastily pulls out her BlackBerry from her suit jacket pocket.

"I don't know, girls," I say. I, somewhat nervous, take a drag on my cigarette. I send the smoke over my shoulder, away from my group of girlfriends huddled around on the small patio out back. "Just because I managed to keep employment for a few measly weeks at a small-time bookstore doesn't necessarily mean I'm ready to earn my entrepreneur badge here."

"We're not talking guns-a-blazing entrepreneur," Lara says in a rational tone, eyes and fingers dancing about her cell phone. "Small startups happen every day. You'd have almost no upfront costs, virtually no risk, and, honestly, I think you could do something with this talent of yours—this passion."

"I don't know," I say again, letting my cigarette hang loosely between two fingers. I cross my legs and shake my bare foot. When I catch sight of the less-than-stellar pedicure job I did myself, I uncross my legs and push my feet under the chair. "Would anyone even *pay* for these services?"

"Sure!" Robin says.

"But if it's all cheap DIY stuff," I say, "why wouldn't they do it themselves? Honestly, if they just got online or watched some of those repair and remodel shows or picked up any number of the magazines I've picked up, they could find out how to do these projects themselves."

"That's true," Claire says. "I'm a major DIY girl and a big part of the DIY craze is that it's Do-It-*Yourself.* You don't hire and pay someone for something that's supposed to be a money-saving project."

"She's right," Sophie says, her face turning down.

"Hold it, hold it," Robin says, hands on hips. "Jackie's proven she can decorate an apartment with class, style, *and* money. That furniture she bought last year for Emily is to die for, and you *know* fashion. You know style, Jack. In fact, I wouldn't even say the DIY deal should be your angle."

"I like this," Lara says, eyes still trained on her phone.

"Okay..." I wait patiently for the next bit of advice.

"All right." Lara finally sets her phone down. "That's exactly it. Jackie, you have an eye for design. You know fashion. You know what works and what doesn't. Robin's totally right. And," she holds up a hand, "this is the seal-the-deal part, the angle you can totally play up."

I wait with bated breath. "Yes?"

"You know how to work within a budget. *Any* budget!" Lara says, face aglow. "You can work with a few hundred dollars and turn drab to fab." She waves her hands behind her, gesturing to the apartment. "You can work with several thousand; if Em's budget was a bit more, you so could have followed through with the sleek and elite style you originally had going with the furniture. So, you're versatile. Any budget, any style, any time! Design By Jackie!"

Slowly I'm beginning to see where the girls are going with this, and I'm becoming as excited as they are.

I tell Lara to go on as I rub out my cigarette and pull my legs into a criss-crossed position on the sticky, plastic lounge chair.

"I just blocked out some of my lunch breaks next week," Lara says, "so I can spend some time figuring out a mini advertising plan for you."

"Advertising?" I say, mouth agape. "That sounds big and fancy."

"If you want to do business, you need to advertise." Lara picks up her phone again. "This'll be a fun side project for me."

"Lara—"

"Hey, we all have hobbies and projects," she interrupts. "I just so happen to love my work so much it's my hobby, work, project, all in one."

"That and a little someone named Worth," Robin says. She dances two fingers across Lara's leg.

"Yes, I have a boyfriend now. Yes, I'm having the time of my life. Yes, I'm getting screwed six ways to Sunday. Or...something like that." She flutters her lashes.

"And you wouldn't have it any other way?" Robin says with a friendly grin.

"Hell no," Lara says. She looks at her phone. "So, a little bit of advertising—we can start with fliers!"

"I can sketch out logo ideas!" Robin offers.

"Ooo, I can put the fliers in my café!" Sophie says.

"I can spread the word at the hospital," Claire says in a sweet voice. "Could get a bite or two..."

"What do you say, Jackie?" Lara grips my knee, smiling wide, her eyes glittering with enthusiasm.

50

"You're going into business?" Dr. Pierce says, his bushy eyebrows knitting together.

"That's right!" I twist around my wrist the orange and brown leather cuff that Emily brought back from her Baltics trip some years back. "I, Jackie Kittredge, am going into business for herself!"

"I have to say, I'm surprised."

"Didn't think I had it in me, did ya, Doc?" I make a clicking sound with my tongue.

"No. I know you're capable of many things, Jackie. I'm just surprised that you're becoming aware of what you're capable of so soon."

I look off to the side thoughtfully, pondering for a moment Dr. Pierce's words.

Ha! I think. *I've surprised the doc! Jackie Kittredge is really movin' on up, and she's knockin' off a few socks along the way!*

I sit up a little taller and pull at the hem of my grey and white pinstriped vest, a bohemian find I got in Paris.

"So a business?" Dr. Pierce leans back in his chair. "What kind of business are you getting into?"

I tell Dr. Pierce all about my design business—Interiors By

Jackie. The name isn't all that creative, but Lara suggested I choose something straightforward. She said I don't want to fall into the kitschy group, trying to call my business something creative and playful and trying too hard, maybe giving off a cheap or throw-together vibe or something. Rather, she said, I should shoot for honest, simple, and approachable. Interiors By Jackie says all it needs to say, and I can be available for a wide range of budgets, since I want to design anything from DIY-fab to sophisticated-chic.

Robin's already designed a logo that meets the simple yet sophisticated theme Lara's talking about. Robin's so excited about the new venture that she spent all her free time over the weekend sketching and playing around on the computer. One of her earliest logo designs, using slate and a Tiffany-blue color with a thin-lined font, the letters 'I' and 'J' standing out boldly, is the winner.

With the logo and name done, Lara had some fliers printed out and even ordered me some business cards. She insisted I make things official and register for a business title and something or other—some kind of tax-related stuff.

I whined about how I didn't know any of that stuff and couldn't care less, but she promptly came over one evening and showed me how I could do it myself on my laptop.

"So this is an official business?" Dr. Pierce says, sounding very impressed.

"That's right! Paperwork's filed, marketing material's on its way, and this week I'm spreading the word!" I clap my hands together. "My friends really came together to help me pull this off so fast. I'm *so* excited!"

"Congratulations, Jackie."

"Thanks. Now all I need is the flood of customers."

"That's the greatest trick," Dr. Pierce says with a kind smile. "Tell you what—how about you give me some cards when you have them, and I'll give them to my landlord."

"Really?"

"Sure. I can't guarantee it'll result in any business, but he owns properties... Perhaps they need a designer's touch." He shrugs. "Can't hurt to try."

"Thanks, Doc!" *Gosh, this owning a business thing isn't so bad. It's a cinch, really!*

Okay, true I've gotten all of my friends to rally to my cause and help get this thing off the ground. But if I get, say, at least one client from Claire giving out fliers at the hospital and one person picks one up from The Cup and the Cake, and then maybe Dr. Pierce's landlord will call and—

"Hey, Doctor," I say, halting my wild train of thought. "Do you have an office or space at home that needs redecorating?"

Dr. Pierce chuckles. "I don't think that'd be appropriate, Jackie."

"Why not?"

"You and I stick to our sessions, how's that?" He wields his pen.

"Breach of ethics or something?" I say with a crooked face, and he nods.

"So," he says, his voice upbeat. "Let's begin our session."

"Hey, Tom!" I greet peppily as I step inside Hodge's Bookstore. It's the first time I've been back since I was let go.

"Jackie!" Tom says, making his slow way around the register counter. "Surprise seeing you here."

I see Shirley's head pop out from the inventory room, and I wave hello.

"This is my son, William," Tom says as a stocky man, much like Tom himself, walks up, extending his hand to shake.

"Nice to meet you," I say as I move the small sheaf of papers from my right hand to my left.

William and I shake and he says, "So this is the Employee of the Month my parents have raved about?"

I feel myself blush as I begin to fan the papers. "Oh, I wasn't that great. They're such nice people to work with." Tom and I exchange a smile.

"William here's taking the bull by the horns," Tom says gaily. He shuffles about a bit before finally resting his weight on the register counter.

"I'll really start plugging away once I can convince these two to go home and enjoy retirement," William says.

"Awww," Tom waves off.

I glance down at my papers and instantly turn to the reason why I dropped by today. "Well, uh, I wanted to come over and bring you something." I look from William, to Shirley, then finally to Tom. "I've found a new job."

"I'm not surprised," Tom says, now maneuvering, slowly, over to a stack of books set messily on the nearby table. "You did such great work here." He pauses and turns around, holding up a knobby finger. "It's not a job that involves alphabetizing, though, is it? Because then—"

I laugh and tell him no. "It's my own business, actually."

Launching into my quick spiel, I hold out my fliers, printed in color with my sleek Interiors By Jackie logo at the top. "I'm trying to spread the word," I explain. "Trying to get some first clients."

"Sure," William says with a warm grin as he takes my small stack of fliers. "We'd be happy to set these out."

"And some day, when we can get our numbers in order," Tom says with a look of dismay, "we might even give you a ring to come on over and fix up this shop."

"When the finances are in order," William asserts himself.

"Definitely. When you're ready, just call me. Here," I say, hastily pulling open my large Louis Vuitton Neverfull handbag. "A few business cards, too, if you like?" I hold out a thumbnail-width's stack. "Hot off the presses!"

The instant Lara called this morning to say my initial box of business cards were finished, I flew to her office downtown.

"I stole some," Lara had said when I excitedly tore open the box and gushed over my very first business cards. I, Jackie Kittredge, a businesswoman!

"Even kept some fliers, too, and I also gave Worth some," Lara added with a wink. "He knows moneyed people and said he'd be happy to help spread the word. You never know."

Would you look at this! People I never imagined are pitching in to help a girl make something of her life, of her newfound independence. Don't get me wrong, it'd be so much nicer if I had my husband to come home to, to swap day-at-the-office stories with, to have around to share my news and excitement. For now, though, I have to do what I have to do, and I need to stay standing—it took long enough to get upright.

I'm enthusiastic when William agrees to lend a hand, too. Pair the fliers and cards here with the ones I'm going to drop off at Claire's next, then the load Sophie's generously agreed to let me set out in the café, not to mention everyone else who's pitched in, and I could very well have my first client come a callin' any day now!

With Hodge's Bookstore checked off the to-do list, I begin the drive across town to Claire and Conner's.

Not only has Claire agreed to pass out some fliers at the hospital, but she's got something else to help me out. She and Conner are in the midst of packing for their big move, and they're taking the opportunity to get rid of a bunch of stuff they don't really need anymore. They want to lighten their moving load, so Claire's gathered a bunch of craft items, furniture, and decorative pieces for me —things I might be able to use for that staging project Lara and I talked about.

I did some Googling last night after Lara and I chatted about my next steps in forging ahead with my business. I found out that many interior designers offer staging—getting a home all dressed up as if it were a model home. It can really help get a house off the market quickly. I read on almost every informative site that potential buyers love walking into a home that feels like it's ready to be lived in. Even if staging isn't something I want to focus on with my business, it can be a great way to make a name for my company.

If I can get one or two people to agree to a staging project—a mini-redecorating gig—then I could take photos and use it in my portfolio, even a website! I have Emily's apartment to start with, even though that's not quite an example of the high-end stuff I'm eager to do. Lara insists it's a start, and while I'm aggressively trying to get my first clients, I should be just as earnest in finding someone who'd be willing to be my second guinea pig, and preferably someone who'd be willing to pay for the out-of-pocket expenses.

It seems daunting at times, and there are moments throughout each day I get really anxious, wondering if I've lost my mind about coming up with Interiors By Jackie. I panic about getting in over my head and want to pour myself a hearty glass of wine or call Andrew up and beg for another chance—I can't do something like this on my own! I've tried to stay standing! Disasters happen! I fail!

Then, I look around me, at Emily's gorgeous apartment, at what I've actually been able to do, and I see the framed picture of my best friends—my supportive team—and I know that I can try to do this. They believe in me, so perhaps it's time I believe in myself. Just take one day, one step at a time.

51

"Hey, Jackie!" Conner says, swinging open the front door to his homey Madison Park home.

Instantly his Jack Russell Terrier mix, Schnickerdoodle, makes a flying leap through the door, yapping incessantly.

"Hey," I say, looking behind me as Schnickerdoodle begins to run rapid doughnuts on the lawn.

"Schnicker!" Conner calls, opening the door wider. "Get in here right now."

Finishing off one last tightly made doughnut, the rambunctious dog shoots back into the house. Conner briskly closes the door behind him.

"Damn," I say, followed by a whistle as I take in the mayhem of boxes stacked about the living room. "You guys really *are* moving!"

Conner runs a hand through his unkempt sandy-blonde hair. "Claire's crying about it every night." He struts into the kitchen, hiking up his baggy brown cargo shorts. "Can I get you something to drink?"

I cast about the room, the realization that Claire and Conner Whitley are actually moving out of town hitting home harder than it has yet.

"Water? Iced tea? Beer?" Conner's voice carries from the kitchen. His head appears around the corner, a carton of milk in hand. "Milk?" He holds the carton up, then takes a sniff. "Nix the milk. Looks like all we've got is water, iced tea, beer, a Coke...coffee!"

I laugh at his offer of beer at half past nine in the morning. "No thanks," I say, setting down my Neverfull handbag on the half of the loveseat that doesn't have boxes covering it. "I'm heading to The Cup and the Cake after this to drop some fliers off. Gonna get my coffee and pastry fix there."

"Damn," Conner moans as he emerges from the kitchen with a can of Coke. "That's definitely a downside to Chad not working there anymore."

I dig through my handbag, searching for the stack of fliers and cards I'd organized for Claire. "Oh yeah?" I say, half-attentive.

"Whenever he'd come over and hang out, like after a weekend shift or something there," he pops open the can of soda, "he'd come with cupcakes and cookies and crap like that. Awesome." He takes a quick sip, followed by a satisfying smack of the lips.

"Yeah, well," I say, still searching in the never-ending depths of my handbag for the fliers. "Maybe if he didn't sleep with his coworkers then he'd still be playing cupcake delivery boy." My fingers finally alight on the papers, and I declare an "Aha! I found them!"

"Coworkers?" Conner asks, his voice a hint unsettled.

"Yeah." I brush a hand over my hair.

"Co-work-*ers*?" he says slowly.

I crinkle my brow. "Yeah."

"Shit, he and Sophie didn't...again?"

I look to my left, my right, then back at Conner, completely nonplussed.

"I knew he still had it bad for her, but no way in hell did I think he'd *actually* act on it. That *she* would!" Conner brusquely shakes his head and takes a drink. "That's why she fired him, isn't it? I knew it!" He smacks a free hand against his thigh. "Knew it!"

I want desperately to hear more of this insanely juicy and totally unexpected gossip. I try not to blow cover that I have honestly no idea what Conner's talking about, so I say in a vague sort of way, "You knew it?"

"I may not be the most astute when it comes to love triangles, but I know my best bud."

I nod slowly and take a seat on top of the cluttered coffee table.

"Sophie didn't fire Chad because he started dating Evelyn," he says with a sneer. "She's—and I don't mean any disrespect; Sophie's a great girl, Claire's best friend, and I like her—but she's a controlaholic, and I can't believe she sank so low." He wags his head and sets his soda down next to me.

"Well...Sophie's a bossy little one..." I say in a distant way. I fake a laugh.

"She fired the poor lovesick guy because she's upset he's with Evelyn now and not her. God! I can't believe her! If she wanted him so badly, why didn't she take him when she had the chance? *Before* he hooked up with Evelyn? That's a real jealous and bitchy move, toying with him like that."

"Lovesick?" I say, feeling beleaguered by what I've just become privy to.

"Yeah—" Suddenly, Conner's eyes grow large and round, his mouth agape. "Shit."

I grip the edge of the coffee table and look down at the tips of my high heels, unable to believe my ears.

"I've just opened my big mouth, and you have *no* idea what I'm talking about. Do you?"

I shake my head quickly.

"Fuck." He runs his hands awkwardly through his hair and lets out a guttural sigh. "Jackie, listen." He leans forward in his seat. "I just thought that when you said *coworkers* you were implying that Chad hooked up with Sophie *and* Evelyn, and I got to wild thinking..."

"Yeah, like a zillion years ago!" I say in a high and a hasty tone. "Back in college! As in, 'has hooked up before'!"

"I know, I know." He continues to run his hands through his hair in anxiety. "I'm so stressed with the move and the new job, and everything's just disorganized and chaotic and— My head's not straight. Just forget all about this."

"Uhh..."

"Please!" he implores. "Besides, it's nothing, really. You said it yourself: Sophie and Chad haven't hooked up recently. So, yeah... guess she *did* fire him because of his deal with Evelyn..."

I raise both eyebrows, trying to follow this bizarre trail of breadcrumbs. "So, to be clear, her firing Chad *wasn't* because she and Chad got together again, had a falling out, and he then hooked up with Evelyn?"

"I thought, but no. Totally wrong. I don't know," he stammers, still running his hands nervously through his hair. "Just a stupid hunch. Like I said, I don't know where my head's at. Forget about it. Please."

"But..." I say, eyes trained back at my feet. "This 'hunch' can't be because you really think there's more to why Sophie fired Chad. Sure she's a control freak, but—"

"Forget about it."

I press on, the breadcrumbs slowly leading me further and faster down the path. "That's not why at all, Conner." I perk my head up and lock eyes with him.

"Forget it."

"You said *lovesick*. You said he still had it bad for her."

"Jackie, please."

"Conner, is Chad..." My voice is small. "Is Chad in love with Sophie?"

Conner doesn't respond.

"Shit," I whisper. "Omigod! But—but—he's with Evelyn."

"And he's happy with her," he blurts out. "Really happy. Him having it bad for Sophie...that's old news!"

"Chad's been in love with Sophie?" I'm in shock. "At some point in time, *has* been?"

"Look." Conner cups a hand to the side of his face. "That's the past. He's with Evelyn now, and I was just jumping to conclusions with the whole coworker plural thing. That's all. Never mind. Forget all of this, *please.*"

"Well." I exhale loudly. "Sure. I guess. I mean...I don't get any hint that Sophie's interested in him... Seems repulsed half the time, really!" I give a nervous laugh. "And Chad's obviously with Evelyn. They seem happy."

"Exactly!" Conner practically leaps out of his seat. "So it's all said and done, and we're moving on. Please, Jackie." His eyes are beseeching. "Please, not a word. No need to cause any drama. For no reason!"

"Yeah," I say with a half-laugh. "You know I *love* my drama, but..."

"Please. For everyone's sake. *No* drama."

"Yeah, well..." I shrug. "All right. Okay..."

"Thank you."

"Besides," I say, standing, "Sophie would flip her lid if she knew, and she'd probably rag on Chad even more, and it'd be just...messy for everyone."

"Exactly! It'd be a total mess. And what with Evelyn and Chad moving in together and—"

"Moving in together?" Another surprise for the day.

"Yeah. It's a big move for Chad."

"Well, I guess good for them?"

"I'm surprised you didn't know already." Conner ushers me towards the hallway, telling me the stuff Claire's gathered for me is in the spare bedroom-turned-office. "I thought Claire would've told everyone by now."

"Nope."

"Ah, well, she probably just hasn't gotten around to it yet. Doesn't have as big a mouth as I do, *apparently.*" He smacks a palm to his head and opens the office door, Schnickerdoodle hot on our heels.

"Didn't know you were the type to spread false rumors and revel in gossip," I tease as we step into the office.

"When you're married to a woman who's slightly obsessed with Lifetime and the CW, what can I say? It rubs off."

"Whoa!" I halt as soon as I take in the disastrous state of the office. "I thought Em's place was a mess!"

The room, much like the living and dining rooms, is stacked with boxes, but in the middle of it all is a large desk, wires protruding from all areas of it, two large computer screens and two laptops on top of it. It looks like there's a printer on one end of the desk, a sewing machine on the other, and papers and fabric are scattered all about.

"It's kind of a disaster," he says. "We sold one of the desks, so it's a little cramped now."

"A little?" I laugh.

"Here," he says, spotting a box on top of an end table. It's marked *For Jackie*. "She said it's just one, for now." He gives a sheepish grin and picks up the box. "She'll let you know when there's more."

"Thanks." I lead the way out of the small disaster site. "Oh, and I'll leave the fliers and cards Claire wanted here," I say, setting them on the dining table.

"I think it's awesome you're starting your own business, by the way," he says coolly. "Congrats."

"It's exciting. Daunting, but exciting. Now I just need a client. A guinea pig, really, for starters."

"Claire mentioned that." He sets the box down by the front door. "Too bad we're moving, because we'd be happy to be your guinea pigs. Lord knows Claire's hated that office for years."

I pick up my handbag. "I should be heading to the café."

"Aww," Conner moans. "Don't make my mouth water. I can't tell you the last time I had one of Sophie's brownies."

"Tell Claire I said hi," I say as Conner puts the heavy box in my car trunk.

"Will do." He rests a hand on my car door. "And good luck with the biz. I bet you'll do great."

I stick the keys in the ignition. "One can only hope." I smile and thumb the Mercedes symbol on my steering wheel. "Hope's kind of what I've been living on for a while now. Getting kind of good at it."

"Hey," he leans down and grins a lopsided grin. "I know it might not be much help what with us moving and all, but if I think of anyone who could be a client, or your guinea pig, I'll let you know."

I start the engine. "Thanks, Conner. I appreciate it."

"And, uhh, about earlier..."

"Swear." I hold up two fingers. "Scout's honor or whatever it is." I hold up four fingers, pressing my thumb against my palm. "I won't cause unnecessary drama."

"Thanks." He's about to shut my door when a look of surprise crosses his face. "Hey, wait a minute."

"Yeah?"

"Speaking of Chad. I've got an idea." Conner rubs at the slight scruff covering his tanned jawline. "It's just an idea. What if you redid Chad's place?"

"Chad's place?"

"Yeah."

"His houseboat?"

"Why not?" Conner slips both hands in his front pockets and leans back on his heels, a look of self-satisfaction about him. "It's just like any other home. His roommates are moving out; Evelyn's moving in soon. The place is kind of a bachelor pad." He pans around the yard, as if giving me time to contemplate the suggestion.

"Hmmm."

"Maybe you could help him make it more...woman-friendly." He sniffs a laugh, then ducks his head down and nearer, leaning one hand on the car door frame. "Just an idea. I can ask him for you if you like."

"Sure," I say at last. "That's actually not a bad idea."

52

"You're *what*?" Sophie says, exasperated, empty teacups in both hands. She pads to the front counter of her café, and I follow closely behind.

"It's not the worst idea," I say.

"May not be the *worst*, but it's just weird." She sets the cups down, her voice now lowered so as not to disturb her customers.

"Look, Lara's right. I need to do some staging. I'm never going to get this company off the ground if I don't have something to show. No portfolio, no proof of what I'm capable of."

"And Emily's place?" Sophie begins to wipe down the counters and the espresso machine, moving about quickly, unable to hide her state of annoyance. "Why can't you use Em's place as a staged example?"

"I am." I turn the café's tip jar around in circles. "That's just a start. Besides, showing super-budget revamps isn't really going to be the best model for my business. If I want to make some real money with this thing—actually survive—I need to show I'm capable of a variety of styles and budgets. And I *need* money." I raise high my eyebrows.

"And Chad's *house*boat is going to be that step to the upper class?" Sophie gives me a blank look. "*He's* going to let you flip that place into a swanky, *feminine* place?"

"Look," I say, keeping my voice down. I look to the front of the café. All the customers are keeping to themselves, either lost in conversation, enjoying a baked good or a coffee, or immersing themselves in their morning read. "Conner's going to ask him for me. If Chad's up for it, I'm doing it. I need the help, Sophie. I can totally flip that place!"

She folds the damp cloth in quarters and heaves a sigh. "It makes sense," she finally says, but her tone sounds like I'm twisting her arm.

I won't lie. The instant I waltzed into the café and saw Sophie, my mind instantly flashed back to my gossip fest with Conner. I promised I wouldn't say anything about his hunch/slip-up, and if it was all matters of the past there was no point in gossiping anyway, really.

But I still couldn't help but feel edgy the moment I saw Sophie, and certainly when I brought up the renovation issue with Chad's home. I know deep down there is no way what Conner's idea was any more than a silly hunch, but it's still weird. Really weird.

On second thought, there's no harm in working out some hunches of my own. Just to clear the air—settle my mind. Maybe if I just asked Sophie if she had any romantic feelings for Chad then I would know for sure the unnecessary drama I promised to keep under wraps with Conner would really be unnecessary.

"What's the problem, anyway?" I ask Sophie in a casual tone. "So I redo Chad's place. What's it to you?"

"Nothing!" she exclaims rather loudly.

"You wouldn't..." I turn my tone up a notch in pitch, coquettish, "be harboring feelings for him, now would you?"

"Chad?" she practically spits.

I nod and say, "Yeah, you know? You two had an encounter back in college, and now that he's moving in with someone—taking things seriously for the first time in his life—you're a little...jealous?"

"Ew, no! Jackie!" She squeezes the cloth in her tightening fist. "You think that one little encounter with Chad has left me pining away for him all these years?"

I purse my lips, awaiting her answer to her own question.

"Please," she splutters. "How's this? You two had your own 'encounter.' You pining away for him?"

Immediately my face twists into an expression of disgust, and I voraciously shake my head. "Okay, okay!" I hold up two surrendering hands. "I get your point. Moving on. So sorry I brought it up."

"Yes, thank you." She heaves a dramatic sigh and tosses the cloth onto the counter.

"You just looked a little upset with the news of Chad and Evelyn moving in together, and me working on his place." I backtrack over the whole unnecessary parade of drama I've started and decide Conner was right: It was all rumors, gossip, hunches... I'm causing more harm than good when clearly that's not the issue here. "Is there *something* wrong, Sophie? You seem upset."

"I'm just—" Her aquamarine eyes turn a tick glassy as she looks just past my ear.

I tug at the sleeve of her shirt and she looks to me. "Talk to me," I say. "What is it?"

"It's stupid." She reaches back for the cloth and squeezes it in her tightening fist some more.

"Sophie?" Evelyn calls out as she emerges from the kitchen. "Oh, sorry. I didn't mean to interrupt."

"No, no," Sophie waves off with the hand clutching the cloth. "It's fine. Jack and I are just chatting. No biggie. What's up?" She stands up a little taller, posture perfect.

Evelyn produces a pink to-go box and says, "The assorted cookies for the pickup you asked for?"

"Excellent." Sophie eagerly takes the box from her and sets it by the register. "They should be by any minute," she says as she checks her gold watch.

Evelyn's about to turn back towards the kitchen when Sophie

blurts out, "Actually, I need you up here now, Evelyn. I'll take care of things in the back."

"All right." With an understanding smile, Evelyn assumes the role of managing the front of the café, and Sophie nudges me to the kitchen.

"Sophie, what is going on with you?" I ask once we're in the back, out of earshot of possible eavesdroppers, our voices registering at normal levels now.

I watch Sophie make her way to the refrigerator. She pulls from it a pink recipe card affixed with a magnet. "Look," she says, sounding incensed, "it sounds silly and totally stupid, but hearing that you'll be doing Chad's place just adds salt to the wound."

I scrunch my nose and say with a shake of the head, "What? What wound? What salt?" I pause. "It's just an idea at this point. Chad may not even go for the idea."

"Oh, the oaf'll go for it." She flies a hand up. "He's got more money than he knows what to do with. He'll be happy to be your guinea pig. *And*, he's so damn smitten with..." She gestures to the front of the café.

"Awww." I wander over to a free barstool. "Are you really jealous of the new girlfriend? I thought you didn't have any feelings for Chad."

"I'm not jealous," she says curtly. "And you're right, I *don't* have feelings for him. Not at all!" She winces in what is unmistakably pure revulsion.

I suppress a laugh and say, "All right. We've established this. So what's the BFD? So Chad's in what seems like a normal relationship with a nice girl. *That's* a first!"

Sophie sighs, leaning against the refrigerator. "A first for what? The normal relationship or the nice girl?"

"*Touché.*"

"I'm just being dumb." She methodically thumbs at the corners of the recipe card.

"Is it Evelyn?" I query. "She not good enough for Chad or something? You don't approve?"

I'm grasping at straws. I really don't know what the problem is. So Chad's got a girlfriend, and a nice one at that. So Evelyn works for Sophie; Chad doesn't anymore. There's no longer that distraction she's got to contend with. I don't see the problem.

"She's *too* good," Sophie says with a chortle. "But that's not it."

"Okay. Then what *is?*"

"It's everyone."

"Everyone?"

"Everyone's finding their someone, Jackie. Everyone's finding love." She presses her lips firmly together.

"Ohhh," I say in a low note. "I see."

"I told you it was stupid."

"It's not stupid. It's not entirely true, but it certainly isn't stupid."

"Uhh." She gives me a wide-eyed, obvious look. "Look around, Jack. Everyone's Noah's Arking it around here, and then there's Sophie. I mean, even world-trekking Em's got someone she's in love with!"

She walks over, takes a seat across from me at the stainless steel island table, and looks into my eyes. "I never would have thought I'd be twenty-eight and single. And what's more, I can't even believe I'm bellyaching about it."

"Oh, Sophie."

"No, it's true. I've been fine with it for a long while. Honest, I have." She pauses, looking at the recipe card. "I was angry that Nathan and Lara didn't work out," she blurts, "but elated once she and Worth started seeing each other. Emily with Gatz...that's great. Super!" She pats the card. "I couldn't think of a better match for those two. Claire and Conner, that's been in the stars for centuries. Robin and Bobby...thank god the girl caught a break and she's all peachy. And you and—"

"And who? Andrew? Me and Andrew?" I give her a vacant expression. "Yeah, and *that's* a love story."

"Oh, it'll get figured out."

"Well, fine, if it does. In the meantime, I am the *last* woman who has a fairytale love story to share."

"I guess." She hugs one arm to her waist. "You know, I was even fine with Chad dating Evelyn."

"Oh, yeah," I say sarcastically. "That went over *real* well."

She rolls her eyes. "Aside from that, I grew to accept it. If they want to date, go for it! He's not working here anymore so it doesn't matter. Who am I to stop them? But this moving in thing... This—this—"

I step down from the barstool, walk over to her side of the table, and lean against it.

"It hit me hard for some reason," she says in a small, childlike voice.

"It's a more serious move," I say.

"Exactly."

"And Chad's not the serious-move kind of guy."

"That too." She begins to rub the sides of her head. "It just all kind of became real to me when Claire told me the news. Like, he's the last one in our group of friends, aside from me, to take a serious step." She pushes the card away from her and hugs both arms to her waist. "And I never pictured I'd be the last one in line. Selfish, hah?"

"Ha!" I shriek. "You want to talk selfish? I know all about selfish, babe." I give her a side hug. "Come on, you'll find your love when the time's right."

"I know. I mean, I need to be realistic here." She surveys the kitchen. "I have a business to run and barely enough time as it is. Where am I going to find the time to meet someone, get to know him, fall in love...?"

"I may only be starting my business," I say encouragingly, "but I'll find whatever damn time I can to try to work on my love life. That is, whenever Andrew's back in the picture." I sigh. "When you find the right one, you'll make the time, too." I give her a reassuring pat on the arm.

"Still no contact?" Her face goes long.

"Oh, the world will hear from me when that happens. *If* that happens," I say. "Ha! Listen to me, being all optimistic."

Sophie pokes me in the ribs.

"I tried calling him," I say, voice barely above a whisper.

"And?"

"I can't do it. Chicken out every time." I look down at my hands. I no longer have acrylic nails, and the manicure job I gave myself isn't exactly artwork. I finger my wedding ring. It's still just as sparkly as the day I first wore it. It still holds just as much meaning as it did the day Andrew slipped it on my bony finger, promising me he'd be there, for better or worse.

"How's this?" Sophie peers at me with a suspicious expression. "If we're both...oh...say, forty, and neither of us have found love—"

"I found mine," I quickly assert. "Just to be clear."

"All right, all right." She rests both elbows on the table, the side of her head in one hand. "If we're both forty and still aren't with our true loves. If we're still unattached, then we'll be old maids together."

"Oh, god, Sophie," I say through a throaty laugh.

"Come on, promise."

"Like a couple?" I raise a curious brow.

"Like a 'we're both old maids and a good friend helps another friend' kind of thing."

I consider the proposition for a second, then shrug and casually say, "All right. If we're both forty and neither of us are married and aren't with anyone serious..."

"Exactly."

"Then we'll be each other's backup."

"Deal?" She holds out her hand.

"I can't believe I'm agreeing to this," I say as I take her hand in mine.

She pumps it strongly then briskly makes her way across the kitchen. "Maybe all I need is some cleaning to get my mind straight, you know?" she says as she reaches for a broom.

"I don't but...whatever floats your boat." I jump into her seat. "Well, I came by to drop off the fliers and business cards. And for a little breakfast snacking." I point at the arrangement of chocolate muffins atop a glass cake stand. "May I?"

"Go for it. And when you're done you can help me tidy up back here, if you don't mind."

"Ohhh, Sophie," I whine as I pull back the muffin's wrapper. "You're not seriously going to make me *work* for this muffin, are you? I do have a job now." I give her a playful wink.

"Jackie, I love you, and I'm glad to see not *everything's* changing, but..."

I take a bite of the succulent, moist muffin. "Me, too," I say with a full mouth. "Deese muffins aw good."

She laughs and continues sweeping. "Come on. I set out your fliers, you help wash a few pans."

"Aww, Sophie." I take another bite, crumbs spilling about the table.

"Okay, if not for that then how about for the company? It's quiet back here." She looks at me with imploring eyes. "I'm still trying to digest this whole 'I'm going to be an old maid' thing."

"You made the deal," I say in a teasing way.

"You know what I mean." She crosses over to the opposite side of the kitchen and begins sweeping her way back towards the middle. "Evelyn knows I know about the move, and she's been saying she's excited to take this step—her first move-in with a guy, you know?"

I roll my eyes and lick my index finger and thumb. "God, been there, done that a zillion times. Don't envy her that journey one bit." I lick my pinky. "And with Chad. Oh, god help her. He can be such a pig."

"I know, right?" Sophie says with a high-pitched laugh. "Well, she's a sweet girl, and I'm trying my best not to rain on her parade."

"Rain comes, parades come, and they go." I take another bite of muffin and page through the morning's newspaper. Sophie continues her sweeping as I turn to the horoscopes page.

"Claire's going to be leaving soon," Sophie says more to herself than me. "I've got this Chad and Evelyn thing shoved in my face... I'm trying to be a good sport, but I just don't care to hear about it..."

"Life'll blow sometimes," I say, careful not to spit muffin out onto the newspaper. "Oooh! You're a Pisces, right?"

"Yup."

"Okay. Here's your horoscope for today."

"Oh, Jack, you're such a goofball. I appreciate what the Zodiac signs predict, but seriously, I think time's just going to have to do its thing for me to get over this loveless state of my life right now."

"It says..." I go on, ignoring her babbling, "Oh, and this is *so* good. You should definitely listen. It says, 'Pisces: You've encountered some resistance on some of your undertakings. It is advised you let them go, because it's possible your goals have changed. It's time to consider alternative actions. Perhaps a new career? A new hair color? A new attitude?'"

I make a *tsk*ing sound and poke a finger repetitively at the newspaper. "You really should read this daily. I've gotten so behind. Em's right—the Zodiac's got some very wise pointers."

"Thanks, Jack," Sophie replies with a long, drawn-out sigh. "But a new career? I've got it. This place is my passion. A new hair color? I've been a natural brunette forever, so I'm not changing now. A new attitude?"

"Oh, and your lucky numbers today are thirty-three, thirty-five, one, and seven." I look up from the paper.

"Thanks again." She sweeps the crumbs into a dustpan. "I appreciate your help, but I hardly think my horoscope is my answer."

I look over my own horoscope, jut out my bottom lip in consideration, and say, "Now if mine isn't truth-telling then I don't know what is. It says, and I quote, 'If you feel like you're not making enough money, now is probably the time to do something about it. Are you maximizing your earning potential? Are you being paid what you deserve? Perhaps you've wanted to change careers for some time but have felt held back. Now is the time to break free and make a change.'" I look to Sophie, my eyes round with awe. "Fascinating, isn't it? God, these things are so amazing."

"Jackie." She walks over and puts a hand over the paper. "I agree, they're fascinating, and sometimes totally accurate."

"I know, right?"

"But," she keeps her hand over the paper despite my attempt to

435

read more, "I think this *maximizing earning potential* means I need to make you a coffee and you need to help out with a few dishes. I'm not done whining, and my nerves are a little too frazzled for me to be alone with Evelyn right now."

"Got it." I say, cramming the remains of the muffin in my mouth.

53

That night, right before I turn out the lights well past midnight after a long and exhausting day of getting all my fliers passed out, my cell phone rings. I lean over Bella, who's snuggly situated between my legs on top of the comforter. "Could be my first client," I tell her as I reach for the phone. "Cross those paws!"

I glance at the screen—it's a long number I don't recognize. *Who on earth could this be?*

"Hello?"

"Jackie?"

"Emily!" I bellow. "Omigod! Emily! Is it really you?"

"The one and only," she says, her voice sounding somewhat distant. "The connection's not the best. I'm using the computer, and the speaker's pretty old."

"Oh, I don't care. Omigod! How are you? What are you doing? Where are you? How's Gatz? How's Australia?"

"Brisbane is *awesome*," she says. "Gatz is just super. The Center for the Blind is amazing. Those kids are teaching me so much— Oh, erm... I know I'm way ahead of you, time-wise. Is now an okay time to call?"

"Uh, yeah!"

"I'm just so bugged up excited with your news I couldn't wait to call! What time is it there?"

"Who cares?" I sit up higher in bed. "I'm so happy to talk to you, I'm not going anywhere!"

"So you're starting your own business, eh?"

"That's right," I say, proceeding to tell her all about Interiors By Jackie in that hyper, super-summary, excitedly rushed-out kind of way you do with a best friend whom you haven't talked to in ages.

"Interiors By Jackie," Emily says. "It definitely is to-the-point. It sounds classy, sophisticated. I like it."

"And Em, I think you're really going to love your apartment when you see it."

"Of course I will."

"So just when *is* that? Gatz decided to stick with the semester, or are you shooting for the full academic year?" I bite down on my tongue, nervous to hear her answer. She sounds so happy over there in Brisbane, though, that I'm sure a year is probably what she wants deep down.

"Oh, I don't know," she says, sounding cavalier. "It still feels like we've just gotten here, and Gatz is so crazy into his work. The guy's like ridiculously inspired over here."

"Oh yeah?"

"He's cranking out some really good poetry. Some inspired stuff."

"Writing you *loooove* poems?" I titter.

"He's even started a novel."

"Wow. That is impressive. It sounds like you guys are having a blast. Good for you."

"And it sounds like you're keeping yourself busy," she says. "Good for *you*, Jackie."

"Busy, indeed. Now all I need is my first client. I swear, if I don't get one soon I'm going to cry into some tequila shooters."

"All in good time, Jackie. Starting a business takes a lot of work, a lot of dedication."

"I've got the time; I need the work. But trust me, I'm dedicated. I'm making this work. Something's got to pan out in my life, right?"

Emily sighs, then says she knows I can do it. "Look how far you've come. Don't give up now."

I tell her things with Interiors By Jackie could be shaking and rattling sooner than I expected, thanks to Chad possibly offering up his place as a staging project.

"Seriously?" she asks with a cackle.

"Yeah. I know, sloppy Chad and his frat boy roomies." I sink back into the pillow I've propped up against the headboard. "Who would've thought he'd want his place all spruced up? But he's asked Evelyn to move in with him and—"

"Huh?"

"More juicy gossip news for you. God, girl, you have *got* to come back here. It's just not the same without you."

"So Evelyn's moving in with Chad?" she gets straight back to the point.

"Yup." I stroke Bella's head. "Guess they're taking the next step. Sophie was miffed a little today—had to calm her down, poor thing...think she's got it rough with Claire moving away and all. Her emotions are out of whack."

"Why was she miffed?"

"Oh, you know... Last single girl standing kind of thing. Of course, she insisted she has no time for love anyhow, but still..."

"Ahhh. I see."

"I told her she's being ridiculous. Not *everyone's* finding love. I mean, look at me, right?"

"So he's really moving in with her?" Emily says, sounding taken aback.

"Yes," I say with a furrowed brow. "It's no big deal."

"Yeah, I know. I'm just surprised, that's all."

"Anyway." I hug an arm to my stomach and begin to finger the silky camisole left over from my Parisian shopping spree. "The neat thing is that *I* just might get to design his place. Wouldn't that be great?"

There's a bit of dead air for a moment, and I'm not sure if the line's cutting out—the connection has been getting scratchier—or if Emily's attention has been drawn elsewhere.

"Emily? Emily, you there?"

"Yeah. Sorry."

"Is the connection bad?"

"Yeah." A pause. The scratchiness subsides a bit. "Guess we should go."

A yawn sneaks up on me, and I make a loud noise as it escapes. "Probably," I agree.

"Well, good for Chad. Good for Evelyn, too," Emily says. "Definitely tell Sophie not to worry. Her time'll come. It always happens when you least expect it, love."

"So true." I fluff my pillow and lie down, eyes fixed on the ceiling.

"And good for you! Best of luck with redesigning Chad's place, and with getting those clients!"

"*If* they ever call." I push out my bottom lip in slight disappointment as the line crackles louder.

"They will. Just be patient. And until then, stay away from the tequila shooters. Tell the girls I say hi."

"Will do. And say hi to Gatz for me."

"I'll talk to you later, Jack. Love ya."

"Love ya, too, Em."

I disconnect the call and close my eyes, letting the exhaustion of the day finally get the best of me, but not before I see the image I usually call forward before I fall asleep these days.

Nestling down into the plushness of the bed, I slowly begin to see Andrew's face—his crystal blue eyes and those wrinkles around them, the wrinkles along his brow, his mouth...they're a map of his worry, his fear, his happiness, his love. I see him grin, then break out in laughter, low and slow at first, then deeper, head shaking, eyes closed, and he motions for me to sit on his lap. He wraps his arms around me, kisses the top of my head, then presses his cheek to mine. He tells me how much he loves me, how I'm his entire world. And as he rocks me back and forth, leaving a trail of kisses from the nape of my neck, up to my chin, down my throat, to my shoulder...I fall asleep.

The following day I spent a good portion of my time at The Cup and the Cake, enjoying breakfast with Sophie before Evelyn and the usual Monday morning rush arrived.

I spent the rest of my day working on design ideas for Chad's place. It's going to be quite a project, and thank god he's agreed to be a guinea pig. Even though I wish he could let me get my hands on the kitchen and really sink my teeth into a full-on, top-to-bottom project, I'm going to have my hands full with the rest of his place. He wants me to brighten it up, make it look more mature and like a real home. As for the feminine touch, he agreed to let me change the color palette of the dark bedroom, trading in the dark charcoal-grey, and black for a softer tan, cream, and light blue. It's not obviously feminine, but at least not so obviously masculine.

The following day, while I'm busily gathering ideas for Chad's two bathroom remodels, running up and down the aisles at Randy's, setting up a makeshift office in the café portion of the bookstore, I get my very first biz bite.

"Excuse me?" a woman's voice says from the adjacent table. "Are you working on a home renovation project, too?" She gestures to my stacks of materials.

"I am," I say jubilantly. "Just about everything except for the kitchen."

"Oh, lucky you!" The woman, whose blonde-grey hair is pulled into a sophisticated chignon, removes her thin-rimmed reading glasses and sets them on top of an interior design magazine. "That's exactly *what* I'm working on."

"Are you doing a complete kitchen overhaul or just sprucing some things up?" I query interestedly. "Switching out some old appliances?"

"Overhaul, I fear." She makes a worried face and glances at her magazine.

I lean forward in my seat to read the magazines title: *Exclusively Kitchens*. "Looks like you're starting out on the right foot with your homework," I tell her.

"I have no idea what I'm doing, what I'm in for." She turns in her seat to better face me. "I thought taking one room at a time would be the best way to eventually turn my home *completely* around."

"I couldn't agree more." I scoot my chair nearer hers. "I've found taking one thing at a time is the *best* way to tackle any interior design project."

The woman gives me a warm smile and says, "I've found it's the best way to tackle any project in *life*."

"Correction," I say, deciding I like this woman and her outspokenness, her friendliness, "*now* I couldn't agree with you more."

"Suzanne Lakin." She holds out a manicured hand, her French tips sporting that once-familiar sparkle of a new fill.

I hold out my hand, feeling a hint of shame at how un-Jackie they look, and say with a shake, "Jackie Kittredge. Nice to meet you."

Suzanne retrieves her magazine and holds it out for me. "I don't even know if this magazine is too advanced to start or if it's even what I should be looking for."

I lightly page through her magazine, determining quickly that *Exclusively Kitchens* is more of an inspiring publication than one that will help you get a leg up on knocking out some cabinets, ripping up some old backsplash tiles, or installing the most suitable oven hood.

"What I really should be looking for are interior designers," Suzanne says. "I considered it, but what with my tightwad of a husband—erm—*ex*-husband." She picks up her reading glasses, folds them closed, then looks at me with a slightly sheepish smile. "Oh, listen to me babble. So divorcée of me, right?"

I only give a close-lipped, kind (and, sadly, seemingly understanding) smile in return.

"He's not *that* tight, I suppose..." Suzanne runs on, fingering the rims of her glasses. "I just know a complete home facelift will not come cheap, help or no help. A professional designer would be great, but I figured I could try it myself."

She points to the magazine I now have on my lap. "That's why I'm doing this. The renovation. The complete one-eighty of my home." She giggles lightheartedly. "I'm ready for a change; time to let go of the past." She giggles again, this time not as lightheartedly. "I haven't changed more than a few throw pillows and rugs in the twenty-three years I've lived in that home. I think it's time for a change."

"I think you're right," I say spiritedly. "Suzanne?" I set the magazine down on top of my large stack. I take my coffee mug in hand and wrap all of my fingers around its warmth. "You've come to the right place."

"Randy's?" She surveys the open café area. "I admit I haven't been here more than a couple times, but—"

"No, no." I cross my legs and begin to excitedly shake my foot. "You, me, running into each other like this. A good friend of mine would say fate or Kismet's done its thing, and I think she's spot-on."

Suzanne just looks on at me with a puzzled expression.

"I'm Jackie Kittredge, of Interiors By Jackie." I hastily pull a business card from my handbag.

"Oh, wow!" Suzanne examines the card with a pleased and surprised face. "Kismet, indeed."

"I'll be upfront with you." I lean in in a mock-surreptitious way. "I have some sample projects I'm working on." I shrug. "For friends. You'd be my first client, but...I'd give you a nice deal."

I take a fast sip of my coffee in a moment of slight nervousness. This is the first business encounter I've had. I was hoping (and expecting) potential clients to just drop into my lap. Now that one actually has, I'm taken aback. Is this really happening? Am I going to blow it?

The jittery nerves are here, because I know, as Lara sagely told me the other night when I bawled about how I was sure I would *never* get a bite, that nothing is a for-sure deal. I may have simply gotten lucky with Suzanne, because, let's face it, competition is heavy, and my experience is minimal.

Lara, the career guru, is right. Outside of luck, the work won't come to me; I have to go to it. Even though I've been busting my tail putting out fliers and business cards—working harder than senior year at U Dub when I had to cram for the toughest two weeks of finals ever—running a business is going to be hard work. I'm nervous, I'm scared, but I'm eager to try it out. I mean, what have I possibly got to lose at this point?

With Suzanne here right now and interested, it's all up to me, clueless and wide-eyed Jackie Kittredge, to take that next step towards my dream. Suzanne could run on about how interested she is in my services and how grateful she is that we met like this, yet she could never call—drop my business card in the trash or leave it to collect lipstick smears and wrinkle about in the depths of her handbag. The fear of that possibility is almost suffocating.

I clear my throat and scoot a little closer, determined to somehow seal the deal.

"I've never overhauled a kitchen, but it'd be a dream!" I tell her enthusiastically and honestly. "Or, if you don't want to start with a kitchen, we could start on *any* room of yours. It'd be my pleasure. I can see your place, come up with some different design ideas, quote you a price, and I can work with you."

Suzanne's eyes focus on my card.

"And, for what it's worth, I *totally* get where you're coming from with the tightwad of a husband."

Her head darts up, and she looks at me with a questioning face.

I roll my eyes and wrap my hands back around my mug. "My husband and I are separated right now. *Not* by choice, but what can a girl do? It's tough."

Suzanne gives a lifeless shrug, and I blurt out, "Take one step— one room to redesign—at a time."

Her eyes brighten, and she says, "Well..."

"If you want to do the project yourself, I understand," I say quickly, terrified I'm going to lose my first shot at a client. "If you

444

wanted to do fifty percent of the work and I the other, say, or have me come in for assistance... Or!" I bounce up in my seat. "I could do one room, show you how it's done, and you could do the other..."

A grin is growing across Suzanne's face as I tell her in a flurry my gaggle of ideas.

"You know what?" she says. As I watch her slip my business card into her handbag my heart begins to sink. *There it goes,* I think. *A kind smile, a slip of the card, and burying of this conversation. I have got to figure out how to be a saleswoman. Damn all those disasters working frontline retail—all those opportunities wasted!*

Suzanne then slips her reading glasses into her handbag, and when I'm thinking I've scared her off for good—she can't even bare a single second more in this awkward situation—she withdraws a brick-red day planner.

"I like you, Jackie, and I think your friend's right," she says. "Fate may have brought us here today—two women in need of some help right about now—and far be it from me, a bitter divorcée, to step in fate's way." She clicks her pen and flips about some pages.

"You're actually interested?" I spit out the first thing that comes to mind. Instantly, I feel like a fool.

Suzanne just smiles, though, and presses the ball of her pen to a page in her planner. "Would you be interested in coming over and taking a look at my home next Saturday?"

"I can't believe it, Lara! I just can't!" I shriek into the phone as I pull a thick handful of my design magazines and books from Emily's refurbished bookshelf. "My first potential client!"

"I am so proud of you, Jackie!" Lara exclaims. "See, what did I tell you? With some patience and hard work—some determination— you could totally do this!"

"Yeah, well..." I heave the stack onto the sofa next to Bella. "You said it would take a while, and this woman just *fell* from the sky!"

Lara laughs and says that of course my first bite could take a while. She then pours on more wise and attentive business advice.

"And I am *so* taking you up on that tip," I tell her. "First thing next week I'm going to look into that staging certificate."

"Those interior design symposiums, too."

"Yeah, yeah," I say hurriedly. "All that."

"And if the entry fee is too steep or if the certificate program is too pricey, I can—"

"Bail me out again?" I cackle.

"*Assist.* Or call it an investment!"

I find a book about kitchen and bath revamps in preparation for my first potential job and tell Lara she can call it what she wants, but

I can't run to her *every* time I need help. She's the one who said that'd be, oh...what'd she call it?

"Wouldn't that be enabling?" I say.

"Yeah, I know giving you handouts at every corner is like me enabling you and the bad habit. But if it's for work, and cash is the only thing standing in your way to become certified or trained...to help with your business..."

"It's no biggie, really," I say. "Yes, I *so* need a mani-pedi and spa weekend and just *hate* the way my nails look. So trailer-park-chipped."

"Oh, Jackie."

"And, yes, I definitely miss my cable, but I've gotten used to PBS. If I need some spare cash I have plenty more designer things I can hock, and I'd get a wad for them."

I glance at my Neverfull GM handbag across the room—the one Louis Vuitton item I'd probably choose to keep if worse came to worst, opting to donate a kidney or some vital organ before parting with my most favorite handbag.

"Anyway," I say, "I'm sure I'll get *much* more than I think for my Chanel pumps and coordinating jacket I plan on hocking. Oh! And even these *so* last-season Louboutins. They kind of hurt my feet, anyway, even though they're *totally* do-me-now shoes."

"Wow!" Lara gasps.

"I know, right?" I giggle. "They *so* are those kinds of shoes. Total sex-kitten."

"No. I mean 'wow' as in you're hocking more of your stuff for cash. Damn, Jackie."

"To buy the new season's YSL one-of-a-kind trench coat I can't afford? Absolutely!"

She flaps her lips in an exasperated way.

"Trust me," I say, paging aimlessly through the illustrative book. "If you *saw* the golden buttons and slim-waist and back pleats and—"

"I get it. It's amazing. Your priorities, as much as you're working on things, Jack, are still a bit skewed."

"Hey now," I say in jest. "This is a positive zone. Dr. Pierce wants me to stay positive and work through shit. Positive zone, Lara."

"All right, all right," she says through a laugh.

"No need to get your financial panties in a twist, anyway," I say. "I am *also* planning on hocking things to help with business and living expenses. And...well...the must-have trenchie is just a little bonus. It'll be a celebratory bonus for the first client!"

"Okay. Sounds like you've got a plan."

"I *so* do! And you've got no reason to worry, because the jacket is completely sold out—that's how *fab* it is—so I'm going to just put in a hold request for when the next shipment comes in. By the time it does I'll *so* be able to afford it! See, total plan!"

"Because thousand-dollar jackets are a priority."

"Lara. Be happy for me."

"Okay, okay. I'm sorry. You're right. Good job, Jackie."

"One step at a time," I say in a peppy tone.

"One step at a time."

<hr />

For the past few days I've spent nearly all my time working on different possibilities for both Chad's home renovation and Suzanne's potential kitchen job. It's still a good week before Suzanne and I'll meet, and I still don't know if I'll get the job, but she did text me the other day saying that she was so happy she met me. She said she thinks we'll be able to do wonders with her home. If you ask me, that sounds like Client Number One.

As fate or Kismet or luck would have it, I didn't have to wait long for Client Number Two to fall from heaven and into my lap.

I'm at a nearby hardware shop looking at wallpaper patterns and border options, just in case Suzanne turns out to be a print-type, when I get a call. A big call.

"Interiors By Jackie," I chime into the phone, remembering in the nick of time not to answer with a habitual, "Hey-o!" or "What's up?"

I don't recognize the number and hope to god it's another potential client.

Please be a client, please be a client, please be a—

"Hello, this is Judy Young," a mature woman's voice sounds over the line.

"Hi, Judy. This is Jackie."

"Hi, Jackie. I'm calling in regards to an estimate."

Omigod! Omigod!

"I came across one of your fliers and I'm interested in your services."

Omigod! Quickly, hands shaking, I say, "That's great!"

I bite my bottom lip a second later, worried I've overplayed this one. I want to be approachable and happy to work with a potential client, not overeager, desperate, and in need of some serious cash in twenty to thirty days when my YSL beauty is expected to arrive.

"What kind of services are you interested in?" I ask nervously.

"I'm actually interested in an entire re-design, top to bottom."

Whoa! I feel like my vision's gone all fuzzy, my head all dizzy. Did she just say an *entire* re-design? Top to bottom?

"I'm very eager to have this job started," Judy says. "So the earliest date you have available for a consult would be excellent."

Trying to gather my wits—in shock over my good fortune of two potential clients within one week—I tell her I can see her as early as tomorrow morning. "What time will work for you?"

"Whatever time works for you. My day is wide open. Your call."

"Nine a.m.?" I fish a pen out of my handbag and begin to take notes on my palm.

"Nine a.m. it is," she says cheerfully. "It's a new space, very plain and not much to it."

"All right." *Great!* I think. *A blank canvas. I can have total license here! And the commission? Unbelievable!* "I can definitely work with that. And the address?"

She gives me the address to a home in Lake Union, not too far from Chad's place, it seems.

"Thank you so much for calling and for your interest," I say, trying to put my best business face on.

"Thank you for working me in so soon," Judy says. "Tomorrow at nine, then?"

"Tomorrow at nine."

Holy crap! I think, staring at my phone once the call ends. *This can't be for real!*

I turn back to the wide display of wallpaper borders and reach for a pearlescent and eggshell *fleur-de-lis* swatch. *I can't believe this...I can't believe this...* The shock just won't dissipate.

My horoscope was right. When I began to gather research material at Randy's the day I met Suzanne I also grabbed the latest issue of *Cosmopolitan*. Minus my YSL stint and my plans to find some way to get a hot stone massage or at least a reflexology appointment booked before the end of the year, I've been a good girl on a budget. I've refrained from the urge to splurge and buy copies of all of my favorite magazines, something I used to do without thinking about it at all, much less twice.

Of course, that doesn't mean I can't leisurely page through some on display over coffee, during a work break. I'm glad I flipped all the way to the end to read my horoscope, though! It said September is my month, and with the stars aligned and in my favor, I shouldn't be surprised to see some big things happening for me.

I've decided to wear my classiest outfit today. I'm meeting Judy, my big potential client, in a matter of minutes, and I want to look my best. I want to look professional and serious, like I'm just the right woman for the job!

I'm still so gobsmacked that I have a consultation today. I mean, the girls, Conner, my horoscope—they were all right! A little bit of patience, some time, hope, and a sprinkle of luck, and everything would work out!

I glance down at myself as I shut my car door. I'm wearing a pair of empire-waisted black, pinstriped pants and a ruffly, cream, silk blouse. I considered going with my pair of black high heels to keep with the whole super classy and sophisticated look, but last minute I just had to slip on my refurbished Balenciagas. The bright yellow color and silver studs add in that bit of flair and flash my outfit was missing. I can be all business and professional, but I'm still Jackie Kittredge, colorful as a parrot, with a mouth like one, too, as Emily says.

"You can do this," I tell myself as I lean down to my car's side mirror. I check my freshly applied pink lipstick one more time. "You can do this."

With my Neverfull handbag snug on my shoulder, a note with the address in my hand, I make my way from the parking lot to the sidewalk.

The address is peculiar, my GPS leading me to some location I couldn't quite reach by car. I parked as close to the address as I could, in a waterside restaurant parking lot in front of a small row of houseboats off to the left. I consider turning left along the sidewalk in search of house number forty-two, but the GPS said my final destination was to my right.

"Forty-two, forty-two…" I walk a few paces along the sidewalk, but when I realize there's a dead-end ahead of me, the walkway spilling out onto a slope of grass and eventually the water, I stop.

"What the hell?" I look from my left, to my right. I pull down my sunglasses and read over the address and directions once more. "To my right?" I look in that direction. "This doesn't make any sense."

Just then I spot a man headed my way. I wave a hand about. "Excuse me! Excuse me!" My sawed-off pumps make chunky clunks against the cement, a very different beat from the sharp *click-clicks* they used to make.

"Excuse me." I successfully get the man's attention, and as I hold out the note for him to look at, I suddenly have a horrifying thought. What if this is a crank call? What if there is no potential client? No house needing a redesign, top to bottom?

"Oh, no," I gasp, startling the man.

"Something wrong, ma'am?" he asks, looking from the note to me.

"Well." I swallow, look at the note, and think, *Maybe I'm really just lost. It certainly wouldn't be the first time...*

"Can I help you?" the man says.

"I hope." I hold the note out further. "I'm a bit lost. Can you tell me where this house is?"

"I can give it a try." He takes the note from me and squints at it.

"It's house forty-two," I say, pointing at the number.

"That should probably read S-42."

"'S'?" I look at the note. "You mean 'S-T'? As in street, maybe?"

He chuckles and says, "No. Definitely not a street. It's slip forty-two."

"Okay. It's a houseboat, I take it?"

He points ahead of him, in the direction I'd just been walking. "With this address," he holds up the note, "it should be a boat you're looking for."

"A boat?" I make a scrunched face. "Are you sure?"

"Forty-two is just three—no—four docks down in this direction." He motions further forward. "Swing a left, onto the dock, and it should be right along there. Evens on the righthand side."

"Thanks..." I say in a drawn-out, slightly baffled way.

Looking down at the note. My mind's completely rattled now. What the hell kind of prank is this? A boat? Judy said she needed a redesign of a new home...

Determined to figure out if I'm being played, I follow the man's directions. Walking on wobbly ground, my heels, even despite their refurbishing, are not exactly ideal for the knobby wooden dock.

"Slip forty-two? What the hell?" I grip tightly the handle of my handbag, stopping at each boat I pass, looking to my left and right. I can't spot any numbers anywhere—no evens, no odds. No forty-anything.

"Ugh, honestly," I mutter, gripping my handbag tighter. I turn around, heading back a few paces, and I search high and low for any sign of an address. I can't find anything! "This has got to be some sort of a joke!"

Even as I retrace my steps, not a single number pops out at me. All I see is one boat after another, an expensive yacht here, a sailboat there...

I'm about halfway down the dock, almost on my last nerve, when I stop.

Abruptly.

Right in my tracks.

"Omigod," I breathe, releasing the tight grip on my handbag. Both hands drop to my side, lifelessly. "Andrew."

55

"Andrew." I take in a quick breath, feeling my fingers tremble, my stomach flipping. "Wh—wh—what are you doing here?"

Towering above me, standing on the deck of a sailboat, is my husband. One hand in his pocket, one hand resting on a long, overhead line, he's wearing a warm smile—that same smile I see in my dreams.

"Hey there, baby doll," he says.

I rapidly shake my head. "Wh—wh—I'm confused." I pan around, trying to piece together what I'm seeing, what's happening.

He lets go of the line and takes two small steps forward on the deck. Both hands now in his pockets, he presses his lips tightly together. I catch his intoxicating gaze.

"What's going on?" I say. "What is this?"

He rubs at the side of his nose, then holds out a hand. "Want to come aboard?"

Completely thunderstruck, I look around once more. "Andrew, I'm supposed to be meeting a client. I don't—" I look at the note in my sweaty hand. "I have work—"

"I am the client, Jackie."

"You're the client?" I slowly look down, feeling kind of goaded, still confused, kind of...happy?

I look back up at my husband, grab ahold of my handbag again, and briskly nod. "Okay," I say more to myself than to him.

Cautiously stepping towards the boat, Andrew rushes forward and helps me climb aboard.

"You and your heels," he says with a laugh as I stumble my way on.

"I didn't exactly expect to be sailing the high seas," I say with a nervous chuckle.

I step down and onto the deck, Andrew's strong hand in mine, guiding me. I meet his eyes again, and a crooked and shaky smile coats my lips. "So you're the client?"

"I'm the client." His voice is low, calm.

"This Judy person doesn't exist?"

"Oh, she exists." Our hands part, his seeking refuge in his pockets, mine back to my handbag's handles. "She's my secretary."

"Your secretary," I say through a heady sigh. "Your new secretary?"

He nods.

Deciding not to beat around any bush, I blurt out, "Nikki's replacement. I heard."

"Worth." Andrew purses his lips. "Mmmhmm."

"Lara told me," I say, at a loss for words.

The corners of his lips turn up. "Yeah."

"So... What's this all about?" I swallow, dismissing the frog in my throat.

I hope he can't sense how nervous I am. Andrew's the last person I thought I'd be seeing today. And the reason I'm so nervous is not just because he's caught me completely off guard, not just because I'm still coming off of my nervousness over meeting a potential client, but because I've been waiting on a hope and prayer that Andrew and I would see each other again and have a talk. I've been dreaming about getting to discuss our marriage and a possible reconciliation—without divorce attorneys present. But this! This? This is coming out of left field.

"Jackie," Andrew says. His blue eyes are penetrating, as if they're speaking to my soul. "It's time I'm honest with you. Completely, one hundred percent honest."

Oh no. I swallow the returning frog. *This is it. He's going to admit the affair. He's going to tell me right here, right now that he wants a divorce.*

I exhale loudly and avert my gaze to the shiny, polished deck.

"Baby doll." He gently lifts my chin, our eyes meeting once again. "About Nikki."

"Oh, no." I clutch my stomach, suddenly feeling the urge to retch.

"I let her go."

"Yeah. I know." I rub my suddenly aching stomach. "Replaced her with Judy."

"Yes. And you know why?"

I fight back the tears I can feel starting to develop and look over his shoulder. Hearing the truth is too much to bear. Having Andrew look at me, touch me, our souls feeling like they're one once again... it's all too much.

"Jackie." He touches my chin again, but I refuse to look at him. I keep my mouth clamped shut, fighting the nervous shaking of my jaw.

"The truth is, there was a job opening in New York," he goes on in his cool and collected tone. "A great opportunity with a solid company."

Oh, can't he just get on with it! Tell the truth already, dammit! Admit it!

"Nikki's learned all she could at the firm, and it was time for a promotion," he explains.

Yeah, promotion! If that's what you want to call it.

"And over these past few months." He exhales, hands back in his pockets. I keep my eyes trained on the row of masts behind him. "These past few months have been the worst of my life."

I look at him at last. *Really? The worst?*

"Not having you in my life, Jackie..." His voice turns weak, almost feeble. "I'm empty without you."

I bite my tongue, staving off the tears beginning to surge forward.

"As important as it was for me to have Nikki working at the firm, doing whatever I could to prove to you that I want you in my life is more important." He attempts to take my hand in his, and I give in, too taken aback to shun. "You're my wife, and you come first."

Still biting my tongue, I avert my eyes to the masts. It's all I can do at this point to keep from falling into a weepy mess.

"Look," he says, squeezing my hand. "We've both made mistakes. We've both acted childish. I'm finished with fighting. I'm ready to fix *us*. I'm taking steps to make things better. Nikki's gone, I'm here, willing to work on our marriage." He draws nearer. "Anything it takes. Couple's therapy, weekend trips, coming home earlier..."

His grip turns tighter and I can't help but look back into those piercing eyes of his.

"But first," he says, "we have to be honest."

Oh god, here it comes. He's going to admit the affair...

"About Nikki. I need to confess."

"Just get it out, Andrew," I blurt. My voice is an octave higher than normal, the fear of the truth sneaking through.

"She's my daughter."

"What?" My hands go numb, my toes go numb, my whole body goes numb.

Andrew closes his eyes and wags his head in disappointment. "I should have told you long ago. The instant I found out. I'm so sorry. I'm so, so sorry. Please forgive me."

"I—I—I'm in shock." I take one step back, breaking free from his grip. I clasp a hand to my stomach, certain I'm going to retch now. "When? How? Wh—what?"

"Twenty-eight years ago," he says with a snort. "I was young, in college, getting my MBA..."

"Omigod." I bring a hand to my forehead, feeling clammy. I

search for a place to sit but just end up settling on the deck right where I'm standing, legs suddenly weakened.

Andrew instantly follows my lead, sitting next to me. "I know. Totally unexpected," he says. "It was a one-time accident. A drunken night."

I gather the courage to look at him. He looks embarrassed, ashamed, his cheeks pink.

"I didn't know she got pregnant," he says. "Then, early last year, this girl, Nikki, comes knocking on my door." He pauses. "Came to the office, said she'd looked me up, her mother had passed away. Nikki'd been taking care of her mother's things, came across her journal, and..." He shrugs. "Next thing I know I've got a daughter I never knew I had, standing there in my office."

A million thoughts and emotions are coursing through my mind, my body. I don't know what to say, to do...

I was somewhat prepared for an admission of an affair, but this? This! A daughter!

"Jackie, I know I should have told you about this the *second* I found out. I never should have put you through the hell I put you through, allowing you to even *think* there was an affair—"

"Yeah, well," I say, finally gathering the courage to speak, "you sure led me on, that's for sure. How could you do that, Andrew?"

"I know, and for this I will be sorry for the rest of my life."

"I mean—I mean—" I look down at my hands in my lap.

In all fairness, Andrew had told me that he was not having an affair with Nikki. He had said he was faithful, but so does every man who doesn't want his wife to out his mistress. What else was I to think with him being so protective of her? So insistent on keeping her as his secretary? Never in a million years could I have expected this.

"When she came and told me," he continues in a soft voice, "I didn't know what to do. I mean, god, *me*, a *father*?" He brusquely shakes his head.

"The paternity test was proof-positive," he says in a deflated way. "Nikki was working a run-down job as a diner waitress, had just lost her mother... I did the only thing I knew how to do: I gave her a job. At first I offered to give her money—throw money at the problem, that's what I'm good at, right?" He snickers ashamedly, giving me a sideways glance.

I press my lips together tightly and weakly raise my shoulders in response, thinking, *We're sitting on one of those very attempts you made to patch things up.*

"But Nikki said she hadn't come for a handout." He cautiously brushes his fingers against the back of my hand.

"Jackie, I'm sorry I didn't tell you sooner. I just—I just—didn't know how you'd handle it. I was worried it would ruin us. So I thought I could keep it hidden, hire her as a secretary, give her a chance—the least I could do as her father." He sighs heavily. "Obviously everything backfired. God, please forgive me, Jackie."

I take a few calming breaths, trying to digest the massive amount of information I've just been fed. All I can do is stare at him in stunned silence.

"Please, baby doll," he says imploringly. "I love you. I know now how foolish my actions were, how wrong I was in keeping it from you...for defending her and letting you make such assumptions. She's my daughter, and I'm the last person in the world who has what it takes to be a father. I didn't know what the hell else to do."

"Why'd she have to be such a bitch to me?" I say, jaw clenched and eyes glossy. "Lying about you being in the office, or out at lunch...wild-goose-chases and her being so—so—so... Well, bitchy!"

He snorts and says, "If you found out your father was married to someone your own age, you probably wouldn't handle it very well."

I give a one-armed shrug. I suppose he's right, but it's still no excuse for the way Nikki treated me.

"I tried to keep it from happening," he says. "What can I say? She's thick-headed like her father."

"That's true," I say with a muffled laugh. "So...what? Now you're a dad? I'm what?" I swallow, a disgusted look overcoming my face, my upper lip curling. "A...mother?"

He chuckles out a no, then says, "Not at all, baby doll."

"So you have a relationship with her... You going to visit her in New York... Are you going to try for some Dad of the Year Award or..." I'm rambling at this point, still so overwhelmed by this unexpected news.

He closes his eyes for a long, heavy breath. His voice is low yet stern as he says, "No. Neither of us are looking for a father-daughter bonding thing. I think the fact that I married someone her age is too much to digest. I mean, Jackie baby, you were *born* when I was in grad school..."

"Yeah, well..."

"Nikki wanted to meet me—wanted to see...family. And I wanted to do something for her." He sighs. "The least I could do, like I said, was give her a job. That's the extent of my fatherly duties."

Suddenly, he claps a hand to his thigh. "I did give her a nice birthday present. Sent her to Hawaii on vacation. Thought that was a nice thing to do."

"Why, you!" I shriek, slapping him on the arm. "*That's* what that was about?"

He crinkles his brow. "Huh?"

"Here I'm thinking you're secretly planning a romantic vaca for us, then I think you're running off for a mistress tryst—"

Andrew's chuckling, rubbing his jaw up and down. "Oh, Jackie..."

"Not 'Oh, Jackie'!" I'm incredulous, but a small smile—a smile of relief—glosses my lips. "I was scared to death! My imagination was running wild!"

"Oh, baby doll. You and your flair for drama. I *told* you I wasn't having an affair."

"What housewife hasn't heard that one before?" I roll my glassy eyes.

"Look, Jackie." He takes both of my hands in his. "I love you. I love you more than you will ever know, and I will spend the rest of my life proving it, making it up to you for all of this mess, all of the neglect, all of the fights."

"But...why now? Why—" I look upwards, trying to abate the

tears. "Why now? Three months! You cut me off, kicked me out, *locked* me out!" He looks off to the side in shame. "You threatened a divorce lawyer, and he never shows up. I'm panicking...waiting around... What am I to think, Andrew? Huh?"

"We *both* needed some time to figure things out," he says simply.

"Yeah. I suppose so. But cutting me off like that, Andrew! I mean, it's like you didn't care about me!"

"I know I shouldn't have cut off the credit cards like I did when you were in Paris. I was just so angry with you. What you did, Jackie—"

"Paris?" I gasp. "It's not just Paris. You cut me off, period. Locked me out!"

"I know, and I'm sorry. I was angry, I was hostile. But Paris? *Paris*, Jackie!"

"I'm surprised you didn't cut me off from Dr. Pierce," I run on, aghast. "Surprised I still had health insurance, could get my meds—"

"I love you, Jackie. I knew you'd be fine without access to credit cards." He holds up a hand. "Not that it excuses what I've done to you, but I knew you'd pull yourself up, figure things out. And look at you, baby."

"Still." I cross my arms gruffly over my chest.

"And I was never going to cut you off from your therapy sessions, your healthcare. I still love you, Jackie. Always have, always will. I'd die if something happened to you."

"And the divorce lawyer?" I raise an inquisitive brow.

"I was never going to call one. Heat of the moment, rash words." He fixes me with a steady, hard gaze. "And as for Paris," he adds in a reprimanding tone.

"I know," I whisper, embarrassed about not only what I put Sophie and my girlfriends through with my lie and immature behavior, but my husband.

"I was worried sick about you," he says.

"I know and I'm so sorry." Tears sting my eyes. "I was thinking about how you're always away on business and I'm left alone and—

and—I thought I'd show you. But I know I was wrong, so wrong. What I did was—was—selfish." I blink some of the building tears away. "It was immature and I'm sorry. I'm trying to work things out now. I'm trying!"

I hug my arms tighter to my chest. "Oh, Andrew. We have put each other through a lot of shit. And for what?"

"I've been asking myself that for three long months."

"Well, where do we go from here?" I look around.

"Well, I'd ask if you're up for a sail," he says with a coy smile, "but I hear you have a client who needs an estimate done."

"Yeah, very funny." I roll my eyes playfully.

"I'm proud of you, Jackie. So damn proud."

I give him a sideways glance.

"Look, I wasn't joking when I had Judy call for an estimate," he says.

"Oh, really?" I look about the sailboat. "Design a sailboat's interior? Andrew, I— Wait a minute, how'd you even find out about my business, anyway?"

His lips curl into a cunning little grin. "What can I say? You and Lara aren't the only gossipers."

"Worth?" I exclaim.

"Lara gave him some of your fliers and...well...the rest is history." He shrugs, a schoolboy expression about him.

"Goodness." I wag my head. "So, you're serious? You want me to do some interior designing on this thing?" I knock on the wooden deck.

"That's the deal here," he says, standing up. "It's my next step to prove to you I want to make this marriage work."

"Oh?"

"I'm really impressed with how you're growing up and going after something you're really passionate about. I need to respect that, need to let you do that."

He waves a hand about, gesturing to the impressive, brand new sailboat. "This boat is yours to decorate, Jackie. Ours to sail. I know you didn't want it before, but maybe I can change your mind this time? Give it another shot?"

He approaches the massive steering wheel. "I know it's another material possession, and when I first came up with it it was another way to try to appease you, sweep anything that wasn't Jennings & Voigt-related under the rug." He grips the wheel firmly. "But it can be more than that. It's a project we can both work on. Together. Like our marriage."

"Okay..." I narrow my eyes, intrigued; a touch of joy is growing inside.

"You design it; I take some real time off and enjoy it with you."

"Really?"

"Really."

"I'd like that," I say.

"I can't expect you to live in a box, Jackie. I can't expect you to be home whenever I come home—"

"Which is always too late," I cut in.

"That's the next step. You know I'm a workhorse; that's who I am."

"I know."

"You married a man who's been in a long-term, borderline-obsessive relationship with his career. You knew that going in."

"Yes," I say with a smile, "and you married a woman in her *twenties* who enjoys an occasional night out on the town, a little dancing, a little fun. *Not* pill-popping slumbers. You knew *that* going in."

He chuckles and leans against the steering wheel. "*Touché, touché*. So how's this? I make a *serious*, heartfelt effort to be more attentive, and you keep up the good work. You grow up, let go of that selfish side a bit—"

"Hey," I say, feeling nettled.

He holds up a single finger and cocks his head to the side. "Your words, baby doll. Your words. Besides, we *both* have issues to work out. Let's work them out together."

"Yeah, well..." I twist at my wedding ring, still feeling miffed, but not blind to the facts. "I have been acting a little spoiled and immature…"

"A little?"

"Hey, come on." I crack a thin smile. "I'm a work-in-progress. You can't expect me to pull a Jekyll and Hyde here."

"We both can't turn around just like that, but we can try. A little bit here, a little bit there."

I nod slowly. "I suppose I can be more…more…"

Our eyes meet, and what was once a thin smile on my lips is now growing broader. I can feel my cheeks redden with excitement and nervous energy as my husband and I share that connection—that shared passion and love for each other—with a single heartfelt and mesmerizing gaze into each other's eyes.

"I will be more understanding of your work," I say. "But now!" I shake my shoulders and hold my head high in pride. "Now *I'm* also a business person."

Andrew laughs and says, "That you are, baby doll. That you are."

"I'm trying; really I am."

"I know. And you're miles ahead of me with this road to a better marriage. Of course, I *am* here on a Thursday morning, nine o'clock —*prime* business hours…" He gives me a sheepish grin, slightly devilish and ultimately sexy.

"That is impressive."

"Look at you." He gestures to me. "You've come a long, long way. You've started your own business, you look great, you look happy…"

I laugh and roll my eyes. "Yeah, right. My roots are seeing the light of day for the first time in years." I pull at my hair. "I'm a hundred years late for my mani-pedi." I wave my fingers. "And happy? Well…I guess I am doing better than I was…" I look into his eyes and lower my voice. "But I'm not as happy as I can be. Without you, Andrew…"

He holds out his hand and I consent, letting him pull me up on wobbly feet.

"Know what?" he says.

"What?"

"I think this just might be reason to celebrate with some bubbly?"

"Oh I'm always up for a little bubbly and celebrating," I say with a flirty expression.

He hitches a thumb in the direction of the cabin, where I can see a bottle of champagne chilling on ice, two glasses set out beside it.

"Pink?" I ask giddily.

"'*Pink champagne. That's the kind of life we've both been used to,*'" he says with a debonair ring, reminiscent of Cary Grant.

"Oh, Andrew." I sniff back the tears.

"And you know what else?" he says. "I think we should start couple's therapy."

"Wha— Are you serious?" I'm stupefied.

"We both have a lot of work to do, and I can't think of a better way than to get a professional's advice to help make sure we're on the *right* track." He tightens his hand around mine.

"God, I've missed you so much, Andrew," I say in a shaky voice, that familiar rush of tears returning.

He places one hand gingerly on my waist and steps nearer.

"A fresh start?" he says softly.

"No."

"No?" His face turns down.

"No," I repeat, resting a hand on his chest. "We've already started. At the jazz bar, when we first met." I bring my hand to the nape of his neck. "These past few months have just been another chapter of our love story." Fresh hot tears run down my cheek. "And now we're starting the next chapter."

"I like that story." He slowly brings his other hand to my back, pulling me closer.

"I do, too."

I breathe in his warm, enveloping scent, redolent of expensive cigars, thick aftershave, and musky cologne, and I press my chest to his, my heart pounding so hard I'm sure he can feel it. I dance my fingers along his neck, up into his salt and pepper hair. I bite down on my bottom lip through a growing smile.

"I don't know *exactly* who I am yet, Andrew," I say in a small, weak voice, "or where I'm going. It's an adventure, and sometimes it scares me. So much change...growing up...life...it's hard."

He pulls me tighter.

"But I do know this much." I look deep into his eyes. "I know that I'm your wife. That's who I'm supposed to be, that's who I want to be. And I know that this is where I belong. Right here, with you, my husband. This is where I've *always* belonged."

"I love you, Mrs. Andrew Kittredge," he says, his lips nearly grazing mine.

I step up onto my tiptoes and touch the tip of his nose. "That's Mrs. Jackie Kittredge, mister."

He makes an *aha* expression as I lean farther in, wrap my arms tighter about him, and kick up a heel.

My stomach fills with butterflies and I feel like I'm rising to Cloud Nine. I think I might even hear fireworks going off in the distance. I feel passionate, I feel hopeful, I feel content and happy. I even feel a little bit scared, but more than that I feel loved. Truly and madly loved...and in love.

"And I love you, Andrew."

As the last of the tepid summer air whips about, causing our sailboat to sway, a new season, a new chapter, is ushered in. It's filled with possibility, with hope, and, as my lips meet my husband's, I know, without a shadow of a doubt, that this new chapter is also filled with a lot of love.

EPILOGUE

Most people only get one shot. I got two. And for that I consider myself the luckiest woman in the world. Well, that and the fact that I married my soul mate.

The story of how Andrew and I struggled through our second year of marriage was certainly not something straight from a charming black-and-white Turner Classic movie. It was the roughest chapter of my life, beating the loudest fight with my mother, the worst insult hurled by my father, the most atrocious of unhealthy habits from my past. Not having Andrew in my life last summer was like missing a piece of myself.

I used to say I felt like I was drowning, slogging it through a really difficult marriage filled with every argument, disagreement, and blowout under the sun. I was screaming at the pool party, and no one was listening.

I realize now that I was the one who wasn't listening, that I was the one who needed to teach herself to swim. I've been my biggest obstacle, falling back on excuses and crutches, complaining and insulting along the way, unwilling to figure out how and when to dive, to take that deep breath, to paddle, to stroke-stroke-stroke, or to just keep on treading. It hasn't been easy getting to this point, but it wasn't impossible, especially when a woman's got love and guidance and such great support.

Those few months without Andrew were anything but easy—they were a whole new level of pain, in fact. Emily says I should take whatever positive things I can glean from the difficult experience, and I know she's right. I'm still the same wild and fancy-free Jackie Kittredge, eager to slip into a party dress and hit the dance floor, but so much of that damaged and frightened and, admittedly, spoiled, woman was a shell of a woman drowning. Now, about half a year later, I'm much stronger, and I'm no longer drowning.

Well, maybe I'm drowning in work. Interiors By Jackie is taking off! With the advertising help from Lara and the investment and business-savvy from Andrew, not to mention the support and encouragement from all my girlfriends, and even Conner and Chad, too, my company's got more clients on the books than I know what to do with. It's not full-blown successful like Sophie's café, but it's exactly what I dreamed it would be. I'm busy, but not workaholic-busy, and I'm doing something for myself *and* other people. I'm in a really good place right now, and I couldn't be happier.

Andrew still spends quite a bit of time at the office, but now that I've got a business of my own, working a couple late nights a week in the home office, I don't give him such a hard time. He has promised to be home before dinner the majority of the time, though, and he hasn't broken that promise once!

We try to take the sailboat out now and then, and I've even started to take sailing lessons! I'm not half-bad, and I can definitely look the part. Oh, I have the most perfect designer nautical wardrobe I've put together from... Well, what can I say? Sailing's turned out to be a *great* hobby for Andrew and me. Even if we can't find the time to break free and get away from it all for an extended weekend, sometimes we'll just stay a night onboard, docked. It's so romantic.

As for the rest of the gang, they're all doing well. Emily and Gatz are in the middle of planning their next globe-trekking adventures. Australia was only the beginning. Now they're talking of sofa surfing their way around the world or something insane. Those two are definitely made for each other!

Robin and her little clan are doing as fabulously as anyone could imagine. Phillip is growing up before our eyes, Rose has turned three! She knows her ABC's, can count without using her fingers, and says she's going to be just like her mommy when she grows up: "the bestest momma in the world."

Lara and Worth are still together, in love with their professional lives, and, more importantly, with each other. Their road's taken some interesting turns, but I have a hunch they're destined for a happily-ever-after.

Claire and Conner are living in Spokane and, to Claire's surprise, really loving it. It's not how any of us imagined it would be, them living outside of Seattle, but they're happy and doing well.

Conner's got a great job and has received a promotion. Claire's settled in just fine in the geriatrics wing at the hospital and she says whenever she gets the baby bug she just wanders over to the maternity ward, gushes a bit, then tells herself she'll be there soon enough. To that I laugh and say, "We'll definitely see." I'm betting anything she'll be calling with exciting news any day now.

Sophie's doing well. The Cup and the Cake is always packed. She's still up to her neck in work, but at least she's not so sour on her love life anymore. She...oh, what am I saying? That's her story to tell. And it's a good one...

Of course, I'd hardly say it's as dramatic as my story, but everyone's got their own tale.

Whenever I think back on last summer's insane string of events I'm reminded to be grateful for my second chance. If Andrew and I hadn't pulled ourselves up from the rubble that'd become our marriage we wouldn't be here today, in love and promising to stand by each other and work through whatever problems come our way.

Like I said, most people only get one shot. Andrew and I are lucky. I let go of him once, but I'm never letting go again. Because when you have something as special and as powerful as true love, when you have that beautiful, pink champagne-filled affair to remember, you can't let go.

THE END

ACKNOWLEDGMENTS

Thank you to my family and friends for all of your love and encouragement.

Thanks to Ginger and Erin for helping me with Jackie's colorful personality and story. Your support and advice are always invaluable.

Many thanks to my fabulous editor, Liam Carnahan of Invisible Ink Editing, for doing a smashing job with this novel.

And thank you to my husband for being the best husband ever. *Ich liebe dich, Christian.*

ABOUT THE AUTHOR

Savannah Page is the author of *Everything the Heart Wants*, *A Sister's Place*, and the *When Girlfriends* series. Sprinkled with drama and humor, her women's fiction celebrates friendship, love, and life. A native Southern Californian, Savannah lives in Berlin, Germany, with her husband, their goldendoodle, and her collection of books. She enjoys jazz, astronomy, and, like Jackie, Cary Grant films.

Readers can visit her at:
www.SavannahPage.com

25552517R00286

Printed in Great Britain
by Amazon